Julia Llewellyn is the author of *The Love Trainer, If I Were You, Amy's Honeymoon* and *The Model Wife*, all published as Penguin paperbacks. As Julia Llewellyn Smith she writes regularly for the *Sunday Telegraph*, the *Sunday Times* and many other publications. Julia lives in London with her family.

# Love Nest

## JULIA LLEWELLYN

PENGUIN BOOKS

PENGUIN BOOKS

Published by the Penguin Group
Penguin Books Ltd, 80 Strand, London WC2R ORL, England
Penguin Group (USA) Inc., 375 Hudson Street, New York, New York 10014, USA
Penguin Group (Canada), 90 Eglinton Avenue East, Suite 700, Toronto, Ontario, Canada M4P 2Y3
(a division of Pearson Penguin Canada Inc.)
Penguin Ireland, 25 St Stephen's Green, Dublin 2, Ireland (a division of Penguin Books Ltd)
Penguin Group (Australia), 250 Camberwell Road, Camberwell, Victoria 3124, Australia
(a division of Pearson Australia Group Pty Ltd)
Penguin Books India Pvt Ltd, 11 Community Centre, Panchsheel Park, New Delhi – 110 017, India
Penguin Group (NZ), 67 Apollo Drive, Rosedale, North Shore 0632, New Zealand
(a division of Pearson New Zealand Ltd)
Penguin Books (South Africa) (Pty) Ltd, 24 Sturdee Avenue, Rosebank,
Johannesburg 2196, South Africa

Penguin Books Ltd, Registered Offices: 80 Strand, London WC2R ORL, England

www.penguin.com

First published 2010
3

Set in 12.5/14.75 pt Monotype Garamond
Typeset by Ellipsis Books Limited, Glasgow
Printed in England by Clays Ltd, St Ives plc

ISBN: 978-0-141-03365-5


www.greenpenguin.co.uk

For Ella Winters. And her mum.

# Acknowledgements

With huge thanks to the National Gamete Donation Trust for all its help in investigating the fascinating world of egg donation and IVF, and especially to Julie Hinks at the Bristol Centre for Reproductive Medicine, who answered so many queries so patiently (and also stood up for nurses' rights!). Anyone who wants to know more can look at ngdt.co.uk. As ever, gratitude to Lizzy Kremer, Laura West and everyone else who works so hard at David Higham Associates. Mari Evans, you are the most brilliant editor and a joy to work with. Ruth Spencer, you're a star, ditto Natalie Higgins, not to mention the entire team at Penguin. Kate Gawryluk, I couldn't have done this without you. Victoria Macdonald, Maryam Shahmanesh and as ever James Watkins. And apologies and homage to Thomas Hardy.

# Prelude

'Ashes to ashes,' intoned the vicar. 'Dust to dust.' It was a glacial February morning and in the south-west corner of the churchyard of St Michael's of All Angels, Little Dittonsbury, Devon, the coffin of Nadia Porter-Healey was being lowered slowly into the frosty ground beside her long-dead husband's.

Their orphaned daughter Grace stifled her sobs with a tissue. She leaned on the shoulder of her brother Sebastian, who was staring straight ahead with a neutral expression on his face, as if he'd broken wind in a crowded lift.

On his other side, Verity, Sebastian's wife, sighed heavily, pulled her cashmere coat more tightly around her and glanced at her slim gold watch. Basil, who was three, clung to her leg shouting: 'What's going on, Mummy?' Alfie, the five-year-old, stood rigid, like a soldier about to be despatched to the Western Front. The gravedigger stepped forward and began shovelling earth on to the coffin. Alfie stuck a finger up his nostril. Verity didn't bother to stifle a yawn. Basil said: 'Mummy, will there be cake soon? You said there'd be cake.'

Grace's sobs grew louder. A dam of grief and exhaustion that had been building up for the past five years was suddenly blasted away. The tears poured out. Her mother was dead. Her beautiful mother whom she'd loved so much. Grace had done everything she could to save her, but it had still been inadequate. As ever, she had failed.

'There, there,' mumbled Sebastian, giving her an ineffectual squeeze on the arm. Sympathetic heads were turning. Grace felt a warm arm around her shoulder.

'Hey, love. Hey. It's all right.'

It was Lou, cleaner, occasional cook and general handywoman at Chadlicote Manor for the past sixteen years. Grace inhaled the familiar smells of bleach and baking – the result of being up since six preparing Chadlicote for the wake. Grace had devoured a whole tray of Lou's sandwiches earlier that morning to fortify herself. She'd blamed their disappearance on Silvester, the spaniel. But she *was* in mourning.

'It's not all right, Lou. Mummy's dead.'

'I know. It's very sad. But *you'll* be all right.'

'I couldn't save her.'

'No one could.' Lou stroked her hair. 'Life is just very cruel sometimes.'

Grace wiped the tears away from her cheeks, aware of her brother hovering awkwardly beside them.

'Ahem, Grace. I think it's time we got going. Showed people the way.'

'Of course.' Grace blew her nose, wrapped her scarf tighter around her neck, readjusted her hat slightly. 'I'll see you back at the house, then.'

'Actually,' Verity chirped up, 'Sebby was wondering if he could drive back with you. As there's so much to discuss.'

'Oh!' Grace was pleased. Since her beloved brother had met Verity ten years ago, she'd rarely had a moment alone with him. He'd been staying for the past couple of days, but he'd locked himself up in the study going over paperwork.

Over the suppers Grace had prepared for him he had been monosyllabic. 'I'm exhausted,' was the most she got from him, although after eating he didn't go to bed but returned to the study, while Grace polished off the leftovers.

As children they had been so close, growing up in the paradise that was Chadlicote, bicycling around the grounds, building bridges over the stream, swimming in the lake, camping overnight in the barn, pretending to be Daleks from their favourite television programme, *Doctor Who*. Her home had always been her favourite place on earth, like something from a fairytale, rambling, beautiful and full of history.

But after they'd been sent to boarding school they'd seen much less of each other. Sebby left school at seventeen, after a mysterious incident involving the groundsman's lawnmower, and went into 'business', although Grace never really knew exactly what that meant. She went to university. Every now and then he'd popped down for an evening, taken her out to dinner and made her feel glamorous and popular, things that – being three (all right, maybe four. Sometimes five) stone overweight – she felt very rarely.

Not knowing what to do with her first in classical studies, she'd stayed on to do a PhD. But after two years she threw in the towel. She enjoyed her research but she'd had enough of teaching bored students, just a few years younger than her but seemingly from a different planet. Students who wore crop tops and cut-offs, miniskirts and flimsy dresses, rather than the Evans smocks Grace had resigned herself to.

They seemed so busy surreptitiously checking their texts, and submitting essays that had been downloaded word for word from the internet, and Twittering and Facebooking, that they didn't have headspace for doughnuts and jelly and Coronation chicken and all the things that haunted Grace's dreams. They looked at her round body with barely concealed pity.

She realized she was getting fatter because she was sad, missing the country she'd grown up in. It was time for a change of career, although Grace didn't know what. The summer holidays were coming and she decided to return to Chadlicote, to think things through. Two weeks before she was due to return, Daddy crashed his car coming home drunk from greyhound racing near Totnes. He died instantly.

Grace resigned from her job. Although Daddy had made a will, the rest of his affairs were in a mess. With Mum in shock, it was left entirely up to Grace to sort it out.

She hoped for some support from Sebastian, who, after all, was tied down to no particular job. By now he'd had various careers. A tapas bar that didn't attract enough trade – bad location, they realized with hindsight. He'd launched a couple of websites, produced one or two films that never got released. Mummy would have loved to have seen more of him; she'd never concealed that Sebby was her favourite – and rightly so, he was better-looking, cleverer and more entertaining than Grace. But around that time Sebby had met Verity and was too busy wooing her (as romantic Grace thought of it) to give Grace a hand.

So Grace single-handedly and not altogether successfully tried to sort out her father's numerous debts. She was too tired and busy and grief-struck even to think about a social life, and nearly a year passed before she could turn her attentions to the neglected house and grounds. It wasn't as if Chadlicote had been in the family for generations – her grandfather had bought it cheaply as a crumbling ruin and set about restoring it. When Daddy had inherited it, the work was only part done and since he was far more interested in who was racing in the two-thirty at Doncaster than in replacing worm-gnawed floorboards, the place had remained ramshackle. To Grace that was part of its charm.

However, it couldn't stay like that. She began to list ways of reviving Chadlicote – converting the outhouses into holiday cottages, opening a restaurant, hiring it out for weddings. She was fired with excitement. Her mother, however, was more dubious. Nadia Briggs, as she was originally known, was the only child of a railway worker and a housewife. They had great ambitions for their beautiful daughter and sent her to finishing school. After that she did a bit of modelling, before marrying Blewitt Porter-Healey, who was seen as a catch because he was the heir to a big house.

Nearly thirty years of living in that same big house, which also turned out to be draughty and unmanageable and four miles from the nearest shop (and thirteen miles from anything even vaguely resembling a boutique or beauty parlour), had only slightly dimmed Nadia's stylishness. In her early fifties, she was still far more striking than her daughter.

Grace adored her mother. She was also a bit scared of her. The awareness that she had failed to fulfil any of her hopes was one of the main reasons she turned so often to the biscuit tin.

'You've lost a few pounds,' Nadia said with a frown as the two of them sat one evening about a year after Daddy's death on the back terrace with its views out towards the lake. 'Have you been doing Scarsdale like I told you?'

'Sort of, Mummy. And just spending lots of time outdoors has helped, I think.'

'Thank heavens.' She slapped her daughter's hand, as it reached for the bowl of rice crackers. 'No! I said you've lost a few pounds. Not that you can go crazy.'

'Sorry, Mummy.'

'Keep up the good work. It might help you find a husband. Lord knows, you're handicapped enough as it is. Young girls shouldn't be living in the middle of nowhere with their parents. They should be sharing flats with other young girls in London. Going dancing and having fun. That's what I did after I left school.'

'But I don't really like London. I prefer the country. And I'm really happy being here with you, Mummy.'

Nadia shrugged. 'And I'm happy to have you here, my dear. After decades of being alone when Daddy was at the greyhounds, it's nice to have some company. It's you I'm worried about. These are your best years. You don't want to spend them locked up with me in the middle of nowhere, your lovely looks lost in a casing of blubber.'

'It won't be like that,' Grace said. And she didn't think it would. She wasn't a weirdo. She was twenty-five; she'd work out a plan to revive the house, she'd lose weight and somehow on the way she'd meet a man.

But her hopes were put on ice again. Because Nadia, who had always been so active, walking at least five miles a day with the dogs, began complaining of joint pains and stiffness.

The symptoms got worse and eventually she went to see a specialist. He ordered some tests and then some more before eventually breaking the news that Nadia had motor neurone disease.

'What, like Stephen Hawking?'

The consultant cleared his throat. 'Well, that's a very advanced form of the disease.'

'So I'll end up in a wheelchair. Talking. Like. A. Robot.' Nadia said the last bit in a synthesized American voice.

'And being a world-class physicist,' Grace added. The consultant didn't laugh.

'There are many, many treatments available to maximize quality of life,' he said.

These treatments began immediately. Nadia popped dozens of pills a day. Saw endless therapists. Grace's days were crammed with ferrying her to various appointments – her mother's hands had suddenly and dramatically got too shaky for her to drive. There was no time for anything else. What choice did she have? This was her adored mother. They couldn't afford nursing care anyway, plus Nadia found that idea intolerable.

'I don't want some man who couldn't get a job anywhere else giving me a bath and helping me into my underwear,' she cried. 'Not when my darling daughter can help.'

Sebastian and Verity had got engaged, so he was tied up with wedding plans. He did call twice a week, and Mummy was always thrilled to hear from him and would spend the rest of the day reporting to Grace: how Sebby was looking into starting a hedge fund, how Verity's bonus from the bank where she worked was going to be more than a million, how they were planning a bash at the Grosvenor House Hotel and a honeymoon in the Maldives. Grace was glad Nadia could live vicariously through them. For her own part, she was so busy just keeping Mummy well that she had no time to look after the house and grounds. Whole sections of the once glorious gardens disappeared under weeds. Wallpaper peeled. Algae stifled the lake.

And slowly Nadia's legs became weaker and weaker until she was confined to a wheelchair. Her arms and hands started to go too, so everyday tasks like turning taps, brushing hair, dressing, doing up buttons became more and more difficult. Her head began to loll as her neck muscles weakened.

Over the final couple of years she found it harder and harder to speak and then swallow as her throat muscles atrophied. In the final days Grace was spoon-feeding her, bathing her, even changing her nappies. Lou helped out as much as she could, and tried to persuade Grace to come out occasionally for the odd supper at her cottage in the village. But so often Mummy would call, frustrated because she couldn't get undressed, or frightened – as her mind began to slip as well – at being alone in the house. Even if she didn't, Grace felt so guilty leaving her that she couldn't really enjoy herself. It was easier to stay at home. And eat. Cakes that Lou baked. Biscuits. Family bars of chocolate wolfed down in a couple of mouthfuls. Jacket potatoes covered in comforting mountains of melted Cheddar. Whole tubs of ice cream, straight from the freezer, that burned her lips and gave her heartburn, but tasted so smooth on her tongue.

*

It was five years between the diagnosis and Nadia's death at the end of a long, cold winter when the house's various boilers kept breaking down and the roof started resembling a colander. Grace could do nothing about her beloved home. She was either helping Mummy, or she was too exhausted to do more than cook a whole packet of pasta, smother it in butter, devour it and collapse.

Now Nadia was gone. Grace was exhausted. She was thirty-four, but she looked far older. She felt some relief that Mummy was, at least, at peace, but all her anxieties were now channelled into the collapsing house that she now owned jointly with Sebastian – Sebastian who had also aged, thanks to the quick arrival of Alfie and Basil, not to mention the folding of more business ventures. Grace told herself something would work out. With Lou's support, she put in place a vague plan to have some kind of holiday – her first since all this had started. Then she would lose four stone and set to work to raise the funds to restore Chadlicote to its former glory.

'So . . .' Sebastian said, climbing into the beaten-up old Land Rover which stank of Silvester, the spaniel, and Shackleton, the pug.

'Are you sure you won't change your minds? Stay the night?' Grace turned on the ignition and backed out of the car park. Verity and the boys had arrived late last night and made a lot of fuss about how cold the house was and how frightened Basil was by creaking pipes in the night. She wasn't surprised when Sebastian now shook his head.

'We've got to get back. Alfie's got a birthday party tomorrow.' He cleared his throat as the car bumped along a winding country lane. 'Now, listen, there's something we

9

need to talk about,' he said hastily. 'What are we going to do with Chadlicote?'

Grace glanced at him as she negotiated the tight bend next to the entrance to Cudd's Farm. 'I know it needs a lot of work. But we'll get there. I can devote myself to it now.'

'Er . . . I'm sorry but I don't think that's an option.'

'What do you mean?' Grace glanced at him sharply as she revved into fourth gear.

It came out in a rush. 'I've been looking at the accounts, as you know. And we have no choice but to sell.'

'Sell Chadlicote?' Grace couldn't take her eyes off the road but her jaw dropped like a cartoon character's.

'I've looked at the figures. It's unsustainable. We have a huge amount of inheritance tax to pay, and even without that we simply can't afford the work needed. And besides . . . even if we did it what would be the point? I mean, what would become of Chadlicote in the long run?'

'Well . . . I don't know. I would live there, I thought. And then maybe . . . well, it would be up to our children to decide.'

'*Our* children?' Her brother looked puzzled. 'Oh, you mean if *you* have any?' His tone made it clear that was highly unlikely. 'Well, yes, I suppose so. But what would they do? They couldn't all live in it together, in some kind of commune. And besides . . . Vee and I need the money. We're feeling the pinch like everyone else. Business hasn't been good for me recently and she's not going to get anything like her usual bonus. Everything has got so much more expensive, and Alfie's really not thriving at the local school, so we've got to start thinking about going private.'

He sighed. 'I'm really sorry, Grace, but it's going to have to go.'

'And where will I live?' she asked, as the car turned the last curving bend and entered the tall metal gates, flanked by the derelict lodge, that marked the drive.

'Vee and I discussed that. Of course you can't be left homeless. I mean, you would be left with a decent sum of money from the sale of the house, plenty to allow you to buy a decent place of your own. But you did nurse Mummy for a long time *and* you're not married *and* you don't have anything even vaguely resembling a career. So we've agreed it would be only fair to let you have the village cottage when the tenant moves out.'

'Oh!' Grace's head was swimming. They were pulling up in front of Chadlicote now: Chadlicote with its beautiful, red-brick Elizabethan façade choked with ivy. Mullioned windows glinting in the sun. Wide stone steps. Perfect proportions. All right, the stonework was crumbling, there were boards over a couple of the windows, but still . . . it was her home. Half hers, anyway. But Sebastian had a splendid home of his own in Wimbledon, near the Common.

It had never occurred to her he wouldn't let her stay.

But there was no time for further discussion. The drive was full of cars, and people in black were standing around the dried-up fountain, wanting to let her know how sorry they were. Grace couldn't face them. She needed time alone. She was still taking in this news, that her brother and sister-in-law were sending her to live in a run-down workman's cottage on the edge of the village, which – as far as she recalled – had a patch of scrubby garden and no central heating.

'Look, do we really have to . . . ?' she began, but Mrs Legan, the village's chief nosy parker, was peering at her through the window. Reluctantly, Grace wound it down.

'Grace. I'm so sorry I didn't get the chance to say it before. But I am truly sorry for your loss.'

'Thank you,' said Grace. She glanced urgently at her brother.

'Do we really have to?' she said softly, winding up the window again.

'I'm sorry. I should have told you earlier. I called the estate agents last night. They're coming tomorrow for a valuation. They think we should have no problem with a quick sale.'

'I . . .' But guests were approaching. Grace gave up and got out of the car. She'd fight this battle later, she told herself, although if Sebby said they had no choice . . .

Grace needed a sausage roll. That would help her think straight.

# I

It was the final viewing of the day and the client was late. As usual. Lucinda stood outside the heavy front door of the converted bottle factory, tapping her heel on the concrete and looking at photos on her mobile. How did people pass the time before they had phones? She smiled at the picture of herself last summer by the pool of the villa in Tobago, wearing a very flattering orange bikini. Mummy and Daddy at the lunch table, sheltered by an umbrella from the Caribbean sun. Ginevra and Wolfie, arms wrapped round each other. Benjie about to do a silly backwards dive into the pool.

Happy memories. Looking up, Lucinda caught sight of herself grinning in the plate-glass doors leading into the lobby. It was the kind of thing you could never admit to anyone, but she knew she was looking beautiful that day. Her auburn hair shone, her green eyes sparkled, her skin glowed. Just lucky, she reminded herself, knowing she was in danger of tipping over from self-confident into smug. She came from a good gene pool. She was young. And going places. She couldn't help it; she smiled again at her huge fortune in being her.

'Lucinda?'

At the sound of her name, she jumped. She swung round. A man – presumably the client – was grinning at her unnervingly, as if he'd read her thoughts. He was about her age. Lanky. Blond, slightly spiky hair. Very blue eyes. Skinny jeans, a Sex Pistols T-shirt and a slightly tattered navy blazer. Very different from the City boys she normally took on viewings. Intrigued, she held out her hand.

'Mr Crex? I'm Lucinda Gresham. How do you do?'

'Lucinda.' He had a northern accent. Rather cute. 'Pleased to meet you.'

She didn't show it, but inwardly she winced. She couldn't help it. Her upbringing might have been too sheltered but she had been taught manners. Mummy had trained her that the right response to 'How do you do?' was 'How do you do?' Ridiculous, but when anyone replied in any other way it made her think less of them and it was all she could do not to correct them. Not that she would have implied that Nick Crex was in the wrong, even if he'd pulled down his skinny jeans and mooned at her. One of the first rules of estate agency was that the customers were always right – at least when you were with them. Back at the office you could bitch about them to your heart's content.

But for now Lucinda would nod and smile if Nick Crex told her Princess Diana had been murdered by aliens. She had to prove Niall wrong. Though he'd never said it in as many words, he'd been understandably wary about taking her on at the Clerkenwell branch of Dunraven Mackie, not least at a time when so many agents were being made redundant.

And quite right, Lucinda acknowledged – even though his behaviour pissed her off – because she had zero experience and owed her job to blatant nepotism. But Lucinda was determined to show her worth, and six months down the line Niall was having to admit that she was pretty good at this selling houses lark, even with the market in its direst straits in years.

'Shall we take a look?' she asked.

'I'm all yours.'

She punched in the code that opened the front door. They crossed the lobby and called the lift. Ping. Up to the first floor. Down a long red-linoed corridor. Lucinda knocked on the green front door of Flat 15. Gemma Meehan had told her she'd be out, but you never knew. She'd had a hideous, though hilarious, experience last weekend when she'd ushered an uptight American couple into 12 Dorchester Place, a cute little Georgian house in a quiet terrace near the Barbican.

Knowing that the owners, the Kitsons, were on holiday in Mallorca, Lucinda had opened the door and marched straight through the hallway to the living room to find Carlotta Kitson wearing nothing but a fuchsia G-string, while a man who was most definitely not Linus Kitson was thwacking her on the bottom with a tennis racquet.

'Oh, whoopsie,' Lucinda cried merrily. 'So sorry!' And she virtually dragged the Americans out of the front door and down the stairs flanked by fake bay trees in a pot. She thought it highly unlikely she'd come across Gemma Meehan in the same situation – she was far too prim. But they did always say the quiet ones were the worst.

No one replied to the knock, so Lucinda unlocked the door and they stepped inside.

'Wow,' he said, before he could stop himself.

'It's a fantastic space, isn't it?' Mimicking his body language, Lucinda looked around the large room. To the

15

left, a kitchen with Italian marble surfaces and a state-of-the-art range. In front of them the dining area. A sitting area furnished with vast zebra-striped sofas occupied the rest of the space. Huge floor-to-ceiling windows on two sides, with views over the slanty roofs of Clerkenwell. It was glorious. Clients always got a great first impression. It reminded Lucinda of Fabio, her sister Ginevra's ex: great on the surface, but a quick viewing immediately highlighted flaws. Still, Ginevra hadn't minded – for a while at least – and maybe Nick Crex was the man who for whatever reason might be blind to the obvious problems of Flat 15 and instead focus on its plus points.

So far, so good. He was turning round slowly. Taking it all in. Lucinda inhaled the scent of freshly baked bread. *Everyone* had latched on to that trick. Fresh flowers on the table. Yawn. Those property programmes had so much to answer for.

'A fencer,' he said, nodding at the left-hand wall where the exposed brick had been decorated with a collection of long, slim blades.

'I guess so,' Lucinda said, surprised. Again, she wasn't being snobbish exactly, but fencing was a posh sort of sport and Nick Crex was certainly not posh.

'I used to fence at school,' he said. 'A "Help Deprived Youth" programme.' His tone was mocking, acknowledging that he'd sussed her and her prejudices. Lucinda blushed.

'Oh, right. What fun.' She twisted the Cartier pearl and diamond bracelet Daddy had given her for her eighteenth birthday round her wrist. She always fiddled with it when she was a bit nervous.

'It was.' Nick Crex turned to a table covered in silver-framed photos. 'And she's a dancer,' he said, picking up a photo of Gemma Meehan in a tutu.

'She used to be. She had to give up. Some injury.' Gemma was attractive in a skinny, dark kind of way. Driving everyone at the agency crazy with all her nagging about why the place hadn't sold, but fortunately the pictures didn't reveal that.

'They've travelled a lot,' he said, picking up a photo of the Meehans grinning on what looked like a Thai beach.

'It's a real party flat,' Lucinda said, eager to steer him back on track.

'Yeah. Especially with that balcony thing.' He nodded upwards.

'The mezzanine,' Lucinda corrected, unable to stop herself. 'It's great, isn't it? Shall we go up?'

He followed her up the spiral staircase, to the upper level. A TV area with a giant HDTV screen and squashy bean-bags. A study area with a desk built into the wall, lit by a genuine Bestlite. Two bathrooms leading off it – this was the point when most people started realizing that there was a catch and asking questions like isn't that a bit of an odd layout and wouldn't it be better if the bathrooms were en suite? Lucinda was all ready with the spiel, that this was a converted warehouse, that the floorplan reflected the layout of the original, historic building, blah blah.

But Nick Crex said nothing. Good man.

While he was looking round, Lucinda stood back. For something to do, she scanned the wedding photos on the wall. Alex in black tie, skinnier than he was now. She didn't like Gemma's dress, far too meringuey. But the look of love in her eyes was very sweet, even someone like Lucinda who categorically did not get the whole bride thing had to admit it.

'So is this a bedroom?' Nick asked, nodding towards the three steps that led down to the master one.

'Yes. It's very . . . original!' Code for blinking ridiculous. She followed him into the room. An empty space. To the right, a ladder leading to a bed perched on top of the – slightly ambitiously named – walk-in wardrobe. A clichéd scent of vanilla candles in the air. Poor Gemma, she wanted this sale so much there was nothing she wasn't prepared to do.

'Isn't it great?' Lucinda enthused. She couldn't think of anything worse than sleeping on a sort of perch, she'd be up and down it all night, wanting to pee, and would inevitably fall off. But maybe Nick Crex had a stronger bladder than her. Or a catheter and bag. 'Look, and here below it you've got your very own walk-in wardrobe. Isn't it fabulous?'

'Mmm.' He definitely liked it. She could tell from the body language. What did he do that he could be in with even the vaguest chance of affording such a place? Even though prices had crashed, it should still have been beyond his league. All she knew about him was from the brief phone call they'd had that morning when she had randomly picked up the phone. He'd said he'd seen the flat on the internet and given a Belsize Park address. Which was smart enough to mark him out as a serious client, rather than a time-waster.

'Would you like to see the other bedroom?'

'Rock 'n' roll swin-dle, rock 'n' roll *swin* . . .'

The sudden noise made Lucinda shriek. Then she realized that it was his ring tone. Impatiently, he pulled his phone from his jeans pocket.

'Hello? Yeah. Hiya.' He looked annoyed. She could just hear a woman's voice.

'Yeah. I'm a bit busy right now . . . Can I call you back? . . . Yeah, I won't be that long . . . I'll call you back . . . I'll call you back, all right? . . . I love you too,' he mumbled like a teenager asked to kiss his mum in front of the school football team. 'Yeah. See ya.' Hanging up, he shoved the phone back in his pocket.

'So, the other bedroom?' Lucinda smiled. It was up a small flight of stairs. Again, a funny shape with another raised bed stuck on a shelf in the corner. But different. Definitely different.

'It's such a great location,' Lucinda said. 'The area just gets cooler by the day. So many bars and restaurants and shops and great for transport links. St Pancras just up the road for the Eurostar . . .'

'Why do they want to sell?'

'They're a couple. I think they want a baby. And . . .' Lucinda gestured towards the mezzanine with its wide-spaced railings and the fifteen-foot drop on to the stone tiles below. No point lying. Anyway, she was pretty sure Nick Crex wasn't into the whole baby thing yet. 'Well, it's no place for a baby, is it?'

'Guess not.' A smile broke over his face, but then suddenly he seemed awkward. 'Well, thanks for that. I'll be in touch.'

'You've got the details, haven't you? No? I'll give them to you.' She rummaged in the lime green Smythson's brief-case which her mother had bought her to congratulate her on her first job. 'Here you are.'

'Thanks,' he said, not glancing at the laminated A4.

'Thanks so much,' she said when they were back out on the pavement. Held out her hand again. He shook it limply. Such gestures obviously weren't the done thing where he came from, Lucinda thought. Snobbish. But true.

'I'll be in touch,' he said, and turned abruptly up the narrow cobbled street. Lucinda watched him for a second and then turned in the opposite direction. It was late enough for her to call the office and say she was clocking off, but she decided to go back and put in at least another hour's work. No one was going to call Lucinda Gresham a slacker.

# 2

Even though her reflexology appointment had run over, making her slightly late, Gemma Meehan was first to arrive at the café where she was meeting her younger sister Bridget. No surprise there, Gemma thought as she took a corner seat and ordered a cup of peppermint tea.

She'd have loved a cappuccino, but caffeine was banned until her future baby, Chudney, as Alex, her husband, insisted on calling it (he'd laughed for about an hour when he'd heard that Diana Ross had cruelly named her daughter that), was safely in her arms. Although then Gemma would be breastfeeding, so caffeine would be off limits too. And then – who knew – but with luck there'd be another Chudney. In other words, no coffee for another – what? – three, four years? Never mind. For her unborn children she would do anything.

'Stop it,' Gemma said, almost out loud. She was getting ahead of herself again. There were no children. And whether there ever would be or not was all down to what happened in the next hour or so. At the thought of the conversation she was about to have, her heart began to pitter like rain on a tin roof. Calm down, she told herself. And by the same token, no negative vibes at Bridget's lateness. Though she could have texted to let her know.

Gemma sighed. She'd spent twenty-one long years making allowances for Bridget. From the moment their mother had returned from the hospital jiggling a screaming bundle, all Gemma could remember was Bridget being a nuisance, albeit a cute one. As soon as she could crawl she snatched Gemma's toys away. Ripped up her drawings. She blew out the candles on Gemma's eighth birthday cake. Every time Gemma cried or complained, her parents told her not to be so silly, that she had to make allowances. That babies couldn't be expected to understand the rules.

But the day never came when Bridget did start understanding the rules. Gemma loved Bridget – the maternal feelings that had always been at her core ensured that – but she couldn't help feeling frustrated at times. While Gemma worked hard at school and even harder at her ballet, Bridget was always bottom of the class. What was worse was she never seemed to care. Gemma was mortified if she came home with an even vaguely bad report for anything, but Bridget didn't give a damn. Mum and Dad would shake their heads and sigh and say, 'Darling, you really must try harder,' but she'd just giggle and the subject would get dropped.

Gemma had gone to ballet school, where she had literally worked her arse off – living for a while on two apples and a glass of milk a day in order to get herself down to the seven stone achieved by the top pupils. Bridget meanwhile had dropped out of school after her GCSEs (two Ds and an E) and gone off to Spain, where she'd worked in a bar for a couple of years.

By the time Bridget had returned with a fiancé, Pablo, Gemma had a job in the corps de ballet of a small company based in Manchester. It wasn't the fairytale life she'd envisaged – the work was physically gruelling, the money was rubbish, and with every day that passed her dream of making prima ballerina became less likely.

But she'd never know if that dream might have come true, because shortly after she'd met Alex, who was up in Manchester working on a case, she'd badly sprained her foot, and that was the end of Gemma's professional career. But it didn't really matter because she was so deeply in love. Five months after they met Alex had proposed to her with a vast diamond and sapphire ring, which his grandmother had been given by her Rajah boss while working as a governess in India just before the war.

Gemma resigned from the ballet company, moved to London to be with Alex and found part-time work teaching dance to toddlers, which left her plenty of time and energy to plan their wedding.

Meanwhile, Bridget had discovered that Pablo had another fiancée back in Malaga, and was working in a shoe shop, although she got fired after a few months for unpunctuality. She went off to India for a while and came back with a gastric disorder that made her farts smell of rotten eggs and a dolphin tattoo on her left shoulderblade. She quickly found a job as dogsbody at a small business selling bras online, which Gemma thought sounded fascinating, but again she was sacked after a few months for spending too much time in chatrooms. Mum and Dad were very sympathetic and let her move into their house in Norwood until she sorted herself out.

It didn't bother Gemma. She was used to it. But it infuriated Alex.

'Here we are declining all offers of financial help for the wedding and there's your sister still getting your poor mum to do all her washing and make her vegan meals,' he fulminated.

'But I don't want Mum to do my washing,' Gemma pointed out. Mum was a terrible cook, after all, and never properly sorted the lights and darks. Anyway, she was blissfully happy with Alex. They could look after themselves, why begrudge her sister?

She and Alex had got married in a beautiful ceremony at the Orangery in Holland Park. Alex and Bridget had a bit of a spat on the day because Bridget insisted on wearing black. Gemma let it ride. She was too busy having the happiest day of her life; or the happiest day until Chudney was born.

On honeymoon in South Africa, Gemma threw her pills away. Six months passed. Then another six. Gemma was only twenty-seven, so she was sure there was nothing to worry about. Nonetheless, she decided after another six months that they'd see a doctor. In the meantime, they put the flat on the market. Around that time she lost her job, when the ballet school she worked for went under. Although she was upset, she decided not to look for another one. She hoped not working would minimize stress levels and boost her chances of conception. It also gave her plenty of time to find the perfect family house.

'Don't you think you might be jumping the gun?' asked her friend Lila, having sat through another lengthy summary of the properties on the short list.

'Absolutely not. John and Alison only started looking for a new place when she was six months pregnant and they had a nightmare. Builders in with the baby, all that drilling and dust. I'd hate that.'

In the end it took five months of surfing the net, tramping round estate agents introducing herself, poring late into the night over school league tables. But then just three weeks ago – the day before their first appointment with fertility doctor to the stars Dr Malpadhi – she found 16 Coverley Drive.

Gemma couldn't resist. She reached into her bag and pulled out the glossy details that by now were etched on her heart. The four bedrooms so beautifully decorated, one for her and Alex, one for each baby and one for guests – even Bridget, if she cooperated today. The lovely light kitchen/diner with its granite work surfaces and Mexican tiles and flagstone floor backing on to the seventy-foot mature, west-facing garden. Gemma wasn't quite sure why west-facing was so good, but everyone's voices dropped in a hushed kind of way at the mention of it and, as for mature, well, that had to be better than immature, which made her think of a garden making fart jokes and crying when it didn't get its own way.

Then there were the things you didn't see, though they were reflected in the price – the Ofsted-rated outstanding primary school just down the road. The town with its cutesy shops, where people still greeted each other in the street. The station, ten minutes' walk away, with its commuter trains for Alex.

OK, the decor was too flamboyant for her – all primary colours, dhurrie rugs and strange metal figurines. Gemma was a more restful, neutrals kind of girl. But such details were cosmetic. She wanted this house so much. And amazingly, picky Alex wanted it too. Terrified that the market was bottoming out and soon prices would start to soar again, they put in an offer for a hundred grand less than the asking price and, after a week of haggling, managed to settle on a discount of fifty grand.

It was theirs. Except it wasn't. Because they still had to sell Flat 15. Flat 15, Alex's bachelor pad, which had seemed so quirky and cool when she'd moved in, but which was now a millstone that no one wanted to buy, that was holding them back. Flat 15, which was all wrong for a family – because families didn't live in city centres and open-plan lateral spaces, they lived in two-storey houses in the suburbs where there was fresh air and good schools and no tramps slumped asleep in doorways. That was how Gemma had grown up and it was what she was determined to provide for her own babies.

But luckily the Drakes of Coverley Drive were still looking for a property of their own, so for now they were happy to wait. And Flat 15 had to sell eventually. In fact, a viewing was taking place right now. Gemma shut her eyes, focusing all her energies into making this one a success. She'd done everything the programmes advised, made fresh coffee that morning, left vases of flowers everywhere, put out photos of her and Alex looking fun-loving and carefree. She'd even lit some sodding vanilla candles that made her sinuses ache but that were allegedly irresistible to home buyers. This time it had to work.

Gemma regrouped. Selling the flat was not her only concern. She had work to do with Bridget too. Time to focus on that.

The door opened, letting in a blast of freezing air.

'Hiiii!' called Bridget from the threshold.

She was wearing a rainbow-striped jumper, a blue beret

with sequins on it and no make up. She had two pigtails tied with rubber bands and she had put on a bit of weight since the last time Gemma had seen her at Christmas, before another long trip to India. Weren't you meant to *lose* weight there with all the curries and dysentery and stuff? 'Stop it,' Gemma told herself. Bridget wasn't a dancer, she could be any weight she wanted.

Most of the time Gemma felt a bit sorry for Bridget, but every now and then she couldn't help being just the tiniest bit admiring of the casual way she flouted the norms. Sometimes she suspected her sister was a much braver creature than her. Alex, of course, disagreed.

'She's not brave. She's lazy, rude and disrespectful.'

'That's harsh.'

'Well, look at her, gadding off to Goa for six months whenever she fancies it, to discover herself. She treats life like a holiday.'

'Why shouldn't she?'

'Because holidays have no meaning unless they're a break from reality.' Sometimes Gemma wondered if her husband was jealous of Bridget's falafel-munching, festival-attending, anti-globalization-marching existence. After all, it couldn't be more different from his own, which was like a hurdle race. Swotting to win a scholarship to Belfast's top private school and then to get into Oxford. To qualify as a barrister, to fight to get a pupillage and then win tenancy of his chambers and now his sixty- to seventy-hour weeks working late almost every night and at weekends, to be on top of his briefs, rarely taking a holiday in case a big case came up.

But if Bridget agreed to Gemma's request, he'd have to

change his tune. She hadn't told him they were meeting. The plan was to surprise him with the most incredible news.

'Oh, sorry!' Bridget cried, as she trod on the foot of an elderly lady, who tutted in annoyance. Bridget steamed on, having not even noticed.

'Hey!' She pulled her sister to her bosom in a clumsy, patchouli-scented hug.

'Great to see you. You look *fantastic*. How are you?' Gemma suspected she was going overboard on the gushiness but she was nervous. Everything hinged on the next twenty minutes or so.

'*Really* good!' Bridget cried, sitting down. 'I'm thinking about doing a degree. I've been looking at all the different courses.'

'Oh, wow!' Gemma said, though more from duty than real enthusiasm. For years announcements like that had fired her up. She'd get all excited on Bridget's behalf, helping her pursue whatever her latest dream was by investigating it on the internet, sending off for brochures, making calls on her behalf. But by the time all the information was placed in front of her Bridget had long moved on to the next fad, so Gemma had stopped bothering.

'I'm thinking of doing a course in popular and world music. There's one at Leeds. Or maybe film and television. Or women's studies. Hi.' Big smile to the waitress. 'A cappuccino, please. Ooh and maybe a slab of that yummy-looking chocolate cake. Anything for you?'

'I'm fine.' Gemma waved the waitress away with a polite smile. To stave off the nagging of '*Why* not? Are you eating enough?' that inevitably accompanied such exchanges, she quickly added, 'So no more travelling for now?'

'Oh no, definitely some more travelling. The plan's to earn some money – there's a job in a sandwich shop going. Once I've earned enough I thought I'd go to Indonesia for some meditation. But not for a while. Say September, when the weather cools down a bit. So you're stuck with me for the next few months.'

'But what about the university course? Doesn't term start in October?'

Bridget waved airily. 'I wasn't planning on starting this year. Maybe next year. There are more important things than courses and qualifications, you know.'

'Mmm,' Gemma said, congratulating herself on not inviting Alex to this meeting. Those kinds of comments irritated him like a case of prickly heat. 'So . . . any news from Mum and Dad?'

'Only the email they sent both of us.' Their parents had moved to Spain three months ago. 'Sounds like the neighbours are being a bit arsey about the extension.'

'They'll win them round, I'm sure.'

'I hope so, because once it's built, I'll be out there like a shot. They won't be able to get rid of me. Dad said he'd send me a ticket.'

Typical. Gemma smiled serenely. 'And where are you living now?'

'At my friend Estelle's in Acton. Remember Estelle? Amazing woman. You should ask her to do your Tarot some time. I'm sleeping on her sofa. Not the comfiest but it's really near this community centre which does subsidized yoga for jobseekers, so I've been going there every morning.'

Gemma took a deep breath. She'd ask her now. But she was thrown off beam by her phone ringing. She looked at the caller ID, planning to ignore it, but it was Dunraven Mackie. 'Excuse me,' she said, grabbing it. 'Hello?'

'Hi, Gemma,' said Lucinda, in her upper-crust tones. 'Lucinda Gresham here. Returning your call.'

'How did it go?'

'Really well! He's definitely interested . . .'

'But he didn't make an offer?'

'Well, no. Not yet. But it's very unusual to put in an offer on the spot. I'd say he'll almost definitely be coming back for a second viewing.'

'Right.'

'So I'll keep you posted. Fingers crossed. Goodbye. Have a lovely day.'

''Bye.' Gemma hung up, bitterly disappointed.

'Offer on the flat?' Bridget asked.

'Not yet.' She pulled herself together. 'But looking good, apparently.'

'You're not *still* obsessed with getting that family house?' Bridget sounded amiable enough but she had that look in her eyes that drove Alex mad, a look that said, 'Christ, how bourgeois.' As if there was somehow something wrong with wanting to live in a nice house in a nice street. As opposed to a friend's futon in an area where it was easier to buy class A drugs than fresh fruit or vegetables.

'It'll be perfect for children,' Gemma retorted.

'I guess.' There was the tiniest pause and then Bridget asked gently, 'And how's all that going?'

The moment had come. Gemma could hardly speak; she felt as if she'd been punched in the mouth. She sipped some tea, then, looking her sister in the eye, said: 'Well . . . we sort of know what we're up against now.'

'What do you mean?'

'The specialist . . .' She couldn't help it, a big tear plopped down her face and into her tea. 'The specialist says I've got the eggs of a nine-year-old.'

'Meaning?' Bridget looked shocked.

'Meaning they're never going to mature.' *It's so unfair,* her inner voice screamed, as it did all day every day. But she didn't say it.

'You've never really had periods, have you?' Bridget said, as if she were an esteemed gynaecologist. 'I always thought that was the dancing, though.'

'Well, it wasn't. It's just the way I was born.'

'You never ate much though, did you? And that can have an effect on your menstrual . . .'

'I always ate plenty!' Gemma snapped, then immediately regretted it. 'Sorry, I didn't mean to sound so cross. I'm just allergic to so many things.'

'Like what?'

'Like butter.'

'You're not allergic to butter. Does it bring you out in a rash? Does it make you vomit? You just don't like eating it because it's full of calories.' Right on cue, the chocolate cake appeared. 'Oh thank you! Yum. Are you sure you don't want some?'

'No thanks. I had a late lunch.' Gemma wasn't going to have an argument about her allergies. They needed to get this conversation back on track. 'So the doctor said the only way forward is egg donation.'

'Using another woman's eggs?'

'Uh huh. Mixing them with Alex's sperm and planting them in my womb.'

'So it wouldn't be your baby?'

'Not biologically mine. But it would be Alex's. And I'd carry it, I'd give birth to it. But it's not so easy. There aren't any eggs in this country. The government changed the law so donors lost their anonymity. Which means hardly anyone is prepared to donate any more in case a child turns up on their doorstep eighteen years later. And the waiting lists are horrific. So now if you want an egg you basically have to go abroad. But of course you have no idea whose eggs you're getting. I mean they *say* you do but you can't be sure and there are these rumours about girls from eastern Europe being forced into it and . . .'

'Right.' Bridget reached out and squeezed Gemma's hand. She'd had a new tattoo done on her knuckles, Gemma noticed as she squeezed back, took a deep breath and blurted it out.

'So I was wondering if we could use one of your eggs.'

'Sorry?'

'One of your eggs.' She shrugged. 'If you'd be OK with that.' She made it sound as if she was asking to borrow a jumper. Not that she'd be seen dead in one of Bridget's moth-eaten numbers knitted from sustainable llama's fur, but anyway . . . 'I mean, I know we could adopt but we want a *baby* and it's practically impossible to find a newborn and I'd like to have *some* blood tie and if it's your egg . . .'

She looked expectantly at her sister's face. She'd anticipated delight, disgust, dubiousness, but Bridget seemed merely amused.

'I don't see why not. I don't want kids. Not yet anyway. So why shouldn't you have them?'

Hot, salty tears flowed down Gemma's cheeks. 'That's so kind of you. I can't believe it. I don't believe it. I . . .'

''s OK,' Bridget grinned, pink in the face and obviously chuffed with herself.

'It's wonderful!' Gemma checked herself. 'Before you definitely commit you need to know exactly what will be involved. It's quite an ordeal. You'll have to take all sorts of drugs and . . .'

'Well, it won't exactly be the first time,' Bridget chortled.

That laugh brought Gemma right back to earth.

'Bridget, you can't take drugs if you're going to be an egg donor. It would be *incredibly* irresponsible.'

Bridget laughed again and waved a dismissive hand. 'Chill, Gems. I was only joking. I mean, you can't discount what I've done in the past but I'm clean now. Well, pretty clean . . . I mean, I do the odd spliff and things but . . .'

'You couldn't do that if you were giving me an egg.'

There was a moment's silence, then Bridget said, 'Um. Sorry. I thought I was helping you out. But obviously not.' She stood up, wrapping her scarf around her neck.

'No, sorry, sorry! I didn't mean it like that. I'm sorry, it's just this means so much to me and I can't . . . I've lost my sense of humour.'

'You mean you once possessed one?' Bridget teased, sitting down again.

Gemma tried to get a grip. 'Listen, you don't need to make your mind up straight away. Have a think about it. Read up on it. I can send you some links.'

'Sure,' Bridget shrugged, good-naturedly. 'But I'll do it. Why ever wouldn't I?'

Gemma's phone rang again.

'Oh sorry, I'd better take this, it's Alex. Hi, darling! Yes, Lucinda says he's definitely interested ... No, I won't get my hopes up but it's looking good ... I know, we'll see, but I might as well be optimistic, for once. And ...' She looked at Bridget, who gave her a perky thumbs up. Gemma was infused with love for her sister and the world in general. 'I've got some other news ... I'll tell you later. Do you think you can get home early tonight?'

# 3

It was Friday morning in the offices of the *Sunday Post* newspaper and Karen Drake, deputy editor of the *All Woman!* magazine supplement, was trying to edit an article that had just popped into her inbox about how egg-cosies were now gracing 'the hippest dining tables' – Kate Moss was a huge fan, apparently, while simultaneously browsing Net-a-porter and listening to Sophie, the features editor, on the phone to one of her mates.

'I've decided I'll get into jam-making during my maternity leave. As well as doing a bit of painting. And arranging all my photos in albums.'

Karen smiled. Sophie was four months pregnant, and fantasies about what motherhood would be like never failed to tickle her. Karen hadn't the heart to correct her. She was still grinning as she picked up her ringing phone.

'Hello?' she said, tucking the handset under her left ear.

'Sweetheart!' said Phil, her husband. 'Fantastic news.'

'Oh?' Phil's definition of fantastic news was not always the same as hers, his usually concerning the fortunes of Tiger Woods or the English cricket team.

'Scott's just sent me details of a new house. It's perfect. Even better than Doddington. And guess what – we can have the first viewing. Before it even goes on the market.'

'Ah,' said Karen. She tried to sound thrilled, but she

felt as if she'd just been punched in the stomach. Talk about bad luck. Secretly she'd been delighted when Doddington had fallen through, the sellers having decided, for some bizarre reason, that they didn't want to leave the rustic ruin, after all. She'd thought it would take months – no, maybe years – before they found a similar property. For the past couple of days she'd even been allowing herself to feel guilty as she wondered how to break the news to the Meehans, who were desperate to buy 16 Coverley Drive, that they weren't selling after all. But goddammit if Scott, the property finder her husband had employed, wasn't doing everything in his power to earn his fee.

'It's in Devon,' Phil burbled on. 'An Elizabethan manor house. Nine bedrooms, ten acres, needs plenty of TLC. A real opportunity to turn it into a viable business. And Scott reckons we can do a deal on the price because they want a quick sale.'

Devon. So they were talking at least a three-hour drive from London. She'd never be able to commute from there.

'I'll email you the details, shall I? Ideally we'd go and see it tomorrow.'

'Bea has a birthday party,' Karen protested.

'She can miss it,' said Phil, as if such a change of schedule were of no consequence, rather than life-shattering, for a nine-year-old. 'There'll be other parties. But there won't be another house like this.'

'Right,' Karen said, already bracing herself for Bea's freak-out. She swallowed hard, as an email pinged on to her screen. Chadlicote Manor, Little Dittonsbury, Devon, read the header. 'I'll call you later when I've read the details. It . . .' she swallowed. 'It sounds very exciting.'

Karen examined the particulars. Just as she feared. A vast ancient pile with room after room after pointless room set in acres of muddy countryside. Tons of expensive and disruptive work needed to restore it to its former glory. What was the postcode? That would be the litmus test. Karen tapped it into the Ocado website. Great. Just as she'd suspected. They didn't deliver there. Plus the chances of Ludmila, the au pair, joining them there were as likely as Britney Spears solving the Israeli/Palestinian question.

In other words, Chadlicote signified the end of everything that kept Karen's life on track.

Karen had never for a second believed in the rustic idyll dream peddled by media offshoots like her own, because she knew the truth. She had been born in a remote corner of Wales where it rained virtually every day of her childhood. There was nothing for miles around except sheep and trees, and the highlight of the year was when a black family stayed in the village B&B and everyone dropped round with excuses just to get a look at them.

At school she was bullied for being clever, so she put her head down and worked hard, determined to get out of that hole at the earliest opportunity. But if term times were miserable, the holidays were even worse. Weeks of boredom with nothing to do but ride her bike up and down the hills and hang out at the bus stop waiting for the twice-daily charabanc into Swansea. Drink cider in copses with her best friend Andrea, flicking through copies of *J17*, which they hoarded like treasure, studying the fashion shots, fantasizing about London, where high culture didn't consist of a tractor show and Londis wasn't rated as a shopping experience.

She was determined to get out at the earliest opportunity, and that opportunity came earlier than she'd anticipated, when she was sixteen and Mum and Dad split up. Dad disappeared to Australia, never to be heard of again. Mum had some kind of nervous breakdown and went to live in a commune. She was much better now and worked for the council in Ludlow, but Karen had never really recovered from her abandonment at that crucial stage in her life.

With no one caring and a clutch of O levels (God, that dated her), Karen had headed off to London to seek her fortune. Things didn't quite turn out the way she'd hoped. Initially she'd stayed with a distant family friend, but after a row when she left her underwear dripping on the radiators she was kicked out.

For eighteen months Karen found herself living in a hostel for the homeless, surrounded by alcoholics and addicts. They were desperate, unpredictable people. Whenever Karen needed to count her blessings – which had been often over the past year – she looked back on that period and thanked God she hadn't been mugged or raped. So many inmates were. She coped by detaching herself from the situation, pretending it was happening to somebody else, by making herself look as unattractive as possible and stomping around with her keys clutched between her knuckles. She earned a meagre living, waitressing and doing odd jobs. Eventually she got out of there, but things didn't improve.

Over the next two years she managed to live in seventeen places, each more of a dive than the last. In one the landlord, who had nine convictions for offences like arson and GBH, used to bring his wife and kids to the house every day, lock them in a room and beat them up. Karen had to wear earplugs to block out the screaming. Then there was the council flat on the eighteenth floor of an east London block where people with guns and knives hid behind every pillar and the lifts also served as public toilets. She tried to treat the experience as a great adventure, but her nerves were becoming more and more frayed.

And then she met Phil. And he saved her. Cheesily, he was a customer in the restaurant. She didn't even register him the first few times he visited; after all, what was there to notice about a man she later – objectively – summed up as 'ish': 'tallish', 'plumpish', 'fairish'. But he kept coming, leaving her bigger and bigger tips, and eventually they got talking. After about a month of this, they went to the cinema together. Not on a date. Purely as friends. He was a venture capitalist, which, he explained, meant he invested in other people's businesses in return for a large percentage of their revenue.

'That sounds grown-up,' she said as she climbed into his – even more grown-up – BMW so he could drive her home. 'You don't look old enough to be doing something like that.' That, she realized, was why she didn't fancy him – his cheeks were too peachy smooth, his voice a little too lispy, to take him seriously as a man. He was more like an over-grown schoolboy.

'I'm twenty-four,' he said. 'And I've been doing this since I was eighteen.' He put his foot on the pedal and the car gave a satisfying roar. 'Where to, madam?'

When they stopped outside the tower block, Phil was appalled.

'You can't live somewhere like this.'

'Why not?' she shrugged.

He gestured at the ten-foot-high graffiti saying 'Suk your father's cock, bitch, Alisha.'

'I can't afford anywhere else.' She wondered what he'd make of her bleak little box with the broken toilet and boiler she couldn't afford to fix.

'I've got a house,' he said. 'You can live there.'

'I can't live with you! I mean . . . I barely know you.'

'You won't be living with me. It's one of my houses. I'm a landlord too on the side, you see. Come on. No strings attached. Look at me. Do I look like a pervert?'

'I'll think about it.'

The next day, a fifteen-year-old girl was stabbed in the lifts. She called Phil, trying hard not to cry.

'If I could stay in your house just for a bit that would be great.'

So she stayed in his house in Kensal Rise for three years, three years during which Phil never laid a finger on her, but – thanks to his never-ending public school contacts – wangled her a job as a PA at the *Daily Sentinel*.

She began writing the odd article when no one else was available and within two years she'd been promoted to a reporter. In her eyes, it was pretty much a dream job. She got to travel all over the country and sometimes abroad on press trips. She knew the inside story on which politician had a lovechild with which TV presenter. She earned a salary, not loads, but enough to pay Phil's rent and allow her London dream to finally crystallize into a reality.

She went out every night, she drank in the hottest bars – often with a complimentary tab. She saw films months before they were released. She also went out with a series of attractive, louche men who were great fun and who, one by one, broke her heart. It was after yet another humiliation from one of them, Ryan, who revealed a secret partner and two children, that Phil took her out for an expensive meal and several bottles of wine.

At the end of it, sozzled and keen to heal the heartbreak, she fell into bed with him. The next morning they were a couple. At least Phil thought they were. And Karen didn't argue. Because she was tired. Tired of unreliable men and of having to find someone who wasn't a cowboy to fix the plumbing and of always secretly worrying that somehow she'd wind up back in the tower block. Phil would take care of everything, make it easy for her. There was no such thing as romantic love anyway, only hormones. Her heart might not sing at the sight of Phil but that was far better than allowing primal urges to blind you. What she'd have now would be mature, sensible, adult. Safe.

They went out for two years and when she was twenty-eight, she accepted his proposal. Around the same time she was headhunted by the *Sunday Post* to become the magazine's deputy. More money. More status. Lots of free meals in restaurants that wanted a mention, discounts on clothes, complimentary holidays in return for a flattering write-up. Two years later Eloise was born. It was the fairytale ending, only of course it wasn't because with their first child came the first inkling of discord in the Drake marriage.

'We can't live here any more,' Phil said, gesturing round the living room of their huge flat in a Clapham mansion block.

'Why on earth not? I love it here.' All those restaurants

41

and cute shops full of fripperies that had been so important to her pre-children and that she hoped she would be able to frequent again one day without falling asleep in her miso soup or Eloise pulling over a display of tea glasses.

'Children shouldn't be brought up in the city. They need country air. Space to run around in.'

'Phil! You know how I feel about the country. Everyone's on drugs at twelve, because there's nothing else to do. Anyway my job's here.' Karen couldn't admit it but she'd been thrilled when her six months' maternity leave ended. Her colleagues said: 'Ah, back so soon, don't you miss the little one?' (Jamila, who'd now left, had said, 'I do admire you braving it back here when everyone's so shocked at you leaving the baby.') She shrugged and said, 'Yes, well, we don't have a choice,' even though everyone knew Phil's money meant she could quite easily never work again. But it simply wasn't acceptable to say you found long days with a small baby duller than watching a darts match.

It was exhausting working all week with no down-time at weekends, but Karen far preferred it that way to the alternative of coffee mornings spent comparing episiotomy stitches and standing shivering in the playground.

Work kept Karen sane. Work was what had made the compromises involved in marrying Phil bearable. It gave her her own identity outside her marriage and children, which made her feel she hadn't completely lost all of her old self. But her work wouldn't be possible anywhere but London, where the newspaper offices were.

But Phil still wasn't happy. He'd always been keen on muddy walks, always yearned for a dog, for easy access to a golf course, shooting and fishing. Of course, he'd been brought up in Croydon, so he had no idea what the real country was like. The argument went on for the next two years until she became pregnant with Bea, which settled it.

'Look, there really is no room for four of us, and even with the money I'm earning we couldn't afford the kind of house we'd like in London. But what about this . . . ?'

'This' was 16 Coverley Drive, St Albans. When Karen saw the particulars, her initial reaction had been to scream. St Albans? Could you get more suburban than that? A five-bedroom detached property with double garage. Yuk. But Phil persuaded her to go and look at it and to both their surprise she was seduced. The house was twice the size of anything they could have afforded in London, and attractive in a retro kind of way with its gabled roof, and the town, which she'd envisaged as some backwater with a Spar selling overpriced rotting vegetables and a war memorial covered in hoodies drinking cider, turned out to be lovely, with plenty of boutiques and delis.

Karen was already coming to terms with the fact that her priorities had changed. Easy access to the tube and dozens of bars were no longer top of the list. After all, she had started obsessing about the Lakeland catalogue, promising herself that one day she would treat herself to an avocado slicer and wondering what could ever make her worthy of a Remoska cooker ('A joy to use', 'What a gem'). It would be nice to have some outdoor space.

So they'd moved.

And it was fine. She'd redecorated the house so it seemed less staid, with colourful objects from her travels, bright walls and ethnic rugs. They found an excellent nanny. There was a good train service, so getting to work only took about fifteen minutes longer than before.

After Bea started school there were three or four pretty much perfect years, with Karen adoring her job (even though it irked her that her boss Christine was never going to stand down and she'd be a deputy for ever), the girls in a brief valley between stroppy toddlerhood and adolescence. They didn't need a nanny any more – an au pair was fine for drop-offs and pick-ups from school – and apart from Katerina, who totalled the car, and Liljana, who they found having sex with her sailor boyfriend on the living room sofa, it worked pretty well.

Phil's business was going brilliantly – he'd sold off most of the houses he'd bought for thruppence ha'penny in the Nineties at a four or five hundred per cent mark-up. They went on fabulous holidays, had big lunches at weekends entertaining friends. For the first time in her life Karen felt complete. She had her family and the broken nights bit was behind her, so she also had some freedom again. She went to the cinema or theatre once a week to keep up with what was going on, and joined a book group. So her job wasn't perfect – a lot of the stuff they published made Jordan's memoirs look like Proust and Christine was always demanding freebies and she wasn't paid the market rate because she was too pussy to ask for a rise. And Phil annoyed her sometimes with the way he always watched telly with his hand down the front of his trousers and – on the rare occasions when she was enjoying something like a film – he would switch to the Teletext cricket scores without any consultation or warning. He always walked forty paces ahead of her and the girls down the street, and if she ever sent him to the supermarket he always ignored her detailed lists, coming back with sackfuls of things like potatoes because they were on special which then sat in the cupboard for weeks going off.

But no life was perfect, and no marriage. Give and take was the key. So she was surprised and somewhat miffed when one night in bed, after the twice-weekly sex which she had decided she'd compromise with, he said, 'I'm bored. Work doesn't offer any challenges any more. I've done it all, made all the money I want to make. It's time to climb off the ladder and smell the roses.'

Another thing that annoyed Karen. Phil's fondness for clichés. But she just said, 'What would you like to do?'

'Well, I know you've always been against it but I really do want you to think about moving to the country. The proper country. I'd like to find a wreck. Do it up. Be a bit of a squire if you like.'

Karen stiffened. 'I couldn't work in the country,' she said.

'Of course you could. They've got broadband there now. You could freelance.'

Karen cringed. She knew what freelancing from the country involved: writing articles about other women who'd also migrated from the city and had set up their own business making hand-embroidered high-chair slip covers. Begging nineteen-year-old work experience girls to listen to her ideas. Earning about seventy-three pounds a year. No, thank you.

'We've had this discussion. I have to be in London. I really enjoy my job, Phil.'

'But I don't any more. I hate the commuting . . .'

'You were the one who wanted to live in St Albans.'

Phil gave her one of his rare icy looks. 'I hate the commuting,' he repeated. 'I'm bored with sitting at a desk number-crunching. I want open spaces. A new challenge.'

'Darling, we'll talk about it in the morning. I'm bushed. Goodnight.'

She hoped by the morning he'd have forgotten all about it but to her annoyance, he brought it up again. And then again and again in the months that followed. She found him browsing property websites.

'Darling, the girls are so happy at their schools. You're not seriously suggesting we uproot them?'

It was annoying, but Karen never really took it seriously. Generally Phil tried to please her – it had always been that way. She'd made a compromise in marrying him and another in moving to St Albans; he couldn't ask any more from her.

And then everything changed.

Phil kept getting colds that he couldn't shake off. Was constantly exhausted. Had bad headaches. Was losing weight. Eventually the doctor did some blood tests.

The diagnosis came back – leukaemia.

Karen would never forget the night after he'd received his diagnosis, her trying to keep it together. Phil, who'd always been so calm, so logical, losing it. Shouting about how his body had betrayed him. 'Now it knows how to grow a cancer,' he'd yelled, until drowsy Bea had come downstairs, wanting to know what the noise was, and they'd told her Mummy and Daddy had been chopping onions and it had made them both cry and a bit cross.

46

In the days leading up to his first consultation he would lash out viciously and irrationally. Then he'd lock himself in his den, watching old golf DVDs and snarling at Karen even if she dared ask him something like what he wanted for supper. 'Who cares?' he'd yell, his face crushed with fear. 'None of this means anything.'

Karen reminded herself that illness affected men differently from women. As a mother she had already experienced huge changes in the body, was more familiar with hospitals and embarrassing procedures. Knew how it felt to give up your body to strangers. But of course her pregnancies had had joyful outcomes. She couldn't know how it must feel to think you were dying. Inasmuch as she'd ever envisaged it, she'd always imagined herself brave, long-suffering, cheery, but Phil had been reduced to a snivelling, self-pitying, aggressive wreck. It wasn't pretty to watch and it was virtually impossible to live with.

But then who could blame him? Over the next eleven months he went through two rounds of chemo, two of radiotherapy. Rapid weight loss. His hair falling out in handfuls. Puking in an orange plastic washing-up bowl at the side of the bed. But there was a happy ending. Karen would never forget the consultant breaking the news that Phil's latest tests had come out clear. Cue weeping and rejoicing, though inside Karen simply felt numb. And of course it wasn't so simple – was anything in life? – because he was only in remission, which meant another four years or so of blood tests before he would officially be cancer free.

During those eleven months, Phil had had plenty of time to think. He'd decided that his life needed a complete makeover, that he was going to offload the last of his businesses and use the cash to start afresh. He would have made much more if he'd sold three or four years earlier, but they still ended up with a ridiculous lump sum in the bank.

'Neither of us need ever work again,' Phil boasted.

Now, looking at the seven-figure price of Chadlicote Manor, Karen doubted this. Even if they negotiated a big discount, it would still eat hugely into their capital. And the restoration would cost millions more.

Phil hated it when Karen raised such objections. 'Money is for spending,' he'd say airily. 'Haven't you realized, even now, how short life is?' He had a point. But then he'd never grown up wanting anything. Karen, still remembering how they'd had no central heating eleven months of the year because Dad was too skint to turn it on, found such comments terrifying. Money wasn't for spending. Not all of it, anyway. It was for putting aside for a rainy day.

Sophie peered over her shoulder. 'Ooh. Is this house on the radar now? You're not going to move there, are you? What would you do for your daily sushi fix? Catch a trout in the lake and skin it?'

'Not if I can help it,' Karen shrugged.

'The grass is always greener, isn't it? I'd kill for a garden and here's you turning your nose up at a million acres of land.' Sophie's tone was philosophical rather than bitter; she was a contented soul.

Karen's phone rang again. 'Hello?' she said, guiltily aware that she really should be calling Issie, their cookery writer, to beg her to next week please try to do recipes that didn't feature Jerusalem artichokes, as readers kept writing in complaining of the terrible wind they gave them.

'It's me. Great news. They can do a viewing tomorrow. The estate agent's going to a wedding but the owner's happy to show us round herself. So we can have a day out – drive down early, see the house, then maybe go and have lunch somewhere. What do you think?'

'I think that's lovely. But we'll still have to cancel Bea's party. Do you want to ring Isobel's mum? Her name'll be on the form list pinned to the fridge.'

'Oh. Can't you?'

Karen gritted her teeth. Now Phil wasn't working he was far more involved with the girls' day-to-day lives, but he was still reluctant to participate in the nitty-gritty of organizing playdates, making headdresses for the school play, liaising with teachers.

'I'm quite busy here, darling.'

'But, but . . . she's a *mum*. You *know* her. I'd be embarrassed.'

Karen glanced at Sophie, now hammering at her keyboard. The innocent. She had no idea motherhood was going to be like this. Karen remembered how, occasionally, before Phil got ill, she had occasional meltdowns at all the stuff she had to do. 'When I'm a goner you realize *you'll* be the one who'll have to make lunchboxes and buy all their friends' birthday presents,' she'd shout.

She could never say anything like that now.

'All right, I'll do it tonight,' Karen said firmly, knowing she'd regret it. 'But you can break the news to Bea.'

'OK. Karen. I'm so excited about tomorrow.'

'Me too,' she lied.

'Love you.'

''Bye, darling,' Karen said.

# 4

Arriving home, Gemma looked around the flat for signs of a viewing. As usual, everything was exactly as she'd left it. Not that there was exactly anything to hide: her knicker drawer was always orderly, the bathroom cabinet full of Lancôme and Jo Malone, with any embarrassing bits and pieces locked away.

Still, she was paranoid, knowing a stranger had been in her home judging her taste, asking what possessed anyone to buy a flat with a bed on a platform and the bathrooms a schlep down a ladder away.

She was tempted to leave a note. *It wasn't me. It was my husband. He was a boy about town when he bought it and he wasn't bothered about en-suite bathrooms. Can't you see what a cool party flat it is? A bit ironic since my husband doesn't really do parties any more. He may only be thirty-one but he's too tired after a day in court and prefers to see people over dinner in a quiet restaurant. But hey ho, it fitted with the image he had of himself when he'd just been accepted by his chambers.*

*And do you know what? We've been really happy here. Watching films up on the mezzanine. Holding big dinner parties downstairs. Lying all day in the funny platform bed, reading the papers and eating croissants and making love, then stepping out of the door and being right in the middle of London. I've always thought of it as our love nest. It's time for us to move on now but I'm sure you could be just as happy here too.*

Obviously she wouldn't do it. Yet maybe she should stick around and waylay viewers. But Alex would pooh-pooh such an idea. Alex, who wouldn't be home before eight at the earliest. Who would probably eat dinner and then head straight for his desk. Such was life as a criminal barrister; he'd be stepping out of chambers when his clerk would chuck him a brief for the following morning, involving defending an alleged rapist in Bromley, and the evening would be gone.

Gemma had got used to seeing films alone, turning up at dinner parties unaccompanied. To cancelling holidays and weekend plans at the last minute. She was an expert at making nutritious meals that could be reheated the moment she heard her husband's key in the lock. To going to bed without him, to be wakened around three for sleepy sex.

She never complained; it was what she had signed up for. And right now she was glad of his absence, giving her time to indulge in her secret obsession. She went into 'her' bathroom – since the flat had two, side by side, she'd bagged the one with the bath while Alex got the shower – and unzipped her handbag. At the bottom, concealed beneath her purse and a copy of *London Lite*, just in case her husband should decide to stop and search her, was a pregnancy tester.

She knew, she knew. She'd rationed herself to just one test a week. Because at one stage she was doing at least one a day and it was bankrupting them, not to mention keeping them on a constant rollercoaster of raised and dashed expectations. After a showdown with Alex, Gemma really had tried her hardest to cut down, to limit peeing on the stick to Friday morning just after breakfast. But every so often, when she was feeling nervy, she cracked and today was one of those days. She knew what the answer was going to be, she had the eggs of a nine-year-old for heaven's sake. But she still couldn't resist.

Her hand shook as she unwrapped the foil. Expertly she crunched it and the box inside an old loo-roll tube in the bin and covered them with the newspaper, which she should recycle really. She'd fish it out later.

Gemma was obsessed with having a baby. But she was also obsessed with not letting her obsession affect her marriage. She'd read so many articles about women desperate to conceive, who'd ended up childless *and* manless, because of their nuttiness. Consequently, she initiated sex *at least* every other day regardless of how tired or not-in-the-mood she was, so as never to commit the terrible crime of baby-making fornication. Initiated sex, even though she had no desire for it whatsoever, now that the body she'd honed so carefully all these years had betrayed her. But Alex would never know as she wriggled under him, faking earth-shattering orgasms.

Every time the tests showed negative or a rare sparse period came, she didn't cry – she knew Alex would feel guilty and resentful. She just shrugged and brightly said: 'Oh well.'

But while Gemma stayed perky on the surface, inside she knew that infertility had warped her. She used to consider herself a generous person, but now every time she saw a pregnant woman she felt twisted like the roots of an ancient apple tree. When friends called to break the news, she tried to sound delighted. But inwardly she was notching up scores on a mental chart, a chart where points were allocated to people she knew had had other hardships in their lives or suffered several miscarriages. Those who said things like 'To be honest, it was a bit of a happy accident' plummeted straight to the bottom and from then on Gemma did her utmost to avoid them.

She'd been dreading the news from Dr Malpadhi, but in a funny way actually knowing it was never going to happen naturally came as a warped relief. At least now she had something to work on. Before that she had been taking her temperature every morning, spending a small fortune on ovulation kits and travelling round the country to be with her husband at the 'right' time, while pretending she just wanted to keep him company in bleak hotel rooms. But now she knew that – barring a miracle – there would never be enough of her eggs to commune meaningfully with Alex's sperm, she'd had to move on and investigate the alternatives. Starting with adoption, which Alex opposed violently.

'I'm just not sure I could love a child that's not my own.'

'Everybody says you do. That it's just the same. Even more intense sometimes.'

Alex shook his head. 'It'd have to be a last resort. Let's exhaust the other options.'

And the only real option was egg donation. The problem was finding an egg. Hardly any were available in the UK, so they'd have to go abroad. Gemma was fine with this, Alex wasn't.

'You don't know what you might be getting. The kind of woman who's desperate enough to want to sell her ovaries . . . well, I don't want her genes in my babies.'

'No, it's not like that. I've been on some of the American websites. You can choose a donor who looks like you, who has a college degree . . .'

'It's still too weird. That half the child would have nothing to do with us. The better half,' he added, tousling his wife's hair.

'But it would be bathed in my hormones, in the womb.'

'Doesn't convince me,' he said, as if she were one of his clients trying to explain why the man in the CCTV throwing a brick through the wall might look exactly like him but actually it was his long-lost twin visiting from Patagonia.

The idea had come to her in the middle of one of her reflexology sessions. Of course! Bridget! After all, they shared exactly the same DNA. And although the pair of them were so different – both in character and in looks – Gemma was convinced that the combination of Alex's sperm, not to mention the latent genes of a family who, bar Bridget, made the Waltons look like a bunch of swinging crackheads, would ensure a more . . . reliable . . . child than her sister had been.

And now she'd agreed, it was all systems go. She just had to get Alex to say yes, but that was a mere formality. Before she told him, however, she'd just do one final test, to be totally sure that a rogue mature egg hadn't been fertilized.

She unwrapped the plastic and peed on the stick, thinking it would be sod's law that – having secured Bridget's services – she'd be up the duff. But even as she was hoping this, a red line was filling the bottom porthole. The top hole stayed empty.

Shit.

Downstairs, the door slammed. Gemma jumped as if she'd heard a gunshot.

'Hi, Poochie!' Alex called, using their old nickname, one that went back so long she'd forgotten its origins.

Why was he back so early? Whatever. No time for secret tears, for mourning yet another non-existent baby.

'I'm in the loo!'

'I don't want to know!' One of Gemma and Alex's longest-standing jokes involved never seeing each other on the throne. She had friends who happily took a dump while their husbands were in the bath. Personally Gemma couldn't bear even to acknowledge she had bowels, which was a bit of a problem in a flat where the bathroom was situated directly off the living area. She'd become an expert on running the taps at full volume – though what that was doing to the environment and Chudney's future world she hated to think. She didn't know how she'd manage giving birth, when sometimes you pooed – but she'd be so grateful for the chance to push a baby out, she'd deal with it.

She shoved the stick under the paper in the bin, flushed the loo and ran out to the mezzanine. Alex was standing in the dining area below, looking up at her, hair tousled, tie slightly askew.

'Hey, Pooch. How are you? How was your day?'

'Busy. But that doesn't matter. What about you? What's this news?'

There was a look of anticipation on his face that Gemma recognized. Oh God. She'd given him the wrong idea. Now she was going to have to disappoint him.

'Oh, Poochie. I'm not pregnant.'

'Oh.' Alex rubbed his nose vigorously, as he always did

at times of great emotion. Alex really wanted children – originally he'd said four but he knew better than to go on about that. 'Right.'

She hurried down the spiral staircase and kissed him full on the lips. 'It doesn't matter! I saw Bridget today.'

'Oh yeah?' Alex looked puzzled. What possible good news could relate to Bridget unless it was that she was emigrating to the moon?

'She wants to be our donor.'

There was a pause and then Alex said, 'Bridget?'

'Yes. She's going to give us one of her eggs. Isn't that fantastic?'

'Does that mean I have to sleep with her?'

Gemma laughed at his appalled expression. 'Of course not, darling. They harvest the eggs from her like they would from any anonymous donor and then they mix one in a test tube with your sperm and put the embryo inside me. It means the baby will have a genetic link to me.'

'But we're talking dotty Bridget here. With a druggie past, who freeloads off everyone and can't stick to anything for even five minutes.'

'Just because Bridget *used to be* a bit of a loose cannon does not at all mean her . . . mean *our* baby would be the same way. It's just as likely to be like me. After all, she and I are exactly the same gene pool, just differently shaken up.'

'But still . . .' Alex ran his hands through his hair. 'I just don't know, Poochie.'

For the second time that day Gemma felt tears pricking. 'Darling. What other option do we have? I can't give you a baby, you won't adopt. You don't want an anonymous donor egg from Spain.'

'A tortilla? No thanks.'

'Don't call it that.' Gemma took a deep breath. 'It's *got* to be Bridget. It's an incredible offer. Why can't we be grateful for it?'

'I'm not being difficult. I just think we can't rush into any of this. You need to look before you leap.'

'What's to look at? We want a baby, we're being offered a great chance of having one. The only chance we have.'

The tears started to fall now. Damn. She'd been really hoping she could keep a lid on things. Awkwardly, Alex put his arms round her. She pulled him close.

'Poochster,' he said into her hair. 'It's OK. I'm not saying no. I'm just saying Bridget is not a reliable person and should we embark on such a life-changing journey with her at the steering-wheel?'

She tried to stop the sobbing, but the tears kept coming. She felt his warm breath against her hair. His body sagged.

'OK, OK. We'll accept it. It's incredibly kind of her. Though, I mean . . . We're still not guaranteed a baby, are we?'

'No. But the chances are around fifty per cent. Much higher than with normal IVF. And we can freeze any surplus eggs, so if it doesn't work the first time, we can try again.'

'Does Bridget understand what it involves?'

'More or less,' Gemma lied. 'She's looking into it.' She flung her arms round Alex's shoulders. 'Thank you, darling. Thank you so, so, so much.'

He kissed her back, placing both his hands on her bony dancer's bottom. Gemma wasn't in the mood: she felt too emotionally exhausted for sex and she wanted to be online delving into the pros and cons of home birth. But, sticking to her rules, she wiggled responsively, placing her hand on the fly of his trousers.

'Come on,' she said, leading him by the hand towards the bedroom with the funny layout that nobody wanted, but which – right now – she was too happy to care about.

## 5

In the spare bedroom of his plush rented flat in Belsize Park, Nick Crex was lying back against piles of pillows, a notebook on his knee and a pen in his mouth. He'd been working on a song all day and the chorus had only just fallen into place. A chorus that was fine. But not a classic. And Nick hated producing anything that wasn't of the very highest standard.

Not ideal when the label was putting on huge pressure for the second album to be delivered. Studio time was booked for next week and Andrew, the Vertical Blinds' manager, had instructed him several times that he'd better come up with some 'fucking magic' by then. But so far he had only two songs that were anything like good enough. It was bugging him. His ambition was to write a song like 'Imagine' that made your brain ache at its simplicity.

There was a gentle tap on the door. Kylie stuck her head round. As usual, she was dressed in her green velour track-suit and her Ugg boots, which she always changed into when she got home from her job at the beauty salon. She smiled at him, her huge blue eyes creasing into her pink, plump face.

'Tea's almost done. It's sausages and chips. Your favourite. Then afterwards I thought we could watch a DVD.'

'I've got to finish this song.'

'You've been in here all day. You need a break.'

'I've got to finish this song. You watch something.'

There was a tiny pause and then she said, 'OK. I'll give you a shout when tea's ready.'

The door shut. His phone bleeped in his pocket. He pulled it out. It was a text from Ian.

Going to premier party in Docklands. Wanna
join us?

Nick was tempted. Usually he enjoyed a party. But if he didn't corral the chords that were running untethered around his brain, he wouldn't be able to relax. Plus, there was the question of Kylie. It would be tricky going without her, but if they went out together she stayed glued to his side, too shy to talk to anyone new, too aware that she was too small, too plump, too – somehow – ordinary to be a rock star's girlfriend. But if he did go alone, she'd still be texting him hourly, asking when he'd be back.

She'd always been up for a laugh back in Burnley, but London seemed to have stolen her mojo, made her shy almost to the point of agoraphobia. She'd found a job as a nail technician, but she'd made no effort to get to know the other girls in the salon.

For Christ's sake, Nick thought, staring out of the window at the dark communal garden. He had to summon the nerve to tell her it was over. He'd tried to confide his desire to end it to Ian, who was his best mate in the band, but he hadn't understood, saying, 'Yeah, mate, there's so much totty you're missing out on by not being single.'

But it wasn't just about missing out on the totty, it was about moving away from his roots, roots which Kylie kept him attached to. Nick's thoughts moved on to the estate agent who'd shown him Flat 15. She wasn't immediately sexy in the way Kylie was. But she had an untouchable aura, which of course made you want to grab her, rough her up a bit. She'd smellt great too – mysterious and spicy. Kylie smelled like an air freshener.

He'd see her again tomorrow at the flat, where he'd arranged a second viewing. Nick smiled. He still couldn't quite believe that he – a boy from a small, dead-end northern town – could find himself in the position of buying a flat in the middle of London, as if it was a litre of milk off the supermarket shelf. But then who could have believed that the band would have taken off like it had?

After all, only two years ago they'd been playing in the back rooms of pubs to their mums and two old men. Nick had been working for a small office supplies firm, writing songs on his PC when he should have been doing spreadsheets, living in a tiny studio flat with Kylie, in the same tower block as Mum. But then the band had been spotted – first by Andrew, who'd become their manager, then by the A&R guy from Prang Records.

Before they knew it, they'd been recording their demo, then they'd got the contract for the two albums, then their first single, 'Mercury River', had gone nuclear on the downloads and was being played non-stop on the radio, and suddenly – within the space of a year – they were the hottest band on the planet. Well, OK, maybe planet was an exaggeration, but they were the biggest in Britain and planning to take on America soon.

And suddenly his Lloyds Savers, which had only ever had about £25 in it before, had climbed into quadruple figures. Then quintuple. And then one day there was nearly a million pounds sitting there. Andrew took him aside for a word.

'You need to do something with that money. Not just leave it, especially when interest rates are so pathetic. Or jizz it away on drugs and cars, which is what the others will do. Get a financial adviser. Invest it. Then you'll have something to fall back on long after the party's over.'

Nick had found a financial adviser called Charles, who'd told him to get into property while the market was low. So Nick had started to look at property on the internet, in the furtive way most men looked at porn. And he'd begun to conceive an escape plan from Kylie.

Kylie. Nick thought back to the first time he'd seen her, across the room at the George IV. He was seventeen, she was sixteen, flicking back her blonde hair and laughing at someone's joke. Fantastic tits complemented by a low-cut T-shirt. A short skirt showing off shapely if rather short pins. Pretty face, if a little chubby. Too much make-up – but all Burnley girls wore too much make-up. It didn't detract. She was gorgeous. She was also, as Nick discovered, his mate Shane's new girlfriend. But Nick wanted her, so Nick was going to have her.

It took a couple of months. At first Kylie ignored his glowering looks and barely responded to the few comments he tossed in her direction. Nick realized he was going to have to work a bit harder than normal to get her. He didn't mind, it was fun to have a challenge. One night he'd toss a compliment in her direction, the next time he saw her he'd ignore her completely.

Worked a treat. When he waited at the bar he could feel

her eyes boring into the back of his neck, then when he arrived at the table with drinks she'd pointedly ignore him. It went on for about a month, until one evening when they were in the pub and Shane said, 'Guess what, guys? Me and Kylie have some news.'

'Oh yeah?' they all chorused. Kylie blushed and looked down, then looked up and caught Nick's eye.

'Well, go on, tell them, Kyles.'

'No, you tell 'em.'

'All right, I will. We're engaged.'

'Oh, wow!' Shrieks from the girls, handshakes from the boys. Nick set his lips in contemptuous amusement as Kylie held out her left hand and everyone admired the ring from H. Samuel. 'Ooh, look at that diamond! You're so lucky.' In the flurry of congratulations, Kylie got up and headed towards the toilets. Nick stood up too. When she came out he was waiting in the dingy little corridor outside, next to the cigarette machine.

'Congratulations,' he said.

She jumped theatrically and laid a hand on her chest. 'You frightened me!'

'Sorry.' He smiled. 'I hope you'll be very happy.'

'And what's it to you, Nick?'

'Nothing. Nothing at all.' He pulled her to him and kissed her hard on the lips, just like he'd seen Clark Gable do in that film his mum watched all the time. For a second she responded passionately, then she pushed him away.

'What the hell do you think you're doing?'

'Something you've wanted for a long time.'

'You cheeky wanker! I'm engaged.'

'Why are you kissing your fiancé's mate, then?'

The moment was so electric, they could both have been dressed in head-to-toe nylon. Then she flounced back to the bar, waggling her arse provocatively.

That was seven years ago, Nick thought. Seven years during which many tears had been shed, voices raised, insults exchanged across the street, rather unconvincing death threats made by Shane Vranch. Seven years during which he and Kylie had initially been blissful, when he'd written poems to her and they'd done things like dance barefoot in the moonlight on the North York Moors. Nick had always sensed he was special. A romantic. His relationship with Kylie sat perfectly with that feeling.

After they got their flat, life was slightly less bohemian. Still, they were happy enough, eating curries in front of obscure foreign DVDs he insisted they watched and going on cheap holidays to Spain, which had been only a qualified success as Nick couldn't swim and the sun disagreed with his pale skin. But still they'd had a laugh drinking cheap sangria in seedy bars off the beaten track, looking at white adobe churches in quiet squares.

Then the third phase, when the band was beginning to get its act together and habits of Kylie's he'd always found endearing, like burning the toast, began to irritate him. They squabbled about the fact that he spent so much time with the band, that he didn't really want to look for a new place to live because he had other things on his mind, that he couldn't make her cousin's wedding because it coincided with a gig, that he wouldn't even discuss getting married even though loads of their friends were settling down and Shane Vranch was a dad now.

Things were getting really tense when the band was

spotted and contracts signed. He didn't consult Kylie, he just quit his day job and announced he was moving to London, leaving the decision of whether she should follow entirely up to her. Inwardly, Nick was torn – he couldn't imagine life anywhere, let alone London, without her. But at the same time he was beginning to feel that a girlfriend with a curly blonde perm and a fondness for *This Morning* was not the kind of girlfriend he should have. He was pretty sure she wouldn't come – she was devoted to her family and loved being near the Moors. Once things were long-distance Nick hoped he'd meet someone else.

But to his surprise, Kylie said she was coming.

'What about your job? Your mum? Your sisters?'

'There are beauty salons in London, aren't there? There are phones. Trains. I love you, Nicky. I want to be with you.'

And like an idiot, he'd gone along with it. It was Nick's darkest secret, but for all his wearing of mascara and covering his arms in mystic tattoos, he was actually a bit of a coward. A childhood spent cowering in front of the TV while Mum and Dad screamed at each other in the bedroom had left him with a hatred of confrontation. Before Kylie, he'd never dumped anyone directly, he'd just stopped calling and ignored them when he'd bumped into them. They got the message, even if they didn't like it very much. Now he both hoped and feared Kylie would quickly get homesick and hurry back to Burnley, but eight months had passed and – although she was miserable in the south – she was showing no sign of upping sticks.

Hence his secret viewing. It was pathetic, but the only way he knew of getting the message across that he'd outgrown her was to move into a new place and not provide her with the keys.

It wasn't that he didn't love her any more, because in a way he did. Kylie was warm and soft; she knew exactly how he liked his tea and how many fillings he had and that he was afraid of dogs. She had a dragon tattoo, matching his, on her left arm and she adored Jammie Dodgers. She washed his underpants and bought him new socks. There was nobody kinder, nobody more understanding of his moods. But as a rock star's girlfriend, she was simply all wrong.

It wasn't just Nick who sensed this. Andrew was putting pressure on him too.

'You mustn't tell anyone you have a long-term girlfriend,' he said, as soon as they started to hit the big time. 'It doesn't go with your maverick image.' He didn't have a problem with the other boys. They were all having it off with models, starlets, reality TV stars. Jack, the lead singer, was having a heavily publicized on-off thing with Myrelle St Angelo, who was *the* model of the moment. Their days were a round of drugs and private jets. But all Kylie wanted was a pint in the local followed by an evening in front of the telly.

Nick hadn't been entirely faithful – there'd been a handful of one-night stands on tour; you'd have to be a robot not to succumb to the temptation. But essentially he was a monogamist. He wanted to be in a couple, but just a smarter one.

Once again, an image of the estate agent's face passed through his mind. She was the kind of woman he ought to have at his side. Haughty. Cool. Clearly well bred.

A plan began to formulate.

'Nicky!'

'Coming.'

Tea was on the oak table in the huge sepulchral dining room. Kylie had said they should turn it into a den, but Nick refused and insisted they ate there as often as possible.

'Looks good,' he said, suddenly realizing how hungry he was.

She blushed happily. 'Well, it's your favourite, ducks.'

A bottle of white wine was opened. Drinking wine was a new thing for both of them – really they preferred lager, but Nick had decided that was no longer acceptable. The sausages were delicious and the chips were fat and greasy. Nick was fussy about food. He hated all veg except carrots, all fruit except apples, and loathed sauces. Dinners with the Prang execs were an ordeal, as they always ordered things like sashimi and oysters. He would toy with them and then stop the limo on the way home for a MaccyDs.

He knew he had to work on making his palate more sophisticated, but the prospect of anything outside his comfort zone made him gag.

'Did you get anywhere with the song?' Kylie asked.

'Not really, it's bloody hard.'

'Poor you, love,' she smiled. There was a pause. Trying to sound relaxed, she continued. 'I spoke to Becky. Apparently Ian says you're going to be touring America later this year.'

Nick paused too, before saying, 'Did she? Yeah, well, that is the plan.'

'I've always wanted to go to America. New York. The shopping's meant to be brilliant.'

That familiar feeling of being slowly suffocated. 'I don't

know if we'll go to New York. Nothing's certain yet.'

Kylie didn't react. 'I was thinking maybe we could go by ourselves some time. For a weekend. Becky and Ian went a couple of weeks ago for her birthday. Drank champagne all the way. They said it was amazing.' Her voice softened. 'It would be good for us to get some time alone together.'

'Maybe,' Nick said, feeling like the most evil man in the world.

The following morning, Kylie was up early and out of the flat by eight. Nick rose an hour later and took the Tube to Farringdon, revelling in the stares of an office worker, a young woman, in a shiny grey suit. Brazenly he stared back at her. Immediately she looked away. Nick grinned. He could see her puzzling – is it him? No, it can't be. That was the joy of being the lead guitarist/songwriter. You got all the perks of wealth and fame, but you could still travel more or less anonymously on the tube. As lead singer, Jack couldn't step outside his front door without a volley of paparazzi bulbs exploding.

But without Nick, Jack would be nothing. Nick wrote the songs, and the songs – despite what Jack's groupies might argue – were what made the Vertical Blinds so hot. They were also what brought in the money. All right, the other guys were doing fine, but Nick got the royalties every time their songs were played on the radio and a way bigger percentage than the rest of them every time a disc was sold or downloaded. Hence his ability to pay cash for that amazing flat and still have plenty left over to buy his mum a house.

Like last time, Lucinda was waiting by the front door. If anything, she was sexier than he'd remembered: in a dove grey trouser-suit, her hair tied back in a neat bun. Her cheekbones seemed almost to point through her skin, heralding her genetic superiority. She was so sleek and glossy, like a racehorse. Kylie – well, Kylie was like a pit pony in comparison: cute, amiable but uninspiring.

'Hello,' she said. 'How nice to see you again.'

Nick didn't quite know how to respond to this. 'Yeah,' he muttered.

'Shall we go in?'

Just like Lucinda, the flat was even better than he remembered. To own something like that would be the apex of his dreams. But one of Nick's rules of life was always to play it cool. Show eagerness and Lucinda would be off spinning a line about how many buyers were after it, the stiff competition, blah-di-blah, maybe he should put in an offer straight away or risk losing the place by morning. He looked around in silence and – unlike last time – she kept her comments to a minimum. At the end, he said, 'I'm going to have to have a think about this.'

'Of course.'

'Yeah,' he said and then suddenly deciding it was time to change tack, he added, 'I like your suit. Very Katharine Hepburn.'

'You didn't strike me as a Hepburn fan.' She looked amused.

'Why not?' Snooty cow. Still, she had a point. One of the advantages of having a mother addicted to black and white movies, he guessed.

'Well, you know. You're in a band and . . .'

'Have you ever seen us?'

'What? Your band? No! I'm not that into music.'

Not that into music? Nick just couldn't understand how anyone could say that – it was like saying I'm not that into eating to stay alive, I'm not that into washing (actually Nick hadn't been that into washing for a big chunk of his teens, but whatever). Not that into breathing, into having a beating heart. Kylie loved music. It had been one of the things that had oiled their early years together, going to gigs, making up obscure playlists, tuning in to far-away radio stations. Some of her favourites were a bit dodgy, but she was always open to new stuff and had, in fact, introduced Nick to quite a few bands who'd become his greatest influences. But he banished such thoughts.

'You should come and see us some time. Might convert you.'

'I'd like that.'

'We're playing a Valentine's Day gig next week. Shepherd's Bush Empire.'

'Where's that?'

Er, hello! If Kylie had asked something like that, Nick's reply would have been so scalding you could have boiled an egg in it. But because he had decided to target Lucinda, he politely answered, 'Shepherd's Bush.'

Lucinda flushed. 'Oh! You must think I'm an idiot.'

He smiled non-committally. 'I'll put your name on the door.' He paused a second and added, 'And a plus one.'

'Great. I'll bring my brother.'

So no boyfriend. No ring on her finger. 'You can come backstage afterwards if you like.'

'That could be fun.' They were in the corridor by now,

waiting for the lift. As the door opened, their elbows brushed against each other. In the enclosed space he could feel her body heat.

Outside, he said, 'I'll see you around, then.'

'Looking forward to hearing from you,' she replied briskly, and tapped off.

Was she interested? Nick wasn't sure. Which only spurred him on. Lucinda represented a challenge. Already he was planning how to handle their next meeting.

# 6

Lucinda strolled confidently back to the office, enjoying the unusually balmy February air on her face. The sale was in the bag. She could tell by Nick Crex's body language. And having done her research and knowing he was the songwriter for the Vertical Blinds, she was confident he wasn't a time-waster, that there was money in the bank he was eager to spend.

He was quite attractive, she realized, with his snakelike hips and blond hair. Lucinda was so focused on work that usually her clients barely registered. But Nick Crex was a bit more glamorous than her usual City-boy clients. After all, even *she* had heard of the Vertical Blinds, and her idea of good music was more in the Michael Bublé range. But it was hard to miss this lot. They were always falling out of nightclubs, high on drugs, and having affairs with models and winning awards. Quite exciting to be connected to them, however vicariously, though she wouldn't mention them to Daddy. He'd be horrified.

She pushed open Dunraven Mackie's plate-glass door. Niall, the residential manager, was on the phone explaining to an American buyer about the differences between leasehold and freehold. As usual he looked ashen. Niall had one-year-old twins who never slept and a very cross wife who rang at least three times a day to tell him how lucky he was to be at work.

Gareth, the lettings manager, was talking too, explaining that it really was very bad form to remove all the lightbulbs at the end of a tenancy (though plenty of people did. As well as door handles. Never loo brushes, though – no one had *ever* stooped so low as to take the loo brush).

'All right, Marsha,' Lucinda smiled at the secretary. 'Got you a frappuccino.'

Marsha's skinny face lit up as Lucinda plonked the paper cup in front of her.

'You're a darling.'

It had taken Lucinda fifteen seconds to realize that if she didn't butter up Marsha her future at Dunraven Mackie would last about as long as an ice cream on a sun lounger. Nobody except Niall knew who Lucinda really was, but she was acutely conscious it was going to come out sooner or later. And when it did she had to have everyone in the office on side. They were already a bit suspicious of her accent, which – she recognized – was like a 1950s duchess, but she'd been brought up in this weird multilingual environment where everyone spoke like that, and she couldn't start dropping aitches just to try to fit in with the gang.

And then there was the question of where she lived. She'd had to give Marsha an address. Joanne – who lived in South Norwood – had overheard.

'South Kensington. *Very* naice.'

'My brother's a student at Imperial and the campus is nearby,' Lucinda said, which was true after all. Then she added a huge porkie pie. 'We managed to find a uni place at student rates.'

'You *were* lucky,' Joanne said and Lucinda had cheerfully agreed, while wanting to punch her lights out.

'No problem.' Lucinda smiled now. 'Hi, Gareth. How are you?'

'Simply spiffing,' Gareth grinned. Lucinda grinned back. She loved Gareth – not in *that* way, obviously, but she loved his round face, his white-blond hair, his near-permanent smile and his local yokel west-cunnrrrry accent, which made him sound as if he should be chewing a piece of straw and sitting on a tractor, not showing wideboys round penthouses. 'Where've you been?'

'I did a second viewing of Flat 15 with the chap from the Vertical Blinds. I think he's going to bite.'

'I hope he's got a bladder of steel, sleeping up that ladder.'

'Not our problem.'

'The neighbours'll be thrilled when they hear Britain's most notorious junkie's moving in,' sniped Joanne from her desk. She was wearing a bright blue minidress over leggings, and a chunky necklace that looked as if it were made out of boiled sweets. As usual, Lucinda felt wanting. She was a classic dresser, favouring shift dresses, chinos, white shirts, little scarves round the neck and loafers. In the circles she'd grown up in everyone dressed like that. But English girls had a much bolder style. Lucinda felt like a maiden aunt around them, especially when they boasted about getting ratarsed and puking in their handbags. In Geneva, you had a glass of wine with your meal, two max, and you vomited if you had food poisoning, not six vodkas and Red Bulls. London was a different world and sometimes she struggled to feel at home in it.

'He's not a junkie. I think that's the lead singer,' she replied, with as pleasant a smile as she could muster.

'I'm amazed you recognized him. I mean, you're the one who didn't know who Sharon Osbourne was.'

'That's not a crime,' said Gareth. 'In fact, Lucinda deserves a medal for not recognizing the old hag.'

'It's because I haven't lived here for long,' Lucinda apologized. They were always teasing her for not knowing Cheryl Cole, Jordan and Kerry Katona, to name just a few.

'Oh yeah, I forgot. You went to college in *America*. Sharon's big there too, you know. Or are you telling me you were so poor as a student you couldn't afford a television?'

'Excuse me,' said Lucinda. Smiling fixedly, she got up and headed towards the loo. The door shut behind her, she stared at her reflection in the fluorescent light. Why couldn't Joanne be nice to her? She was trying so hard. It wasn't her fault she hadn't grown up here and didn't get the references to cheap English chocolate and children's TV programmes that seemed to send the rest of the office into raptures.

She jumped as the door opened, flicking a tap and pretending to wash her hands. But it was only Marsha.

'All right, Luce?' At least she had a big smile for her.

'Fine,' Lucinda said, trying to sound as chipper as she could. 'How about you, Marsha? How's Dionne's appeal going? Did she manage to find something to keep the bailiffs at arm's length?'

'Yeah, she offered to shag 'em both. That did the trick.' Marsha stopped at the cubicle door. 'Don't worry about Joanne. She's just insecure. It takes at least a year before she accepts you into the team.'

'A year?' Oh, great! Only six more months to endure.

'She's just jealous because you're so pretty. And posh.' Marsha winked at her in the mirror. 'Don't let it get to you. The rest of us love you. If it's any consolation Gareth was asking about you yesterday.'

'What do you mean asking about me?'

'Wanting to know if you had a boyfriend.'

'Really?' Lucinda dwelt upon this for just a moment. Just the faintest flicker of a smile crossed her lips. Not that she was interested in Gareth *at all* – but still. Somebody liked her. 'And what did you say?'

'I had to break the news to him that you did. He took it on the chin, said he wasn't surprised.'

'But why did you say that?' Lucinda was confused. 'I don't have a boyfriend.'

'Yes, you do! Who's that Benjie you live with?'

'He's not my boyfriend! He's my brother! God, does everyone think I'm going out with him?' Lucinda laughed as she thought of Benjie, aged nineteen, zoology student, inveterate dope smoker, not to mention being gayer than all five of the Village People at a Liza Minnelli concert, being her boyfriend.

'That's more like it. Keep smiling. Coming to the Fox later?'

'Of course.' Everyone went to the Fox & Anchor on Friday night. There was no way Lucinda was going to miss it.

She returned to her desk, reinvigorated, like one of Henry V's soldiers on the eve of Agincourt. It was nearly the end of the day, and one by one the others shut down their computers and donned their coats. Lucinda was going to join them, show she was part of the team, but before she left she tied up various loose ends, sending emails, calling anxious clients, checking her diary for Monday's viewings. Before long, it was just her and Gareth left. Surreptitiously, she peeked at him over the top of her computer.

So he fancied her. She'd known it anyway, but it was good to have it confirmed. She looked at him again. No. Sorry. Those rosy cheeks were just too wholesome and there was that silly accent. Nice guy. Make someone a very good boyfriend. But not Lucinda. Her best friend Cass always teased her about being fussy, and it was fair to say she was picky about men.

At twenty-four, Lucinda was proud to say she'd never been in love and she was very happy with that situation. Obviously she wasn't a virgin and she certainly enjoyed flirting. But as soon as she'd reeled the guy in, she lost interest.

The fun was all in the chase, she'd realized. Who wanted all the grief of a relationship? What was the point? Either you ended up heartbroken like Cass or married like her mother, going for endless facelifts in the hope of keeping your husband happy. A forlorn hope, as Daddy had had mistresses for as long as Lucinda could remember. Or you were like Ginevra, shopping all day long and forever talking about setting up a business selling children's clothes with her friend Stacey but never actually getting round to it, because her haircare took up so much time.

It was all so pointless and old-fashioned. This was the twenty-first century for heaven's sake, you didn't need a man for anything apart from breeding, and now they were manufacturing sperm, so even that would be unnecessary.

Lucinda did want kids in an abstract sort of way. But she wanted to take over her father's empire much more. She was so proud of how well she was doing, given how easy it would have been to have ended up as just another spoilt trust-fund brat. Men would only distract her.

Gareth looked up and caught her eye as she brooded on her plans for world domination. 'Coming to the pub?' he smiled.

'Yes.' She turned off her computer. 'We'll just lock up, shall we?'

They switched off the lights, checked the windows, activated the burglar alarms. Lucinda liked the methodical way Gareth went about it all. He was a good worker. Not one of life's leaders but definitely someone you'd want on your team. Her phone rang.

'Hello?'

'Hello. It's Nick Crex.'

Yes! Just in time for close of play.

'I want to make an offer.'

The figure he named was a hundred grand below the asking price. Alex Meehan wasn't going to like it. But a first offer was just a first offer. A calling card.

'I think that's a bit lower than my client will entertain. But I'll certainly put it to him and get back to you.'

'OK,' he said, sounding taken aback by her frosty tone. Good. She wanted to unnerve him. 'Um, look forward to hearing from you, then. Don't forget my gig.'

'I'll have to see if I can make it. Goodbye, Mr Crex.'

She hung up, smiling. One nil to Lucinda. Now time to call the Meehans. She'd dial their landline, then with any luck she'd get Gemma. Lucinda always communicated with her if she could, because she was the nervy one who would jump at any straw. Alex, on the other hand, would have none of it. He was logical and nitpicking. She pitied the agent who was dealing with him when it came to the house they wanted to buy. He was exactly the sort who'd pick up on the tiniest thing in a survey and run with it for months.

'Hello?'

Shit. What was he doing home so early? But, of course, it was Friday. No court tomorrow.

'Mr Meehan, hello. Lucinda Gresham here. I've some good news. The viewer's put in an offer.'

'But is it good enough?' he snapped back.

Lucinda named the price.

'That's too low.'

'Well, in today's economic climate . . .'

'It's too low. It's a no.'

'Okaaay. I'll tell the client that.'

'If you would. Thanks very much.'

'Goodb . . .' But he'd gone already. Lucinda rolled her eyes, imagining the furore at Flat 15. She was sure Gemma would be desperate to accept.

'Enjoy your weekend, guys,' she said into the silent handset.

'Ready?' Gareth asked.

'Just one final call.' She dialled Nick's number.

'Hello?' Loud music playing in the background. Well, he was hardly going to be listening to a bit of light Chopin. Lucinda told him the response. He laughed.

'We knew that was going to happen. OK, I'll up it another fifty. But that is my final offer.'

'Best and final?' Lucinda smiled, keeping the tone as friendly as possible.

'Best and final,' he said brusquely, and he was gone. She called back Alex Meehan.

'OK. We'll think about it over the weekend. Get back to you on Monday.'

'Done and dusted!' Lucinda exclaimed, hanging up. She took her trenchcoat from its peg and tied her Hermès scarf around her neck. 'Shall we?' she said to Gareth, who had put on a nerdy grey anorak.

'Absolutely.' He locked the main door. 'So what are you up to this weekend?'

'Going to hole up at my friend Cassandra's. She's been dumped. Needs cheering up.'

'Oh? Sorry to hear that.'

'Don't be. He wasn't worth it. I knew that from the time I overheard him at a party describing Cass to someone as "my current girlfriend".'

Gareth sucked his teeth. 'Nice.'

'I know. Anyway, I'm going to get in all the clichés. *Bridget Jones* DVD, *Sex and the City* box set. Tubs of ice cream.'

'Bottles of Chardonnay. Tissue multipacks.'

'You've got it,' she laughed. She didn't know what came over her, because the next thing she said was, 'I don't have a boyfriend, you know.'

'Sorry?' Gareth stopped and stared at her.

'I don't have a boyfriend. I know you asked Marsha if I did and she said yes, but I'm single. I live with my brother.'

'Oh. Right.' Gareth walked on, head bent against the winter wind.

'Yes . . .' Lucinda continued a bit more shakily. She wasn't quite sure why she'd felt the need to start this conversation. She'd wanted to set the record straight, she supposed. Just a tiny voice at the back of her head told her that perhaps she'd also wanted some kind of further confirmation that Gareth was interested. That she'd been showing off, pandering to her own vanity. Basically, being a pricktease. 'Just wanted you to know.'

'OK.' They had stopped on the kerb of Farringdon Road, looking right, left, right for traffic. But Gareth then looked directly at her.

'So . . . um. Would you like to go for a drink?'

'We *are* going for a drink,' she said lightly.

'Er. No. I meant . . . alone.' Already, his confidence had shattered and he looked unsure of what to say next. Lucinda had seen it all before. She needed to put a stop to this at once.

'Gareth, I don't think that's a good idea,' she said gently. 'I mean, you shouldn't date people you work with. I just didn't want people thinking my brother was my boyfriend. I mean, yuk!'

'Oh, right.' Gareth began crossing the road. She followed him as fast as she could in her Roger Vivier heels.

'Sorry!' she gasped as they safely reached the other side. 'I didn't mean to embarrass you. I just didn't want to give the wrong impression.'

'It was a bit of a funny way of going about things,' Gareth said. He sounded kind, but still she felt she was being attacked.

'No, it wasn't! I just . . .'

'Look.' He stopped suddenly and so did she. 'I'm not

sure what message you're trying to communicate. Do you want to have a drink with me? Or don't you?'

'I . . .' Lucinda felt unsure of herself. This straight talking made Gareth seem very manly. Perhaps he *was* quite attractive. He obviously sensed her changing mood, because he smiled. He had surprisingly good teeth.

'I could show you some hidden corners of Clerkenwell. There's some amazing bars round here I bet you have no idea about.'

'Hmmm.'

'And restaurants too . . .' His voice was teasing, coaxing. He had very long eyelashes, she noticed. But . . . well, it sounded awful, but she was Michael Gresham's daughter and he simply wasn't *enough* for her.

'No, I couldn't. Thank you, though.'

Gareth went a little pink. 'OK, then. Um. Do you still want to go to the Fox with the others?'

She smiled at him to show she still liked him, that there were no hard feelings.

'Absolutely.'

They walked the rest of the way in an awkward silence. Lucinda felt bad for Gareth. No one likes rejection, and she'd lured him straight into this one like a hunter with a baited trap. She hoped they could stay friends.

'I heard the funniest thing today . . .' she tried, before launching into an anecdote about a client's vibrator falling out of her bag. But Gareth barely cracked a smile. Well, sod him. It wasn't Lucinda's fault she didn't want to be his girlfriend. But still she felt a little cold inside. She liked people to like her – especially at work – and now she'd ballsed things up with her closest ally.

It was a bit silly really, she didn't *need* friends to climb to the top of the tree, but the truth of it was that Lucinda wanted them. She could barely admit it to herself, but she was lonely living in London. Apart from Cass, she had no old friends there – they were in France, or Switzerland, or America, and she didn't quite know how to make new ones. She had Benjie to hang out with, of course, but so much of his time was spent having sex with anonymous men on Clapham Common, where Lucinda hardly felt welcome.

She was just about to try another tack with Gareth when a tall, rather grumpy-looking man in a grey raincoat stepped in front of them.

'Gareth. How are you?' He had a South-Efrikan accent, which to Lucinda's ears always sounded humourless and cold.

'Oh, hello, Anton.' The men shook hands energetically. He was in his forties at a guess, quite good-looking, just with a decidedly irritable air to him. She wondered what was making him so cross. 'How are things?' Gareth was asking.

'Busy as always. They said the credit crunch was going to send us all tits up, but it hasn't been the case. Demand's still exceptional.'

Gareth noticed her standing there expectantly. 'Anton, this is Lucinda. She's just joined us. Lucinda, this is Anton Beleek. He's a big property developer. You know the Craig-hill building? That's his.'

'Oh yes? I just took on a flat there today.'

'Did you.' He barely registered her, eyes still on Gareth. Sexist twat, Lucinda thought. Probably he'd dismissed her as an irrelevant secretary. 'So how are things, Gareth? What's your reading of the market?'

They stood talking. Slow rain was starting to fall. Lucinda shuffled uneasily from foot to foot. They carried on talking. She hugged herself rather dramatically to make it clear she was damp and cold and a bit bored but they ignored her. Eventually, she cleared her throat.

'Guys, since you've got so much to talk about I'll leave you to it. Gareth, I'll see you down at the Fox in a minute.'

Gareth had the grace to look a bit embarrassed. Anton whoever-he-was didn't. Well, bugger him.

'No, no, I won't keep you standing in the rain, Anton. But very good to see you. We should have lunch soon.'

'We'll do that,' Anton said. They shook hands. He nodded at Lucinda. ''Bye.'

'What a rude man,' she said, watching his retreating back.

'That's just his manner,' Gareth said, rather brusquely.

'And he's some big-shot property guy?' she asked, still stung. 'I bet he's not like that when he's wooing investors.'

'Apparently he is. Doesn't seem to make any difference. He owns half of the area. Must be worth trillions. He is a nice guy underneath it all, though. He's just a little serious.'

'Is he married?'

For the first time in their brief but eventful walk, Gareth laughed. 'Typical woman's question. No, he's not. He's had a few girlfriends, I hear, but it's never worked out. Too much of a workaholic.'

'Too much of a rude pig more like,' Lucinda said, pushing open the door of the Fox & Anchor and enjoying the warm blast of air that hit her face. 'Hey, everyone,' she said, approaching the gang at the bar. 'Who'd like a drink?'

# 7

Late on Saturday morning the Drake family's Volvo drove through a large rusting iron gate and on to a twisting, potholed drive, flanked by beech trees naked in the February air. The sky was a dull yellow that threatened snow, the ground was hard. Apart from the engine there was an air of total, slightly menacing silence.

'Daddy, this is amazing,' said Eloise, craning her head this way and that. 'How much land is there?'

'Lots,' said Phil, grinning at her in the driver's mirror. 'Easily enough for you both to have a pony.'

For the first time since hearing she was going to miss Isobel's party, Bea smiled.

'Two ponies!'

'Could we have a swimming pool?'

'I don't see why not. Plenty of space.' Before he'd been ill, Phil had been very firm about not spoiling the girls. But since his recovery he basically gave them whatever they asked for. It drove Karen nuts.

The girls squealed and grasped each other.

'A swimming pool! Amelia will be so jealous.'

Phil grinned from ear to ear, as he glanced sideways at his wife. Karen replied with a grin that was – if anything – even wider. Only it didn't extend to her eyes.

'This is just what we need,' Phil gabbled. 'Country living.

Fresh air. We could grow our own vegetables. No more stress. Loads of family time.'

The car swept round a final wide bend, and standing before them was Chadlicote Manor.

'It's like a fairy castle,' cried Bea, who – to her mother's bemusement – at nine was still in the throes of the pink, Disney-princess obsession.

'No, it isn't,' Eloise contradicted. 'Does it have battlements? Or a moat? Or a drawbridge? It's a Tudor manor house, isn't it, Mummy? We did them in history last term.'

'That's right, honey,' said Karen, trying to adjust her look of horror. The house was undeniably beautiful. But you didn't exactly have to be a master builder to see that it had been horribly neglected.

Car parked, the girls scrambled out and ran screaming towards the wide front steps guarded by two moss-covered stone greyhounds. Phil seized the huge brass knocker in the shape of a lion's head and banged it against the oak door.

There was a sound of barking, a faint cry of 'Coming', a rattling of bolts and a clanking of locks and slowly it opened. On the threshold stood Miss Porter-Healey. Karen had imagined a petite old lady, smelling of violets, in a moth-eaten tweed suit. But this woman in a shabby green tracksuit was a few years younger than her. Yet oh, how different. While Karen was slender, with a raven's-wing slick of dark hair, Miss Porter-Healey was mousy, tallish and – there was no politer word – fat. A pretty face, yes, but her blue eyes and cupid's bow mouth were obscured by layers of blubber. A fat black pug wheezed asthmatically

at her side, while behind it a skinny copper-coloured spaniel barked excitedly.

'How do you do,' she said in a soft voice, holding out
her hand. Her nails, Karen noticed, were bitten to the quick.
'I'm Grace. Excuse my get-up, you're a bit earlier than I
expected. I was just trying to get things shipshape for you.
Come in, come in.'

They shook hands, muttering introductions, then
followed her into the vast entrance hall.

'Cool!' cried Bea.

'Mum, look, there's a minstrels' gallery,' cried Eloise. 'It's
like *Romeo and Juliet*.' She turned to Miss Porter-Healey.
'That's my favourite Shakespeare play.'

Miss Porter-Healey probably wanted to slap the preco-
cious brat and tell her to go and play with a Barbie, but to
her credit she smiled kindly. 'My brother and I used to do
plays up there. You could do the same. Your mummy and
daddy could sit down here and watch. Oh, down, Silvester,
down.' She grabbed the spaniel, who was happily humping
Phil's leg. 'I'm *so* sorry.'

'Quite all right. No problems,' Phil laughed. The girls
giggled. Silvester rolled on to his back and Bea started
tickling his tummy.

'Mummy, if we lived here could we have a dog?'

'Um. Maybe, darling.' Karen looked around. It was
certainly an impressive space, with that huge staircase in
the middle dominated by a dusty chandelier with no bulbs.
Perhaps Miss Porter-Healey had removed them, hoping
the dim light would conceal the ancient paper with fleur-
de-lis pattern flapping off the walls. Or the crack in
the floor by Karen's feet. The girls were inspecting a

ping-pong table in the far corner, held up by a pile of Penguin books.

'Would you like to play?' Grace asked. Karen felt embarrassed for her. Eloise and Bea didn't play, they Wii'ed and MSN'ed. But to her surprise, they said, 'OK.' Seconds later they were laughing as the plastic ball skittered across the table.

'What lovely girls,' Grace said, sounding as if she meant it. Karen looked at her with fascination. Yup, there was no doubting it, she was in the presence of a full-blown spinster of the sort she'd thought existed only in Miss Marple novels. Grace looked around the space, smiling wistfully. 'My brother and I had so many wonderful times here. It really is a magical house. But now my mother is dead and so . . . it has to go.' Another timid smile. 'It would need a lot of work done to restore it to its former glory. A lot of time and money. But it could be fabulous again.'

'And . . . er . . . you?' Phil said cautiously, not knowing how to phrase it. But Grace caught his drift.

'I would love to stay here. Chadlicote is a very much loved home.' She paused for a second, then rallied. 'But the rest of the family want me to sell. I shall move into a cottage which belongs to us in Little Dittonsbury. So I shall always be close by if you need any advice.'

Phil's eyes were sparkling. It was his ultimate fantasy come to life, shored up by months of convalescence spent watching *Grand Designs* and *Property Ladder* on More 4. Already, Karen could see him fantasizing about their struggle being turned into an hour-long narrative sandwiched between ads for building societies and loo roll. Couple buy crumbling pile. Couple have several hilarious misadventures as they painstakingly restore it. Couple go several hundred thousand over budget and work takes two years longer than scheduled, but eventually all is well and Kevin McCloud appears to announce he has had his doubts but is now bowled over by the owners' creative vision, their loving attention to detail. Cue credits and trailer for next week's episode.

Karen shivered.

'I'm sorry,' Grace said, scanning her flimsy top. 'I turned the central heating on full this morning but it takes a while to get going. Would you like to borrow a coat?'

'Oh no, I'm fine,' Karen lied, resisting the urge to hug herself.

They followed Grace round the house. Karen noted the creaking floorboards, disintegrating window frames with paint scattered beneath, the spiderwebs, the mould on the wooden shutters, the holes in the plasterwork that made it look as if it had been under fire from the SAS. It was all so shabbily un-chic, so depressing. Karen took in the piles of *Doctor Who* videos (not even DVDs!) in the tiny sitting room called the den, which Grace clearly inhabited year round in preference to the vast and draughty living room.

Her heart tugged as they moved on to Grace's tiny bedroom on the second floor. Sometimes Karen berated herself for having never truly appreciated her old single life of lie-ins and cocktails and weekend shopping trips to New York. But that, she realized, was the urban version of spinsterhood. If you were living in Devon, it meant four walls with drab flowery paper. A bookcase filled with ancient children's paperbacks of *The Secret Garden* and *The Wolves of Willoughby Chase*. A mantelpiece covered in kitsch china ornaments that would have been incredibly amusing in a Hoxton living room but here just spoke of a lifetime shopping at village jumble sales and an inability to throw tat away.

Phil peered out of the small window. 'Look, Karen, you can see the lake.'

'That's why I stayed in this room,' Miss Porter-Healey said. 'I mean, it was mine as a girl and when I came back as an adult I could have moved into a bigger one, but there's nothing like waking up in the morning and seeing the water. And besides . . . it reminds me of my childhood.'

Phil nodded enthusiastically. He grew even more excited after he'd seen the master bedroom, the 'nursery', the six other bedrooms, the two studies and so on and so on and so on. 'Imagine what you could do,' he said quietly to Karen, though not so quietly Miss Porter-Healey couldn't hear. 'We could install a cinema. Have a games room. The heating's knackered, we could rip it out and put in under-floor throughout.'

Karen thought back to her own upbringing in the tiny two-bedroom cottage where they received regular visits from cousin Genette, who owned a massage parlour in Swansea, and her great-auntie Noreen, who'd turned up at Gran's funeral with bare gums because her Dobermann cross had eaten her false teeth, and marvelled that she'd come so far. Why was she so ungrateful? Why didn't she want to live in this mansion?

After the tour, they inspected the dying, tangled wilderness that was the grounds. Somebody had once worked on them planting irises and roses, encircling the lawn with yew trees, but now it was all a haze of dense bramble. Still, the girls were in heaven, as if they'd been given £200 each to spend at Claire's. Karen gazed at them in astonishment. Surely this couldn't be her own offspring getting so excited about nature?

'Look at this,' Phil said contentedly, as they stopped for breath beside the gazebo, at the highest point in the property, with its dizzying views of rolling hills and, just there on the horizon, a slice of sea. The country light enhanced his gauntness. The weight he'd lost during his illness hadn't even started to come back on and his hair hadn't grown back yet – the doctors said it might never happen. His pocket started bleeping loudly.

'Oh!' Miss Porter-Healey exclaimed. 'What on earth is that?'

'My alarm,' Phil said, digging in his pocket and pulling out an envelope marked 'Noon'. He shook some pills out on to his palm, opened the bottle of water he always carried and swallowed them.

'Sorry. I need to take so many vitamins to keep myself in shape and the best way to benefit from them is to have a few every few hours or so.'

'Of course,' said Miss Porter-Healey. Karen felt embarrassed, like she always did when Phil went through this pantomime. She could understand why; he'd been at death's door, after all, but the fussing and obsessing still – quite unreasonably – annoyed her.

Phil put his arm round her shoulder. 'There seems to be a very special energy here.'

'I think so,' said Miss Porter-Healey.

'I've been very ill, you see.' He held up a hand to silence any platitudes. 'Don't worry, all is well now. But it's forced me to take a good look at my life. Make many changes.' He smiled ingratiatingly at Grace in the way he used to when he wanted to persuade someone to hand over a huge percentage of their company for a tiny sum of money.

'I hope you don't mind me saying so, but this place seems to hold so many opportunities. It could be opened to the public. Weddings. Corporate bonding days.'

'Absolutely.' Grace smiled, although she seemed a little sad. 'I was considering ventures like that, but then my mother got ill and nursing her took priority. But it would make me so happy to let everyone share Chadlicote's beauty. And it would certainly help with the overheads, which are substantial, I'm afraid.'

'Well, that's pretty obvious,' Phil said, but in a very friendly way, and everyone laughed. 'But it sounds as if it could be ideal for us. Karen's a bit apprehensive about jacking in her job and this would be a project for her.'

He said it as if restoring Chadlicote was the equivalent of – say – buying and wrapping forty Christmas presents, a bit of a hassle but fun really. Another rictus grin from Karen. Her jaw was aching from so much fake smiling, her head from calculating what this would all entail. Years, probably decades, of builder hell; long, freezing winters. And all for a future discussing marquees with stressed brides and bulk-buying white wine to serve junior executives on away-days.

A lifetime of being exiled from the friends she'd taken such an age to make, who'd promise to visit but wouldn't. Of seeing the career she adored knocked brutally on the head.

Of being stuck in the middle of nowhere with a man she was no longer sure she loved.

Karen would have forever to live with the secret that although she was obviously overjoyed her husband was still alive, she sometimes fantasized about life if he had died. She and the girls would have been devastated, of course they would. But she would have been alone, starting again.

For Karen was in the nightmarish position of being still married to a man who bore virtually no resemblance to the one she'd married. The Phil who had survived his cancer was nervier, more anxious about silly little things and careless about big issues like money. He said he wanted to spend more time with the girls, to appreciate the finer things in life, to watch the grass grow, but then he wasted hours slumped in front of sport, or – worse, in Karen's opinion – on the internet communicating with other cancer 'survivors', swapping tips about vitamin supplements and homoeopathy.

All the burdens he had used to shoulder, like dealing with bills or little household repairs, tended to get passed to Karen, because he said stress was bad for him. He wouldn't go on holiday to hot places any more because he was frightened of the sun, and he insisted on a vegetarian or vegan diet, which was tricky since the girls ate virtually nothing but sausages, chicken and bolognese sauce (which Bea inspected forensically for any trace of hidden vegetable).

The result was that Karen had changed too. She was a far angrier person than she had been. Angry with her husband for suffering so unstoically. For his demands – which, while being utterly reasonable, were still infuriating.

Then she was even angrier with herself for being so unsym-pathetic.

Of course everyone told her how brave they both were. It was one of the ways people coped with cancer, to see it as an ennobling experience. But the truth was cancer hadn't enlarged their spirits, it had reduced them, made them both petty-minded and cross.

But then she looked at Phil again. His cheeks were ruddy. He looked the happiest Karen had seen in months.

She was going to have to go along with this plan. She'd been studying the ground, but now, looking up, she caught Grace's eye. The pain there made Karen feel slightly sick.

But that couldn't be Karen's problem. Throwing her shoulders back, she said, 'Absolutely. There'd be plenty to keep me busy here. And there's nothing I love like a challenge.'

Phil realized they'd gone too far, made it a bit too obvi-ous that they were gagging for the place. Time for a hasty retreat if they were going to get it at the knockdown price he had in mind.

'Of course we need to have a serious conversation about this.' He looked at his watch. 'Crikey, is that the time? We'd better be making tracks soon if we're going to make it back to London in time for *Robin Hood*.' They walked back along the drive, hugging themselves against the cold. When they reached the car, hands were shaken again.

'We'll be in touch very soon,' Phil promised.

'Oh my God, Dad. We're going to live in a . . . castle,' said Bea, as they drove off.

'*Not* a castle. An Elizabethan *manor house*! Mum, why does she keep saying castle?'

'Well, we don't know that for sure, darling,' Karen said. 'We just need to do the maths.'

'But Daddy's rich since he sold his company,' Bea said.

'God, Bea, you don't go around at school telling everyone Daddy's rich? That's sooo embarrassing.'

Phil laughed as they headed back over the little stone bridge. 'Not rich, darling. Well, not very rich. But we can afford this place. Would you like it? Would you really like to live here?'

'Yesss!' the girls clamoured. Phil laughed again. And Karen's last vestiges of hope withered and died. If his little princesses wanted it, there would be no argument.

'Where shall we go for lunch?'

'Somewhere that does spaghetti bolognese,' Bea said.

Eloise rolled her eyes. 'Not spaghetti. Penne. Much nicer.'

'And vanilla ice cream,' Bea continued undeterred.

'Pistachio for me. That's my favourite.'

*You'll be lucky getting pistachio out here in the sticks*, Karen thought. But she just smiled again as Phil cried, 'Ladies. Your wish is my command.' It was amazing how obedient her facial muscles could be.

# 8

Lucinda spent virtually all weekend with Cassandra, her old schoolfriend from La Chêneraie, watching cheesy films, listening to her weeping and periodically saying, 'There, there.' Privately, she thought Cass was well out of it. Tim, the dumper, had so clearly been an arse. Lucinda remembered the first time Cass had introduced them at a party. There was a smugness about him, a look in his eyes that said, 'Hey, I'm good-looking, I work for a bank, I earn ludicrous amounts of money in return for screwing the economy, therefore I'm every woman's Holy Grail and don't I know it?'

'Hi,' Lucinda had said brusquely, determined not to boost his ego further.

'Lucinda's an estate agent,' Cass had said, eyes shining, obviously thrilled to be introducing the two most important people in her life to each other.

'Oh yeah,' he'd smirked. 'What do you call twenty estate agents chained together at the bottom of the sea?'

'I don't know,' Lucinda replied, thinking, *Yawn, yawn, yet another one who thinks I've never heard an estate agent joke before.* 'But I know what you call twenty bankers. A damn good start.'

He'd laughed brittly. 'Touché,' he'd said and turned away.

From then they'd hated each other. Not in a sexy, really-we're-so-attracted-to-each-other-and-this-is-how-we-show-it way, just good old-fashioned dislike. Cass, of course, had been oblivious. She'd bought Tim an expensive watch for his birthday, treated him to a weekend at Babington House for their month's anniversary. She bunked off work early to get her hair done for him, she came in late with stubble burn on her chin and got bollocked by her boss. Lucinda heard about it bemused. OK, Cass was an over-privileged girl, who – like virtually everyone from school – saw her job in the press office at Sotheby's as a cute little hobby like ballroom dancing that could be put on the back burner whenever. But still Lucinda just didn't see how such a loser could take priority over work, however trivial.

'Honestly,' she said at some point on Sunday morning, when Cass's snivelling had been temporarily abated by an almond croissant. 'I know this all seems shit now. But he wasn't worth it. I never liked him anyway.'

Cass looked up suspiciously. 'Didn't you? Why didn't you tell me?'

'Because he was your boyfriend, not mine. I hoped I'd change my mind.'

'What do you think I did wrong?'

'Nothing. He's the one who made the mistake, letting go of you.'

'Do you really think there's no one else? I bet he's met someone and he's just too chicken to say.'

Privately, Lucinda was sure of that, but she just made mmm-errrr noises. Cass continued. 'Oh, Luce. What am I going to do? I loved him so much. I know he's an idiot, but it was just something about the way he sme – he- he- he – helled.'

Lucinda patted her back as the sobs started again. She felt sorry for her friend and yet she genuinely didn't understand.

Maybe something was wrong with her that she had so little interest in what seemed to obsess every other woman in the world. But why should that bother her, Lucinda decided. She wasn't the one with the swollen eyes and dripping nose.

'And it's Valentine's Day on Tuesday. I'd bought him a card and a present. Booked Le Caprice. And now I'll be home alone.'

'No, you won't,' Lucinda said briskly. 'I'm going to a gig. The Vertical Blinds. You can come with me.'

Cassandra gaped. 'The Vertical Blinds! They're a bit cool for you, aren't they, Luce?'

'One of them's a client. I was going to take Benjie, but he won't mind. He's always blowing me out at the last minute when he gets GayDared.'

'Cool.' For the first time that weekend, Cassandra looked as if life might still be worth living. 'Thanks, Luce. Their lead singer is gorgeous. Will we get a chance to meet him?'

'You never know.' Lucinda stood up, delighted she'd finally made Cass smile. 'Look, it's getting late. I'll head off. But call me whenever you need to vent and we'll go to the Valentine's Day gig.'

Gemma and Alex had argued all Friday night about whether to accept the revised offer from Nick Crex. Alex said it was still way too low. Gemma pointed out, smiling all the while, that it was the only offer they'd had in five months; the market was going down but if they accepted it Alex would still have made a profit on the place since he'd bought the flat ten years ago.

'But I feel I've been cheated,' he protested. 'Those estate agent shysters told us to put it on at that price to get our business and now they're doing all this "Oh well, the market's falling, I'd accept it if I were you . . ." They've conned us. It pisses me off. *And* he's a rock star.' Nick and Gemma had been thrilled initially to discover the identity of their buyer, but now it annoyed them that someone with so much to waste on ketamine and fast women was haggling over the price of a flat.

'They haven't conned us, darling, just misled us.' Gemma stroked his brow. 'And all rock stars are mean. I read Mick Jagger's as tight as a pair of his leather trousers.'

Alex grunted. He was in a bad mood anyway. He was a very successful barrister but over the last year his workload had been dwindling, thanks to the government changing the system so that a load of his colleagues were now employed in-house by the Crown Prosecution Service, creaming work away from freelances like himself.

'I'm poorer than I was a year ago, that's why we can't just say yes to this lower offer,' he explained on Saturday morning, as they sat eating porridge at the breakfast bar. 'The fertility treatment is costing a small fortune.' He held up a hand before she could protest. '*Not* that I begrudge it, but we have to factor it in. The bank's not going to keep increasing our mortgage because there's no guarantee I'll be making enough to pay it off. There's a certain figure we just can't go over. Now I've got to work. I need to start preparing my new case.'

'But you said it wasn't for a few weeks.'

'It isn't. But it's huge. The guy I'm defending is about as dodgy as they come. He's from the Holmes family. They're one of those big East End Kray-type families, string of convictions that go from here to China. If I get him off this, it'll be mega. All the bad-ass mafioso types are going to be queuing for my services. Gunning each other down in the street.'

Gemma wrinkled her nose. She didn't need to say anything, they'd had this argument a thousand times before.

'If you want Coverley Drive that's the way it goes, Poochie. I'm a taxi for hire. If my light's on then I have to take whoever flags me down. So let me start preparing.'

'OK. I'll go for a swim.'

There was a drawn-out pause, like in *Who Wants to be a Millionaire?* before you learn if the contestant got the two-hundred-and-fifty-thousand-pound question right or wrong. Then Alex said crossly, 'Oh, bloody hell. All right. I'll accept the offer on Monday. You realize this means we're never going out for dinner again, though. Can't afford it.'

Gemma screamed, just like the happy contestant would.

'Oh, thank you, darling. Thank you.'

Her husband grinned sheepishly as she showered him with kisses. 'That's OK. I guess when Chudney comes along, restaurants will be out anyway.'

'And foreign holidays. And nice clothes. Too stressful to fly. Or risk wearing cashmere.' They often played the 'when Chudney comes' game, listing all the downsides of babies. It helped distance them from how much they both wanted one.

'Now go and swim, so I can try to earn an honest bean. Or a dishonest one, if you prefer.'

Thank God Cass had reminded her about Valentine's Day, Lucinda thought the following morning on her way to work. After she emerged from the Tube at Chancery Lane, she popped into the newsagent's to buy two Valentines. One for Daddy, another for Benjie. The same one – a bit camp but very pretty with a silver background and a fat satin heart appliquéd to the front.

But in the office, when she opened them, she realized her mistake. Inside, both bore the legend *Marry Me*. For Benjie, it was fine. She added, smirking: *And we'll move to a trailer park in Kentucky and be right at home ?? xx*. But for Daddy, it was all wrong. He wouldn't find her joke funny in the slightest and if she crossed it out it wouldn't look perfect – and everything Lucinda did for her father had to be just right. She'd buy him another one when she went out for her 10.45 viewing. But in the meantime what to do with the spare Valentine? It was too pretty to waste.

Briefly she considered Cass, wondering if it would cheer her up, but no – she'd think it was from Tim and that would be cruel. Lucinda mentally listed the men she knew. No. Absolutely no one she even remotely fancied. Which, perversely, brought her thoughts to Gareth. He wasn't at his desk. Lucinda was relieved. Cass's histrionics meant there hadn't been much time to think about him over the weekend, but whenever she'd gone there she'd felt horribly guilty. Why had she deliberately humiliated him like that by letting him know she knew how he felt about her? Answer: because she was vain. And at sea in this alien environment and in need of reassurance. Even though Marsha had already told her how Gareth felt, him confirming it had given her a kick.

Lucinda felt a faint flush around her earlobes. Basically she wasn't a nice person. She would have to try harder. Her ringing phone dragged her away from such dismal thoughts.

'Hello, Dunraven Mackie.'

'Lucinda? It's Alex Meehan.'

'Oh, good morning. How are you?'

'Fine, thanks. Listen, we discussed the offer over the weekend and even though it's lower than you'd led us to believe we'd get, we're going to accept it.'

Lucinda's mood instantly lifted. 'OK. I think you've made a sensible decision there.'

'I think we had no choice.' God, he was rude. 'But we don't want to lose the house we want and we can't keep them waiting for ever. Anyway, I've told our solicitor and he'll be in touch. Look forward to hearing from you later.'

'Absolutely.' She hung up with a soft 'Yes!' But there was no one to boast to. Niall, with a big patch of babysick on his shoulder, was on the phone. So was Marsha. The others were all out. Well, never mind. They'd all hear later at the midday meeting. Lucinda couldn't wait to see the expression on Joanne's face when she discovered she'd sold the unsellable flat. Immediately she called Nick Crex. Voicemail. Not that surprising. Rock stars didn't get up until the afternoon. She left a message for him to call, then took out her notebook to start listing clients to contact.

The agency door opened. She looked up to see Anton,

the South-Efrikan property developer. Just like Friday night, he had that gloomy look on his face. Lucinda watched as Niall hung up, jumped to his feet and held out his hand.

'Anton! Good to see you.'

'You too, Niall. I was just passing and I thought I'd drop by. Take the market's temperature.'

'Not as bad as it looks,' Niall said, and they launched into a conversation Lucinda knew backwards, upside down and inside out, about how the market had bottomed out and was definitely on the rise again. She listened for a moment or two, then picked up the phone and called her first client. Voicemail. She left a message, in perhaps a slightly louder voice than was necessary. She hung up. Anton still wasn't looking at her. Rude man. He hadn't even acknowledged her and Marsha.

She decided to stare at him. See how long before he noticed. But a whole minute passed and he carried on talking to Niall, oblivious. You could tell he was the sort of guy who'd never care about a woman's opinion. Sexist pig

Surreptitiously, Lucinda stuck out her tongue. Turning back to her keyboard on impulse, she googled him. She couldn't remember his surname and *Anton, property developer, Clerkenwell* brought up nothing. She tried *Anton Craighill building EC1*. Of course, Anton Beleek. Funnily enough he didn't have a Facebook page. But his offices did have an address. Just down the road from them behind Clerkenwell Green. She looked up at him again. He didn't seem to register her. Looked down again. Looked up.

Looked down. At her Valentine.

Something came over Lucinda. She grabbed a pen and

wrote 'Can't stop thinking about you' under the *Marry Me*. Then a big ?. Then XXXooo.

Then she shoved it in its envelope and scribbled Anton's name and address on the front, adding 'PRIVATE'. Sealed it, stamped it and stuck it in her bag. Time for her appointment.

'Niall, I've got a viewing at Finsbury Square. See you later.'

Walking out of the door, she bumped straight into Gareth.

'Hi, how are you?' She couldn't quite meet his eye.

'Good, thanks. Good weekend with your mate?' He seemed his normal, smiling jovial self.

'If you call listening to "I Will Survive" on a loop good, then yeah, I suppose so.'

He laughed. She laughed too. Great. No hard feelings. For a second Lucinda wondered about fixing him up with Cass. But no. The yokel accent again. What was it with the men around her and funny accents? First Gareth sounding like he was sitting on a tractor, chewing a piece of straw, then Ent-on.

'See you later. Maybe pop out to Pret after the meeting?'

'Yeah,' he smiled. 'Why not.'

She walked off happily. Paranoia unnecessary. Gareth was still her friend. Reaching the postbox she stopped and considered her actions. It was ridiculous to send a Valentine to a man she didn't know purely because she had a spare one and he'd wound her up by ignoring her. Lucinda twiddled her bracelet. The same voice that had admonished her for playing with Gareth's feelings now told her she was being a show-off – again. But then her phone rang. Aha. Nick Crex.

'Hello? Lucinda speaking.'

'Hiya, it's Nick Crex here. I got your message. So the flat's mine?'

'Well, not quite. But subject to contract and blah blah, then yes. Congratulations.'

'Nice one. So what do I do now?'

'Inform your solicitor. I'd advise you to commission a survey and we can get the ball rolling.'

'How soon do you think I can move in?'

'Well, as I understand it the Meehans have an offer in on a property in the country. Depending on whether that's chain free or not – I don't know. A month. Two months?'

'*Two months?* Shit. I thought I'd be in by the end of the week.'

'I'm afraid not. Buying a property can take a while, especially if there's a chain. But don't worry, I don't foresee any huge problems. Why don't you call me with your solicitor's details a bit later and I'll get on to him.'

'OK,' he said sulkily. ''Bye.'

Shit. Nick Crex obviously had no idea how long this whole process could take. Suppose he changed his mind? She'd tell the Meehans they needed to act immediately.

She chewed her lip, calculating how to phrase it and without thinking dropped the Valentine into the post-box.

Damn.

But then Lucinda laughed. Did it really matter? Anton South-Efrikan's secretary would probably open it and bin it before he even saw it. And even if he did – so what? She hadn't put her bloody name on it. He'd have no idea it was from her.

Reassured, she continued to the viewing.

# 9

Outside a tall Georgian building just off Harley Street Gemma stood, coat wrapped around her tiny frame. The day was dank and gloomy, as if someone had thrown a tarpaulin over it, but her heart was full of sunshine. They were going to accept Nick Crex's offer. And – though she'd kept this from Alex – today Bridget was meeting their fertility guru, Dr Malpadhi. Gemma had been a bit presumptuous, making the appointment before Bridget had actually agreed to anything, but she had been happy to go along with it. Gemma was not allowed to attend the meeting. The clinic was very firm about that. But there was nothing to stop her making sure her sister arrived on time. Or meeting her afterwards for a debrief.

She checked her watch again. Her blood pressure began to rise. Even though she'd called to check Bridget was on her way, Gemma was certain she'd still get waylaid, miss her slot and Dr Mapadhi would set the whole process back another month. But no, there she was, bustling down the pavement in paint-smattered jeans and a tie-dyed T-shirt.

'Bridge! I can't believe you've worn that.'

'Why does it matter? They're interested in my reproductive abilities, not my dress sense.'

'I know but . . .'

But what? Bridget was right. Gemma hugged her.

'Thanks so much for coming. Off you go inside. Hopefully Dr M'll be running late and you can enjoy all the magazines.'

'You know I hate magazines. They set up impossible standards for women.'

'OK, OK! Sorry! There are free biscuits and tea and coffee.'

'Bring it on!'

Gemma squeezed her arm. 'I'll be in the Lebanese café on Wigmore Street. See you there.'

Gemma spent an hour trying to read the paper but really staring out of the window at the parade of buggies. Bugaboo was still the brand of choice, she noted. Gemma guessed that that was what she too would go for, even though she knew it was a bit of a cliché. Although maybe she should buy a Phil & Ted's to convert it to a double buggy if they had a second child . . . If Bridget was willing. If . . .

She had to get a grip. Even if Bridget's eggs were fine and she handed them over, they might not take to Gemma's womb. She might miscarry. Gemma's heart clenched as she mentally listed the disasters that could befall them – the baby might be stillborn or deformed or develop a passion for the works of J. R. R. Tolkien or grow up to be a Christian fundamentalist. But what was the alternative? Carrying on with her life of meals out, films, holidays. All lovely, obviously. But the thought of there being nothing more terrified her. Life seemed to stretch before her in an endless unbending line, like a road through the desert. She *needed* motherhood to intervene, to throw things off at a tangent.

Still, at least Coverley Drive would be a bend in the road, the dawning of new possibilities.

'Heeey!' said Bridget's voice behind her.

Gemma was instantly suspicious. 'That was quick. Did he see you? What did he say?'

'Oh, you know.' Bridget smiled up at the waiter. 'A double espresso please. All the usual crap you'd expect – how delighted he was to meet me, what a wonderful thing I was volunteering for. Then did I know exactly what was involved. I told him I'd read about it online but he said he still had to go through it all with me, so he talked me through the whole IVF procedure when I have to say I did nod off a little. Then he told me I was going to have to have all these physical tests and counselling. I told him that was unnecessary, that I've spoken to dozens of healers in my time. But he said it was obligatory.'

'I told you it was.'

'I know, but I was hoping I could talk him round. Save us all the aggro. I asked him what kind of issues we needed to talk about and he said well, there's the fact I didn't have children, which made me laugh. I was like: "Yes, thank God!"'

How could she be so flippant? Though it was true, it *was* just as well.

'I told him I didn't want children, that I found them a drain on the earth's resources and that anyway too many issues with my own parents are unresolved. But he said, "Fine, but that might change." And if for whatever reason I decided I wanted kids but I couldn't have them then the fact I'd given you my baby might prove tricky.'

Gemma shut her eyes and squeezed her nails into her palms. But Bridget was chortling.

'I told him not to worry. But he said, whatever, I still had to do it. One session on my own and then one session with you guys all together. So we've been booked in for a fort-night today.'

'A fortnight? That's ages away.'

'The counsellor's on holiday. In the meantime there's various medical tests they'll do on me – blood, hormones, they've got to measure me, weigh me. I was like – woah! – are you sure? You'll regret it when I break the scales and you have to buy a new pair.'

'Don't be silly,' Gemma said shortly. The weight issue was worrying her, it might interfere with ovulation. At least Bridget was drinking black coffee instead of one of her usual milky sugary confections. Gemma would rather she wasn't drinking coffee at all, but this wasn't the time.

'That's what they told me. So I'm going in on Friday for all of that.'

'It's really kind of you,' Gemma said, filled with one of her sudden rushes of fondness. Bridget was doing so much for her and doing it for nothing. Just love.

'Ah, it's my pleasure. Fancy another . . . what are you having? Coffee? Tea?'

'Herbal tea. No thanks, I'd love one but I've got to get going. Got a reiki appointment.' That was not strictly accu-rate; she did have a reiki appointment, but it wasn't until four. The truth was that now the deal was nearly done, Gemma had an overwhelming urge to scarper. She was anxious Bridget might annoy her and she'd snap and every-thing would be off. Best to leave on a high.

'Oh, that's a shame. Well, before you disappear, just help me choose a Valentine.'

'A Valentine?'

'Yeah. C'mon, Miss Organized Knickers, you're not

going to tell me you've forgotten what day tomorrow is.'

'Of course not.' Gemma had bought Alex's card a week ago, along with the tasteful gift – a small print from a gallery in Islington – and the ingredients for a special dinner. She'd never go out for a meal on the night itself; could you imagine anything tackier than being stuck in a restaurant with an overpriced set menu and dozens of other couples being forced to gaze romantically into each other's eyes?

'Who are you buying one for?' she asked, pulling on her coat.

'Oh, just this guy.' Bridget gave a most un-Bridgety giggle. It was soft and sweet and positively feminine. She turned to her sister, smiling. 'He's called Massimo and he's a barrister.'

'A barrister!' Gemma was stunned. Bridget went out with minicab drivers and asylum seekers who wanted to marry her to get a passport. Gemma was the sister who went for men with prestigious, lucrative careers. Half of her was delighted that Bridget was seeing the light, another half of her felt oddly threatened by this news.

'Yeah, he's gorgeous. Blond hair, blue eyes.'

'Where did you meet him?'

'In Costa Coffee in Ealing. Where he works.'

'Where he works? What, with his laptop?' Gemma imagined a bewigged and gowned man sitting among the dossers tapping notes about his latest case into a dinky Mac, as he sipped on a frullato.

'Not with his laptop. Behind the bar.' Bridget gave her an odd look and then started to giggle. 'Oh no, you didn't think I meant he was like an Alex boring barrister. He's a *barista*. He makes coffees.'

'Oh.' Gemma began laughing too. 'I did think it sounded unlikely.'

'Imagine me with a stuffy lawyer! Oops, sorry. I didn't mean it that way.'

'It's OK.' They were in the newsagent's now, browsing over the card rack. 'So . . . has anything happened between you and this guy?'

'Not yet. But we always have a great laugh when I go in. I just think he needs a bit of kicking in the right direction.' She held up a card. 'Here, how about this one?'

It was a monstrosity of hearts and flowers, purple and gold, sequins and glitter. The kind of thing Gemma loathed.

'Yeah, that'll do,' she shrugged diplomatically.

'The message is "I Love You". Do you think that's OTT?'

'No, it's a Valentine, that's the whole point of them,' Gemma lied. After all, it wasn't as if this would go anywhere, it would be the same as Bridget's last eight million relationships.

'You're right, it is, isn't it?' Bridget squeezed Gemma's arm. 'I'm so happy I'm doing this. I really feel it's going to bring us so much closer together. Closer than we've ever been before.'

'We've always been close.'

'I guess.' She shrugged. 'But I don't know. Sometimes I haven't felt it. Last time I was in Goa I talked a bit to my meditation teacher about our relationship.'

'We haven't always seen as much of each other as we should,' Gemma conceded. 'But you're never here. Look, I'm sorry but I really have to dash.'

'OK.' Another one of Bridget's clumsy bosomy hugs. 'I'll call you, let you know how the tests went.'

'Thank you,' Gemma said and felt the damn tears prick again at her eyes, overwhelmed by genuine affection for Bridget for being so big and shambolic and genuinely kind.

But still, it was time to go.

'Don't sign the Valentine, will you?' she called over her shoulder, as she opened the door. But Bridget's reply was swallowed by the roar of traffic.

# 10

It was Tuesday morning. Nick was turning cartwheels naked on a beach. Seagulls were crying, the sand was soft under his hands and there was a strong smell of . . . burning. Was it his pale skin in the tropical sun? But then a siren started wailing. Were the police chasing him? Or was it an ambulance?

'Nicky! Nicky, wake up!'

'Oof.'

'I've set off the smoke alarm trying to make your breakfast,' Kylie squealed. 'Help, I can't reach it.'

'Oh, shit!' Nick jumped out of bed and ran naked into the kitchen. He climbed on to the table, wrenched at the jangling smoke alarm and ripped out the battery.

Silence.

'Fucking hell, Kylie, you got to stop burning the toast.'

'Sorry, sorry,' she apologized. 'I just can't get the hang of this De' Longhi thingy. I'll go to Argos and get us a new one.' She grimaced ruefully. She had a very pretty face, Nick thought, as if seeing her for the first time. 'Now get down from there. I've got a Valentine's surprise.'

Valentine's Day. Nick hadn't forgotten; he'd have had to have been deaf, blind and imbecilic given the hints she'd been dropping for what seemed like months. Kylie wasn't materialistic but she did set a lot of store by soppy cards and teddy bears to mark things like anniversaries. He'd asked Andrew to organize a big bunch of flowers to be delivered at some point in the day. That should keep her happy. After all, there'd be no romantic dinner because it was the Shepherd's Bush gig that night. And before that they were busy with a magazine shoot, followed by some studio time.

'Come on,' Kylie said, taking his hand and leading him – still naked – into the dining room.

'Ta dah!'

'Oh, shite.' Nick looked around. Huge pink balloons hung from the ceiling. Pink glitter dusted every surface. There were pink candles on the mahogany table, which was laid with pink plates, pink flutes filled with . . .

'Champagne at this time in the morning? You must think I'm a rock star or something.'

Kylie threw her arms around his neck, laughing. 'Oh, Nicky, you're so funny. Happy Valentine's Day, my love. Now I know we can't go for a meal tonight but I thought we could have a special Valentine's breakfast instead. Look what I've done!'

He looked at his plate. A fried egg had been cut out in a rough approximation of a heart shape. There was a lump in his throat. He bet Jack and Myrelle St Angelo were snorting cocaine off each other's buttocks. But Kylie's gesture was undeniably touching.

'Do you want to eat it in the altogether? Or shall I get you a T-shirt?' She grinned lasciviously. 'I know which I'd prefer.'

'A T-shirt. We're not in a bloody nudist camp.'

She laughed again and bustled off to get one. Nick

looked at his plate. A fuchsia envelope sat next to it. Before he could open it, Kylie returned.

'I know there'll be all those groupies bombarding you with their knickers tonight at the gig, so I thought I'd stake my claim on you first thing.' She kissed him. 'Eat up.'

As she spoke the door dringed.

'That'll be the car.'

'It's only nine. They're early, aren't they?'

'No, nine was the pick-up.' He gulped down the tea and pushed the untouched egg away. 'Listen, thanks for this. See you later, eh?'

'At the gig.'

'Yeah,' he said, remembering his invitation to Lucinda. The thought of her bumping into Kylie made him cringe. She'd surely think less of him if she saw how ordinary his girlfriend was. But why would they talk to each other? There'd be thousands of people there. His phone rang.

'Hello?'

'Nick. It's Charles.'

'Oh, hiya,' Nick said furtively. His financial adviser, only a few years older than him and already jowly and red in the face, but with a confidence that Nick could only dream of, the result of an expensive education. Charles was in awe of Nick because he was in a band, but secretly Nick was far, far more in awe of Charles.

'How's it going with the flat?'

'Um, just a minute.' He walked into the bedroom and closed the door. 'I've put in an offer and it's been accepted,' he mumbled into the handset.

'Sorry?'

'My offer's been accepted.'

'Excellent. I've checked it out online and it seems a very sound investment. Congratulations, mate. So now you have to instruct a solicitor.'

'That's what the estate agent said. How do I do that?'

'I'll do it for you. And you need to arrange a survey.'

'A what?'

'A survey. To check the flat isn't about to fall down or anything. It's important, Nick, don't skip it.'

'Can you sort it out for me?'

'I can. But I'll have to bill you for it.'

'That's fine.'

'So what does your girlfriend – Kelly, is it? – think of the flat?'

'Um, she loves it.'

Kylie banged on the door. 'Nicky, your car's waiting!'

'Got to go, Charles, talk to you later. Thanks, mate.'

'You're welcome. All part of the service. I'll get a surveyor on the case.'

'Who was that?' Kylie asked as he emerged.

'Just work. I'll see you at the gig, yeah?'

'I can't wait.'

He was sitting in the back of the chauffeur-driven Merc when he realized with a pang that he'd left Kylie's Valentine on the breakfast bar. She'd be so hurt.

Oh, for Christ's sake get over yourself, he told himself.

The shoot was at a studio somewhere in west London. Nick thanked the driver (he had read somewhere always to be 'kind to the little people') and pushed his way in through the revolving door.

'Nick?' A tall, skinny girl with a blonde pony-tail that

scraped her buttocks stepped forward. 'Hi, I'm Zinnia from *Fashionista. So* great to meet you. Like, all my friends and I are rarely into you.'

'Rarely into us? So who are you into the rest of the time?'

She threw back her head and laughed hysterically. 'Not rarely. *Really. Really* into you. Ha, ha. Come this way.'

He followed her into a lift that carried them up to a kind of penthouse: a huge white room opening on to a big balcony with views across London. Not unlike Flat 15, Nick thought. A man in jeans and a checked shirt was faffing about with cameras, the make-up girl was setting up in the corner and a skinny Indian man in flares and a blue sequinned top more suitable for a honeymoon in the Maldives than February in London was sorting through a rack of clothes. Nick waved at Paul and Ian, who were lolling on beanbags, drinking tea and helping themselves to trays of Danish pastries. As ever, Andrew was on the phone, one finger jabbed in his ear. Andrew crapped while making phone calls, had sex while making phone calls and would no doubt still be making phone calls from the grave.

'Morning!'

'Look what the cat's dragged in.'

'Fuck off,' Nick replied. 'How is everyone today?'

'Knackered. Been having a fine Valentine's morning.' That was Paul, who was straight out of I'm-in-a-rock-band central casting. He was short, carrot-haired and arguably had a too-big chin, but since their ship had come in he'd been making the beast with two backs with any-one with two X chromosomes. 'This cute model that I met in Mahiki. She did this amazing thing with her little finger . . .'

'Too. Much. Information.' Nick cuffed him ineptly round the head in a you're-my-mate-and-I-don't-know-how-else-to-display-emotion kind of way.

'What about you, Nick? Been making the sweet, sweet lovin' on this special lovers' morning?' It was Ian, whose new girlfriend Becky, a glamour model, was the closest thing Kylie had to a friend in London.

'Yeah, course I have.' Nick rolled his eyes and picked up another cup of tea from the hospitality table.

'Hope it hasn't got in the way of your songwriting,' said Andrew, slipping his phone in his pocket. He sounded jocular, but Nick knew he was worried. Fucking leech. All he did was sit around eating free cakes and drinking free coffees and for that he took twenty per cent of their money. It was ridiculous. Maybe they should get rid of him? Manage themselves. If the bloody Spice Girls had done it, it shouldn't be beyond their capabilities.

'Nick. Andrew asked you a question,' Ian said.

'It wasn't a question. It was a statement. And yeah. Some progress.'

'Anything to take into the studio next week?'

'Plenty!' He looked around, trying to find a distraction. 'Where's Jack?'

'That is a very good question,' Andrew said grimly. 'Been trying to raise him. Time to try again now.' He picked up his phone and jabbed in a number, but without much confidence. But then . . .

'Hello? Ah, Jack, you fucker, where the fuck are you? . . . No! That is not good enough! . . . Mate, you're needed for the shoot now . . . And what about the gig tonight?'

The band caught each other's eyes, like naughty school-boys summoned to the headmaster. Jack had been doing a lot of this lately. They'd all grown fond of the recreational extras that were one of the perks of the job, but Jack had fallen hopelessly, passionately in love with them. Increasingly, he was up all night, coked out of his skull, and then found it impossible to go to sleep without a handful of downers. It was usually impossible to raise him before noon, so his absence today came as little surprise.

'OK, OK. Fucking hell, Jack . . . Well, this morning we'll work something out. But this evening . . . what are we supposed to do? . . . No, I'm not going to fucking chill about it. We'll have to cancel the fucking gig. Well, fuck you then.'

He threw the phone across the room, narrowly missing the Indian boy, who wailed, 'Lawksamercy.'

'Fuck!' Andrew yelled. 'Arsehole.' He made a gesture of tearing his hair out, then, 'Right,' he said with an eerie air of calm. 'Well. We're just totally fucking fucked, aren't we? We'll have to cancel the fucking gig. I'll call the promoters.'

Andrew strode out of the room. The three of them looked at each other uneasily. Cancelling gigs was obviously not ideal.

'Becky'll be pleased,' said Ian, who had always been a glass-half-full sort of man. 'I can take her out for dinner tonight. Do ya think Andrew'll be able to get us a table at Nobu?'

'It's probably not top of his priorities right now,' Nick said, watching their so-called manager gesticulating on the other side of the glass door. He'd better organize something with Kylie now. Another thought struck him. Lucinda. He'd invited her to the gig. Normally he wouldn't give a toss about such niceties, but for some reason he disliked the thought of her turning up at an empty Empire. He pulled out his phone and dialled Dunraven Mackie.

'It's Lucinda's day off,' a sneery woman told him.

Briefly, Nick imagined her curled up among white sheets, in the arms of a lover. But she'd said she was going to take her brother to the gig.

'I'll try her mobile.'

He was sort of relieved to get her voicemail. Lucinda was annoyingly intimidating. But that was also why she turned him on.

'Um, Lucinda. It's Nick Crex here. Er, our gig tonight's cancelled. Sorry about that. Just thought I should let you know. So . . . and I'm getting on the case and everything with a solicitor and whatnot, so I'll hear from you shortly then. So. 'Bye.'

He hung up, oddly unnerved. Zinnia stood in front of him.

'Ready for make-up now?'

'I guess,' he muttered. While they smeared foundation over his cheekbones, he found his mind darting between irritation at the cancelled gig, concern that Jack was doing this far too often and a niggle at the back of his head about when he was going to see Lucinda again. She made him feel like his teeth when he'd come out of the dentist's, having had them professionally cleaned for the first time in his life – stripped of a layer of plaque so they tingled and he couldn't stop bothering them with his tongue. But the sensation had died down rapidly, and so would this interest. She might be posh, but she was still only an estate agent, for fuck's sake. Nick needed to get a grip.

## 11

Lucinda was sitting at the breakfast bar of the mansion flat in the block Daddy owned in South Kensington, eating muesli and gazing out at the communal gardens bathed in weak, but promising, early spring sunlight. It was Tuesday – Valentine's Day, not that the date meant anything to her – and her day off.

The night before, she and Benjie had stayed up late watching a bad movie about a dog from space, so she'd slept late, until nine. It wasn't what Benjie would call a lie-in – he thought noon was an early start. Lucinda, on the other hand, considered a morning in bed a morning gone for ever and was now berating herself for her laziness.

She ran through her plans for the day: check her investments online and perhaps trade some shares. Go to the gym. Catch up on her reading that afternoon – thanks to Cass's woes she still hadn't had a chance to get through the Sunday papers – and then tonight was the Vertical Blinds gig, which could be fun. Her phone rang. She looked at the Caller ID, hardly daring to believe it.

'Daddy! Hello. How are you?'

'Mummy and I are in town,' barked her father, as ever ignoring her attempts at social niceties. 'We'd like to take you to lunch.'

Typical. Anyone else's parents would have acknowledged that their daughter had a job, that she might not be available at a moment's notice. But not Michael Gresham. Such a big cheese it never occurred to him that any of the mice might not be eager for a nibble. And anyway, of course Lucinda was thrilled at a chance to see him. So often she'd discovered from a newspaper article, or an offhand remark, that he'd been in London a whole week on business and not bothered to look her up. She tried not to let it bother her, she knew how busy he was, but it still hurt, just as it had hurt when he'd never appeared at school concerts, or plays, or at her graduation ceremony.

'You're lucky, Daddy, it's my day off,' she said, determined to play it cool. 'Normally it wouldn't have been possible at such short notice.'

She'd been angling for a 'Why?' but all she got was: 'What about Benjie? Is he about?'

'Um. He's not here. I think he's in the library.' Hearing his only son was dead to the world after a heavy night on Hampstead Heath might not go down too well with Michael Gresham.

'Well, please get in touch with him. Unless I hear otherwise I'll see you both at Claridge's. One.'

''Bye, Daddy,' Lucinda said softly into the silent handset. 'See you later. I'm really looking forward to it.'

She banged on Benjie's door.

'Fuck off!'

'Fuck off yourself. Daddy's in town. He wants us all to have lunch today.'

'Oh, shite.'

She opened the door to be greeted by that smuggy boy smell of old socks and semen, which even a raving queen like her brother, who probably spent at least two-thirds of his trust fund on aftershaves and moisturizers, couldn't banish from his bedroom. Benjie pulled himself up on his elbow revealing his buff torso, achieved by a daily hour in the gym when he should have been in a zoology lecture.

'It may be shite, but if you want your allowance next month I suggest you come along.'

'But I've got college! What does he want to see us for?'

'Um . . . possibly the fact that we're his children.'

'Like that's ever motivated him. Must be his annual attempt at playing the paterfamilias. Will Mummy be there too?'

'Yeah,' Lucinda said without enthusiasm.

'Great. That'll make it slightly more endurable.'

Lucinda shrugged. The battle lines had always been drawn very precisely in the Gresham family. Benjie and Ginevra were Mummy's little boy and girl, Lucinda was Daddy's. She found herself both scornful and sorry for Gail Gresham. She had come from a fairly humble background, had dazzled Daddy with her youthful beauty and had spent the rest of her life trying desperately to hang on to her looks and to him, turning a blind eye to his philandering. For the past nineteen years she'd not eaten more than five hundred calories a day, ever since Daddy had remarked that she was looking a bit chubby after the birth of Benjie and ought to watch it. Her diary was crammed with appointments for facials, hairdos, manicures, fillers, an annual spot of surgery.

But Daddy was still bored with her, and no wonder when Gail never read anything but *Hello!* Lucinda always did her best to make sure she'd read *The Economist* before she saw her father and had opinions on the issues of the day, so they had plenty to talk about. Why couldn't Mummy see that, she wondered, as she clicked on to the *FT* website for a hasty mug-up.

But as she skimmed an article about developing finance initiatives in Islamic banking, her thoughts kept returning to her father. Lucinda was incredibly proud of him. All right, he wasn't one of these 'I were born in a barn, we had it reet poor, walked ta school barefoot, had ta eat me brothers and sisters for tea one winter' types. His father had been a stockbroker, he'd been to public school and Oxford.

But he'd still taken the family money on to the next level, buying up rows of condemned houses in Cornwall, demolishing them and turning them into chi-chi retirement villages. After that his tentacles began to spread everywhere. He owned huge chunks of London, a massive slice of the north-east, had empires all over Europe, Australia and the States. By the time Lucinda, the middle child, was born, he was a tax exile. She'd grown up in Geneva, world capital of milky chocolate and cow bells, and attended an international school where her fellow pupils were sheiks' sons and oligarchs' daughters.

Even though Daddy was rarely around, he'd always been her favourite parent. As a little girl she remembered dancing around when he came into the room, hoping he'd notice her. Which he did vaguely – patting her on the head, saying she looked pretty. Lucinda wanted more than that. Very early on she clocked that the only thing Daddy really paid attention to was money, and the only way she was going to make an impression on him was to make some herself.

Of course there was absolutely no need to ever go out and earn a bean – the three Gresham children all had trust funds, and even though their access was limited until they were twenty-five, they could still basically have whatever they wanted. But Lucinda still wanted to work. Gail wouldn't allow them to have any kind of holiday job; she was worried they'd be kidnapped or something, and anyway Geneva wasn't the kind of place where you could find a job delivering papers from château to château, so Lucinda had to wait until she left school.

'What would you like to do with the rest of your life?' Daddy asked when he took her out to celebrate her Baccalauréat and her place to study economics at Brown University in the US. Blissfully, it was just the two of them – the rest of the family had chosen to go to their villa in St Tropez for the weekend, as one of the neighbours was having a party.

Lucinda glowed. 'Well, Daddy, if it doesn't sound too cheeky, I'd like to do a Master's in business and then come and work for you.'

The 'if it doesn't sound too cheeky' was a sop. Of course Daddy would want Lucinda to work for him, she thought. But to her surprise, he didn't give her his usual indulgent if distracted smile. Instead he put down his cutlery and looked at her severely.

'You would, would you?'

'Well, yes, of course,' she stammered, wrong-footed. 'I mean – who else would I want to work for? You're the best. And I'd really try my hardest for you.'

Michael laughed. 'But why would I want you to work for me? You've got no experience.'

Now Lucinda was flustered. 'But nor does anyone who's doing their first job. I'd learn quickly, Daddy.'

He eyed her over his glass of Châteauneuf. 'I'm flattered you want to work for me, though also slightly concerned about your sanity. But it's not going to happen just like that. You need to go off, get some experience of your own and then – if you really can impress me – I'll take you on. But it's not going to happen automatically. I didn't get to be Michael Gresham by hiring my children.'

'You're not going to hire Benjie or Ginevra. Just me!' Infuriatingly Lucinda's eyes were full of tears.

'Maybe you,' Daddy said gently, picking up her hand and kissing it in the candlelight. Lucinda saw an old lady at the table next to them stare in fascination. Clearly she thought she was his mistress. Oh, yuk. Loudly, to make the situation clear, she said, '*Je t'aime, Papa.*'

'What? Oh. I love you too, sweetheart.' He smiled. 'But you know better than to think you can get round me that way. I'm telling you. Go off. Get your degree – you'd bloody better after the amount I've spent on your education. Find a job. I might help you with that bit but it won't be at HQ. Amass experience.'

So that was what Lucinda was doing now, amassing experience. She'd got her degree, she'd got her Master's and then she'd gone back to Daddy, hoping he'd have changed his mind. But if anything he was more resolute than before.

'I want to see you out in the real world for a bit. I think a spell in an estate agent's would be a good start. Maybe in the UK, you've never spent any time there. You should know a bit about where your old dad comes from. And it'll give you a feeling for how the market moves, what people are looking for in a property. I'll pull some strings.'

Lucinda was infuriated that she couldn't find her own job. She felt stuck in a no man's land – unable to join the family firm and take the nepotism taunts square on the chin. But also unable to go out and find a job like a normal person – even though she was more than qualified to do so.

It was the same with the South Kensington flat, she thought, pulling a Ralph Lauren slip dress over her head. Daddy went on and on about not spoiling his children, but then insisted they lived in one of his properties 'because otherwise your mother's frightened you'll end up in some arse end of nowhere being burgled and stabbed'. Lucinda would have relished the prospect of finding her own place, of – burgling and stabbing aside – living like most people. She'd already been surprised at the satisfaction she derived from doing her own laundry and cooking, though not cleaning – because that would mean tidying up after Benjie – so she paid Honoria nine pounds an hour for that.

Still, resentment was pointless. Daddy was what he was, and if Lucinda wanted to be his number two she would just have to work her hardest at Dunraven Mackie and do brilliantly. And once she'd served her apprenticeship, she'd win her rightful place at company HQ in Geneva working as his right-hand woman. And – although she wished Daddy a long life – one day the company would belong to her alone.

It wasn't as if she'd have to fight the others for the job. Ginevra was happy being a corporate wife in Mum's image, and all Benjie cared about was ketamine-fuelled nights in

Old Compton Street. Neither of them needed the cash, neither of them possessed the ambition that burned inside Lucinda. Sometimes she thought it might be fun to compete with her siblings as if they were in the cast of *Dallas*. But looking at Benjie now, checking his MSN for messages from his various paramours, Lucinda knew that the chance of him fighting for a stake in the family business was about as likely as snowfall on their house in Tobago.

Not that Benjie wanted to totally piss off his father – he needed his allowance. Which was why today he'd eschewed his normal combo of pink T-shirt under a studded leather jacket in favour of a blue button-down Thomas Pink shirt and chinos. Benjie's homosexuality was taboo in the Gresham family. You'd have thought it would be impossible to ignore the sexuality of a man who'd always preferred his sisters' Barbies to his toy soldiers, but if Michael Gresham had his suspicions, he had never voiced them, continuing to use terms like 'poofter' and 'bender' to describe any man he didn't think much of. For his part Benjie did his best to act manly, even if he couldn't prevent himself from squealing in admiration if Mummy had a piece of new jewellery.

She was just having a before-going-out pee when Benjie yelled.

'Your phone's ringing!'

Lucinda jumped up, Princesse TamTam knickers round her ankles. 'Quick, hand it to me!' she yelled round the loo door. She hated missing calls – you never knew when someone might ring with a cash, asking-price offer on a property. But by the time Benjie tracked down her phone on the kitchen table, it had stopped. She listened to the message.

'Oh, that's a shame,' she said.

'What?'

'Our gig tonight is cancelled.'

'What gig?' Then Benjie remembered. 'Oh, the Vertical Blinds? Fuck, I was looking forward to that. Their lead singer is so sexy.'

'Never mind.' Lucinda was pleased. Now she wouldn't have to tell her brother she'd actually offered his ticket to Cassandra. Who'd be disappointed, but what could she do? She turned her head as the post thwocked on the door-mat.

'Wicked!' Benjie screeched, gathering it up. 'Please God, please, let there be something from Sergei.'

'Uh?' It took her a moment to work out what he was talking about. Then she remembered. Of course. Valentine's Day.

'Yes!' Benjie was kissing a card emblazoned with a romantic image of an erect penis. 'He loves me, he lervs me. He loooves me!!' He opened Lucinda's Valentine and laughed. 'Thanks, sis.'

'How did you know it was from me?'

'Er, the message. And the handwriting . . .' Lucinda laughed. In school they'd all learned to write the French way, in big loopy curved letters, very different from English people's anarchic scrawl. Not that you saw people's handwriting very much these days when everyone emailed and texted. Uneasily, she thought of the Valentine she'd sent Anton South-Efrikan. Would he be able to recognize her from her handwriting? Oh, but sod it. Lucinda had already been through this. His secretary would bin it, and that would be the end of that.

'Shall we go?'

'Wait, there's one for you!'

'For me?'

'I don't see any other Lucinda Gresham in the room. And you are a gorgeous young woman of twenty-four. Why shouldn't you get a Valentine?'

True. Intrigued, she opened the hot pink envelope. Perhaps it was from Daddy, she couldn't help thinking, but he'd never observed Valentine's Day before – even with Mummy – so why should he now?

A card fell out. It was cheap and cartoony, the sort you might find in your local garage displayed next to the Ginsters' pies and tubs of Pringles.

'I love you a lot, I love you almighty. I wish your pyjamas were next to my nightie,' Benjie read over her shoulder. 'Ooh, classy.'

'This coming from the man whose favourite programme is Jeremy Kyle.' Lucinda opened the card. *'To the Greatest Trainee Estate Agent in the World. ? XX.'* She smiled. 'It's from Gareth.'

'Gareth?'

'A colleague.'

'Ooh, is he fit?'

'No,' she said briskly. 'He's nice but not fit.'

'So nothing's going to happen?'

'No.' But Lucinda was pleased. The card had struck exactly the right tone – it made it clear Gareth was still interested, but in such a joky way that neither of them would feel embarrassed. 'Now come on. You know what'll happen if we're late.'

They arrived at Claridge's fifteen minutes early. Ginevra

was already waiting for them in the bar, wearing a Dolce & Gabbana peasant top and skinny black jeans tucked into boots.

'Ooh, look! A Russian hooker,' Benjie hissed. 'This place is really going downhill.'

'Shut up,' Lucinda nudged him. 'At least we're being spared Wolfgang.'

'Such a shame. Because I was really looking forward to talking to him about corporate bonds and the Ryder Cup.'

'You could have asked him for some fashion tips,' Lucinda sniggered.

'Ah, yah!' said Benjie, in an unkind but accurate impression of their Austrian banker brother-in-law. 'So ve are vearing ze primrose yellow sweater with white jeans today, Wolfie? Und ze cravat, of course.' Brother and sister sniggered.

Ginevra jumped to her feet. 'Guys! Hey! So good to see you.'

'You too, Gins.' Kissing her, Lucinda felt guilty for her bitchiness. Ginevra and Wolfie might have offended many sensibilities with their Eurotrash outfits and inanely dull conversations about which was better, Klosters or St Moritz, but they hadn't shot Bambi. She should be more charitable.

'What are you doing in London?' she asked.

'Wolfie's over here for some meetings. And remember Princess Marie-Carolina of Bulgaria who was in my class at La Chêneraie? It's her baby shower this afternoon – she's marrying some hedge fund guy, so I thought combine it with lunch with you guys and then go on and see her. Look, let me show you what I've bought her.' She bent down and reached into a Selfridge's carrier bag, revealing an – admittedly cute – yellow cashmere cardigan and bootees. '*Adorable, n'est-ce-pas?*'

'*Très joli*,' Lucinda yawned, as Benjie clapped his hands together with genuine rapture, crying: 'That's gorgeous, Gins! Do you think they do them in adult sizes?'

'Good, good. So you're all here.'

Michael Gresham. Tall, solid, with a thick, silver head of hair. At the sound of his booming tones, heads swivelled and conversations stopped dead.

'Hello, Daddy,' Lucinda said, offering him her biggest, most beaming smile. But he looked right through her to her – arguably prettier – big sister.

'Hello, darling.' Kiss, kiss. 'How are you? Looking lovely, I must say.'

'Thank you, Daddy,' Ginevra smirked.

Lucinda tried to ignore the envy that always flickered inside her at such exchanges and instead turned her attention to Gail. As usual she was standing a few respectful paces behind her husband, looking pretty but boring, in a grey tweed suit. Her lips were definitely more swollen than last time they'd seen each other, her hair a couple of tones blonder.

'Mummy, how are things?'

'Wonderful, thank you, darling.' Kisses were exchanged to an overwhelming pong of Y by YSL. 'Benjie, my darling little boy. And Ginevra! Oh, I love that necklace. Is it Bulgari?' Lucinda rolled her eyes.

'How are things with you, Benjamin?' their father asked as they made their way to the dining room. 'Working hard?'

'Of course, Dad,' Benjie smiled. 'How about you?'

Michael laughed, as he always did at his son's teasing. 'You know me. Your mother's fussing over me as usual. Says if I carry on like this I'll have a heart attack. I say I'd rather be dead than bored.'

'You look in great shape to me, Daddy,' Lucinda said. Michael continued to address Benjie.

'So when are you going to quit that namby-pamby degree of yours? Stop cutting up dead animals and do something serious? Like economics.'

'You've already got an economist in the family,' Lucinda pointed out, but her father ignored her. Benjie's decision to read zoology had been the bravest move of his short life. Daddy had been incredulous that anyone – not least his only son – would want to study anything that didn't focus on money and how to make more of it, but Benjie had been adamant. For a week or so, Daddy had hummed about whether he'd fund such an airy-fairy decision, but Mummy had intervened, Benjie had made an insincere promise about doing a Master's in finance and – until now – there had been no further discussion.

'I'm doing well, Daddy,' Benjie said quietly. 'Predicted a first.'

That was an outright lie. But Michael's attention span was short and it had already moved on to his firstborn.

'And what about you, Ginevra? Enjoying Madrid?'

'Daddy, I love it there. I'm doing a Spanish course and I'm thinking about launching my own internet business with my friend Pia. We were thinking hand-made Madeiran lace christening gowns.'

Lucinda snorted involuntarily. Daddy looked at her stonily.

'Sorry, got some water up my nose.'

'And you, Lucinda?'

'I got the office commendation last month.'

'Did you?' A tiny flash of approval in his eyes. 'Well done. Right, shall we order?'

Lunch passed in the usual fashion. Ginevra, Benjie and Mummy had a heated discussion on whether Tory Burch's wedges were suitable on a yachting holiday. Lucinda meanwhile tried to discuss emerging Far Eastern markets with her father. Michael didn't appear particularly interested, though, looking at his BlackBerry and snorting, before bashing out a reply.

'So, Lucinda?' Ginevra asked as the main course was served (the others had all gone for steamed Menai Straits bass – typical low-calorie nonsense, in Lucinda's opinion. She had the roast beef, because that was what Daddy was having). 'Are you seeing anyone right now?'

'She got a Valentine this morning,' Benjie snitched.

'No! Who from?'

'The whole point about Valentines is that they're anonymous,' Lucinda pointed out, annoyed.

'But you do know. It's from a guy she works with. It was horrible. Cheap and tacky.'

Ginevra smirked. 'Does he know who you are, exactly?'

'Of course he doesn't. Nobody knows.'

Daddy frowned. 'Are you sure? You've got to be careful.'

It was the threat that hung over all of them. Fortune

hunters. People who were only interested in them for the Gresham money. Of course at La Chêneraie that hadn't been an issue – all the pupils had been the children of moguls and the Greshams were virtually the poor relations. But in the outside world, as she couldn't help thinking of it, you had to watch out.

'This guy doesn't know who I am.' She thought of Gareth, with that open, trusting face. Way too decent to be an estate agent. 'And even if he did, well . . . he's not like that.'

Gail tried – and failed, thanks to all the Botox – to frown. 'I don't know, darling.' She turned to Michael. 'Do you really think this is a good idea? Maybe Lucinda shouldn't be doing this job.'

Lucinda felt a flash of panic. She loved being in London, being free to live like an ordinary person. What was the alternative? Finding a husband, like her sister.

'Mummy, Daddy, everything's fine! I love what I'm doing here. Don't worry, no one's being a fortune hunter.' Eager to change the subject, she turned to Ginevra. 'I love that nail polish. Is it Chanel?'

# 12

A week had passed since Valentine's Day. A milk-white blur of snowdrops lined the drive to Chadlicote Manor. In the kitchen, Grace and Lou stood leaning against the Aga rail, clutching mugs of coffee (with skimmed milk for Grace – she always drank skimmed milk, just like she consumed litres of Diet Coke) and discussing the Drakes.

'They've moved very quickly,' Grace said. 'They visited on Saturday, put in the offer on Monday, Sebby and Verity accepted it on Wednesday . . .'

'Sebby and Verity *and* you,' Lou corrected her.

'Yes. Well . . . I thought it was rather a low offer but Verity said the market's still very unpredictable and we should move things as fast as possible. So the survey's happening tomorrow and . . .' Grace shrugged.

Lou eyed her with exasperated affection. 'So what are they like?'

'The Drakes? Delightful. He's a rather serious chap, he's been very ill and wants to completely change his life. She was very pretty. Thin.' Grace hovered on the last word longingly, then continued. 'A bit quiet, but then she had to take plenty on board. Lovely girls – that'll be a change for this big old house. Brighten it up.'

'Should be your children living here,' Lou said quietly, just as there was a loud banging at the front door. The dogs started barking.

'Far too early for the post,' Grace said, puzzled. The banging grew louder as she ran along the cold passageway to the front door. The dogs were nearly frantic by the time she opened it. A stocky man with red hair, an even redder complexion, lots of freckles and a broad grin stood there. He wore a faded Barbour and orange cords. He held out a stubby-fingered hand.

'Morning. Miss Porter-Healey, I presume. I'm Richie Prescott, the surveyor. How do you do?'

'Surveyor? But that was meant to be tomorrow, wasn't it?'

He looked puzzled. 'I don't think so. Tuesday ten a.m. That's what was written in my diary.'

'I had Wednesday. I must have made a mistake.' Grace was baffled. She didn't get things like appointments wrong. There were few enough of them, after all. She must be even more befuddled than she realized.

Richie Prescott frowned. 'Well, if it's not convenient we can always reschedule.'

'No, no. Today is convenient. No problem at all. You'll just have to tell me how I can help you.'

'Good lord.' Mr Prescott looked around the echoing hall. 'Isn't this just the most marvellous house in the world? I remember coming to the fête in the grounds here with my parents when I was a little boy. It's a great privilege for me to be able to survey it.' He patted Shackleton, who was slobbering on his trouser leg. 'Hello, boy. Delighted to meet you.'

Grace glowed, like other people did when their babies were admired. 'I'm so glad you like the house. I mean, it's a bit of a wreck, obviously, but it still is very special. To me. At least.'

He glanced at her. 'Why are you selling? If you don't mind me asking.'

'Well, my mother is dead and after death duties . . . my brother and I simply can't afford the upkeep.'

'I see. I'm so very sorry. But what a marvellous space. The National Trust would be slavering to get their hands on it. Did you apply for any grants?'

'I thought about it. But it's so complicated and time-consuming and . . . my mother was very ill these past few years. Looking after her took up most of my time.'

'Of course.' A tiny pause, then, 'Well. Where to start? It's going to be a long job, I'm afraid. Are you all right just to leave me to it?'

'Certainly. You tell me where you'd like to begin and I'll guide you in the right direction. And would you like some tea or coffee to help you on your way?'

'I'd love a coffee. How kind! Milk. But no sugar. Sweet enough, you know?' He winked. Grace blushed as if she'd just opened an oven door.

'I'll start in the attic and work my way down, if I may,' Mr Prescott was saying.

'Of course. Shall I show you up there?'

'No need. I assume I just keep climbing!'

As he headed up the stairs the phone rang on the hall table. Grace picked it up. 'Hello?'

'Is that Grace?' trilled a nasal woman.

'Yes.'

'Verity Porter-Healey on the line for you.'

Grace never quite understood why picking up the phone and dialling was too challenging for Verity, but she said: 'Hello?'

'Hello, Grace.' As usual Verity sounded utterly affronted at having to talk to her.

'Hello, Verity, how are the boys?'

Deep sigh. 'A *nightmare*. God, if only I'd known what I was letting myself in for. Still, I suppose you think I'm lucky to have them. Anyway, never mind. I was just calling about the surveyor's visit tomorrow.'

'Actually he's here now.'

'What? But he was due tomorrow.'

'That's what I thought, but he swears the appointment's for today.'

'Oh, Grace! You are being nice to him, aren't you?'

'Of course! I'm making him coffee right now.'

'This sale has got to go through. Otherwise I'm not sure I'll be able to have a holiday at half-term and my heart is set on the Seychelles. I've been reading how vital Vitamin D is for the bones. I'm shattered, you know, I worked my arse off all last year and then I didn't get a bloody bonus, as if world financial meltdown was somehow my fault.'

'I know. Poor you. But really, the Drakes seemed very keen, I don't think a bad survey will put them off.'

'It had better not.'

'All right, love to the boys, I . . . Oh!' Grace peered into the handset, surprised. 'She's gone.'

Lou, who'd been pretending to plump an ancient armchair's cushions, rolled her eyes.

'I don't know, Lou. I do my best to be nice to her. But she can be so tricky. She's always so distracted, and she snaps at the boys, which I hate, and she puts Sebby down all the time.'

'Mmm,' said Lou neutrally.

'But she's right. We do need to sell the house as quickly as possible. Little Alfie needs to be transferred to a private school, the primary he's at won't prepare him for the eleven plus and if he doesn't get into a private school he'll be bullied terribly because he's so sensitive and . . .' Grace shook her head. 'I'd better get that coffee up to Mr Prescott.'

Grace took the coffee up the stairs, stopping on the way to glance into the nursery, as Mummy had – with slight affectation – called it. The rocking horse, the doll's house, the tiny children's chairs – all sitting there like something from a museum. Grace tried not to think too much about children. They were her secret dream. But nobody was interested in her, or ever likely to be now. It was all right. Basil and Alfie loved the rocking horse and – who knew – maybe Verity would have a girl one day and she could have the doll's house. It would be lovely to have a niece. She could read her the stories she'd enjoyed as a child: *Ballet Shoes* and *What Katy Did* and the entire *Chalet School*. She was sure Sebby would like another one, but Verity always laughed at the idea, saying unless he started to help out a bit with childcare two was more than enough. Which was very unfair; Sebby was a marvellous father, always playing monsters with the boys. It wasn't his fault work exhausted him and he needed a lie-in at weekends.

But perhaps all was not lost, she thought, stopping to catch her breath on the landing. She was only thirty-four. She just needed to meet some men. She'd considered online dating, or the personal columns in the *Telegraph*, but she couldn't quite summon the nerve. She felt the same about finding a job. Grace was used to the air of faint pity in people's eyes when they regarded her. She'd seen it in Karen Drake's. It made her ashamed. And it made her more inclined than ever to lock herself away and eat and eat.

But that could change. She'd start a diet tomorrow, she decided. Tonight she'd finish all the bad foods in the house – the cheesecake in the freezer, the pizza in the fridge, the tin of Quality Street. Tomorrow morning she would start afresh. Ryvita for breakfast. Ryvita and cottage cheese for lunch. Cottage cheese on salad for supper. She'd take the dogs for a long, long walk and in the evening she'd do sit-ups in front of a *Doctor Who* video.

She pushed open the attic door. Richie Prescott was crouched under the eaves, surrounded by hatboxes, trunks bulging with faded linen, broken garden furniture and bad watercolours. He turned to her, smiling.

'I bet you played wonderful games of hide and seek up here.'

'We did,' Grace agreed shyly.

'Marvellous. Ah, thank you!' He took the coffee and inhaled in mock comic-book style. 'Just what a man needs on a winter's morning.' He reached in his pocket and pulled out a slim silver hip flask. 'Hope you don't mind,' he said, catching her eye. 'Just a drop of the Scottish stuff to warm my cockles. It is freezing up here.'

'Oh, I do apologize!' Grace exclaimed. 'It . . . well, of course we don't heat the attic. But I'm afraid it doesn't get much better as you go downstairs. Would you like to borrow a coat? A jersey?'

'No, no, don't worry.' He drained his coffee in one. 'Plenty of padding on me, more's the pity. And like I say, a little bit of the amber nectar never goes amiss, ha, ha.

Now don't you worry about me again. This is going to take several hours, so shall I just come and find you when I finish?'

'Do. I'll probably be in the kitchen. Or my study.'

But downstairs again, she felt oddly self-conscious. She knew there were still a million things to do, but with Richie in the house she couldn't settle to any of them. She flicked through her diary. As she'd thought. Richie Prescott was down as coming on Wednesday morning. She must be going batty. She went back to the kitchen. Lou had gone by now but had left one of her game pies warming in the oven. Automatically, as Grace had always done, she set the table with a knife, fork, spoon. A napkin. A glass of water. Salt and pepper grinders.

Then she stopped. The lonely setting for one struck her as utterly pathetic. Suddenly, angrily, she removed everything. Tucking the dish under her gloved arm, she began forking pie into her mouth. Great mouthfuls of crust, lumps of meat that moved painfully down her throat, failing – as usual – to heal the pain in her heart.

She'd just finished when she heard a tap at the door.

'Come in,' she cried, putting the dish down and wiping the crumbs from her mouth.

Richie Prescott stuck his head round.

'Only me! Terribly sorry to bother you, but could I trouble you to use your phone? As you know, there's no mobile reception here and I want to check my messages. Just worrying a touch that this appointment *was* meant to be tomorrow and today I should be somewhere else.'

'Oh! Well, I did wonder.'

He shook his head. 'Forget my own head if it wasn't

145

screwed on. But if you don't mind . . . I'm just going to call my mobile and pick up my messages.'

'Of course.'

Richie dialled, chattering away all the while. 'Crocuses are starting to show already. Spring's definitely on its way. Oh, hang on, now I have to jab my pin in, what is it again? Oh yes, I remember.' He listened intently, then struck his head with his hand. 'Idiot!' He hung up. 'You were right and I was wrong. I was meant to be here tomorrow and at a house in Totnes today. And the lady in Totnes is very angry.'

'Oh, dear,' said Grace solemnly.

'So if you don't mind I'll pop over there now and come back here tomorrow at some point.' He smiled. His eyes were bloodshot, like the bloodhound belonging to the Narl-bys who lived over in the next valley, and his teeth were a bit yellow. But he was a man, smiling at her.

'Of course,' Grace said.

'Cheerio then. *À demain*!'

He disappeared back down the corridor. Grace stood at the threshold, watching his retreating form. She felt foolish. Why couldn't she have been funnier? More clever? Told a joke? Discussed the world energy crisis?

Why couldn't she have been thinner?

Tonight she would eat nothing. And she'd brush up on conversation topics. Grace's life was moving on relentlessly, like a boat being swept downriver, and she needed to at least try to seize the helm.

Nick was sitting in the back of a Prang Records people carrier on his way home from the studio. The past few weeks had been up and down for him. Finally, ideas for songs were trickling in. Hardly like a mountain stream, more a leaky tap. But all the same. Inspiration was working again. He'd stayed up four nights in a row, with Kylie fussing around him, trying to make him come to bed or offering him cups of tea and sandwiches.

He'd had to swat her off like a midge as he attempted to get the ideas down on paper before they vanished, like bath bubbles down the plughole. Nick forgot all about Flat 15, ignoring calls from his solicitor, the surveyor, even the sexy estate agent. Who gave a fuck? Somehow he had to wrestle these ideas out of his brain and turn them into guitar chords.

Finally, after what seemed like almost a physical struggle, he'd succeeded in getting four good songs down. Two OK ones. One that was shit but which Andrew claimed to like and which Nick hoped he could improve. Nothing great yet. Nothing in the 'Imagine', 'Life on Mars', 'Virginia Plain' vein that would ensure his place in the hall of eternal fame. But enough to be getting on with. Nick felt as if he'd been forced to bang his head against a wall for months and then suddenly allowed to stop.

But now the next round of problems started. The studio time started on Monday. All that week Jack turned up either hours late or not at all. Even when he was there he was often so off his chops that his input was useless.

Andrew was furious.

'You have got to get yourself together, mate. Give the drugs a break for a bit. You can get back on them when the album's in the bag.'

Jack looked indignant. 'What are you talking about, man? I ain't touching drugs. I'm just hung-over.'

'Yeah, right,' Nick snapped. 'That's why your eyes are like pencil points and you're talking even more shite than ever. Give it a break, mate, just for a few days.'

But he wouldn't. Or couldn't. Whatever. Nick didn't care about his old friend's obvious addiction problems. He cared about the fact that his songs weren't going to get recorded.

'Can't we just sack him and get in another singer?' Paul asked on a Tuesday morning, as – again – they sat around the studio waiting for Jack's car to arrive. Yet again, the driver was reporting that he wasn't answering the door. His phone was off.

'No,' Andrew said. 'Unfortunately, Jack is the face of the band. A very pretty face. And a good voice too. Without him, we'd lose the fanbase overnight.'

It seemed unfair, as the rest of them weren't bad-looking lads, but Andrew was right. They'd all tried singing at some point in the old days when Jack had been too bladdered to go on. None of them had his magic, his way of mesmerizing the crowd. So they just had to bide their time and wait until he did deign to turn up, usually around six p.m., and then cram in as much recording as they could.

Often Nick didn't get back until the early hours. Kylie would be asleep in her Winnie-the-Pooh pyjamas, but as soon as he crept into the room, she would sit bolt upright and smile.

'Hiiiya! How did it go?'

'Fine,' he would mumble, and no matter what time it was, they'd always have sex.

But this evening was different. It was only half ten when Nick stepped out of the car. Time to eat something, maybe watch some telly with Kylie beside him. He was looking forward to the prospect – even though he shouldn't have been. He should have been prepping himself to leave Kylie behind. But one more night snuggled in front of the telly wasn't going to make any difference either way, was it?

Stepping into the flat, he was hit by the silence. Astonishingly, the telly was off. She must have gone out. Well, that was a turn-up. Kylie starting to get a social life. That would help when he finally broke the bad news.

'Hello,' said a little voice in the dark.

Nick jumped.

'You scared me!'

She was sitting in the corner armchair. From the neon street-light peeking in through the window he could just see that her face was streaked with mascara.

'What's going on?'

She handed over a large envelope. 'You got this.'

'You've been opening my letters?'

'It was an accident, I thought it was for me.'

'Yeah, right.' He pulled out a document. The survey on Flat 15. He'd forgotten all about it.

'Who's thinking of buying Flat 15, Summer Street?'

He didn't allow his expression to flicker. 'It's something I've been considering. Charles told me to invest my money and this is one option.'

'So we're going to live there?'

'Um . . . Probably not. *If* I buy it, I was planning to rent it out.'

'Well, can I have a look at it?'

He sighed. 'You can if I decide to follow it up. But probably I won't. Now what's the news?'

'Why didn't you tell me?'

'I meant to. I forgot. You know how insane it's been.'

She looked hard at him, then sighed. 'So you don't want me to look at this flat.'

'No point until I know I want to buy it.'

'Right.'

She seemed to have swallowed it. They shared a pizza, then went to bed and had energetic sex. But Nick was shaken. It had been a narrow escape. The following day, while a drums solo was recorded, he read the survey. Even he could see it didn't look good. All sorts of problems with the building: a dodgy roof, rising damp, new windows needed throughout, which the tenants were going to have to pay for over the next few years. He still wanted the flat but he'd be crazy to go for it at the current price.

His phone rang.

'Hello, Mr Crex. Lucinda Gresham here. Have you seen the survey?'

'I have. It's pants, isn't it? So I'm going to reduce my offer by fifty grand.'

'I see,' Lucinda said smoothly. 'Well, I shall put that to them and find out what they have to say.'

'You do that,' he said and, hanging up, he smiled. He had them right where he wanted them. Now he just had to find the energy and guts to leave Kylie. To move on to the life he believed should be his. He should start planning his seduction of Lucinda. He'd work out a strategy tomorrow.

# 13

Lucinda and Gareth had a morning appointment for a house near King's Cross, in a square which used to be full of dosshouses and brothels but which was now being colonized by couples with dreams of kitchen-diners leading on to the garden and utility rooms.

The house had belonged to an old man who had just died, who'd been living there for the past thirty years with his middle-aged, dope-smoking son. The walls were yellow with nicotine and piles of newspapers covered every inch of floor space. All the same, it was an entire house, rather than one that had been converted into flats, which made it a rarity in the area. Developers would be all over it like orange-skinned girls round footballers in a nightclub.

'I value this property at nine hundred and seventy-five thousand pounds,' she said.

'Do you think?' The son looked disappointed. 'I thought it would be more like two million.'

'I think this is an excellent price, given that the property does require some – ahem – modernization.'

'But I had it valued when Dad was still alive and they said one point two. And it should have gone up.'

Gareth shook his head. 'I'm afraid the market's slumped a bit since then. I mean, it's on the way up again now but it's still got a way to go.'

Walking back to the office, they shook themselves as if exorcizing a demon.

'People are so bloody greedy!'

'Probably won't get the instruction now, it'll go to Bleeker & Wright, they'll lie to him, tell him he'll get five million, and he'll go with it. He's the type.'

'Fair dos to them. If they want the fun of dealing with Mr Malodorous they're welcome to him.'

Lucinda glanced sideways at Gareth. She'd been touched by his Valentine and she'd thought about saying something, but in the end she'd decided not to. Though she liked him more and more as a mate every day, she just didn't fancy him and never would.

She turned the corner heading to the office. Standing outside it was Anton Beleek. Automatically Lucinda blushed and looked away. OK, so he'd never know the Valentine was from her, but it had still been a stupid thing to do. Attention-grabbing. Pathetic.

'Anton,' Gareth called merrily. 'Good morning.'

'Morning, Gareth. I was just passing and hoping to have a word with Niall.'

'He's out on a viewing,' Gareth said, unlocking the door. 'And I'm afraid our PA is . . . busy.' Marsha was in court again – one of her children was up on more GBH charges. 'Shall I ask him to call you?'

'Actually I'll call him, if you don't mind,' Anton said, following them inside. 'Could you give me his mobile number?'

'Sure.' Gareth was busy disabling the burglar alarm. 'Lucinda, could you give Anton Niall's number?'

'Of course.' She searched Niall's desk for some business cards but he appeared to have locked them away in his drawer. 'I'll write it down for you,' she said. She called up Niall's number on her mobile, scribbled it down and – trying to be professional – wrote his name and 'Dunraven Mackie' on a page of A4 and handed it to Anton.

'Thanks,' he said brusquely.

'You're welcome,' Lucinda replied sarcastically. Her desk phone started ringing. 'Sorry, excuse me. Hello, Dunraven Mackie.'

'Lucinda, it's Gemma Meehan here.'

Lucinda's heart plummeted. She'd been planning to call her to break the news that Nick Crex had dropped his offer, but she'd wanted to do it once she'd outlined her speech. 'Gemma, hello! How are you?'

'Well, thanks. Just wondering when we're going to hear something more from Mr Crex, now he's seen the survey.'

'Ah, yes. I was going to call you.'

Her tone alerted Gemma. 'Why? What's happened?'

Lucinda took a deep breath, and told her.

'What? But we'd already accepted far below the asking price from him! How can he do this to us?'

'I'm very sorry,' Lucinda said. 'It's his decision. You are, of course, entirely free to turn the offer down.'

'I don't believe this! Bastard! I've got to call Alex.'

'I'm very sorry.'

'For Christ's sake.' Gemma sighed. 'I'll get back to you. In the meantime here's my new mobile number if you hear anything. I've had my old one stolen . . .'

'I am sorry to hear that,' Lucinda said. She scribbled

down the number, writing Gemma next to it. Idly, she added: *Chase up solicitor*. Then, as Gemma ranted a little bit more, Lucinda started on a to-do list. *Birthday card for Ginevra. Organize getting windows cleaned in the flat. Email Lily at Harvard.*

Lucinda's spine was tingling. Someone was watching her.

'The survey was a little negative, you see,' she said loudly, glancing over her shoulder.

Anton Beleek was standing right behind her, staring down at her piece of paper. As she swivelled round in her chair, his solemn face turned scarlet and he instantly looked away. Lucinda's own face flamed. She stared into the mouthpiece as if it contained nude dancing pictures of Brad Pitt. Fuck. He'd seen her handwriting, first on the piece of paper she'd given him and then on her doodles. Her distinctive, curvy French handwriting. He'd worked out she'd sent the Valentine. This was hideous. Lucinda hadn't been so embarrassed since Cassandra had caught her blowing herself a kiss in the mirror and saying, 'You're gorgeous,' in a fruity American accent.

'Yes, yes, I'll let you know as soon as possible,' she said loudly to cover her confusion. Out of the corner of her eye she saw Niall walk in.

'Niall,' Anton hailed him. 'I was hoping to grab you.'

They started talking. 'Goodbye, then. Take care,' Lucinda said to Gemma and hung up.

'Um, Lucinda, do you know how phones work?' Gareth asked, grinning. 'Your voice is carried by cable or satellite to the other phone. They're not just a megaphone to allow yourself to be heard on the other side of London.'

'Get lost' is what she'd normally have said, but Anton's proximity intimidated her, so she simply laughed nervously, then turned flummoxed to her screen. But Anton, conversation with Niall over, began approaching her. Horrified, Lucinda picked up her handset and gabbled into it.

'Hello, Mr Masterson. Yes, it's Lucinda here from Dunraven Mackie. Just calling to confirm our appointment later today . . .' She glanced over her shoulder. Anton was standing there again. There was a smile on his serious face which creeped her out. Smiles didn't suit him. He looked like a politician trying to get down with a posse of teenage rappers.

'Of course, I'm looking forward to seeing you. Yes, I'll take some details . . .' Christ, he wasn't going away. What was she supposed to do? 'Obviously, it sounds like a fascinating property,' she continued. 'Seven bedrooms? Marvellous!' At this ears began pricking up. A seven-bedroom house was as rare as a Mandarin-speaking donkey. Lucinda saw Joanne's face pucker with suspicion. Damn. 'Oh, sorry, I misheard you. Three bedrooms, ha-ha, yes, that's more like it.'

*Diddle-dah, dah-diddle-dah, dah, diddle dah, dah, dah!*

Shit, the phone was ringing loud in her ear. She answered, her face the colour of hell's hottest pit.

'Hello?'

'Hey, it's me. Listen, I just can't decide between these two pairs of boots. One is Jimmy Choo and the other . . .'

'Ginevra, I'll call you back,' Lucinda hissed, then, for the benefit of her smirking colleagues, 'You just cut me off on an important call.'

'How could I have done that?'

'I don't know. The line must have gone dead and I must have been talking into thin air. How embarrassing. Ha ha ha!' Her giggle sounded feeble and airy, but Anton Beleek didn't seem to care: he was grinning at her in the moony sort of way old ladies smile at ugly babies in prams. 'I'll call you back,' she repeated and hung up.

'Goodness, I can't believe I got cut off when I was talking to Mr Masterson,' she said loudly. 'How embarrassing.'

'Um, are you sure you were talking to Mr Masterson?' Joanne sneered. 'Only while you were on the other line he just called me and he said he hadn't spoken to you for ages.'

'Really?' Lucinda tried to look confused. 'How can that be?'

'I don't know,' Joanne said stonily. Niall frowned. Gareth looked rightly concerned for her sanity. Lucinda cringed. And Anton Beleek still stood there. *Go away! Don't you have a successful business to run?* Hastily, she picked up the desk phone and this time called Benjie.

'Hi, what do you want?'

'Mr Silver,' she said. 'It's Lucinda Gresham here. Just calling to chase up the quote on your property.'

'What the fuck are you talking about?'

'I know you weren't sure if you wanted to put it on the market, but . . .'

Out of the corner of her eye, she saw Anton Beleek reluctantly move off. He pushed open the door of the agency. Lucinda exhaled with relief. Why had she been such a prat? What had she been thinking of? But Anton would take it no further. He must realize the Valentine had been a joke. Surely?

*

The Drake family were all in a high state of excitement about their imminent purchase of Chadlicote Manor. All, except Karen.

'I can't believe we're going to live in a castle,' Bea kept saying, while Eloise yelped, 'It's *not* a castle – Mummy, tell her not to be so silly!' She was more excited about the new school she'd be going to, a school selected after another long drive down to Devon, which would accept both sisters as day girls but which also took boarders. 'Can we board, Mummy?' she kept asking. '*Please*. It would be so much fun. There'd be midnight feasts and we'd put on plays and I could do lacrosse.'

After an hour's solid whining on the theme, Karen was severely tempted , but she continued to repeat calmly, 'No, darling. Mummy and Daddy would miss you too much.'

Phil was the most animated he'd been since he received his diagnosis, calculating first how much to offer, then commissioning his survey and spending hours on the internet contacting other people who'd renovated country houses for tips.

'We can have our own vegetable garden,' he told Karen as they lay in bed. 'And keep chickens. Goats maybe. Be totally self-sufficient. Have an utterly holistic lifestyle. It'll be amazing.'

'But what will we live on?'

Phil made a sheeshing sound. 'Stop worrying about that. We'll be OK. I can't believe this house came to us. It must be something cosmic. Giving us a second chance.' He placed his hand on her bottom, their shorthand for 'How about it?' Karen winced. Only six bloody hours until morning; how could he not crave sleep in the way that she did?

But then, like most men, Phil's need for sex had always been pretty feral – she'd known he'd been really sick when he hadn't wanted it, and as soon as he was better it had shot straight back to the top of the agenda.

'Darling, do we have to?' she said. 'I've got that headache again.'

'I'm getting worried about you and your headaches,' Phil said crossly. 'I think you should see the doctor.'

That was another problem with having a husband who'd knocked at death's door, you couldn't invent symptoms to get you off nookie duty. Not without being eaten by guilt.

'If I get any more, I will,' she lied miserably, as his hand slid along her thigh.

In the Parenthope Clinic's plush waiting room, the only sound was the purr of the credit card machine from the lobby. Alex frowned over a thick brief. Gemma attempted to read a magazine, but she couldn't concentrate. She felt as if a drawer had been pulled out of her stomach. Where the hell was Bridget? How could she do this to them on today of all days? All right, it was only ten minutes, but suppose Dervla saw this as a sign of not being committed and declared them unfit for parenthood?

Dervla was their counsellor. She was in her forties, skinny, dark and mesmerizingly well dressed. Just a glance confirmed that she was the kind of woman whose soufflés always rose and who had views on contemporary art. She would also be a Pilates devotee. Gemma had found it hard to concentrate during their session with her, wondering if her dress could really be Marni and if so what could her husband do – there couldn't be that much money in counselling, surely? Then she'd found it hard to focus because she'd been worrying that entertaining such shallow thoughts instead of focusing on your unborn child's welfare might lead to instant expulsion from the clinic.

Still, she'd taken in something. Dervla had made them discuss their expectations of parenthood, what role they expected Bridget to play in Chudney's life, how and when they'd tell the child everything about its origins. ('When Chudney's two weeks old and then we might fail to refresh its memory,' Alex had joked on the way home and Gemma had cried, 'Al! You know we must never hide anything from our child.')

They'd discussed how they must be prepared for disappointment every step of the way, how even if Bridget's eggs were good enough quality, there was still only around a thirty-five per cent chance that the embryos formed from them would attach to Gemma's womb. They'd talked about how, with Bridget's permission, they would like any extra eggs produced to be frozen in order to give them a chance at having a second child.

Alex moaned that the counselling was all a formality and the clinic would pass any couple who could find the money and weren't obvious child abusers. Gemma disagreed; she was sure they'd be failed but it seemed her husband was right because Dervla had approved them and – more miraculously – approved Bridget. Now they were all back for their final session together.

'Stop tapping your feet,' Alex said in the soft voice people always use in waiting rooms.

'Sorry.' Gemma picked up a copy of *OK!* and flicked through it, while subtly eyeing the beaming couple sitting on the leather sofa. They were holding hands and occasionally exchanging soft words. Making eye contact was the worst possible faux pas in this situation, but Gemma was sure she could spot just the tiniest bump under the woman's purple shift dress. Cow. The woman was old – well, not *old*, but over forty, and she'd obviously hit the jackpot. Why was Gemma such a freak to be still in her baby-making prime but unable to produce?

'Sorry! Sorry!' boomed Bridget on the threshold.

'Hi,' Gemma said. She wanted to snap: 'Why are you late?' but she bit her tongue and instead said, 'You look great.' And Bridget did. Her hair was shiny and swingy, she'd definitely lost weight, and she'd dressed far, far more elegantly than usual in black trousers and a grey cardigan that Gemma was amazed to find she coveted.

'Thanks for making the effort,' she smiled.

'Oh, it's not for you,' Bridget giggled, as the forty-something pregnant couple pretended not to listen. 'It's for the barrister.'

'The who?' For a confused second Gemma thought her sister was trying to please Alex. She was touched.

'The barrister, remember. The guy I sent a Valentine to. It worked! We're an item. Hardly been out of bed since.'

Now the forty-somethings couldn't disguise their fascination.

'Did you tell reception you were here?' Gemma asked hastily. 'Because we are a little late.'

'Yeah, sorry about that. I couldn't find my keys. I was locked in the house. Too many Es when I was in Kerala last, they've obviously killed my memory. Or maybe just too much sex.' The forty-somethings' jaws were dropping. Gemma tensed, expecting her husband to explode. He loathed her sister's cheerful references to drugs. 'Doesn't she realize they're at the root of all the evils in the world?' he'd rant. 'Doesn't she care that the fair-trade peasants she claims to support are having their lives devastated by the coca trade?' But this time he merely smiled serenely. Good man.

Bridget gestured to the door.

'Anyway, I'm here now. So shall we?'

Dervla was sitting in an armchair by the large sash window. She was wearing a sheath dress – possibly Jil Sander, Gemma thought, as she took her place in a leather armchair and accepted a cup of camomile tea.

Dervla sat back and smiled like Blofeld might before lowering James Bond into a shark pool.

'So. Bridget has made you an incredibly generous offer. You must be thrilled. Alex?'

Startled to be put so suddenly in the spotlight, Alex cleared his throat.

'Um, yeah. Yeah, of course. Knowing the baby will be genetically as close as possible to Gemma is obviously a great help.'

'How do you feel about fathering what is in essence going to be your wife's sister's child?'

'I prefer not to think of it that way,' Alex said, looking distinctly put out. 'After all, Gemma is going to carry the baby and give birth to it and . . .'

'And breastfeed it,' Gemma interrupted. 'And change its nappies.' She couldn't wait. Couldn't understand people who told her it might not be all it was cracked up to be, that babies could be boring and hard work. Ungrateful sods. They didn't deserve children.

'But you will both always have to live with the knowledge that biologically Bridget is the child's mother. And the child will know that, we hope, since we advise you in the strongest possible terms to be open with them from day one about their origins.'

'From day one?' Bridget chortled. 'Can you imagine? Baby: "Scream, scream, fill my pants." Gemma: "Oh darling, I can't be doing with all this. But it doesn't matter because I'm not really your mummy, that'll be auntie Bridget." Yes, I can see the baby really caring about that.'

'Bridge!'

'I apologize if I didn't express myself accurately enough,' said Dervla. 'What I meant was that as soon as the child can communicate it must be explained to them that they are not biologically the mother's, but they were very much wanted and loved.'

They all nodded gravely.

'Now something we need to discuss,' Dervla continued. 'Money. You are all aware, I take it, that the Human Fertility and Embryology Authority emphatically forbids payment to donors. Although expenses can be covered. And the interpretation of expenses can be somewhat *liberal*.' She gave an unnerving Sarah Palin wink.

'That's all right,' Bridget said. 'I wouldn't want Alex's ill-gotten gains anyway.'

'My ill-gotten gains?'

'Yeah. You know. Prosecuting the innocent. Defending the guilty.'

'Everyone is innocent until proven guilty,' Alex sighed. 'My job is to help the jury make up their mind.'

'Yeah, right.'

'Well, what alternative do you suggest?' Alex said, still icily polite. 'Letting rapists and murderers walk the streets? Or would you have everyone accused of committing a crime thrown in jail?'

'It's a fascist system.'

'What a brilliantly sophisticated argument, Bridget. Do you have any idea about the definition, or indeed, the origins of fascism?'

'Please!' barked Dervla. They all froze. 'We're not here to discuss the merits of the criminal justice system – though for what it's worth there is clearly still a disproportionately small number of black lawyers – we're here to discuss payment. To underline the fact that it's not acceptable. That the motives for donation must be entirely altruistic.'

'We already talked about this,' Bridget said.

'I know. But we all need to go through it together, I'm afraid. Many women would expect a financial reward for this service.'

'But not me! I'm doing it for love. I love my sister. I want to give her the one thing she wants and can't have.'

'How do you feel about this, Gemma?'

'I feel very honoured.' And she did. Tears were swimming in her eyes. 'I'm moved that Bridget will put up with all this, to help me and Alex. I . . . I just wish there was some way to repay her.'

'Don't be silly.' Bridget took her hand. She'd filed her nails, for the first time ever. 'It's what I've always said. Despite what you two might think, life is about more than buying and selling, running round on a hamster wheel. People are good. People help each other out because they want to.'

Alex raised an eyebrow. If Dervla saw it, she said nothing, just scribbled something in a notebook with a paisley cover.

'Good. Well. Thank you for coming. I'll be in touch shortly.'

'Have we passed?' Bridget asked.

'I'll be in touch shortly. Goodbye.'

## 14

It was a still-frosty March morning. Lucinda was taking Daniel Chen to see a flat to rent in the Arlington, a development near the Angel. She didn't normally do rentals but Melanie, the lettings manager, had come down with tonsillitis and everyone else was busy. Lucinda didn't mind. A chance to prove herself.

Daniel was twenty-four, a banker who looked straight out of central casting: tie slightly askew, stripy shirt, brogues, self-satisfied air. Lucinda had no doubt he had a red Maserati and an account with a high-class brothel. Where did they clone them? Weren't all bankers supposed to be selling the *Big Issue* by now? He was the kind of guy Cass would adore. Lucinda wondered why those types did nothing for her, as she stretched out her hand, smiling broadly.

'Daniel, hi. I'm Lucinda. Shall we get going?'

In the lift, she decided to try to make even more money out of him. 'Have you thought of buying instead of renting?'

'I want to wait until the market cools.'

*Um, it's practically frozen, my friend.* 'All the signs are that prices are starting to rise again. There are some properties on our books right now, which . . .'

'I want to rent for now,' he said rather harshly.

OK. In that case Lucinda decided she'd make him rent

the flat, whatever it took. She rang the bell and knocked firmly, before unlocking the door. They entered. Lucinda inhaled new plastic and dust. It reminded her of sitting in the back of one of Daddy's cars, being driven by the chauffeur, Thierry, to school. She looked around. Typical bachelor pad, huge HDTV, kitchen full of stupid gadgets Daniel would use once and then forget about. Slate floors, granite worktops, remote controls to turn on the fire and run the bath taps. Everything would break down, get jammed, drive him crazy and Melanie – who would be called upon to sort it out – even crazier. Daniel, naturally, was enraptured.

'Wow. Great entertaining space.'

He fiddled with the coffee machine inserted in the wall and the juicer that didn't need cleaning (allegedly), tapped on the walls and put his ear to the maple flooring. Lucinda didn't have a clue what he was doing and she was pretty sure he didn't either. He then pushed on into the bedroom, which was slightly untidy. Lucinda made a note to have a gentle word with the tenant to tidy before viewings, but Daniel didn't seem to mind.

'Like the blinds. Is this the en suite?'

'Yes. Do you want to take a look?'

'Of course.' He tried to open the door. 'Oh, it's locked.'

'It can't be locked. It must be jammed.' Lucinda tried. It did indeed appear to be locked. She gave the door a gentle kick with her heel.

'How odd.'

'I'll try,' said Daniel, who clearly fancied himself as something of a macho man. He threw himself against the door, which – being the flimsy work of a developer – flew open to the sound of screaming. Lucinda stepped forward.

Someone was cowering in the shower, wrapped up in the plastic curtain.

'Hello?'

'Please don't hurt me.'

'We're not going to hurt you. I'm . . . the lettings agent.'

The curtain slowly unravelled. A young, pretty Asian-looking woman stared up at them, terrified.

'It's OK,' Lucinda said again. 'I'm from the agency.'

'Oh my God. I thought you were burglars. I heard you come in. I hid in here.' She stood up, looking mortified.

'I'm so sorry I broke the door,' said Daniel, equally abashed.

'I thought you were out,' Lucinda said. 'I do apologize.'

Much grovelling later, she and Daniel descended in the lift, both giggling.

'I feel terrible,' Lucinda said. 'I did ring the bell. And knock.'

'It's all right. I still want the flat. And I'll pay for the damage.' The door pinged and they emerged still laughing into the lobby. Daniel's phone started to ring, just as Lucinda spotted Anton Beleek.

'Sorry,' said Daniel, holding up a hand. 'Hello? Hi, mate! Yeah! Yeah, we really went large. It was like the old days. Shorty got so hammered he pissed in the wardrobe in the middle of the night. And they say we're meant to be grown up now!'

'Hello!' said Anton, like Lucinda was his long-lost best buddy rather than someone he'd never even exchanged the time of day with.

'Good morning,' she replied nervously. 'What are you doing here?'

'Waiting for a contact. Showing her Flat 21. This is my development. Didn't you know that?'

'No, I didn't. I should do my homework.' Lucinda giggled like a bimbo. An awkward silence fell. She glanced at Daniel, willing him to get off the phone, but he was chatting away oblivious to her. 'So then we had a vindaloo and I tell you, my arse the next morning . . .'

'So it's full-on at the moment . . .' she said, just as Anton said, 'I was wondering. Are you free tonight by any chance?'

'Oh! Oh. I'm so sorry, I'm afraid not.' Lucinda should have stopped there. Not given any excuses. But she was so embarrassed, she gabbled on. 'I'm going to the cinema with my friend Cassandra. This new film with Cameron Diaz. The reviews are terrible, but it still looks like fun . . .'

'How about tomorrow night?'

Shit. 'Ummm . . .'

'Or Wednesday? Or Friday? I'm afraid I'm busy on Thursday.'

What should she have done? She should have said, 'Listen, I suspect you're about to ask me out but I'm not interested, you're at least fifteen years older than me and you're South Efrikan and – worse – you don't know how to smile, except when you look at me and then your eyes glaze over like you're a member of a cult.' Or at least a polite version of that.

But she couldn't think properly. She felt trapped. And he hadn't actually *said* he wanted to ask her out, just enquired if she was free. Perhaps she was being presumptuous and he was asking because there was a seminar for novice estate agents he thought she ought to attend. Daniel was still chatting obliviously, so, twisting her Cartier bracelet round and round her wrist, she said, 'Tomorrow's fine.'

'Good. Because I'd love to take you out for dinner. To the Bleeding Heart. Do you know it?'

'Um, no, I don't.'

'Well, that is a great omission in your education which we must remedy at once.' He didn't smile. Was he trying to be funny? He continued. 'It's very near here. Wonderful place. I'll book a table for eight, if that's convenient.'

'Fine,' she said, as Daniel finally hung up. Lucinda smiled as brightly as she could. 'Well, we'd better be on our way. Contracts to sign. Goodbye, Mr Beleek.'

'Please. Call me Anton.'

She didn't say anything, just hurried away as fast as her Bally court shoes could carry her.

'See you tomorrow,' Anton called after her.

A harsh March wind was blowing, so rather than go to their usual café, Karen and Sophie were sitting in the Post Newspaper Group's canteen, eating tuna salad (disgusting oily dressing, no wonder they came here so rarely) and discussing upcoming editions of the magazine.

'So the week after next we've got "Why I Gave Up Work and Found Untold Happiness" by Elinor York,' Sophie said.

'Fantastic. Christine will love that.' Christine was the magazine's editor, a Dries-Van-Noten-clad, childfree fifty-something, with a much younger husband who 'wrote screenplays', an immaculate house in Camden and two pampered long-haired dachshunds.

'And then we've got Naomi Jones on "My Breastfeeding Hell".'

'Excellent too!' Christine ranked breastfeeding with devil worship.

'And Anne Moncrieff on "Botox – A Disaster".'

'Tick again.' Christine had more plastic in her body than a recycled robot – most of it blagged as a freebie from various Harley Street consultants desperate for publicity. But she still loved to scare readers with tales of faces twisted for ever in Jack-Nicholson-as-the-Joker smiles.

For a brief second, Karen wondered why she was so desperate to hold on to her job. Phil was right – she'd surely be better off growing organic vegetables than acting as Christine's mouthpiece. Christine, who'd not exactly been sympathetic about Phil's illness and the amount of compassionate leave Karen had taken, who'd made it clear that she was going to die at the helm of *All Woman!* magazine, leaving Karen stuck in her shadow.

She'd considered looking for another job, but newspapers were sacking everybody right now, so Karen decided it was best to hold tight and restrain her sense of déjà vu at the sight of yet another article about working mothers, depicted by a harassed woman in a Versace skirt suit with phone at her ear and baby on her hip, the vomit and poo-stains and elasticated waists that made up Karen's experience airbrushed away.

But even though Karen knew her job wasn't exactly contributing to the sum of human wisdom, she still loved it. Loved the challenge of getting the supplement – however frothy – together every week, of having a team around her who made her laugh far more than her husband did. It gave her a sense of control, control that was lacking in every other department of her life.

'Karen?' said a voice above her head.

It was a man. Early thirties. Tall. Fair, quite long hair. A pale, thin face. Elegant pin-stripe suit.

'Max!'

'How are you?' they exclaimed at the same time, then laughed awkwardly. 'I was planning to look you up,' he continued. 'But now here you are.'

'What are you doing here?'

'I've just started on the *Daily Post* as a news reporter. Replaced Toby Maitland. Today's my first day. I still haven't got a clue where the loos are.' He grinned. 'Might get embarrassing.'

'I had no idea. I mean . . . I can tell you where the loos are, but that you were joining . . .' She turned to Sophie, who was looking quizzical. 'This is Max Bennett. I used to know his older brother, Jeremy. Max, this is my colleague Sophie Matthewson. I'm deputy editor of *All Woman!* now,' she explained.

'I know. I've been following your career, like a stalker.' He and Sophie nodded hellos. 'Do you want to join us?' she suggested.

Max sat down, plonking a bottle of water and a sandwich on the Formica. 'So, Karen. What's the news? Last time I saw you I still had all my own hair and teeth. You look great though, you haven't changed a bit.'

'Don't be daft.' Karen rolled her eyes. 'How old are you now? Twenty-four?'

'A bit older than that,' he grinned.

'Married?'

'No.' A short pause. 'Jeremy is, though. Or rather was. He's divorced. I'm sure you knew that. Has three sproglets and lives in Barnet. Good grammar schools, apparently.'

'Right,' Karen said. The memory of Jeremy wasn't altogether a happy one – they'd had a six-monthish or so fling when they both worked at the *Sentinel* before he'd made the 'I can't commit' speech. About a fortnight later, he'd been engaged – presumably to his babymother. Karen hadn't truthfully been madly in love with him; she'd been seduced by his good looks – very similar to Max's, only a bit fleshier – and his pukka background, so different from her own. But it had still been deeply humiliating.

'How about you, Karen?'

'Me? Oh, I'm married, yes. Got two girls.'

'Right.' He turned to Sophie with a smile. Everyone fancied Sophie, with her curvaceous body and perfect teeth. 'So what about you? Any kids?'

'Not yet.' Sophie pointed at a tiny, yet definite bump. 'But soon.'

'Oh. Right.' Max blanched, a little uncomfortable. 'Congratulations.'

Sophie filled Max in on every detail of her pregnancy. Karen watched his polite nods with amusement. Max Bennett. Last time she'd seen him he must have been around twenty, spending his uni holidays with his parents in their lovely rambling house in Highgate. He'd had a rather silly Liam Gallagher goatee but he'd seemed amiable enough, much more laid back than Jeremy, who was always in a state because someone had stolen his byline. He'd lost the goatee now, in fact he'd grown into a rather handsome man.

Karen was bludgeoned with a sudden sadness. She'd been so young then, so hopeful. She'd come through so much and had entered into what – in hindsight – was a golden age of freedom. But instead of enjoying it, she'd wasted it worrying she was never going to marry and have babies, never imagining that a husband and family might not lead to a happy ending, but instead to the start of a whole new set of problems. Then she'd been a babe, now she was an office has-been; stuck in a respectable but unexciting gulag, permanently exhausted, considering Botox, unhealthily fixated on school league tables.

She stood up. 'Sorry, but I need to get back to work. Max, see you around some time, eh? We'll have lunch.'

'Definitely,' he smiled at her. She smiled back. But as she edited an article on 'Great Investment Buys' (Karen knew at heart that a £50 lipstick wasn't really an investment, but that was what kept the advertisers sweet), she felt oddly uneasy. And that unease accompanied her home on the train and through supper of Quorn veggie bake, as it called up memories of the happy, free person she used to be.

## 15

The same morning, Bridget and Gemma were standing outside the Parenthope Clinic hugging themselves in the chilly breeze. After a sleepless night waiting for Dervla's verdict, the clinic had called to say they were satisfied the Meehans had made a mature and well-thought-out decision and the egg donation could take place.

So this morning the sisters had returned to meet Donna, the impossibly tall, blonde nurse, who gave them both a special nasal spray to harmonize their cycles, ensuring Bridget's eggs were at their best just when Gemma's womb was in optimal condition to receive them.

Now, on the pavement, Bridget jumped up and down.

'Yay! Finally it's legal to inhale.'

Gemma refused to rise to the bait.

'Fancy a coffee? Or a herbal tea?' Bridget asked.

'Well, I . . .'

'Actually, it's not a question. It's an order. I've got someone waiting for us. Someone I really want you to meet.'

'Who?'

'The *barista*? Remember him? Because it's all happening. We're in love!'

A Filipina nanny holding an angelic blonde girl's hand stopped and stared at them. Bridget started waving.

'Hey, look, there he is! Massy, darling. Hey. Stay there!'

The man on the other side of the road raised a hand

as he stepped out into the traffic. He had short, stubby fair hair and wore a navy parka. Gemma was taken aback. He seemed astonishingly clean-cut for Bridget: most of her boyfriends had dreadlocks and tattooed pierced faces.

'Heeeey!' cried Bridget as he arrived safely on their piece of pavement. She hugged him. 'Isn't this *great*?'

Gemma held out her hand. 'Hello, I'm Gemma.'

A warm hand grasped hers. 'Massimo.' She'd been expecting an Italian accent but this was pure Larn-don Town. 'Nice to meet you.' He had piercing blue eyes, far more alert than Bridget's usual stoners. Gemma was reminded of the pictures of Jesus in her children's Bible.

'Shall we go for a coffee?' Bridget asked, slipping her hand into Massimo's. Gemma cringed. Wasn't she a bit too keen?

'So long as it's not Costa,' Massy said. 'Shithole.'

'How long have you been working there?' Gemma asked politely.

'About eighteen months. Before that I worked in my dad's coffee bar in Alperton, but the rents kept going up and business was dying, so he had to close it.'

'Oh. That's tough.'

'Yeah. It was. He came over from Italy when he was nineteen, he put everything into the business and now he's sixty-seven and he's got . . . basically nothing. A state pension.'

'Massy's parents are amazing,' Bridget interrupted. 'They're so friendly and welcoming and his mum's the *best* cook. She made these meatballs in a spicy sauce that you just have to try.'

'I thought you were vegetarian.'

'Oh Gems, that's old news. I've eaten meat for ages. It's the healthiest thing to have as rounded a diet as possible.'

Gemma remembered the row last time Bridget had come out for dinner with her and Alex. He'd ordered a steak, triggering a lecture about how beef clogged up the large intestine and cow's farts were destroying the ozone layer. After that Alex had announced he was never sharing a meal with his sister-in-law again. But love was a powerful force. In its path, Bridget's colon, let alone the future of the planet, was irrelevant.

'Massy's family really know what's important,' Bridget yabbered on, as they pushed their way through the door of a chintzy-looking establishment. 'Like . . . family. They treat me like their own daughter. Asked me to move in with them.'

'I still live with them,' Massy explained, with an embarrassed shrug.

'But instead we've decided to look for a place of our own,' Bridget said, seizing his hand. Gemma felt her buttocks tingling. 'It won't be anything special – just a studio, but it'll be ours, won't it, sweets?'

'It will,' he smiled. 'Just got to go and . . . you know.'

'So what do you think?' Bridget hissed. 'Isn't he great?'

'Yeah. He seems really nice.' Gemma hesitated. 'Isn't it just a little bit soon to be moving in together, though?'

Bridget ignored her. 'I just didn't think of myself as the kind of girl who finds a boyfriend. I thought those kind of things only happened to you. It's all . . . it's amazing. I mean, you wouldn't have thought someone so special would be interested in someone like me. But something just clicked between us. Like destiny.'

'I'm really happy for you,' Gemma said. And she was. But she also felt weirdly off balance, as if she'd performed a dance step wrong.

'Have you told him about . . . you know . . . what you're doing for us?'

'Mmm. He says it's wonderful. Says the fact I'm prepared to help you like this is one of the reasons he's fallen in love with me. Made him realize what a generous person I am. Doing this for nothing. But love.' Bridget paused and then said, 'Though I did wonder this morning. Should I tell the clinic?'

'Tell the clinic what?'

'Well, that I've got a . . . partner now.'

Panic clutched at Gemma's chest. Her life was like a video game – as soon as she'd slayed one gremlin another three popped up. Suppose the introduction of Massy meant they had to go through the counselling again?

'He's not exactly your partner, is he? I mean, you've only been seeing him a few weeks.' Massimo was returning. She continued rapidly, 'I don't see the need to tell them unless you do. It would just be a hassle, wouldn't it? And you being with Massimo's not going to change anything, is it?'

'Talking about me?' Massimo said, sitting down.

'Yeah, just saying how supportive you're being of my egg donating.'

Gemma's heart thudded, but he smiled. 'I think it's an incredible thing to do. But that's my Bridget. Always think-ing of others.'

'Mmm,' said Gemma and then, 'Oh, excuse me,' as her

phone rang in her pocket. 'Hello?' she said, pulling it out.

'Hello, Mrs Meehan. It's Lucinda here. How are you?'

'I'm well,' Gemma said cautiously, because Lucinda's tone was too breezy to be trusted.

'Good, good. Just wondering if you'd decided what to tell Nick Crex.'

'Alex is still making up his mind.'

'I hate to hassle you but he's expecting an answer soon.'

'Well, he can wait. He keeps messing us around. If he doesn't want it, he can go elsewhere.'

'I'm so sorry, Mrs Meehan. I know how frustrating this must be.'

'I'm sure you do,' Gemma snapped, hanging up.

'Problems with the flat sale?' Massy said. 'Gemma's told me about it.'

'Yeah, the buyer's reduced his offer again.' She tried to smile.

Bridget snorted. 'But you'll still be getting some extortionate price for it, Gems. I mean, it's a crime really. They say property prices have fallen but Massy and I can't even afford a box.'

*You might be able to if you had a job,* Gemma thought, but instead she said, 'Yes, well, property in London is so overpriced, even now when the market's supposedly on its knees. Everything costs far, far more than it ought.'

'Yeah, it's tough,' Massimo said, but seemingly without self-pity. 'Gemma says your pad's amazing. Two bathrooms just for the two of you.' He whistled. 'You're lucky. And this IVF business is costing you a fortune, isn't it?'

Gemma squirmed, as she always did when money was mentioned. 'Yes, but it's worth it. I mean, what price a child?

You can't start bean-counting when something so important is concerned.'

'I couldn't agree more.' He stood up. 'Babe, sorry to be a party pooper but I've got to get going. Someone to meet.' He held out a hand to Gemma. 'Very nice to meet you, Gemma. See you again, soon, yeah?'

'I hope so.' Gemma meant it. After all, he seemed perfectly amiable.

Bridget flung her arms around her. 'Aren't I the luckiest woman in the world?' A sloppy kiss landed on Gemma's cheek. 'I'll see you soon, babe. Start the sniffing tonight. Hey, Massy, I've got to show you this inhaler thing the clinic's given me. It's wild. Gems, I'll call you. We should all four of us go out some time.'

'Great idea,' said Gemma. She watched them walk off, arm in arm. She still felt disoriented. To her horror, she realized it was because Bridget suddenly seemed so together. Wasn't that her role?

Gemma shook her head. She was a disgusting, warped person. This baby-making was doing horrible things to her. Please God, let the egg donation work. Because she needed a child. Needed to be fixed.

After the film (which was just as bad as the reviews had promised), Lucinda and Cass sat in a bar on the King's Road working out how to remedy the situation.

'Call him and say you're ill,' Cass exclaimed, as if she'd just solved the world energy crisis.

'But he might see me round and about. Or drop into the agency. Anyway, he'd just make the date for another night. I know the type. He's persistent.'

Cass giggled. 'Why don't you go wearing one of those peel-off face masks? And halfway through dinner start fiddling with it and slowly peel it off and plonk it on your side plate.'

'Yeeurch!' They chortled, but Lucinda said, 'I can't.'

'It would put him off you.'

'It would also put everyone in the restaurant off their food.'

'Pick your nose throughout the meal, burp loudly, try and squeeze out a fart.'

'Cass!'

'Well, you want him not to like you.'

'I don't want him to *dislike* me. And he works with so many people I know. I can't have it going round that I burp in the middle of my meals.' It was the usual thing: Lucinda's vanity. She didn't like everyone, but she wanted everyone to like her.

'Well, you're just going to have to go, then. And be very boring. And if, after that, he asks you out again because he doesn't care what you have to say anyway, he just wants to get in your pants, then tell him you have a boyfriend.'

'But anyone can tell him I don't.'

'Then just tell him you want to be single for now or whatever. He's not going to destroy your career, he just wants a quick slap and tickle and when he realizes he's not going to get it, he'll go elsewhere. He's a multi-millionaire, isn't he? Women must be fighting over him.'

'I doubt it,' Lucinda said. She couldn't admit that just a tiny bit of her was flattered by this attention. Anton Beleek might be a freak but he was also a powerful and rich man. And he liked her. A voice in the back of Lucinda's head whispered that a shrink would have a field day with the daughter of a powerful, rich man wanting to attract the attentions of another powerful, rich man, but she pushed that to the back of some dusty mental top shelf, the same place where she'd stored the fact that Anton had only realized she existed because she'd sent him a stupid Valentine in a moment of pique.

'I've got something to tell you,' Cass said coyly, interrupting her thoughts.

'Oh yes?'

From her expression you'd have thought she'd cured cancer and discovered why one sock never returns from a wash. 'I'm back with Tim!'

'Oh!'

'Don't look like that,' Cass said happily.

'Sorry. I'm just . . . surprised, that's all.'

She was immediately defensive. 'Why?'

'Well, last week you said he was a loser and a cuntbag.'

'Did I? Oh well, yes, maybe I did. But . . . you know, he called me last night and we had a really good chat and he explained how much pressure he'd been under at work and then he asked if he could come over and . . . ' She shrugged. 'I really love him, Luce. I've got to give him a second chance. I mean, we all make mistakes.'

'Right.'

'You look pissed off.'

'What, me? No! I'm not pissed off. Just a little . . . tired. A lot on at work. We should be going.'

'OK,' Cass said extremely eagerly. Lucinda looked at her suspiciously.

'Are you meeting Tim tonight?'

'Well . . . he did say he might come over. If I got home early enough. By the way, that reminds me. You know we were going to go to Brighton this weekend? Do you mind if we go some other time? Only Tim said he'd take me away somewhere. To make things up to me. You don't mind, do you?'

*Of course I bloody do.* Lucinda smiled tightly and said, 'That's cool.'

'I knew you'd understand. Thanks, Luce.'

'You're welcome.'

Grace was sitting at the kitchen table, a half-eaten packet of Jaffa Cakes in front of her, frowning as she scanned a jobs site on her computer. She knew she had to find work, but it was so confusing. The obvious career for her would be teaching, but the vision of standing up in front of a class, teaching a dead language nobody cared about, made her dizzy with fear. She'd investigate some other prospects first.

**Customer Services Helpline Manager**

We're looking for an enthusiastic and proactive Helpline
Manager to guide and develop our Contact Centre Team
Supervisors and the wider Helpline team. You'll ensure that KPIs
and productivity targets . . .

KPIs? Well, she could find out. Grace was clicking on the link when the phone rang. Probably Verity wanting to know if they'd heard any more from the Drakes. Now there was some sort of problem with the chain, the sale was moving slower than anticipated and tempers were fraying.

'Hello?'

'Is that Grace?'

A man's voice. Local accent.

'Yes?'

'It's Richie Prescott here. You remember? The surveyor.'

'Oh, yes, Mr Prescott. Is there a problem?' The survey had been damning but it hadn't seemed to put the Drakes off – they'd stuck at their initial offer.

'No, no problem. Actually I was ringing about something quite different. I hope you won't find it too cheeky but I was wondering if you fancied dinner some time?'

Was this a joke? Grace said nothing.

'Hello? Are you still there?'

'Yes, yes, I . . .'

'I mean, if you're too busy, I quite understand. Or . . .'

Grace laughed. 'I'm not too busy.'

'So you'd like it?'

'Yes.'

'Good. Good! I was thinking Friday night, if you're free. The Chichester Arms in Hyddleton? Seven thirty suit?'

'Lovely.'

'Good! See you then. 'Bye.'

''Bye,' Grace said. She stood for a long time, holding the silent phone. Shackleton nudged her leg inquisitively.

'Shacky,' she said, kneeling down. 'I'm going out to dinner with a man.'

Shackleton buffed her ankle with his domed head. Grace took it as a sign of approval. She was shocked. Women like her didn't get asked out; that was the kind of thing that happened to normal women, women like her students and Verity. So Richie Prescott must consider her normal. Must

183

have seen through the layers of padding to the good heart that Grace knew lay at her core. They would have dinner. She would have to diet all week in preparation, but they would have dinner. And then . . . A bubble of happiness swelled in Grace's chest. Who knew what might happen next?

# 16

After her evening out with Cass, Lucinda was too furious to sleep. Furious with her friend for being such a wimp, and also furious for herself. She'd been looking forward to their weekend in Brighton. And it wasn't just that: now Cass and Tim were back together she'd have no one to hang out with. The loneliness that had accompanied her first few months in London was back again and it made Lucinda feel cold inside. Young, attractive, rich, high-flying women weren't meant to be lonely. It was an embarrassment, like suffering from piles. 'Get a grip,' she told herself, rolling over and taking a sip from her glass of water. She wasn't in London to make friends, she was here to do a good job and win Daddy's approval.

But rattled by her friend's desertion, she took more care dressing for dinner with Anton Beleek than she would have admitted to. Joseph wool trousers, a black T-shirt, a black velvet jacket. Nothing provocative or revealing, but definitely not frumpy either. After all, she had work to get through first and she didn't want to frighten the clients.

Terrified of the others discovering her date, she lingered late in the office. One by one they put on their coats and left, until finally only she and Gareth remained.

'You're very industrious today. As ever.'

'Mmm. A lot on.' Lucinda stared fixedly at her screen.

'Fancy a drink when you've finished?' He sounded casual enough.

'I'd love to.' Lucinda's reply was heartfelt. 'But I'm meeting a friend.'

'Never mind.' Gareth seemed unbothered by her perpetual rejections. 'We'll have to go out some time soon, though.'

'That would be great!' She thought wistfully of a night with Gareth, gossiping in the Fox & Anchor, as opposed to what lay ahead of her. Oh well, better get it over with.

'Need me to escort you anywhere?'

'Uh, no! I'm fine, thanks. Just meeting my friend near the Tube.'

'Have fun. See you tomorrow.'

'See you tomorrow.'

Heart thudding, she left the office. The Bleeding Heart was in a tiny courtyard just off Hatton Garden. She walked there slowly. She'd be ten minutes late, not rude, just fashionable.

The restaurant was surprisingly adorable, in a cellar consisting of several rooms running off each other like a warren. All candlelit. Very cosy. Very atmospheric. Dared she think it, very romantic. The waiter led her into one of the smaller rooms. Anton was waiting, of course. He stood up as soon as he saw her, his swarthy features contorted in a nervous smile.

'Howzit! I was a little concerned.'

'Sorry. I was just running late at work.'

'Right, right, of course.' There was the traditional awkward moment when they decided whether or not to kiss. Lucinda dealt with it by stepping backwards. Anton gestured to the chair.

'Sit. Please.' She obeyed, like a well-trained dog. 'I've ordered champagne,' he said. 'Moët. I do hope that's agreeable to you. I'm sure you know that the "t" at the end of Moët is not silent, as so many seem to think.'

'Of course. And it's pronounced Chan-don, not Shawn-don.'

'Well done.' He grinned. Suddenly he looked sweet, almost vulnerable. Lucinda realized this evening might not be such a dead loss after all.

She drank the first glass quickly, the second a bit more slowly. She dithered a bit over her order. First the gazpacho, then . . .

'I think I'll have the chateaubriand. Oh! No, never mind.'

He'd been watching her attentively. 'Why not?'

'I think I'd just rather have the salmon . . .' She couldn't bring herself to say the real reason. But he'd sussed her.

'Because the steak's for two? I'll share it with you.'

That seemed cringingly intimate. 'No, no, honestly, the salmon looks so delicious and . . .'

'Really. It would make me so happy. The steak here is superb. It's why I chose this restaurant. I'm a big carnivore.'

'More used to giraffe and hippo, aren't you?'

Anton laughed. 'Are you judging me on national stereotypes? How cruel. But fair as well.' He ran the last two words together, so they sounded like 'aswell'. 'I *have* eaten giraffe, though I can't say it's a favourite.'

'Mmm. It's a bit stringy.'

'You've eaten it too?'

'In Kenya. My father – er . . .' Lucinda didn't want to get

187

into who her father was. 'My family went on holiday there a few years ago and we went to this restaurant called . . .'

'Carnivores. I know it well. Did you like Kenya?'

'I loved it . . .' She hadn't actually particularly enjoyed that holiday. Daddy was constantly announcing he was going to stay in the hotel because he had to work and then Mummy cried a lot and got drunk at dinner. But that wasn't Kenya's fault.

'There's nothing like it, is there? Actually seeing animals in the wild.'

And suddenly the conversation was flowing as they discussed which of the Big Five they'd seen. The waiter had to clear his throat several times before he was heard.

'I'm sorry!' Anton exclaimed eventually. His eyes were shining; he looked like a teenage version of himself. 'Let's order.' So they did, with him asking for a fantastic bottle of Gigondas. Lucinda had to say, she was enjoying this. It was almost like being with Daddy, drinking good wine, eating good food, talking. She'd thought they'd have a turgid conversation about the housing market, but instead they gabbled on about fine wines, then the conversation somehow moved on to movies.

'I really love the old black-and-white weepies but now I work I don't get time to watch them any more. It's an afternoon indulgence, isn't it?'

'Is it? I don't know. I've always worked pretty hard. Not much room for indulgence in my life. Though I am partial to the odd session with a pile of *Star Trek* DVDs.'

'Oh. Right . . .' Lucinda had known there would be a catch. Anton was a Trekkie. It figured. She'd never watched an episode in her life but she knew it was for socially challenged people. Her phone rang. Surprised, she checked the caller ID. Shit. Cass. She'd forgotten she was her get-out clause. Lucinda thought about not answering, but she knew that then she'd pester her all evening , so she said, 'I'm so sorry. Urgent work thing. Do you mind if I deal with it quickly?'

'Not at all.'

'Hello?'

'How's it going?' Cass giggled.

'Fine, thanks.'

'Really? He – llo! So you're not running away?'

'Everything is fine,' Lucinda said tightly. 'May I call you in the morning and give you more details?'

'Are you going to shag him?'

'No. But I'll call you in the morning. Thank you. Good-bye.' Lucinda thought she'd hit the off button, but in her confusion she pressed speaker instead.

'Luce fancies the old South African! Luce fancies the old South African!' Cass's voice chanted.

Heads turned. A woman tutted. Scarlet, Lucinda managed to turn off the phone and shoved it in her bag. She looked up at Anton.

'Oh my God, I am *so* sorry.'

But he was laughing. 'The old South African, eh? Is that what you call me?'

'No, of course not!'

'Ach, shame. It's OK. I *am* South African. And I guess, to you, I do seem old. Forty-six. Bloody ancient, izzit?'

'No, no . . .'

'How old are you, Lucinda?'

'I'm twenty-four,' she said, defiantly.

'So young,' he said, looking wistful. Patronizing arse,

Lucinda thought. 'So much to learn. So much to do.'

'I don't *feel* that young.' After all, she wasn't the one enamoured of an ancient series involving men with pointy ears, in a galaxy far, far away.

'Oh but you are. Believe me. Enjoy it while you can, Lucinda.'

'You don't strike me as ever having been young.' Embarrassment combined with the wine was talking now. She threw her hands up. 'Sorry! That sounded awful.'

'It's OK.' He smiled again, but more ruefully this time. 'I know. I give off a very serious impression. I've not had an easy time of it these past few years. My parents both died, pretty long, horrible lingering deaths. It took it out of me.'

'I'm so sorry to hear that.' He held up a hand in acknowledgement.

She was intrigued now. 'And have you ever been married?'

'Never. I was engaged. A long time ago. She ran off with a good friend of mine.' His tone was deadpan. 'Broke my heart.'

Lucinda's heart tugged. Poor man.

'But maybe that's changing now,' he continued with a big wink.

Oh, shit. Being with Anton was like playing snakes and ladders. Every time he rose in her estimation, he stepped on some metaphorical serpent and plummeted back to the bottom. Lucinda smiled weakly.

'Lucinda,' he said, a sudden urgent tone in his voice. 'Why did you send me that Valentine?'

OK. Now they were definitely back at square one. She squirmed in her chair. 'Sorry about that.'

'No, don't be! I'm so happy you did. How else would we have got to know each other?'

'I was just being silly,' Lucinda mumbled, suddenly understanding what Anton had meant about her being very young. And stupid, she told herself furiously. 'It was a sort of joke.'

He looked pained. 'A joke?'

'Yeah. I had a spare Valentine and . . . you looked so unhappy and . . . I thought it would be funny.' Lucinda looked at her watch miserably. 'Listen, I'm sorry, Anton. I've had a lovely evening but I'd better get going. You know, early start and all that!'

Another pained expression. 'You won't stay for some dessert? Cheese? Coffee?'

She considered performing Cass's burp trick. 'No, honestly, I'm stuffed. Couldn't eat another thing. I have to get going.'

'All right.' He made a cheesy scribbling 'bill, please' gesture. Lucinda scrambled in her bag.

'Please,' she said as the bill was put in front of him. 'Let's go halves.'

He looked as if she'd just suggested they had a quick freebasing session in the loos. 'Don't be ridiculous,' he said sharply.

'Please.'

'I won't be hearing of it.' He placed his black Amex on the tray. 'Can I offer you a lift?'

Lucinda cringed at the thought of him expecting to be invited in for coffee. 'No thank you, I'm fine. I'm miles away. South Kensington. I'll get the Tube.'

'At this time of night? I won't hear of it.'

'OK, I'll get a taxi.'

'I'll ask them to order one.'

Bollocks. Now Lucinda would have to pay for a cab, when the Tube would have cost £1.60. She could afford it, of course, but that wasn't really the point. Lucinda had been brought up to be frugal. Daddy said people who wasted money wasted fortunes.

Waiters helped them into their coats. Outside two black BMWs sat one in front of the other. Lucinda turned to Anton.

'Thank you for a lovely evening.'

'The pleasure' – *plizhir* – 'was all mine. Perhaps we could do it again some time?'

Really, she should have said no. But she didn't know how to.

'Yes, that would be lovely.' Lucinda stood on tiptoes to kiss him on the cheek. He smelt musky, rather nice. She felt a brush of stubble against her face.

'I'll be in touch.'

'Look forward to it,' she said, before she realized how that might sound. As the cab pulled off, she exhaled loudly. It had been much more enjoyable than she'd expected, but still she was glad it was over. And after Cass's call there was no way they'd be seeing each other again. He'd suggested it, yes. But he was only being polite.

Since that unexpected call from Richie Prescott, Grace had forgotten her job hunt and concentrated all her energies on a crash diet. For breakfast a glass of hot water and lemon juice. For lunch a plate of undressed lettuce, tomato and cucumber. For dinner, because she recognized the need for protein, a plain grilled chicken breast or salmon fillet and a side plate of steamed vegetables and lemon. Even though she thought of food constantly, she managed to resist temptation. She took the dogs for long walks. And it had worked. All right, she had only lost four pounds but that still enabled her to squeeze into the pink Monsoon dress she'd bought for her graduation ball.

Grace drove to the Chichester Arms, leaving behind two somewhat indignant dogs. All the way her stomach growled beneath her ruched waistband and she wondered what she would eat. She'd been so good, she deserved a bit of a night off. She'd have a bread roll, but no butter. A starter if Richie did, ditto pudding. And a main course of . . . she felt weak at the knees just wondering what low-calorie options the menu might offer. Sea bass maybe. With plain boiled potatoes and plain spinach. Nothing naughty. But still a bit of a treat.

Her destination was a thatched pub with low ceilings. Richie was waiting at the bar, wearing a suit and tie, a glass of what she took to be gin and tonic in front of him. At the sight of her, he jumped up.

'Grace! How very wonderful that you came. I was worried you'd change your mind.'

'Oh no. Why would I do that?' She simpered as he squeezed her hand. His fingers were like sausages, she thought uncharitably. She was a fine one to talk.

He looked her up and down. 'You look lovely.'

'Thank you.' Her ears tingled with delight.

'How about a swift one here? Before we sit down.'

'Gosh! I'm driving, so I can only have a glass.' And alcohol had tons of calories.

'I'm driving too. But a drink now, and then a bottle of wine between us should be perfectly fine. Gin and tonic all right with you?' Grace nodded, too embarrassed to ask for tonic lite. He turned to the barmaid. 'Two G&Ts, gorgeous.' He downed the glass in front of him. 'By the way, that was Perrier,' he said, turning back to Grace. A beat, then he added, 'Try it if you don't believe me.'

'No, no, of course I believe you.'

They had their gins and tonics. The alcohol went straight to Grace's starved head. By the time they sat down she was so hungry she feared she might snatch one of the daffodils out of the vase and gobble it. Normally she ate at six, because that was what Mummy had liked – and because it was the best way of filling a lonely evening. How dull she had become. How institutionalized.

'Red or white?'

'Whichever you prefer,' said Grace. 'I really shouldn't have any.'

'A drop won't hurt!' He ordered a bottle of Macon something or other. '*And* a bottle of sparkling water,' he continued with a wink at Grace. 'Or would you prefer still?'

'Sparkling's fine.'

There were a few awkward moments while they puzzled over the menu. Grace's head swam, her stomach performed a drum solo. Fortunately, the piped Charles Aznavour drowned it out. Honey-marinated chicken skewers on a bed of leaves, she read. Lovely, were it not for the honey. Farmhouse bread, thick cut, served with olive oil and balsamic vinegar. The prospect of biting into a wodge of carbohydrate, feeling the tang of oil on her tongue, almost made her swoon.

'It's got to be the chicken liver terrine,' said Richie. 'Love a good pâté, me.'

Oh help. A terrine was pure fat. But everything else was just as bad. And it would be rude to sit and watch him. And the creaminess of pâté on her tongue . . .

'I'll have the same.'

'And then I fancy chicken with bacon, shallots, and rich red wine sauce.'

Sea bass. She would have the sea bass. All right, it came on a bed of buttery spinach and mashed potato, but she'd toy with those. They ordered. Silence fell. Grace smiled shyly at Richie, while trying to avert her eyes from the groaning bread basket. He downed his glass of wine and poured himself another. She floundered around for safe topics of conversation.

'So . . . been to see any interesting houses lately?'

'A few,' he said. And he was off. He told her about the bungalow in Loddiswell with dodgy foundations, the cottage with outbuildings in Malborough that would need complete modernization, the penthouse in Salcombe with rising damp.

'I love Salcombe,' Grace said. But Richie didn't hear. Grace's head swam even more. She kept staring at the bread. The starters were a long time coming. Eventually she could help herself no more. She took a seeded white roll, broke it open and began spreading it with a pat of Anchor butter.

'Of course I saw there were potential problems with the basement, but the buyer didn't seem to care . . .'

God, it tasted good. The butter was salty and cold, the bread soft and crunchy at the same time. She finished it, then started on another one, just as her starter was put in front of her.

'Oh, splendid,' Richie said. But he made no move to eat, instead picking up his wine glass again. 'Of course, it's rare to survey a house as glorious as Chadlicote. I've already told you, it's such a shame you're selling it.'

'And I've already told you, there's no financial alternative. I desperately need to find a job as it is.' It would be rude to leave the remnants of the roll, she decided, cramming it in.

'I think we'd better toast that.' Richie looked at his glass accusingly, as if it had somehow emptied itself, then turned to the waitress. 'Thank you. Delicious. Might we have another bottle of the Macon, please, darling?'

'I'm quite all right,' Grace said hastily.

'Well, I wouldn't mind a wee drop more. I can always get a taxi home. Red wine. Very good for you, you know. Full of anti-wotsits. Thin the blood. Sure you won't join me?'

'No, thank you,' Grace said. 'So you grew up in Thribble Pington?'

'Born and bred there. You know, I'm sure if you held out you could get a better price for Chadlicote than the Drakes are paying.' In the candlelight his face was shining with sweat, though the room wasn't particularly warm.

'I'm sure. But we need to sell quickly. And they're cash buyers.'

'Possibly another cash buyer could be found. Ah, cheers.' The waitress uncorked the new bottle and poured. Richie tasted it perfunctorily. 'Very good, thank you. To new jobs.'

Grace had meant just to play with the terrine but it was looking at her so invitingly. She had a mouthful. Oh! So rich. She had another. Before she knew it she'd eaten it all. She stared longingly at Richie's half-touched plate. Maybe he was on a diet too, she thought, as he pushed around the salad leaves. She couldn't bear to see the waitress remove it. Fortunately, the main courses followed quickly. Richie had chosen better, she thought, gazing longingly at his chicken in its rich sauce. But these potatoes were delectable, from the early Jersey Royals crop – and even more so if you added another butter pat.

'So . . . ' Grace asked, after her plate was cleared. Richie's – infuriatingly – was only half touched again. 'Do you have any hobbies?'

'Hobbies!' He seemed amazed. 'Not really. Do you?'

'Well . . . I'm very fond of opera.'

'Opera!' he snorted. 'All fat ladies singing about their lost loves. Serves them right. They should lose some weight. Oops. Sorry. No offence.'

Fortunately, the waitress rematerialized. 'Would you like coffee? Dessert?' Grace decided she'd ask to see the menu. Why not? She'd broken the diet already, so she might as well go for it. She'd make it up by starving tomorrow.

'No pud. I'm stuffed. But I'd love a coffee. An Irish one, I think. Treat myself.' He smiled at her. 'Wake me up for the drive. How about you?'

'I'll have a filter coffee, please. Black. No sugar.'

'You sure no pud?'

'I'm fine, thank you,' Grace said tightly.

They drank their coffees and chat creakily resumed again.

'Do you watch television ever?' Grace tried. She kept thinking about the missed dessert.

'Far too much! I'm a huge *Doctor Who* fan.'

'Really! Me too.' Her heart soared. Something in common after all. Finally conversation flowed. Who was their favourite Doctor (obviously Tom Baker), what the new one would be like. Grace began to relax. She hadn't been wrong. There *was* a connection.

'And have you . . . Do you . . . Is there anyone in your life?'

She emitted a short, surprised laugh. 'No! Goodness me, absolutely not.'

'It's not that funny, is it?' He drank a little more. 'I was married. Broke up two years ago. Divorce coming through now. All very sad but life goes on.'

She nodded gravely. 'It does, yes. Indeed.' So he'd been married. Was that a bad thing? Did he want to be reconciled with his wife? Or did it mean he had loved and wanted to love again?

'We'd better get going, I guess,' he said, as the dining room cleared and the waitress began to stash chairs on top of tables. He had polished off the second bottle of wine and was slurring slightly. He gestured for the bill. Grace made a motion for her bag.

'No, no. Don't be silly. I won't hear of it.' He got out his credit card and plonked it down.

'You need to ask them to call a taxi,' Grace reminded him.

'Oh yes. So I do.' He looked in the direction of the waitress, who was at the till.

Grace dared to voice the thought she'd been toying with. 'Or I could always give you a lift.'

'Could you? Marvellous!'

So he climbed into the old Mini which reeked of damp Shackleton.

'Sorry about the smell,' she said as she reversed out of the car park.

'Don't be silly. You know I love dogs.'

He loved dogs! Another shared interest.

It was a beautiful night, with a clear sky full of stars and three-quarters of a moon. As Grace drove him down the twisting country lanes that led to Little Bedlington, where he lived, her heart felt as if it was struggling to escape from her ribcage. She was going back to his house. What would happen next? Would he invite her in? Would he try to kiss her? Or something more? She didn't know what she wanted to happen, all she knew was she mustn't blow it.

'It's a left here,' he said.

She'd expected a sweet cottage with hollyhocks outside and roses around the door, but in fact they were in front of a block of new-build flats. She turned off the engine. He turned his head towards her.

'Thank you. That was a lovely evening.'

'Thank you for dinner.'

'And thanks for the lift home. You're a star.' He opened his door and climbed out. ''Bye,' he said, bending down. The door slammed and he turned his back to her, fumbling in his pocket for his keys. For a second Grace stared after him, then, hand shaking, she turned on the ignition and began driving back towards Chadlicote.

## 17

Lucinda was sure she'd never hear from Anton again and that suited her just fine. But in fact he called her just two days later in the office.

'I have a craving for top-notch Japanese food, and knowing your adventurous streak I thought you might like to join me.'

'Oh!' Lucinda felt uncharacteristically flustered. Joanne was watching her suspiciously, which made her even more undecided, so she said: 'Yes, OK. Why not?'

They went to a cute little place in Soho, where she stuffed her face with sushi and gyoza and tsukemono. Anton told her about how he used to live in Tokyo. He made her laugh with tales of crazy Japanese behaviour. They discussed his developments.

'Luxury is still where it's at,' he told her. 'The more ridiculous the gimmick the more the clients go mad for it. Even with the downturn, they're still demanding twenty-four-hour room service, floor-to-ceiling fridges. Panic rooms. Eyeball scanners. Bulletproof windows. The latest thing is mirrors with a time delay. You can stand with your back to it and then turn round to check out your rear view. Everybody wants one. Everyone wants to live like a billionaire.'

He didn't mention Cass's phone call or the Valentine, and at the end of the evening he put her in a cab with just a kiss on the cheek. After the Gareth debacle, Lucinda was relieved. He still liked her. They could be friends. A bit of an odd friendship, admittedly, but so what? In keeping with her upbringing, she sent him a brief thank-you note but she heard nothing back. She was a bit surprised, but relieved. So that was that, then.

But then, a week later, he called to invite her to Covent Garden.

'I know my love of opera firmly betrays me as an old git,' he said with a smile in his voice. 'And you may find the idea abominable. But I thought it was worth a punt.'

'I'd love to,' she said. 'I adore opera. Sometimes I go with my father. What is it?'

'It's *La Traviata*.'

'One of my favourites.'

'Really?'

Cass laughed when Lucinda told her. 'This is your third date, right? And we all know what's expected on the third date.'

'It's *not* a date.'

'Oh yes. What is it then, exactly?'

'He knows I'm not interested in him in *that* way. He's like a kind of mentor.'

'Mentor?' Cass snorted. 'I suppose that could be another word for sugar daddy.'

'Don't be stupid. You know I don't need a sugar daddy. I've got a *real* dad.'

'I know that. But *En*-ton doesn't. Just watch it. That's all.'

'Yeah, yeah,' Lucinda said in a teenagery voice so Joanne looked up and glared at her. The opera was the following evening after work, no time to change. She wore a grey slip dress and kitten heels, very conservative, not remotely provocative. They had the best seats in the house. It was a fantastic production and by the interval Lucinda was enraptured. She should go out more. This was what London was all about.

They fought their way through the crowd to the bar. Two champagne flutes were standing next to an ice bucket labelled 'Beleek'.

'That was fantastic,' Lucinda exclaimed, as a white-haired middle-aged man with a huge stomach, only partly concealed by his blazer, tapped Anton on the shoulder.

'Mate! How absolutely marvellous to see you!'

'Giles!' They shook hands. 'You too. I didn't take you for an opera buff.'

'Can't say I am. Contacts dragged me along.' He nodded condescendingly at Lucinda. 'And who is your girlfriend?'

Lucinda expected Anton to explain the situation. But instead he just said: 'This is Lucinda Gresham. Lucinda, meet my dear old friend Giles Wakeham. Lucinda's an agent at Dunraven Mackie, you know.'

'Oh yes? So tell me, Anton. Any news about the Prior Development . . .' And they were off: jaw-jawing while Lucinda stood completely ignored. It reminded her of the first time she'd met Anton and of what an unevolved, old-fashioned *man* he was. Just like Daddy, she realized with a jolt. To be fair, he was trying to include her, turning to her and asking her opinion, but Giles wasn't remotely interested in anything she had to say and kept talking over her.

Huffily, Lucinda pulled her mobile out of her bag. A text

from Nick Crex. Oh help. The poor Meehans were still arguing about whether to accept his offer. She opened it.

Shep Bush gig rescheduled for Friday. U still on guest list plus
one. Nick Crex

The bell started ringing, summoning them back to their seats. Giles disappeared into the crowd with a 'Good to see you, old chap. We'll have to get you both over for dinner soon.'

'Sorry about that,' Anton said, with a wry shrug. 'Very presumptuous of him.' There was a brief silence and then he faintly raised his right eyebrow, like Roger Moore. Lucinda felt slightly nauseous.

'That's OK,' she said faintly. The bell rang again. She couldn't concentrate on the second act. She was being an idiot, letting Anton take her out. He was ancient, with ancient friends who were jumping to unflattering conclusions about her being his girlfriend. As if. She wouldn't see him again. But then came the second interval and no sign of Giles. Instead a plate of smoked salmon sandwiches was waiting for them, along with two more flutes of champagne.

'Oh, wonderful,' Lucinda exclaimed. 'I was starving.'

'I thought you might be. These things are bloody long.'

They stood at the corner of the bar, munching the sandwiches and chatting. Again, the early unease melted away as they discussed various operas.

'In the summer we'll go to Glyndebourne,' Anton said. 'The perfect combination: sublime music and then a long, long interval so you can have a three-course picnic in the beautiful grounds. I'll get my housekeeper to prepare it.'

'That sounds lovely,' Lucinda said, before she could stop herself.

Throughout the final third she wondered what she was doing. Of course she'd love to go to Glyndebourne, it had always been one of her ambitions, but did she really have to go with Anton? But then again, why not? He was obviously lonely, he obviously enjoyed her company. They liked talking about property. Why couldn't a younger woman spend time with an older man without people thinking it was dodgy? But Lucinda's other voice told her that men in their forties didn't have platonic friendships with women in their twenties. She had to cool things, be unavailable next time he asked her out.

But at the end of the evening as he opened the cab door to her, he said, 'I was thinking of going down to the country next weekend. For some walking. I don't know if . . .'

'Um, yes that could be fun,' she said. 'I'll just have to check my diary, but I don't think I'm doing anything.'

'I hope not,' he said intensely, then he pulled her close and kissed her on both cheeks. He smelt good: of pine and surf. 'I'll call you soon, Lucinda. Thank you for a wonderful evening.'

'No, thank *you*,' she said. She climbed in, the door closed. As the taxi moved off, she resolved that a little trip to the country couldn't hurt. After all, she really did love walking. At home one of her favourite things was following a mountain trail in the Alps. Trotting from the Tube to the office to a viewing and back again was hardly the same. She'd see precisely what Anton was suggesting before rejecting anything out of hand. In the meantime, she remembered, there was the Vertical Blinds gig. But that was a step too far. Imagine Anton's stiff, besuited figure moving jerkily to guitar riffs. No. She'd see if Benjie was free.

But Benjie was going out with a crowd from college. Cass was away skiing with Tim. Sitting in the office the following morning, Lucinda wondered who she could ask. Gareth was sitting at his desk, yakking to a client. She hadn't spent time with him in a while, and the worry that he was cross with her still niggled. This could be a nice goodwill gesture. She approached him.

'Are you free on Friday night?'

She couldn't be sure, but Gareth seemed to go a little pinker in the cheeks. Oh no. Not another guy taking her friendliness the wrong way. She continued quickly. 'The guy from the Vertical Blinds who's buying Flat 15 has put me on the guest list for their gig at Shepherd's Bush Empire. I know you're a huge fan so I was wondering if you'd like to come along.'

'Really? I'd love to.' He beamed. Lucinda beamed back.

'We'll go after work on Friday, then.'

As so often these days, Karen woke around five and couldn't get back to sleep. Worries were banging on her brain like bailiffs at a debtor's door. She didn't want to wake Phil – he was obsessive about his sleep. So after half an hour she put on her dressing gown and went downstairs. Clutching what would be the first of the day's many mugs of coffee, she wandered from room to room. Rooms she'd decorated so lovingly. Rooms filled with memories. Bea toddling beaming across the playroom, then bashing her head on the flagstone floor. Eloise practising her flute in the conservatory. Years of Christmases with the big tree in the living room and the scent of spicy candles. It had been the perfect family home: bright, a bit cluttered, tasteful but in a colourful way – Karen hated anything beige or monochrome.

She moved on to the kitchen. Sitting down at the huge pine table, she remembered her and Phil laughing there with friends. Friends. The illness had certainly shown them in a new light. Some – surprisingly not by any means those she'd considered A-list – had been rocks. They'd brought round casseroles, driven Phil to hospital appointments, listened to him banging on about platelets and blood counts for hours.

But then there'd been others like Jon, best man at their wedding, who'd sent a box of chocolates and then never called again. Or the distant acquaintances who'd suddenly decided that Phil was their closest buddy, but by that token his pain must be their pain, who would burst into tears, saying how devastated they were, how they didn't think they could cope, so Phil and Karen ended up comforting *them*. Who would turn up uninvited and sit around, accepting Karen's increasingly resentful offers of cups of tea, while wringing their hands and saying they wished there was something they could do to help.

People they barely knew wanting to kiss and hug them, and asking questions about Phil's bowel movements and telling them about how they'd heard of a marvellous herbalist in the Congo and how maybe Phil should travel there for treatment – after all, it would be selfish not to do everything in his power to fight the disease. People who told Phil to 'think positive' – as if that was the magic cure that medical science had been missing all those years.

Karen had to accept that the cancer had changed

everything. So why not change houses too? But how could she make the final break from the place where her daughters had played, where they'd prepared for their first day at school? From the place where, for a few brief years, everything had been, in hindsight, perfect.

'You all right?' said Phil behind her.

'God, you gave me a shock!'

He was standing in his green velvet dressing gown, which still hung on his bones like an empty flour sack. 'Sorry. I realized you weren't in bed, so I came to find you.'

Karen decided to try and communicate something of her feelings. 'I'm just feeling a bit sentimental.'

'About leaving this place?' She nodded. Phil stared at her. 'Christ, I can't wait. I feel the whole place is infected by my illness. It's like there's a malign spirit here. Until we're somewhere new, I won't be cleansed of it all.'

'But you know that's just in your imagination.' Her tone was gentle but he shook his head, his voice rising to the whine she'd come to dread. 'It's not. I feel it. God, Karen, how can you say something like that? It's not as if you don't know how I've suffered.'

'OK,' she said angrily. 'OK, you're right.'

They stared at each other for a moment. Then he put his arm round her shoulder.

'Sorry, Kaz. It's just sometimes I think you don't understand how desperate I am to get out of this place. To make a fresh start.'

'I know.' She should tell him how equally desperate she was not to go to Devon. But over the past couple of years Karen had got used to keeping her worries to herself. 'But how can we afford it all?'

'We'll manage. Stop fretting. I have plans.' He turned towards the door. 'Well, I don't know about you, but I'm going back to bed for another couple of hours.'

'Well, I don't know about you,' she snapped. 'But I have to go to work. After the school run. So if you don't mind I'll get on with preparing breakfast for everyone.'

He turned and looked at her, askance. 'Hey! You know I need my rest. Where did that come from?'

'Sorry,' she said, not sounding it. 'Only I do get tired too, you know.'

'It won't be like that in Devon. In Devon, everything will be so much more chilled. No commute. No work to stress you.'

'No money,' Karen retorted under her breath, as he disappeared back up the stairs to the bedroom. 'No escape.' Once again, she flirted with that awful wish that Phil had died, instead of being replaced by this unrealistic, inward-looking creature.

She brooded on her situation as she dropped the girls at school, and then all the way to the office. Sophie was on the phone to one of her mates.

'I mean, I don't know what it is with Natasha,' she was saying. 'Her kids are just so damn fussy. Won't touch anything green, hate cheese. I just don't know why she isn't stricter with them. I'm not going to let my children down from the table until they've finished every morsel on their plates. You just start as you mean to go on.'

Karen dimly remembered her old self, the self who would never park her children in front of the television, never use a dummy, never reward with sweets, and tried to keep a straight face. Her phone rang. An internal number.

'Hello?' she said wearily, suspecting it would be Accounts berating her about her slow payments to freelances.

'Karen?' A voice she didn't recognize.

'Yes?'

'It's Max. Max Bennett.'

'Oh, hello. How are you getting on?' Max Bennett! Since bumping into him in the canteen, she'd wondered occasionally if she should contact him. But why would he want to hear from such a careworn frump?

'Fine. Just wondering if you might be free for lunch some time soon.'

'Oh!'

'Don't worry if you can't, I know what it's like.'

'Well, the magazine does go to press tomorrow, so we're pretty busy. Friday might be good, though. If it works for you, that is . . .'

'I'll see what I can do,' he said. 'I'll call you if there's a lull. Perhaps you could show me one of your local haunts.'

'I'll see what I can do,' Karen said, sounding extremely businesslike. She was sure she wouldn't hear from him. Still, as soon as she hung up she dialled her hairdresser.

'Hi, it's Karen Drake here. Do you think Mandy could fit me in tomorrow evening? Only I'm long overdue some highlights.'

# 18

On Friday afternoon, Anton called Lucinda in the office.

'Lucinda, howzit? I'm really sorry but we won't be able to go for our country walk. I have to go to South Efrika this weekend. Family affairs to sort out. I'll be back towards the end of next week so we can rearrange. I hope you're not too disappointed.'

How bloody presumptuous! 'It's fine,' Lucinda assured him coldly. 'I hope you have a good trip.'

'Thanks. I'll be thinking of you. We'll do something nice when I get back, I promise . . .' And the line went dead.

An hour later, an enormous bunch of lilies and freesias was deposited in front of Lucinda's nose by a grumpy-looking delivery man.

'Hello!' said Joanne. 'Who's the lucky girl then?'

'Oh. Wow.' Lucinda was mortified. Hastily, she opened the card.

'?' it said.

'Who are they from?' asked Marsha.

'I don't know,' she lied, showing her the card, thanking the Lord there hadn't been any kisses.

'A mystery admirer,' Joanne said shortly. Gareth was unusually silent, staring at his keyboard. He stayed silent until everybody else had left for the pub and they were alone together.

'You're still coming to the gig, aren't you?' Lucinda asked.

'Sure,' he said, staring stonily at his screen. 'If you still want to go with me.'

'Of course I do, Gareth. Is everything OK?'

He looked at her. 'People have been gossiping about you, you know.'

'Oh yes?' Immediately Lucinda was on the defensive.

'Mmm.' His voice was very gentle. 'Apparently you're seeing Anton Beleek.'

'I am not!' she said loudly, and then, when Gareth didn't respond, she went on. 'He's just a friend. We've only had dinner a couple of times. And been to the opera once. There's absolutely nothing going on between us.'

'He's a bit of a catch,' Gareth said, but without any hint of sarcasm. 'Owns half of east London, as you know.'

'I don't care about things like that,' Lucinda said impatiently. 'Who said I was going out with him, anyway?'

'Some bloke saw you at the opera and told Niall. Marsha was listening in and . . .'

Bloody Marsha. Lucinda had thought she was her friend. 'We went to the opera and then I went home alone. Kind of like our outing will be tonight, OK?'

The last point was probably uncalled for, but she was hurt. Gareth smiled at her, apparently unruffled.

'Just thought you'd like to know.' He stood up. 'We'd better get going. I'll just get changed.'

A few minutes later he emerged from the lavatories in jeans and a white T-shirt. It was disconcerting seeing Gareth out of his suit and tie, like the time Lucinda had spotted Anne-Marie, Daddy's normally uptight PA, at the

Patinoire de l'Europe, ice skating in a candy pink all-in-one, her head thrown back in laughter. And realized she was her father's latest mistress.

She didn't want to think about it. 'I didn't think to bring a change of clothes,' she said ruefully, looking down at her beige Armani suit.

'You'll be fine,' Gareth said. 'Just take your jacket off.'

They took the Hammersmith and City line to Shepherd's Bush, where – at Gareth's suggestion – they ate delicious pierogi in a funny little Polish restaurant with frilly curtains and check tablecloths. From the Royal Opera House to this, Lucinda thought with a wry grin. She wasn't sure which one she preferred. She was aware that she hadn't done as much young persons' stuff as a woman of her age perhaps ought to. Her student crowd had been pretty sedate. A bit of her wondered what it would be like to – for example – go on a druggy weekend in Ibiza, but that wasn't the kind of behaviour that turned you into a CEO. Sedate outings with Anton to the opera and Michelin-starred restaurants were far more in keeping with the kind of image she wanted to project.

Gareth interrupted her chain of thought. 'I take it you know all about the Vertical Blinds' lead singer. He's a big smackhead. That's why the last gig was cancelled. He was too out of it, apparently. Be interesting to see what state he's in tonight.'

The auditorium was dark and hot. Gareth kept up a stream of chat but it was hard to hear what he was saying. After an hour, the band still hadn't appeared. Lucinda felt irritated and impatient.

'They always keep you waiting, it's part of the mystique,' Gareth said.

But another hour passed. The crowd was starting to get restless. There was a bit of booing, some slow handclapping. Some people left.

'We don't have to stay,' Lucinda said to Gareth, seeing him stifle a yawn. She knew he'd been up at five thirty to show a big-cheese client a penthouse at the Barbican.

He shook his head. 'No, no, I'm enjoying myself. Let's get another pint.'

It was their fourth and she was definitely tipsy, but why not? It was Friday night and she was only twenty-four. They pushed their way to the bar and then squeezed back through the crowd until they were just a couple of rows from the front. The lights lowered. Half the crowd cheered, half booed. The band shuffled on to the stage. First a drummer, then a short red-haired guy with a guitar round his neck.

Then Nick Crex.

To Lucinda's surprise, the sight of him made her feel as if a pilot light had been turned on deep inside her. She'd always known he was attractive, in an academic kind of way. But seeing him on stage in a military jacket and drainpipes, a guitar hanging round his neck, she felt a whoomph of lust, violent and scorching in its intensity, as if a match had been dropped in petrol.

'That's the client?' Gareth nudged her.

'Mmm.'

She couldn't take her eyes off him. He struck the first few chords. The drummer started drumming, the guitarist strummed and a skinny blond guy shambled over to the microphone. Everyone started screaming. Gareth nudged her.

'There he is. Jack the Smackhead.'

He certainly looked out of it. His eyes were completely unfocused. He shuffled around the stage, limbs moving uncoordinatedly, mumbling into the mike. The crowd screamed some more but in an unconvincing way, as if they were extras in a crowd scene following bad directions. Lucinda glanced at Gareth. He was grinning.

'He's off his chops. It's a disaster.'

Lucinda looked again at Nick. He was looking down at his guitar, his mouth in a straight line, his eyes furious. There was something very sexy about a man who looked so angry. He looked up and caught her eye.

Oddly nervous, she gave him a little wave. A faint grin lit up his face for a moment, then it turned blankly angry as he continued strumming. Lucinda's whole body tingled, as if she'd been shocked. Her eyes were fixed so firmly on Nick that she missed Jack tripping over a cable and falling flat on his face. Hearing the audience's 'Ooh', she turned to see him rolling giggling on his back like an upturned turtle. The music halted abruptly. The booing started.

Nick pulled his guitar over his head and threw it to the ground. He ran into the wings. Standing on tiptoes, Lucinda craned to see him. There was a girl waiting there, pretty in a kind of cheap way, blonde and busty. She threw her arms around his neck. He pushed her away. Lucinda watched entranced. Her face, her hands, even her earlobes felt as if they were on fire.

She didn't feel jealous of the girlfriend. She just made her want Nick more. Even though she was a bit drunk, she felt extremely sober. She suddenly knew as sure as she knew her own name that she would sleep with Nick Crex. She wanted him. And whatever Lucinda wanted, she got.

Over the next forty-eight hours Karen found herself thinking about Max constantly. Bumping into him in the canteen had just depressed her. But the lunch invitation had completely rejuvenated her. She moved around the *Post* building with a new self-consciousness, aware that though *Daily* staff rarely trespassed on *Sunday* territory it wasn't entirely unknown. When she talked on the phone to irritating PRs or aggressive freelances she kept a bright smile on her face and laughed a lot, which they must have found most unnerving.

It was odd, because she barely knew him really. Hadn't given him a thought in thirteen years. And today's lunch would probably just be a one-off. Karen knew how these reunions worked: you exchanged news, pulled out a photo of your children which the other one scrutinized and said 'Aah' to, gave a bit of career advice, said, 'We must do it again soon,' and as soon as you walked out the door all thoughts of them were obliterated in a round of online food shops, au pair crises and work deadlines.

She consoled herself with this on Friday morning, when she woke after less than three hours' sleep feeling like a bad-tempered porcupine and looking slightly less pretty. Nothing appealed less than lunch with someone she vaguely wanted to impress. Never mind, the pace on the *Daily* was frantic. He'd never be able to escape.

But he called her just after one.

'I've just finished my first story and I can knock off the

second this afternoon, I reckon. So how about we nip out for an hour? You can show me the sights.'

She took him to L'Amandine, a little deli with a café attached, in the warren of stuccoed houses behind Kensington Church Street.

'This looks nice.' Max looked around at the framed vintage travel posters, the lace curtains, the croissants under a glass dome on the zinc counter.

'The food's good,' she said, a little jittery after the four coffees she'd consumed that morning. 'If you don't mind service with a scowl.' She nodded at Estelle, the proprietor. As usual, Estelle blanked her, as if she had just escaped from prison, rather than having come in here at least three times a week for four years. 'So how are you finding life at the *Daily*?'

'A bit nerve-racking. But nice people. Far less of a labour camp than the *Sentinel*. There seems to be a consensus that it's acceptable to have a life outside the office, which makes me a bit jittery. You know that joke: "Why do *Sentinel* staff die so young?" "Because they want to."'

Karen laughed. 'Though the money's better at the *Sentinel*, I seem to recall.'

'They agreed to match my salary here. I thought that was a good deal given the state of my personal life . . .' This sounded interesting. Infuriatingly, Estelle was hovering above them. Max smiled up at her. 'May I have the croque madame, please? And a tap water.'

'No tap water,' Estelle scowled. 'Only bottle. Perrier. Evian.'

'Oh,' Max said humbly. 'Evian then.'

'Same for me,' Karen said. As Estelle stomped off she

smiled apologetically. 'I warned you this place had charac-ter.' She wondered how she could get him back to the personal life topic.

'I thought it was illegal not to serve tap water. Oh well. So, as I was saying, I thought same money, probably less pressure. Sounded like a win-win.' He looked her in the eye. 'My girlfriend works there, you see, and it was all getting a bit heavy spending all day under the same roof.'

'Do you live with her?'

'No. She wants that but . . . I'm not sure, to be honest. I'm in Essex Road. Got a little rented flat there. And what about you?' he asked as their food was plonked in front of them with an angry grunt.

She cringed as she said: 'St Albans. A cliché, I know.'

'Why cliché?'

'Because it's where everyone goes when they have chil-dren and decide it's time to leave London.'

'What did you say you had? Two boys?'

'No, two girls.' Virtually any woman would have asked about ages and names, but Max was a single man and just nodded. 'And what about your husband? What does he do?'

She thought about not telling him. But then they'd exchange a few more platitudes and lunch would be over. 'Well, he was a venture capitalist. But he was very ill a couple of years ago. Cancer. He's better now,' she continued as Max's features formed into the obligatory shocked and sorry expression. 'But as a result he sold his business. Said life was too short to spend shackled behind a desk. In fact . . . he wants us to move to the country. He's found a house to buy in Devon, he wants that to be our project. So I may not be at the *Post* for that much longer.'

'You'd resign? Oh no, Karen. You can't do that. What a waste.'

'Hardly,' she shrugged.

'Just when we made contact again. I can't bear it.' But his tone was mocking, belying the seriousness of his words. He took a bite of his sandwich, then continued. 'All my friends with kids depart for the country. I don't get it at all. Why do people think it's better to live surrounded by trees and mud and cows, instead of near the shops and a cinema? It's as if because you suffer, it must be good for you.'

'I don't think they think it's suffering. It's giving your children the best start.'

Max shook his head, as if he were disappointed in her. 'The country's horrible. Brown. Depressing. Pylons.'

'Cows,' Karen agreed. 'People who wear Barbours.'

'No shops.'

'Don't be silly,' she grinned. 'What about the Spar?'

'That's not a shop. All it sells is one wrinkled turnip and a packet of Bourbons. The owner would shoot you if you asked for anything else.' He paused and said, 'Do you really think you'll be happy there?'

'I don't know,' Karen said. She paused. 'I know Phil won't be happy if we stay. And if your husband's not happy then you can't be.'

'So when did you get married?'

'About a year after I . . .' *split up with your brother* '. . . left the *Sentinel*. I was twenty-eight. Now I think I was too young.' Where on earth had that confession come from?

'Not that I made a mistake or anything,' she added hastily. 'It's all great.'

'God, I'm thirty-two and the idea of marriage still terrifies me. Much to my girlfriend's disgust.'

'How long have you been with her?'

'Nine months.' He looked her in the eye. 'To be honest, I'm not sure it's going to last much longer. We're kind of at make or break time; like I say, she wants marriage, babies and I . . . I want them one day, sure. But I'm pretty sure I don't want them with her. Does that make me sound like the biggest S H One T on the planet?'

'A bit,' Karen said and then, to her surprise, found herself adding, 'But the most important thing is to get married for positive reasons. I got married because I craved security. I was scared. I came from a dodgy background. I was living a crazy existence. I thought marrying Phil would make me safe.'

'Crazy existence? You were an up-and-coming star, as I recall.'

Karen shook her head. 'I'd been living alone since I was seventeen. I'd been in all these awful squats. I just felt so grateful to Phil. It was so nice having someone reliable in my life. Knowing that if the boiler broke down I wouldn't have to deal with a plumber who'd rip me off. That he'd check the car tyre pressures. Make sure the roof was mended. I felt I had to marry him. Had to show him how much I appreciated what he'd done for me. I still feel that.' She took a sip of her Evian, suddenly shaky at how much she'd just said.

'So that's why you're moving to the sticks?'

'That's part of it. The other part is Phil nearly died. After what he went through I don't see how I can say no.'

'You went through it all too.' Max wasn't looking at her; he seemed annoyed somehow. He finished his sandwich hastily, then gestured apologetically at the clock on the wall. 'We'd better get back. But I've enjoyed this, Karen. Can we do it again soon? No, no, I'll get this.'

'Thank you.' She couldn't see his expression as he stood at the cash desk, handing over a twenty-pound note. Suddenly she felt a complete fool. She'd confided all this stuff in Max, but he clearly had no idea how close to her heart it was. Why on earth should he? She meant nothing to him; she was just a dull, older woman from his past whom he was being polite to, whom he probably couldn't wait to get away from.

They walked back to the office in awkward silence. Swiped their cards through the turnstiles. Waited for the lift.

'Looks like we might be in for a good summer,' Max said.

'Fingers crossed.'

They stepped into the lift. At the first floor Max stepped out.

'It's been good to catch up,' he said through the closing doors.

'Absolutely.' The lift carried Karen upwards. She was furious with herself. Irrationally disappointed, as if she'd gone to sleep on Christmas Eve and woken up to find it was Boxing Day.

# 19

Two days after the Shepherd's Bush gig, the three non-hospitalized members of the Vertical Blinds were sitting in Andrew's tiny flat in Chiswick, arguing about whose fault it was that things had gone so wrong.

'The reviews have been shite, the fans are all blogging away saying we're a joke,' Paul said. 'Why did you do it, Andrew? Why did you let him go on stage when he was smacked out of his head?'

'Ah, c'mon,' protested Ian. 'It's not like he hadn't done it a million times before. How was Andrew to know?'

'It's not like we've ever seen Jack do a gig sober,' Andrew said defensively. But he looked worried. And rightly so. Andrew was in his early fifties. He'd managed various one-hit wonders in the Nineties, but when he'd 'discovered' the Blinds he'd been on the verge of bankruptcy. He had an elderly mother in a nursing home and a load of debt. If the Blinds went tits up, he was going to be selling the *Big Issue*.

Ian yawned. 'Whatever. We obviously ain't doing anything for the next few weeks until he's been in and out of rehab. Better see what parties are going on.'

And sort out buying the flat, Nick thought. And concentrate on seducing Lucinda Gresham. He'd felt her eyes on him that night, and when he'd looked at her he'd known she was gagging for it. He'd shag her and then he'd do his best to fall in love with her. He didn't feel it yet, but it could come.

He needed to call her anyway – she'd been leaving him message after message about his offer and how the Meehans had finally declined it 'but they're still happy to come to some arrangement'.

He did it the following morning, just after Kylie had gone to work. His heart thudded in a way he wasn't accustomed to as he dialled.

'Lucinda Gresham?'

'It's Nick Crex.'

There was just the tiniest pause and then she said, 'Mr Crex, glad to hear from you. I enjoyed the other night by the way.'

'Oh yeah?'

'Yes. I mean, things obviously didn't turn out quite as intended but you were excellent. Really good. So have you an answer for the Meehans?'

'I want to go back to the flat. For another viewing.'

There was another brief hesitation. Then she said, 'Okaaaay. When?'

'Today?'

'How about . . . three? Obviously I'll just have to check with the vendor if that's OK?'

'No worries,' he said. 'If I don't hear from you I'll see you there at three.'

Energized, he spent the next couple of hours writing and actually managed to get a new song down. He played it back a couple of times, getting more and more excited. This was what he'd been looking for, something like 'Mercury River' that would be played on radio stations across the world and be an anthem. He strummed the opening chords again and, tentatively, started singing.

'*Green-eyed princess. In your castle. Watching down on me.*'

He decided to walk to the flat. So he got dressed in his favourite black jeans and Bob Dylan T-shirt and set off down the hill through Camden Town. Yesterday's clouds had parted, revealing a turquoise sky, and for the first time in months the sun's rays warmed Nick's skin. Strains of Bebel Gilberto drifted down from a balcony, people were sitting outside pubs. Spring had arrived – even if it was just for today – and Nick felt the happiest he had in a long time.

He felt even happier when he arrived at the flat. Lucinda was standing outside, her hair twisted up in a chignon and wearing a tight-fitting grey suit and very high black heels. Nick was sure she'd made an effort for him.

'Hello, Mr Crex.'

'Please. Call me Nick.'

'Nick.' She smiled. 'And I'm Lucinda.'

'I know.'

She gestured at the door. 'Shall we?'

In the lift, he could feel tension throbbing between them. She let him into the flat. He looked around in silence.

'I do like it,' he said after a long pause. 'I'll meet them halfway, twenty-five grand off the original figure.'

'Fine,' Lucinda said. 'I'll put it to them later. If I can get hold of them, that is. It turns out they've gone to Belfast for the weekend. Some family party.'

'Have they now?' Nick suddenly turned and began studying the display of swords on the wall. Carefully, he ran his hand along one of them and picked it off its brackets. He looked at Lucinda defiantly, then, when she didn't tell him off for meddling, said: 'Beautiful.'

'Of course. You know about swordsmanship.' The word made her blush. Excellent. 'You did it at school, didn't you?'

'That's right.'

'Let's see then,' she challenged.

For a second, he was thrown. 'Here? Suppose they come back.'

'I told you. They're on the way to Belfast.'

She was gabbling, she was nervous. He considered grabbing and kissing her in a grand romantic gesture. But instead he held up the sword so it glinted in the sun that was slanting in through the huge windows. He slashed it downwards.

'It's all about cutting and thrusting,' he said, glancing sideways at her, enjoying the innuendo. 'Of course this is much heavier than a fencing sword. But basically you cut like this.' He jumped forward. 'And thrust like that.'

The sword whooshed down through the air, and stopped just inches from her chest. She screamed and jumped backwards.

'If you were my opponent we'd challenge each other like this.'

'You're a maniac.' Her eyes were shining.

'Just showing you what I learned.' He inhaled. 'I could show you some proper loose play now. You can be my adversary, except I don't think you should use a sword. So I'll just play around you. You've just got to promise to stand absolutely still.'

'OK,' she said coolly.

He pointed to a spot about a yard in front of them. 'Stand there. Like I said. Do not move.'

She stood stock still in front of him, grinning. Nick flourished the sword. The next thing Lucinda knew was its point darting to her left side, just above her hip. Then suddenly it was on her right side as if it had passed through her body. And then the sword – clean and blood-free – was back vertically in Nick's hands. The whole thing had been quicker than Benjie's response to the question 'Is Tom Cruise gay?'

'How did you do that?' she laughed, running her hands down her body.

'I didn't touch you,' Nick said softly. 'It's like a magic trick. The sword passed behind you. Now, you're not afraid, are you? Because I promise you I won't hurt you. I won't even touch you.'

'You really promise?' She didn't look scared. She looked excited. Nick felt a flicker of admiration for her.

'I really promise.'

'Then I'm not afraid.' She jutted her chin in the air, but then – just as he was about to move – added, 'Is the sword really sharp?'

'It's blunt. But still, don't move.'

The blade whirled through the air, reflecting the afternoon sun. Lucinda watched, hypnotized. A dragon tattoo twisted round Nick's arm. He stood mainly facing her, sometimes turned sideways on, lips closed tight with concentration as he eyed the outline of her body. His movements grew slower and slower, until she could appreciate each one. The only sounds were her breathing growing shallower and shallower, and, somewhere, the buzzing of a fly, swatting the hot glass of the windows. He stopped.

'You've got a piece of hair loose,' he said, nodding at a strand escaping from her chignon. 'Wait, I'll fix it.'

She felt a flash of silver on her left – the sword had descended. A chunk of her hair fell to the ground. Lucinda shrieked, her hand flying to her head.

'You cut it off.'

'You were great. Didn't move a muscle.'

'I had no idea you'd do that,' she laughed.

'Just one more time.'

'No way! You're a lunatic.' But her tone was far from discouraging.

'I won't touch you. But there's a fly on your shoulder. I need to kill it.'

She saw the point aim towards her breasts and – she thought – pierce her flesh. Lucinda shut her eyes tight, inhaling sharply. Then, slowly, she opened them again.

'Look,' Nick said, holding the sword before her eyes. A fat fly was impaled on its tip.

'It *is* magic!' She laughed.

'No. Skill. I ran the fly through and stopped about a millimetre before your skin.'

Lucinda wrinkled her nose in confusion. 'But how could you cut off my hair and spear a fly if the sword was blunt?'

'I lied about that. The important thing was to get you to stand still.'

Lucinda sat down on the zebra-striped sofa.

'I could have been killed and I didn't realize.'

'You could have been killed one hundred and eighty-six times.' He replaced the sword on the wall. 'But you weren't because I know what I'm doing.' He stepped back from her. 'I'd better get going. I'll be in touch tomorrow. About my offer.'

'Oh.' His businesslike manner threw her. 'All right then.'

He stepped closer to her. Bent over her. Kissed her on the lips, fully and firmly, for about five seconds.

'You're beautiful,' he muttered. Then he backed away and repeated: 'I'll be in touch.'

He was out the door, running along the corridor to the lift, which was waiting for him. As it carried him downstairs, he exhaled triumphantly. He could never have planned for as brilliant a prop as those swords.

In the lobby, he collected himself. Slowly, he pushed open the huge plate-glass door and walked briskly – but not too fast – along the street. Like a man who'd just been to a viewing and now had other places to go, certainly not a man who'd pulled off a coup he'd been planning for weeks. He willed himself not to look round, but he could feel Lucinda's eyes burning into his back. He took his phone out of his pocket and – pretending to study a text – saw that she was leaning out of the window, watching him. Wondering why he'd kissed her and then run off. Hoping it would happen again.

## 20

Lucinda could barely get herself back to the office. As she walked along the familiar cobbled streets, she could feel her lungs reacclimatizing themselves to air, her jellied limbs solidifying again. She kept replaying the events of a few minutes ago. Nick Crex had kissed her with warm, firm lips. She'd felt his hard body against her, inhaled his faintly salty smell.

He'd called her beautiful.

Re-entering the office, she found it hard to believe she was the same Lucinda who'd left less than an hour previously, for the third viewing. The same auburn hair. The same grey Carolina Herrera suit. The same Cartier pearls on her wrist. But everything was different. She felt beautiful. Invincible. She looked at her colleagues talking on the phone, going through paperwork, from what seemed almost like a position of power.

'How did the viewing go?' asked Gareth casually, as if it was just another afternoon.

'Uh?'

'With Mr Vertical Blinds. Isn't that where you were? At Flat 15?'

'Oh. Yes.'

'And?'

Did Gareth know what had gone on? She stared at him

for a second before she realized what he was actually asking.

'He's going to meet them halfway. Which I'm pretty sure they'll be cool with.'

'Did he say anything about that junkie lead singer? What a knob.'

'Third viewings always spell disaster,' Joanne interrupted, as Lucinda tried to collect herself. 'He's obviously not happy about something or he wouldn't keep coming back.'

'I know they usually do.' Lucinda turned on her computer, trying to stop her voice from shaking. 'But there's always an exception to the rule, isn't there?'

A pile of emails had come in while she'd been out. But Lucinda couldn't concentrate on them. Instead she called up Google and bashed in 'Nick Crex'. She'd been doing this ever since the Shepherd's Bush gig. Studying the online gallery of him on stage wearing sunglasses, outside a stadium in a football shirt, which presumably indicated he supported some team – she'd never understood the British obsession with football.

There was a Wikipedia entry, telling her about his tough upbringing in Burnley and how he was considered the brains behind the band. Lots of clips of him doing his stuff on stage that she watched surreptitiously with the sound turned down. Since the gig Lucinda had downloaded their album and been listening to it non-stop. Their music would never really be her thing, but she was getting used to it.

She'd also learned:

- The Vertical Blinds' first gig was on 13 June 2005 at the Orange Tree in Burnley.
- Nick's favourite colour is indigo.

- Nick Crex, the lead guitarist and songwriter, and the lead singer, Jack, were neighbours in Burnley and attended the same school.
- His hero is Bryan Ferry, the former lead singer of Roxy Music.

No mention of any significant other. But she knew she couldn't let it rest at that, so she'd googled again: 'Nick Crex girlfriend'. There were three thousand five hundred and ten results, but the first two were reprints of an article, with a line saying how one of Nick's earliest songs was about losing his girlfriend to a boy in the year above at school. 'And so the Blinds' trademark wit and irony, reminiscent of Joe Jackson and Elvis Costello, was born.' Yay! But then she read on. And number three on the list was an article from *The Times*, saying, '*Crex with his childhood sweetheart.*'

Heart thudding, she'd clicked. The article was dated just a month earlier, and was about Jack's problems and his fondness for model girlfriends. 'Crex, on the other hand, is in a long-term relationship with his childhood sweetheart, Kylie, a hairdresser whom he met at school and who avoids the limelight.'

'Lucinda,' Niall had called. Hastily, she'd closed the webpage. She'd felt uneasy, but more than that she'd felt defiant. From the glimpse she'd had of this Kylie at the gig, she knew she was prettier than her. But even if Kylie had been Angelina Jolie's long-lost twin, Lucinda wouldn't have been that worried. Nick had never mentioned her to Lucinda, and if he was buying a flat you'd have thought the question of his long-term girlfriend would have come up. So it was obviously nothing serious.

Now she sat rerunning the events of less than an hour

ago. It had been such a turn-on: him whizzing that sword around. Lucinda had been ready to have sex with him then and there on Alex and Gemma Meehan's zebra-print sofa, but he'd dashed off. She'd watched him go. Disappointingly, he hadn't looked back.

But he liked her. He must do. Or he wouldn't have called her beautiful. No one had ever said that before, not in so many words. Not even Anton. For a second, she wondered about that. Perhaps if Anton had flattered her more directly she'd have more feelings for him. Lucinda's ego was like a thirsty plant that needed constant watering.

But the more she thought about Nick, the more her confidence evaporated. Nick and his girlfriend were serious. He'd just kissed Lucinda on a whim and immediately regretted it. She was beginning to understand what it must be like to be Cassandra, how ambiguous this boy-girl stuff was, how exhausting it was having to decode signals like a cowboy watching Indian smoke rise over the desert. But he'd told her she was beautiful.

Lucinda wondered if she should call him – and if so, what should she say? Pretend it was business? Or be blatant? She chewed her lip in uncharacteristic indecision, then jumped as her desk phone rang.

'Hello?' she said, face on fire, sure it was him.

'Lucinda? It's me!'

Oh, shit. Anton. Anton whom she hadn't given a second's thought to.

'I'm back. A bit earlier than I expected.'

'Hi,' she said guardedly.

'So how are things?' He sounded so warm and needy. Lucinda cringed. 'I was wondering,' he continued. 'Do you

231

fancy dinner tonight? There's this little fish place I know called J. Sheekey's.'

'Oh!' Lucinda said. She gnawed a cuticle as she looked at her computer clock. 5:59. She did not want to spend the evening at home, willing Nick to call.

'I mean, if you're free.'

'I am free,' she decided. 'What time?'

'Really! Are you sure?'

'Yeah, I'm sure.' She felt Gareth watching her. She dipped her head, ashamed. But what was wrong with having dinner with Anton? Just as friends.

To clear her head, she walked from the office to Sheekey's, just off the hubbub of Charing Cross Road. The restaurant felt very clubby: wall-to-wall mahogany and black-and-white photos on the wall. Anton was waiting at a corner table. As soon as he saw her, he stood up. Her flesh crept at his eagerness.

'Lucinda. What a treat. Would you like oysters? I've already ordered champagne.'

'Lovely,' she said, sitting down. He was so old, whole Everest expeditions could get lost in the crevices round his eyes. She thought of Nick and his smooth, hard body and shivered. She shouldn't have come. She was wasting Anton's time and hers.

'Oysters for the lady?' Anton enquired, as the waiter hovered into view. She nodded dumbly. But her silence didn't seem to matter. Anton talked about his travels and some new building projects he was embarking on, and how he'd just seen the new programme for the Opera House and he really hoped Lucinda would be able to join him at *Turandot*.

'Mmm,' she nodded. 'Yes. Could be nice.' After all, she was never going to hear from Nick again, so why not? She might as well enjoy some opera. But then she felt her phone, buzzing in her inside jacket pocket. She whipped it out. Nick's number.

'Excuse me, but I have to take this.'

'I don't think phones are allowed in here . . .'

But she'd already answered. 'Hello? Hi . . . Oh.' She held up a hand to Anton and to a waiter who'd rushed in to protest. 'It's OK, I'll take this outside. Sorry,' she mouthed to Anton, but she wasn't really, she just wanted to be alone, talking to Nick.

'Where are you?' he said, once she was outside in the little courtyard at the back of some theatre.

'In a restaurant,' she said.

'Oh yeah. Who with?' He didn't sound jealous, merely amused.

'A client.'

'Well, leave him at once. You need to come and see me.'

'Excuse me,' she said, grinning so widely she thought her face might snap. 'But I told you I'm busy.'

'I need to see you now.'

'Where?'

'At yours?'

That wouldn't work – Benjie was in tonight, revising. 'Sorry, that's not possible. How about yours?'

'No.' No explanation. She knew why. Her mind contorted like a Cirque du Soleil acrobat as she tried to think of an alternative. And then it came. The Meehans. Away in Belfast. She'd just have dinner with Anton, then nip back to the office and collect the keys.

'I can see you later. Maybe in a couple of hours.'

'But I want to see you now.'

'I'm busy.' She knew she should play harder to get but it was so difficult. 'An hour and a half? Back at the flat?'

'Now!'

Anton stuck his head round the door of the restaurant. 'Lucinda! Are you OK?'

She waved at him apologetically. 'Be there in an hour,' Nick said. 'Or I'll be gone.' And he hung up.

'All done now,' Anton said eagerly. 'Those oysters are waiting for you.'

'Actually,' she said. 'I'm really sorry but I'm not feeling well. I'm going to have to go.'

Anton frowned. 'Are you sure? You look fine.'

'No, honestly, Anton . . . it's women's troubles.' She knew that would have him backing right off. 'I really think I need to get home. I'm so sorry, I thought I'd be OK but I'm not.'

Anton's face contorted with concern. 'Oh dear. Let's get you a taxi.' He turned to the top-hatted doorman, who was watching the scene with an 'I've-seen-it-all-before' expression. 'Here's my card,' he said, pulling his Amex out of his wallet. 'I'll be back in a minute. I just need to find this young lady a cab.'

'Really. I'll be fine on my own,' Lucinda protested. 'You go back in. Finish the oysters.'

'I'm hardly going to enjoy them without you.' He took her arm and led her towards Charing Cross Road, pushing through a crowd of babbling theatregoers. Fortunately, they saw a cab straight away. Anton flagged it down and helped her in.

'South Kensington,' he told the driver in his usual abrupt fashion. She climbed in.

'Will you call me tomorrow? Let me know you're OK?'

'Of course,' she assured him. The cab pulled away and she turned round to see him staring after her mournfully. For a second she felt horribly guilty, but then she thought of Nick waiting for her at the flat. It was if her nerves had been replaced by electric wires. She leaned forward and tapped on the glass.

'We're not going to South Kensington,' she told the driver. 'We're going to Clerkenwell.'

Dear Gwen,

So I had my 'date' with Richie. It went as well as could be
expected, I suppose. I'm not sure we have all that much in
common but he is very amiable. I'm sure I bored him silly,
though! I don't think there'll be a re-run in any case and that's
probably no bad thing, I'm so busy packing up the house
and . . .

Grace stopped typing, suddenly overwhelmed with despair.
The grandfather clock had just struck two, but she'd been
unable to sleep. She'd goofed. Totally and utterly messed
things up. She kept trying to tell herself that Richie Prescott
was not actually so wonderful himself, that sometimes as he
kept on and on about great property deals he'd done she'd
been a little bored. But that didn't matter. He was a man. He
had asked her out. And he wouldn't again. Because she'd been
too fat. The only chance to escape from her ghetto, to join
the world of people who married and had children, who lived
like Sebby and Verity, had eluded her.

Only one thing could fix this. She hurried down the stairs
and along the cold dark corridor to the kitchen. She flung
open the breadbin, pulled out two slices, threw them in the
Aga toaster and slammed the hotplate lid down. The dogs,
asleep in their baskets, stirred in confusion. Grace shushed
them as she stared at the toaster, willing it to hurry up. Why

had she thrown all the biscuits and sweets away? It had all been a waste of time.

Before the bread was barely scorched, she pulled up the Aga lid and crammed the toast into her mouth. Carbohydrates rushed round her body and her mood temporarily soared. She shoved in two more slices as she chomped, and this time slathered them in rock-hard, fridge butter. Then two with peanut butter. Two with jam. Two with cheese.

The bread was finished. She opened the pantry cupboard. A few bags of rice and pasta. It would take too long to cook them. Grace took a handful of dry penne and stuffed them into her mouth, crunching the dusty, dry chips. She washed them down with a pint of milk straight from the fridge.

Then she buried her face in her arms and she cried and she cried.

He wasn't there. Lucinda paced up and down Flat 15, jumping at every sound. She checked her hair in Gemma's bathroom mirror, splashed water on her face to help herself cool down, then decided her make-up needed touching up – but she had none to hand apart from the little compact and tiny bottle of Ô de Lancôme she kept in her bag.

She didn't dare help herself to any of Gemma's cosmetics. She daren't put on music, light a candle – any of the things she might have normally done to create an ambience – in case she left traces.

Television was obviously out of the question, so she picked a paperback about American politics off the crowded bookshelf and tried to read. But after not taking in ten pages, she got up and stared at herself in the full-length mirror on the back of the bedroom door. She looked so square in her suit, like a girl from Geneva rather than a rock chick. She wondered if she should have gone home and changed, but even in jeans and a T-shirt and Benjie's leather studded belt, her skin would have been too clear, her eyes too bright, her cheeks too flushed for her ever to masquerade as Amy Winehouse. And surely that was the kind of woman Nick would be into?

Fifteen minutes later, however, she'd stopped fretting about pleasing Nick and instead was merely wondering why he hadn't shown up. Was he stuck in traffic? Or was he with his girlfriend? She tried his mobile but there was no reply, not even his voice, just the O2 messaging lady. She didn't say anything. She was on the verge of going home when the doorbell rang.

'Hello?' she said tremulously into the intercom.

'It's me.'

As soon as he stepped through the door she was in his arms. They slid down to the floor, with her pulling his T-shirt out of his trousers and grappling with his belt. She couldn't get it undone, so he helped her. She ran her hands along his pelvis, so beautifully hinged, like her school protractor. His eyes were dark and narrow. It was all so quick and hot and he was kissing her all over her face, her neck, her nipples. She held on to him and dug her nails into his back.

'You're so fucking sexy,' he said.

She wriggled out of her trousers, then grabbed his hand and guided his fingers inside her, desperate for him to feel her wetness. Her thighs were dissolving. She opened up her legs for him. It was the best sex she'd ever had in her life, in a different league from all those fumblings with nervous

Pierres and Xaviers in spare bedrooms in ski-resort chalets that a gang of them had taken over for the weekend. She grabbed his buttocks to have him as deep inside her as possible, tilted her hips up at him, biting into his shoulder. She came with a shriek of ecstasy and he collapsed on top of her with a sort of roar. He rolled beside her and they lay quietly for a very long time.

'Oh,' she said eventually.

They both started to laugh.

'Did you like that, then?' he asked.

She shrugged. 'No, not really.'

'Nor me.'

They giggled some more.

Nick looked around the room. Huge, rather spooky shadows from the windows fell across the walls. 'So why couldn't we go back to your place?'

'My brother's there. Why couldn't we go back to yours?'

He was silent.

'It's because you have a girlfriend.'

'How do you know that?' he said, though he didn't sound particularly surprised.

She had enough nous not to tell him she'd been googling him. 'I saw her at the gig.'

'I see.' For a second, he looked uncomfortable, then he said, 'It's all over. We're on the rocks. That's why I'm buying the flat. And she's looking for her own place.'

'Oh. Right.' Lucinda's very highly attuned bullshit detector didn't quite buy this. But she wanted to believe him, so she decided that for now she would.

'You are the most incredible woman I have ever met in my life,' he whispered, running his fingers up her thighs.

'I bet you say that to all the girls,' she joked.

He looked intently into her eyes. 'No. I don't.'

She was thrilled. No one had ever singled her out in this way before, or if they had they hadn't been worth it. To hide her excitement, she traced the edges of his blue-and-gold dragon tattoo with a fingernail.

'What's all this about then?'

'It symbolizes protection. Strength. George V had one, you know.' He flexed his long, thin arm. 'Look, it's as if it's moving.'

'Did it hurt?'

'Not really,' he shrugged.

Lucinda tried to envisage Henri De Villiers, the boy she'd lost her virginity to, with a tattoo hidden under his pinstriped shirt. She couldn't. But she was distracted anyway, by Nick's fingers, which had begun to probe inside her again.

They had a near sleepless night, fuelled by a pizza they found in the freezer. They fell asleep just before dawn and woke around noon and made love again.

'So what is it your dad really does?' Nick asked, when they finally stopped for a breather.

'He works in property. That's why I'm here. Learning a bit before I join the family business.'

'So he's rich.'

'It depends what you mean by rich. What does *your* dad do?' she parried.

'I wouldn't fucking know. He walked out when I was six. Haven't seen him since.'

'I'm sorry.'

'Don't be. He was a bastard. Treated my mum like shit.'

240

'My dad doesn't treat my mum too well, either.' She paused. 'He's always having affairs. Various mistresses. We're not meant to know anything about it, but it's usually common knowledge. I mean, he goes on holiday with them and things. Calls them his PA but they'll be the mother of someone from my class at school. Or the big sister on one occasion. I don't know why Mummy doesn't say anything. I guess she feels there's too much to lose. I mean . . . our house is pretty big and she has lovely clothes and she's very much a figure on the Geneva scene. And she came from a very ordinary background, so I guess she's scared of what she might go back to, even though she'd get a ton of alimony. But I think she's doing it all wrong. I think she should kick him out. I mean I love him. Love him more than I love her, but still. She needs to show some dignity.'

It was probably the longest speech Lucinda had ever made about her family. She stopped, slightly astonished.

'Well, my mum was right to kick my dad out but she's still not exactly Mrs Happy. Living on the sixteenth floor of a tower block watching Jeremy Kyle all day. Stuffed full of Valium.'

'My mum takes Valium too,' Lucinda laughed at the unlikely coincidence. 'Has done for years.' She paused. 'Have you really not seen your father since you were six?'

'Nope. I've had a postcard once or twice. I wish . . . Well, whenever I'm in the papers or whatever, I sort of hope he might see me. When I do a gig I wonder if he might be out there. But I've heard nothing. Maybe he's dead.'

Lucinda was touched. Gently she pushed back a strand of his hair, which had fallen over his forehead. She felt a closeness to him she'd not felt towards any human being for years. She was so used to keeping it all buttoned up.

'Maybe we should go for a walk?' she suggested.

'What for?'

She was a little shocked. Didn't Nick know that Fresh Air was a Good Thing that must be partaken of every day for at least twenty minutes?

'People might see us,' he said. 'And that could be awkward.'

'Oh. Yes. Right.'

For the first time in the past twenty-four hours her bubble was pricked. Why did he care if people saw them? She reasoned she didn't want her family to know about him either. But his situation was different – he had a girl-friend.

'How long have you been with her?' she blurted out.

He looked amused. 'Are you jealous?'

'Of course not,' she lied.

'That's weird. I'd be jealous if you had a boyfriend.'

'You said it was all over between you. Why should I be jealous?'

'Exactly.'

'And how long have you been together?'

'Why does it matter? Seven years.'

'*Seven years*?' Of course. She'd been his childhood sweet-heart. Still, Lucinda felt bruised all down the front of her body, as if she'd been punched. 'So it's serious.'

'It was serious. But we've drifted apart. We like different things now.' Nick hated himself for saying it. But it was true. Wasn't it?

'What does she do?' Lucinda was persisting.

'She's a nail technician. Does manicures.' He pulled her

towards him. 'It's boring. I don't want to talk about it. I want to fuck you again.'

At around five, she insisted she really did have to leave.

'Why?'

'The Meehans will be back at some point. And I have things to do at home. Like laundry.'

Nick felt a sense of anti-climax. He'd begun thinking of Lucinda as some kind of goddess. Foreign. Obviously rich. Exactly the kind of woman he should be with. Why was she talking about laundry? That was a Kylie sort of remark.

'Can you come back later?' he asked.

'No. I can't. I've told you, I'm not sure when the Meehans return.'

More disillusionment. 'OK,' he pouted. 'I'll see you then.' He pulled on his jacket.

'I'll tidy up,' she said, glancing round. 'Make sure everything's exactly as we found it.'

'You do that. See you.' He headed towards the door.

'Nick! Wait!'

'What?' he said, looking bored.

'I'll . . . be in touch about the sale.'

'Yeah, all right then.' The door slammed shut and yet again Lucinda was left terrified and exhilarated, as if her world had just been struck by a meteorite and was now spinning, uncharted, into a black hole.

## 22

Max Bennett was sitting at his desk feeling hungover and irritable. He'd had another row with Heather last night – she'd been on at him again about moving in and he'd finally told her he didn't want it.

She'd cried, and he'd felt like a bastard, but then they'd ended up in bed together and in the morning she'd left while he was in the shower with a merry 'Cheerio, then!' and he'd been left covered in Imperial Leather suds, furious at his cowardice, at his inability to knock this thing on the head and give poor Heather, who really was a very nice girl, just not the one for him, a chance to settle down with a nice man.

Max hadn't met anyone he wanted to settle down with and he wasn't sure that would change. He enjoyed life the way it was.

At least he usually enjoyed it. Max looked at his screen. He'd just filed 600 words on Jordan's new boyfriend. He hadn't gone into journalism for this. He'd been hoping to be breaking scoops à la Watergate. But that kind of journalism had died out along with bus conductors and payphones; his brother Jeremy had enjoyed the tail end of it and then got out and moved into the lucrative world of PR. Max had followed in his footsteps, but these days the industry was in such dire straits he felt like a hansom cab driver after the invention of the automobile, knowing his days were distinctly numbered.

His mobile started ringing. Shit. Heather. Quickly he turned it off and shoved it in his pocket. The office was humming away as ever, but a few people had sloped off from their desks for lunch. Time for a break; Max decided he'd go for a walk, perhaps up to Kensington Gardens, to enjoy the glorious spring weather.

He walked up Kensington High Street and into the gardens. Round the pond twice, dodging necking tourists and gleeful toddlers. He was about to sit on a bench and feel the sun on his skin when he did a double-take. Occupying the bench already was Karen Drake.

For a second he watched her. Like every time he saw her, Max was struck by her beauty. Absolutely nothing like Heather, who was blonde and tall and voluptuous; Karen was almost on the scrawny side. And certainly a lot more tired-looking than when she'd been Jeremy's girlfriend. But there was something so intriguing about her, Max had always thought so, and seeing her sitting there, staring ahead, unaware of his scrutiny, indeed unaware of anyone, he felt as if he was nineteen again: watching from a distance, in total awe.

He wondered if he should run for it. He'd wondered about calling her after their lunch, but she hadn't seemed to particularly enjoy it and then the Heather stuff and the demands of the new job had taken over.

He was about to back away, when she looked up. Straight at him.

'Hello!' She sounded friendly enough.

'Hello. How's it going?'

'Fine.' She pushed her sunglasses up on to her head. 'Just taking a break from the article I'm editing about how *the*

make-up trend for hair this summer will be structure. Whatever that means. How about you?'

'A ten-minute breather. You know what I said about how
life would be easier at the *Post*?'

'Mmm.'

'Well, they conned me. Like someone asking you for
their Tube fare home. And I fell for it.'

Karen laughed sympathetically. 'I didn't want to say
anything, but you did seem a little bit naive about it
all.'

There was a tiny pause and then he said, 'Listen, sorry
I haven't been in touch since our lunch. I was hoping to
do it again sooner, but like I say I've been on the rack.'

'That's OK,' she shrugged.

'Do you fancy a coffee?'

'What, now?'

'If you still have time before you need to get back.'

'Not sure where to go for coffee round here,' she said.

'Let's have an ice cream, then,' Max exclaimed, nodding
at a nearby van. 'A 99?'

He thought she'd say no. But she stood up. 'Did you
know Mrs Thatcher invented 99s? Before she became a
politician?' she asked, starting to walk towards the van.

He did know, but he didn't want to be rude, so he said,
'No! Really? When? When she was a chemist?'

'Mmm, hmm. She was on a team that worked out how
to preserve Mister Softee. Another thing to be grateful to
her for. Or not.' She glanced at him sideways. 'I'm forget-
ting, Mrs Thatcher probably seems to you like Churchill
did to me. Ancient history.'

'Not at all,' he said indignantly. 'My mum used to frighten

me with her when I was a kid. Said she'd come and get me instead of the bogeyman.'

Karen laughed. 'Yes, I remember your mum, she was very . . .'

'Champagne socialist.'

'I didn't say that!' They both laughed. They ordered two ice creams from the van.

'I'll get these,' Max said, as she fumbled in her bag for her purse.

'No, I insist. My turn.'

'OK, the next lunch is on me though. Somewhere nice.' He had no idea where that flirtatious remark had come from. He hadn't planned on another lunch with Karen. Apart from anything, nobody lunched any more; the concept was a throwback to the boom years, like first-generation iPods and waiting lists for handbags. Happily, Karen seemed not to have registered it.

They sat down on a nearby bench.

'Well, this is decadent,' she said.

'Not by your standards. In the old days didn't you always polish off a bottle of wine at lunchtime?'

'Not just me! Everyone. Sometimes two. And then we'd go back and work our butts off all afternoon unearthing scoops, bringing governments to their knees.'

'And then you'd go to the pub and drink some more.'

'It's all true. Your generation are complete wusses in comparison to us: living on a diet of Red Bull and vitamin water. Not that I'm any better. I remember when I used to long to stay up until midnight on New Year's Eve. Now my first thought on receiving any party invitation is: "Oh God, I wonder how early we can leave."' She stopped short.

247

'Sorry. I don't want to frighten you with stories of family life. Your poor girlfriend won't thank me.'

At the mention of Heather, he flinched slightly. 'Jeremy's just the same,' he said cheerily, not wanting to go there. 'Says his idea of perfect happiness is going to bed at nine. So what news on your move?'

Karen looked wary. 'Nothing as yet.'

'You haven't resigned?'

She shook her head. 'The house sale might fall through. I don't want to be jobless until I know for sure.'

'Sounds like you don't want to be jobless at all.'

Karen bit into her Flake. He noticed the diamond ring flashing on her left hand. What had she said her husband was? Venture capitalist? Loaded.

'It worries me a bit that I can get so much satisfaction out of putting together a hundred pages a week on diets and star beauty secrets and the five best flip-flops on the market. But I do. Even with all Christine's histrionics. I love all the daily little challenges, and the people around me and being in control and . . .'

But Max was finishing her sentence.

'. . . And maybe you haven't felt in control so much recently.'

'How did you know?'

'Your husband was ill. My mum died of ovarian cancer. Seven years ago. I know what it's like. You try everything. Spend hours on the internet researching cures, working out who's the best doctor. But in the end, it's out of your hands. We were unlucky. Your husband was lucky. Neither of us could have had a say in the outcome.'

'I'm sorry. I didn't know.'

'No reason why you should.' Max shrugged, as the familiar wave of grief smacked him on the head. 'It just means I know a bit of what you must have gone through. Though for you it must have been one hundred times worse. With young children. I can't . . .' He shook his head.

'It was awful,' she said quietly.

They smiled sideways at each other. She had a lovely smile, perfect, small white even teeth. He imagined them biting down on . . .

Max! She was married and almost old enough to be his mother.

'So,' she said briskly, as if she'd sensed his thoughts and wanted to snuff them out. 'Have you seen any good films lately?'

Gemma was sitting in the 'chill-out' area in the mezzanine, looking out over the sun-streaked back streets of Clerkenwell, phone tucked under her chin as she talked to Bridget. But she couldn't concentrate on the conversation; all she could think about was the latest blow. They'd had a great weekend in Belfast for Alex's dad's sixty-fifth, but on the Monday when they returned she'd received crushing news. Bridget had a cyst on one of her ovaries. Which meant the egg extraction had to be postponed for the time being.

'We need the eggs to be in the best possible condition,' explained the clinic nurse, Sian. 'A cyst is usually only a temporary problem. We've given Bridget some tablets and they should zap it.'

'Everything will work out,' Bridget was assuring her now, down the phone. 'I can just *feel* it.'

'How can you feel it?' Gemma couldn't help the bitterness that crept in.

'I just . . . Don't be negative, Gems. That's not going to get us anywhere.'

'I'm not being negative. I've had a look online and there are tons of things we – I mean you – can do. Maitake mushrooms can help.'

'What?'

'I'll track some down. And pokeroot oil. And you should avoid body lotion because apparently that exacerbates cysts!'

'Yeah, yeah.' Bridget sounded as if she were fifteen and Mum was nagging her to do her homework.

'So how's it going with Massy?' Gemma said, realizing she'd better back off.

'Really well. He says I'm his dream lover and must have been put on this earth to make his happiness complete.'

'He sounds almost too good to be true.'

'He is. So did you fill in all the forms last time you went in?'

'Yes. Both of us.' A green form each, Gemma consenting to having an embryo placed inside her, Alex consenting to have his sperm used to make said embryo. Please let the day happen.

'Me too. And I had to write the baby a goodwill message. And write a portrait of myself. Which is kind of silly because of course the baby's going to know me. But it's nice to think if I was run over by a bus or something, my baby would have something personal to remember me by.'

'"*My* baby?"' Gemma felt herself stiffening.

'My baby. Your baby. Whoever's. We've been through all that. Let's just hope you don't let me down, eh? That you're able to carry it.'

Gemma felt giddy with unease. 'What about you letting *me* down?' she said, trying to sound breezy.

'Absolutely. Dervla went on a lot about that, how I mustn't feel guilty if my eggs weren't good enough, blah blah. As if I would. I mean it's not up to me, is it? How's Alex, anyway?'

'Busy. His trial's started so he's getting about three hours' sleep a night.' Gemma stared out of the window, breathing deeply, determined not to let Bridget know how unnerved she was. Far below she noticed a young woman standing on the pavement staring up at the flats. She had bleached blonde hair, an obviously fake tan and wore a short blue puffa jacket over white jeans. All very bling, not grungy Clerkenwell at all. There was a troubled look on her pretty, round face as she scanned the building.

'Alex works too hard, you know. And what about the flat sale?'

'Oh, we've had a victory on that. Sort of. He's only going to take twenty-five grand off now.'

'Alex hangs tough as usual.'

Gemma had had enough. 'Look, I'm really sorry, there's someone on the other line. I'll call you later, OK? 'Bye.'

She hung up feeling quite ill. What on earth was she doing? Was she doomed to a lifetime of Bridget referring to Chudney as hers? Interfering. Judging the decisions she and Alex made as parents. It was going to be a nightmare. Why hadn't she gone for the anonymous donor?

It was on days like these she wished she still worked, had

something to take her mind off her worries. She'd go for a swim, she decided. She grabbed her swimming bag, put on her raincoat and headed for the lift. Its doors opened and the blonde she'd seen on the street stepped out. She looked around, clearly unsure what to do or where to go. Normally Gemma followed the first rule of London life: never speak to anyone unless you have been introduced to them at a dinner party, and never make eye contact with anyone except blood relations. But now she heard herself saying, 'Can I help you?'

'Yes. I'm looking for Flat 15.'

'Flat 15? That's where I live.'

'Oh, right!' The woman smiled nervously. She had a northern accent. Gemma was unnerved. Was she selling something? Or a Christian?

'Can I help you?'

'I think my boyfriend and I are buying your flat. So I was wondering if I could take a look at it.'

'Your boyfriend? Nick Crex?'

'Yeah, that's him.'

'Oh.' Gemma was surprised. Obviously, she was pretty – very pretty – but Gemma had imagined someone a bit hipper. More edgy. Alexa Chung rather than Jordan's little, shyer sister.

'He really is, do you want me to prove it?' She wasn't annoyed, more pleading. As if she were used to the raised eyebrows. She opened her bag. 'Look, here's our gas bill. We've got all the utilities in both our names.'

Gemma glanced at it: an address in NW3 and Nicholas Crex and Kylie Baxter. 'So how come you haven't seen the flat before?'

'I only just found out he's buying it. And I was curious.'

'But your partner came and had a look on Friday,' Gemma said. 'Again.'

'Again? How many times has he been here?'

She looked stricken. Gemma felt suddenly uneasy. 'Um, a couple of times, I think. I'm not sure.'

'Right.' She paused. 'He said he's buying it as an investment. To rent out.'

'Does he? Well, he's certainly been putting us through the mill over it, so please tell him to make up his mind.'

'I see. I'm sorry.'

'It's all right,' Gemma said, touched by how pale she looked. 'Look, since you're here, come in.'

'Are you sure?'

'Absolutely.' As she headed back down the corridor, Kylie following, it occurred to her that perhaps this wasn't an altogether brilliant idea. That the vendor was meant to have absolutely no contact whatsoever with the seller, that Kylie might not like the flat and talk Nick Crex out of it. But sod it. You had to believe in karma. By being kind to Kylie, the rest of the sale would go swimmingly and the cyst would be cured too.

'Oh,' said Kylie, looking round. 'It's just one big . . . space, isn't it?'

'Mmm.' Gemma closed the door behind her. Already she was regretting her decision. She wondered if she could open a window, but that involved grappling with a scary-looking metal pole, which a buyer might find offputting. 'Tea, coffee?'

'I'd love a cup of tea. But only if you're having one.'

Gemma switched on the kettle. Kylie was still looking around, slightly bemused. 'Are there any curtains for those windows?'

'No.' Gemma decided not to tell the truth, that they looked into the idea years ago and dismissed it as too expensive. 'After all, we're not directly overlooked; there are flats over there but they're too far away to see anything. I mean maybe with a powerful telescope . . .'

'Right,' Kylie said dubiously. Gemma poured boiling water over an Earl Grey tea bag.

'Milk? Sugar?'

'Just milk, please.'

She added some. 'I'm having herbal.' For some reason she added, 'I'm trying to have a baby, so my husband and I are off tea and coffee. Anything caffeinated.'

'Really? Oh! I'll have to remember that when we start trying. Because I want to. Soon. Actually,' she lowered her voice as if the world was listening, 'I'm not that careful already. Leaving it to fate, if you know what I mean.'

*Are you indeed?* Gemma's bitterness was on full alert now. *Let's hope it'll be easy for* you. 'Mmm,' she said.

'Do you mind if I have a look upstairs?' Kylie asked.

'Sure,' Gemma snapped. She followed her up the spiral staircase. Kylie stood on the mezzanine floor, biting her lip.

'Is this what they'd call a loft?'

'Oh no,' Gemma assured her. 'Lofts are just one big space and we've got lots of rooms. Um, the bedrooms are through there.' She congratulated herself on being the kind of person who always made the bed in the morning, unlike Bridget, who said: 'You're only going to mess it up again

254

later, so why bother?' Kylie went into the master bedroom, looked around and came out chewing her lip.

'Did you see the walk-in wardrobe?' Gemma asked. 'Isn't it great? I don't know how I survived without it.'

'Don't you feel a bit funny sleeping up on that platform?'

'Oh no, you get used to it really quickly,' Gemma lied. 'It's fun.'

'I can see why you want to move if you want a baby.'

Silence. Gemma was furious with herself. Why on earth had she thought it was a good idea to let this woman in? She was going to run home to her rock-star boyfriend, point out the obvious flaws that – as a typical man – he'd not noticed, and the whole deal would be off.

'It's a wonderful part of London,' she said hastily. 'So many bars and restaurants and cool little boutiques.'

'Uh, huh. I don't know London that well, really. I miss home, to be honest. I'd like to move back, I don't see why we couldn't have a house in Burnley, but the rest of the band's here and . . .' To Gemma's consternation, a fat tear rolled down Kylie's plump, pink cheek and into her mug of tea. 'Oh, sorry!'

'It's OK. Do you want a tissue?'

Kylie nodded. The tears were really coming now. Gemma hurried into the bathroom and came back with a wad of Kleenex.

'I'm being silly, I know, it's just . . . it's all so hard at the moment. I came to London with Nicky because I love him but I never see him and when I do he's grumpy because the new album's going so badly and I miss my mum and . . .' She blew her nose heavily into the tissue. 'I'm sorry. It's just all getting to be a bit much.'

'Don't worry,' Gemma said, gesturing towards the sofa. 'Here. Come and sit down.'

'I'm keeping you. You must have places to go.'

'I'm in no rush.'

They ended up having two more cups of tea. Kylie confided in Gemma how alien she found London. How the girls in the salon mimicked her northern accent. How she was terrified because she kept reading in the news about all these stabbings. How Burnley was rough too but at least she knew her neighbours, felt people were looking out for her, and her mum and sister were just up the road. How lonely she was sitting in her luxurious flat every evening waiting for Nick to get back from the studio.

'That's why I want a baby. At least then I'd have some company.'

Even though Gemma still hated her for assuming a baby would come so easily, she couldn't help feeling sorry for her. 'I know what you mean. Though . . . you're very young, if you don't mind me saying. Maybe you just need to make a few more friends first.'

'That's what my sister says, but it's hard. The girls at work ask me out sometimes, but I just feel weird when I do go out with them because I'm not on the pull like them. And I'm not really a clubs and loud noise and booze and pills person anyway, I like watching *Hollyoaks*.' Suddenly she stood up. 'Anyway, listen, I've kept you long enough. Bored you rigid most likely. Thanks for letting me have a look round. It's . . . er . . . it's lovely.'

'We've been very happy living here,' Gemma said.

'And where are you moving to?'

'To St Albans. Just a bit north of London. Nice family area, you know.'

'Oh.' A look of yearning in Kylie's eyes. 'I think that's what I'd like too. Anyway.' She held out a hand. Amazing nails, Gemma noted, in fuchsia pink. 'Thanks again, it's so kind of you to take the time.'

'I'll come out with you. I was going for a swim. Get me fit for having the baby.'

They travelled down in the lift together, both feeling a bit awkward after this slew of shared confidences. At the door to the building, Kylie said, 'Sorry, which way is the Tube?'

Gemma was going in that direction but she didn't really want to walk together. They'd had their brief moment of intimacy and she didn't want to prolong it. So she said, 'Um, turn right, then left, then right again.'

'Oh yes! I'll find it. Thanks again. 'Bye.' A shy hand was raised and Kylie hurried off, pulling her jacket snugly around her round frame. Gemma waited until she was a safe distance ahead and then set off herself. A light rain started to fall.

Dearest Gwen,

So lovely to hear all your news. The girls do sound like a handful, though they look terribly sweet. I can't wait to come and see them. Is Amelia enjoying school? I can't believe my little goddaughter knows how to read and write already. How quickly time passes.

I am well, thanks for asking. The sale of the house is still going ahead. Of course I have mixed feelings about this but I do see if Sebby is going to rescue the travel company he invested in and Alfie is going to start pre-prep next term, there is no alternative given how poor state schools are in the area. I haven't heard any more from Richie – I honestly didn't expect to though, it was just a one-off thing. Now I've started the job hunt in earnest. Sadly an heiress's life is not an option. Hope to hear from you again soon.

G xx

The email pinged off. Grace opened the kitchen cupboard. Ever since the dinner she'd been eating and eating. Dieting had got her nowhere, after all. She'd bought some fresh cream yesterday – maybe she'd have that on a bowl of Frosties. After all, she needed some sustenance before she commenced her daily search of job websites. So far, she'd had no luck at all: virtually nothing seemed available apart from jobs as manual labourers in farms round about, or secretarial positions which demanded knowledge of Excel and XP. Grace was a dab hand at navigating a website, but she had no idea what those things meant.

She scrolled down the page, wondering what she'd have for lunch, when her eye was caught by something a bit different.

Gift Shop. Kingsbridge. Assistant needed. Must be available to work Saturdays. Call Carol.

A gift shop. Well, that was something she could do. Might be fun. All sorts of people coming in and out. Grace could advise them on what birthday presents to buy.

Yes, she liked the sound of that.

She picked up the phone and dialled Carol's number.

# 23

Karen stood in front of the mirror, looping a heavy hoop earring through her left earlobe. Today she was having lunch with Max again and she wanted to look her best.

After their halting start, lunch had become a regular thing. Two days after they'd bumped into each other in the park, they'd had tabbouleh in a Lebanese café. The following week shawarma in an Iranian restaurant, followed two days later by burgers and fries. The third week, they'd gone macrobiotic Thai.

In that period Karen had started to make some changes to her life. The weather inspired her. It was only early April, but one perfect spring day was merging into another; in the evenings the air was heavy with the smell of neighbours' barbecues. When the wind was in the east, the strains of James Blunt and Duffy (no hip hop here, this *was* St Alban's) floated over the back fence.

During her commute, she abandoned her usual routine of reading all the papers on the way in and making to-do lists on the way back. Instead she popped in her iPod speakers, shut her eyes and listened to albums by new bands she'd downloaded the night before. Because suddenly Karen wanted to listen to music again. Once it had been the most important thing in the world to her, after all. She'd spent hours sitting in her bedroom in North Wales, rain lashing on the window-panes, listening to Adam and the Ants,

Queen, Duran Duran, the Human League, songs she'd painstakingly taped from the radio on her tiny cassette player. She used to press pause constantly so she could scribble down the lyrics in her notebook. Now of course she could have found them in seconds on the internet – but that wasn't the point.

The point was that in those days music had excited her. Why had that stopped? She wanted to recapture that sense of curiosity. She wanted to know what films were playing at the cinema and to have considered opinions on the latest developments in the Middle East. To be like the old Karen, the one Max remembered, who'd had the world at her fingertips.

After their awkward first few encounters, they now talked and talked, words pouring over each other in their rush to get out. Even before the cancer, she and Phil had never been like that. They discussed how they must get around to having someone look at the leaky shed roof and that they needed to book a holiday, the logistics of getting Eloise to drama club and Bea to her flute lesson, the fact that they ought to invite their new neighbours round for a drink. But they never bounced ideas off each other. They existed. They hadn't lived.

It was crazy, really. She shouldn't be listening to Kasabian when there was so much to do regarding the move. But it would all work out somehow, Karen reasoned.

With the girls, she was unusually jolly, almost self-consciously so, as if someone was watching her. When Bea came home from school with a letter asking her to create a Japanese geisha costume by Monday, she just rolled her eyes and said, 'Oh, all right then,' when normally she would have screamed. When Eloise asked for sweet-corn, a chef's hat and six fresh tomatoes for the following morning, she didn't complain, just got in the car and drove to the nearest superstore.

Karen wasn't stupid. She knew she was behaving – in all probability – like Grace Porter-Healey nursing a crush on the vicar. But heavens, why not indulge herself a little? Why not enjoy the lost sensation of having something to get up for in the mornings? Of looking forward to whatever the day might bring.

She studied her reflection again. She'd dug out the high boots from Bertie that she'd bought on a whim but almost never wore because they aggravated her sciatica, and was wearing them over slim-fitting trousers (almost leggings but not quite, as she worried she was too old for them) that showed off her shapely legs.

A flowery top from Primark that she'd treated herself to the other day when she'd popped in ostensibly to buy some tights for the girls. A handful of chunky necklaces and bracelets from Accessorize that she'd snapped up during a commando-style raid when her train home had been delayed fifteen minutes. Once Karen had spent hours loitering round shops, fingering fabrics, trying things on – now she shopped like a man, in-out and no messing.

She wondered if Phil would comment on her funked-up appearance. But he barely glanced at her as she walked into the kitchen. As usual, he was eating his breakfast standing up next to the radio so as to catch every word of the *Today* programme. Normally Karen wanted to scream at him for doing this; today she let it ride.

*

Sophie, on the other hand, raised an eyebrow when she entered the office.

'You look gorgeous. What's up?'

'Nothing,' Karen said, pleased to have been noticed, but annoyed that her looking good was deemed worthy of comment.

'I haven't seen that top before.'

'Haven't you? It's ancient.'

'Oh, right. Do you fancy lunch today?'

'Um, I'd love to. But I'm lunching a PR.'

'Oh yeah? You're always lunching PRs right now.' Sophie sounded understandably suspicious. Lunch with a PR meant two courses in an upmarket restaurant where, despite all the goodies on the menu, the craziest you could go with your order was a salad and a grilled steak if you didn't want to be dismissed as Mama Cass. You made desultory conversation and at the end of it all were shown a range of hair products or new lipsticks which you were expected to ooh and aah over as if they were the Turin shroud, before hurrying back to the office with a promise to feature them in the magazine to find two thousand new emails waiting for you.

Karen was still trying to think how to explain herself when Sophie's phone rang. Within seconds she was far away. 'So Natasha had an epidural. I mean, I know, each to her own, but I really don't see why such a thing should be necessary. I mean, women managed for millions of years before such things were invented . . . I know, but a natural birth is proven to help bonding with the baby . . . I *am* hiring a Tens machine and I think breathing techniques will seriously help.'

Breathing techniques. Yeah, right.

*

They were meeting at a Japanese place about half a mile from the office. Karen had grown fond of venues like that, slightly off the beaten track. Max was sitting at a corner table waiting for her.

'You look amazing,' he said, also looking surprised, but rather thrilled too.

'Me! What? This? Oh, thanks.' Karen's face flamed up as if she'd opened an oven door. She twisted her head to receive Max's air kisses, except they weren't air kisses, his lips brushed softly against each cheek. 'Sad old lady!' she reprimanded herself, as, heart fluttering, she unfolded her napkin and sat down.

'Now you look much more like the Karen I remember.'

'What do you mean?'

'Well . . . brighter somehow. Don't take this the wrong way, but younger.'

'Just had my hair cut,' she muttered, again both flattered and dismayed. 'The noodles are great here.'

'Then I'll try them. And a beer?'

'Why not?'

'So have you told work yet?' he asked, once they'd ordered.

'Told them what?'

'That you're leaving.'

'No.' Karen cringed. 'I know I should but Christine's away on a spa freebie and she'd kill me if I didn't hand the resignation to her in person.'

'Karen!'

'I know. She's back next week, I'll tell her then.'

'You're going to have to. Because she's going to make you do your four months' notice, you know that.'

'I know, I just . . . I sort of want to pretend this isn't happening.'

Max looked at her for a moment, then said, 'Can I ask you something?'

'I may not answer.'

'When you said that about New Year's Eve. Not wanting to stay up until midnight. Did you really mean it?'

Karen laughed. 'Max. One day I hope you will have children and you will understand.'

'But my friends with children still go out. Not all the time, admittedly, but . . . And you've got a nanny or whatever, haven't you, so no babysitting excuses.'

'Phil doesn't . . .' She looked at her newly manicured hands, confused. 'Phil gets tired and he doesn't drink any more and he's very particular about his diet and he needs a lot of sleep, so . . . It just doesn't seem worth it. And I do go out . . . With other mums from the school sometimes. And Sophie and I used to have the odd drink before she got up the duff.'

'How about the cinema?'

'Why was the DVD player invented?'

Max looked perplexed. Bless him. One day he'd recognize the invention of lovefilm.com as one of the greatest contributions to society since disposable nappies.

'I'm sorry,' he said. 'It's just I remember you as such a party girl. So vibrant. And . . . don't take it the wrong way, you seem much more yourself now, but the first time I bumped into you in the canteen you did seem so much . . . more serious.'

Karen felt a tingling in her sinuses. She looked away.

'Maybe you need to get out a little more?'

'I . . .'

'Have you head of the Vertical Blinds?'

'I . . . uh . . .' She'd *heard* of them. 'Isn't the lead singer a junkie?'

'They're the ones. I'm going to a gig of theirs on Friday. The lead singer's just come out of rehab and they're doing a very exclusive set in Camden. I had to use all my media muscle to wangle tickets. Do you want to come?'

'I'll . . .' *Have to check with Phil.* But she wasn't going to say that. She swallowed. 'Yes, I'd love to go.'

Max's pale complexion turned faintly pink.

'Good.'

Karen knew it was too good to be true. 'Will your girl-friend be coming?'

'We split up. About a week ago.'

'Oh! I'm sorry.' She couldn't remember when she'd last heard such good news.

'Don't be, it was overdue.' He gestured at his bowl. 'Shall we eat?'

'Let's,' Karen said with a big smile.

# 24

Carol at All Thinges Nice had been very friendly on the phone and said she'd love Grace to come in for an interview. 'Though actually I'm closing the shop for a couple of weeks,' she said in a squeaky posh voice. 'We're off on holiday to Antigua. Could you come in a fortnight Friday? Look forward to meeting you.'

In that fortnight, Grace recommended a new diet. She decided to go for one she'd read about online, involving only citrus fruits and protein. After two weeks of it, marred by only one lapse involving an entire packet of Rice Krispies she'd stashed for emergencies at the back of a cupboard, she'd lost ten pounds. So she was in high spirits as she drove to Kingsbridge along narrow country lanes. Spring was definitely arriving, the lilac trees would flower soon, the witch hazel was already out, lambs were frolicking in the fields and the sunlight was pale lemon.

Richie Prescott hadn't called. But that was all right. Grace kept remembering all the things she hadn't liked about him: his blotchy complexion, the fact he was her age but appeared at least five years older, the fact he'd been married before. No. She was better off without Richie. She was going to pursue a career in retail.

All Thinges Nice was on a side street and had a candy pink façade. Its windows were strung with feather-shaded fairy lights and displayed a pile of pink cushions, a pink dressing table topped with a pink mirror and a huge pink bamboo birdcage. Pushing open the door, Grace was assailed by an odour of vanilla, lavender and sandalwood. The caressing tones of Enya tinkled out of speakers. She saw a lace-covered table piled high with magenta silk scarves and fuchsia velvet hats. Grace stared at a rack of birthday cards adorned with glitter and sparkly studs. She glanced at a price sticker. *Five pounds?* Surely that couldn't be right. But it was all terribly pretty, terribly feminine. She reached out to stroke a peach silk camisole.

'Can I help you?'

A tall *thin* woman with long, blonde hair, in a jewelled tunic and jeans, appeared from behind a carved screen. She looked at Grace dubiously, as if she might steal some scented writing paper.

'I'm Grace Porter-Healey. Here for my interview.'

Blue eyes scanned her. 'Oh, Grace! Of course. Hello. I'm Carol.' She extended a skeletal hand. 'It's so lovely to meet you. Welcome to my little empire.' She giggled. 'It's been going about six months – my youngest started school and I had nothing to do, so Bartie, my husband, put up the cash to start this little business. Not ideal timing, what with the credit crunch and everything, but it's always been my dream to own a shop.'

'It's lovely,' Grace breathed.

'I'm so glad you like it.' Carol paused for a second, then said, 'Now, listen, Grace. I don't want to disappoint you when you've come all this way but unfortunately the role of assistant has actually been filled.'

'Oh.'

'I'm so sorry. I tried to call. I didn't get any reply.'

'The answerphone was on,' Grace said. A stone was lodged in the base of her throat. She was too fat for All Things Nice.

'Really? Maybe I dialled the wrong number.' Carol's eyes grew bigger by the second. She put her hand on Grace's arm. 'But listen, Grace. Not all is lost. There is a job you could do for me. I'd only need you for a week or so but it would be an enormous help. And I'd pay you. Cash in hand. Can't do the minimum wage I'm afraid, credit crunch and all that, but I could do six pounds an hour.'

'I . . .'

'It's this way,' Carol said. She led Grace through the crammed shop floor and down a narrow dark flight of stairs into a windowless basement, crammed with cardboard boxes.

'We're putting together eco gift baskets,' she explained. 'One bottle of seaweed shower gel, one cake of soap, one flannel. You need to put them all in one of these wicker baskets, on top of some hay, cover them in polythene and tie a lovely ribbon. We've got about four hundred to do.' She winked. 'I bought a job lot on the internet. With the packaging it'll be a six hundred per cent mark-up.'

'Oh,' said Grace.

'Do you want to start now or to come back tomorrow?'

Grace shrugged. 'I might as well start now.'


'By the way, I won't be back until late tonight,' Karen said casually over breakfast on Friday morning.

Phil looked up, annoyed. 'But *I'll* be home late. I've got yoga.'

'Why didn't you tell me?' Karen said. She was in a vile

mood anyway, because there was no real coffee. No one had told her they were close to running out, so she hadn't ordered more and now she was having to make do with Nescafé, which she hated. Plus her high boots were pinching her toes and it wasn't even eight yet. She was worried about her outfit – a kaftan over leggings, set off with strings of beads. Less than an hour ago she'd thought it gave her an air of jet-set chic but now she suspected she looked like a clown. Then there were her nails – she'd spent all yesterday evening applying polish, then removing it because it looked as if it had been applied by a drunk five-year-old, then reapplying it, then removing it, until the carefully purchased jar was half empty, whereupon she'd decided she was never bothering again.

How could she go to a gig with Max? People would think she'd mistaken the venue for a bingo hall and warn her there was no Stannah stairlift.

'I did tell you. Yoga's been changed to Friday evenings,' Phil said. 'Anyway, I assumed you'd be home at the usual time. You always are.'

'We'll have to see if Ludmila can babysit,' she sighed. 'Go and knock on her door.' Ludmila never surfaced before ten.

'I can't do that. She might think I was making a pass. Where are *you* going, anyway?'

'What's a pass?' asked Bea.

'Nothing,' Karen said. 'I've got a leaving do. Remember Jamila? She's off to a new job.'

'Oh, right,' said Phil. As she suspected, he couldn't remember Jamila at all. Just as well, since she'd actually left the *Post* to freelance four years ago.

Why wasn't she telling Phil the truth about where she was going, Karen wondered as she took her seat on the train, having bribed Ludmila with double pay to babysit. They weren't living in Afghanistan, it was quite legal to go out with an old friend – male or female.

It was legal. But was it innocent?

Once you were married, you didn't have friends of the opposite sex any more. They were the first thing to go after marriage – well maybe not the *first*, that was probably shaving your legs regularly. But friendships were not long afterwards. After all, they only really started if there was a batsqueak of flirtation there, and once you were off the market, that flirtation seemed wrong. In any case, all her old male friends were coupled off too now, and seeing them one on one was somehow taboo. In marriedland you had foursomes in the unkinky sense, or women only. Karen missed those insights into how male brains worked.

She missed friendships full stop. Even before Phil got ill, the girls and work had already meant she rarely had the time or energy to lavish on her mates. It was fine, she told herself, Phil was her friend, the only person on the planet who cared – or pretended to care – that Christine had humiliated her in conference or Eloise's teacher had smirked at the birthday cake she'd made. She'd heard about his business, the companies he was going to invest in, his secretary's new boyfriend. A lot of it had been boring, but it didn't matter. A lot of *life* was boring, but when you had someone else's attention it gave it the veneer of meaning. Of substance.

But Phil's illness had changed all that. All the trivial stuff that had been the fabric of their lives became irrelevant.

They had one sole focus, defeating the cancer. And the cancer had robbed her of Phil, just like another woman might have done; though Phil – surely – would never have got involved with another woman; his faithful nature was one of the things Karen loved best about him.

So how was it that now she often wished he had run off with someone else? Because then she could have left him without anyone thinking worse of her.

Karen shivered as her train pulled into King's Cross. She wasn't going to analyse this. She was just going to enjoy a night out. Go with the flow.

Grace managed to put together eight gift baskets that morning. It wasn't nearly as easy as it looked. It was tricky to pull the polythene tight over the basket and tie a neat raffia ribbon. The hay made her sneeze and the odour of seaweed left a sour taste at the back of her throat. The scratchy baskets pricked her fingers. And her stomach was rumbling. There was a baker's down the road. Grace kept wondering if it sold sausage rolls. She wondered if she'd be allowed a lunch break. She wondered about telling Carol that she had a PhD in classical civilization.

'How are you doing?' Carol asked, sticking her head round the door.

'Fine!' Grace said breezily.

'Um.' Carol's nose wrinkled. 'You need a bit less hay in each basket, Grace. It all costs. You'll have to take some out of each.'

'And redo the polythene cover?' Grace asked, horrified.

'Afraid so. Sorry, Grace. Good thing I checked on you, eh?'

The highlight of Grace's day was lunch, though to her horror it didn't come until three o'clock.

'Sorry, Grace, I'd forgotten all about you down here,' Carol laughed. 'Why don't you pop out for half an hour?' She looked at Grace's work. After redoing the first six gift boxes, she'd managed sixteen more. 'Oh my God! Grace. What's with these ribbons? They're a bit . . . What can I say? They need to be smarter than this.'

'Oh.' Grace looked up at her dejectedly. She'd never been good with her hands, but she'd done her best.

'Never mind,' Carol tutted. 'See you back here at half three.'

To comfort herself, Grace had two sausage rolls. And a packet of crisps. And a doughnut. She sat on a wall, feeling the spring sunshine on her arms. She had a job. Well. Sort of. But if she worked really hard at it, then maybe Carol would overcome her prejudices and realize Grace was a natural shop assistant.

*You could be aiming higher than shop assistant*, she told herself uncertainly. *You have a PhD.* But a PhD in a useless subject. She could teach again, she supposed, but the thought of a room full of young, attractive students sniggering at her was more than she could bear.

She'd start another diet tomorrow. Carol would recognize her talents. She'd promote her to the shop floor, then maybe to assistant manager. Together they'd create some kind of franchise. Take over the south-west. Then England. Then Europe, then America . . .

Carol was waiting for her at the door. She looked serious.

'He-llo Grace,' she said, as if Grace were the village idiot.

'Hope you had a nice break. Now, listen, sweetheart, don't take this the wrong way but I've been inspecting your work. And it's really just not up to snuff I'm afraid. I don't think All Thinges Nice is quite the place for you, my dear. So . . .' She pressed a twenty-pound note into Grace's hand. 'Take this, my angel and let's call it quits. There'll be a better job for you somewhere else. Maybe in an old folks' home? All right? No hard feelings.'

And the pink door was slammed in a stunned Grace's face.

Tears blinded her eyes so much, she could barely drive home. She couldn't even work in the basement of a stupid gift shop. What was wrong with her? She was useless, unlovable. All her education had been for nothing.

Grace focused on biscuits. She'd stop at Mac Maschler's shop in the village and buy some Bourbons. And some HobNobs. Jammie Dodgers. An enormous loaf of bread. And she'd eat it all in one vast gulp. Maybe be sick. And then eat some more.

She pulled up outside the shop, formulating her excuses for Mac. '*Guests are coming. The Drakes are paying a visit.*' She was sure he didn't believe her lies, but she didn't care.

But a sign on the shop door read *Closed*.

Grace stared at it in disbelief. She got out. She rattled the handle. But it was true. How dare Mac? Where could he have gone? It was only four. She'd have to drive back to Kingsbridge. Go somewhere relatively anonymous like Somerfield, where she could pile her basket high. Pretend she had a houseful of guests to feed.

But there wasn't time now. It was the dogs' suppertime. She couldn't leave them hungry. She'd go home, feed them, then return to Somerfield, where she'd buy enough food to last her a month. Well, a week anyway.

She roared up Chadlicote's drive, the Mini's throttle sending flocks of startled birds out of the hedgerows. As she embarked on the home straight, she saw a black Bentley parked in front of the house. Two men were standing in front of it, in dark suits. Grace slowed down. Their faces came into focus.

One was a tall, dark, rather sad-looking man in a pinstriped suit. The other was Richie Prescott.

# 25

The Vertical Blinds gig took place in a tiny theatre off Camden Road. Karen was really enjoying it. Yes, the music was loud, but it didn't make her ears ache. It was really very catchy. She felt herself moving in time to it, then jumping up and down a bit, even singing along to some of the choruses. It helped that she and Max had been out to dinner at an Indian, first, where she had downed three bottles of Cobra, and now had another plastic pint glass in her hand, but still . . . This was her, she thought, as she applauded wildly at the end of a song. She'd rediscovered the real Karen. The Karen who liked noise; hot, dark crowded rooms; being surrounded by strangers. Fields, open spaces were never going to do it for her. *But Karen, you're forty-one. You can't start attending gigs now. Next thing you know you'll be putting your hair in bunches and wearing 'Hello Kitty' T-shirts.*

*If you left Phil you could do whatever you wanted.*

*No, I couldn't*, she told the devil on her shoulder. *Because I'd still have the girls. Broken-hearted girls at that. Girls who almost lost their dad once, who adore him.*

She glanced at Max, sweat shining on his forehead. She couldn't ignore it. He was stirring up all sorts of needs in her, needs she'd assumed had died forever, needs she thought mature adults just learned to live without but which now she realized were as vital as breathing.

Ridiculous. He was practically a baby. Karen had

babies of her own. Who would always come first.

At the end of the evening she'd peck him on the cheek and thank him and run for the last train home. She'd cool off the lunches. She'd be leaving London for good in a couple of months anyway. She'd make a new life for herself in the country, she'd join a book group, maybe learn to ride and . . .

'You OK?' Max shouted in her ear.

'Fine. Just hot.'

'Do you want another drink?'

'No, no, thanks. I'm fine. I . . . Oh, shit!'

A man pushing past her carrying six plastic pints of beer had stumbled, soaking her front, her hair, her feet.

'Sorry, darling! Sorry, love. You all right?' He was dabbing her with his denim jacket. Max pulled a tissue out of his pocket and started to dab too. His hand reached a little too close to her breasts, and he snatched it back. Relieved to see someone had taken over, the man disappeared into the crowd with another mouthed 'Sorry!'

'You're soaked,' Max shouted over the drone of the bass guitar.

'Thanks for stating the obvious. I must stink. How am I going to get home like this?' She should be cross, but actually she found it quite funny.

'Have you got anything you could change into?'

'Funnily enough, no.'

There was a pause. On stage the music roared, but Max and Karen didn't hear it as he said, slightly too casually, 'I only live up the road. You could always come back to mine and borrow a T-shirt.'

*

276

Max's flat was a studio in a block of flats next door to a taxidermist's shop. Through the grilled windows, Karen spotted a stuffed owl, wings poised for flight, several stags' heads, a snarling fox. She hugged herself. Places like this were what London was all about. Entering the flat, however, her buoyancy evaporated. How studenty, she thought, taking in the framed posters on the wall, piles of CDs and old newspapers everywhere, a vast HDTV screen. At least it was impressively tidy. And why were there candles everywhere?

'Sorry, it's a bit of a tip,' he said apologetically.

'It's not, not at all,' she said – thinking, *Candles?* Were they already there? Or was he planning this? As if sensing her thoughts, Max took a box of matches from the mantelpiece and began to light them.

'Would you like a drink?' he said over his shoulder.

'Well, seeing as I'm here.' She'd drunk too much already. But she was scared. Her heart fluttered like sails in the breeze.

'A glass of champagne?'

'*Champagne?*'

'It's all I've got in the fridge. Apart from beer. And you've probably seen enough beer for one night.'

'I think I should get changed first.'

'Oh yeah, I need to find you a T-shirt. Come and have a look.'

Swallowing, she followed him into his bedroom. A neatly made bed. A pile of books by it. No visible trace of porn mags or Nintendos. Max bent over and opened a drawer. Glancing over his shoulder, Karen saw a jumbled mess of T-shirts, boxer shorts and ties.

'Drawers not as tidy as the room,' she said.

Max laughed. 'Nicely spotted. But I didn't think you'd be looking in my drawers.'

They both realized the implications. Marx had been hoping she'd come back with him. Blushing faintly, he pulled out a white T-shirt. 'Will this do?'

'Great.'

'I'll wait for you.'

'OK,' she said. He left the room. Karen exhaled deeply, as if she were seven centimetres dilated. She pulled off her kaftan, which reeked like a brewery, and put it into her bag. She stood there for a moment in her black lace bra, holding Max's T-shirt. Gap. A bit crumpled.

'Are you OK?' he shouted through the door.

'Fine,' she said. 'Only . . .'

'I can find you another one.'

'Maybe you should do that,' she said. As he opened the door, she stepped forward and suddenly she was in his arms. His tongue was in her mouth. Karen's heart was beating so hard, she thought it would pop out of her chest. They kissed and kissed. She felt as if she were shedding a skin, the old calloused layer that proclaimed her a wife and mother, and returning to the Karen she used to be, the one who danced all night on tables and still was at her desk at ten a.m., the one who had overcome her demons and had everything to look forward to, the one who had passionate feelings. The old Karen, whose breasts tingled as if they were electrified when kissed and who was suffused with a sweet overwhelming wetness lower down as she pulled Max towards the bed and down on top of her.

*

Grace woke early. She was starving. She hadn't eaten a thing last night, not after the conversation she'd had with Richie Prescott while his dark-haired friend, who turned out to be a South African called Anton Beleek, was looking round.

'I'm really sorry I haven't been in touch, Grace,' he said. 'I've just been terribly busy, you know. Not that that's an excuse, but I'm not always the most organized of chaps. Love to make it up to you, though.'

Grace muttered something non-committal, her face flaming. All right, he still had a face like a tomato and terrible teeth. But he was apologizing to her. Perhaps she'd been unreasonable to dismiss him so harshly. It had only been a couple of weeks and people *were* busy.

'Perhaps we could go out another time.'

Grace jumped.

'Really?'

'Of course! Don't look so worried, I don't bite!'

Anton Beleek was striding ahead of them, up to the gazebo.

'Fantastic grounds,' he said over his shoulder in his whip-crack voice. 'So much that could be done with them.'

'I had plans,' Grace said, panting as she tried to talk and walk. 'But my mother got ill and . . . you know.'

'They really could be restored to something marvellous. Do you know Garberton House at Yelverton? Reminds me of that, except of course this is on a grander scale.'

'I must go and have a look at it,' Grace said.

'You should. People who are buying, are they keen gardeners?'

'Well . . . they're keen but . . .'

'Hmm. Hope they don't ruin it.' Anton strode on to the gazebo. 'Marvellous view,' he called over his shoulder.

'So Anton is a friend of yours?'

'Old friend,' said Richie, between gasps of breath. 'As I said, very keen on Tudor architecture. And gardens, Lord love him.'

'I see,' said Grace.

They'd refused a cup of tea and left around six, by which time the dogs were howling for supper. Grace, however, didn't eat. Thank heavens Mac's shop had been closed. And that she'd been sacked – if she hadn't lost that silly job, she would have missed the visit. She ate nothing that night. As she mused on fate's vagaries, the phone began ringing at her bedside. She snatched it up.

'Hello.'

'Good morning, Richie P here. Hope I didn't wake you!'

'Oh no.' He *must* be keen.

'Well, sorry to call at crack of dawn but I have something rather unexpected to put to you. Anton adored Chadlicote and, to my total surprise, he called me late last night and asked if he might put an offer on the table for it.'

'An offer?'

'Yes. He'd like to buy it.'

'But the Drakes are buying it!'

'He'd offer you five thousand pounds more.'

'Gosh! I don't . . . No, I'm terribly sorry but we're on the verge of exchanging. I couldn't let the Drakes down like that.'

'But you'd get five thousand pounds more.'

'But the Drakes want the house so much. They'll restore it. Love it. Bring up children here.'

'Anton would do all that.'

'He doesn't have a family.'

'How do you know?'

'I could just tell.'

'But he might one day. Look, Grace, give it a thought . . . Anton's a super chap, well, you saw that yourself. And he has a lot of money. He really could do wonderful things for Chadlicote.' There was a tiny pause and then Richie said, 'Anyway, that wasn't really why I was calling. I was wondering if you fancied another dinner some time.'

She hadn't seen this coming. 'I'd . . . That sounds lovely.'

'Jolly good. I'll book somewhere and let you know. Now think about this Anton business. Just think about it. No pressure, but every penny helps in my experience. Toodle-oo, then.'

Karen was on the morning train to King's Cross. She'd had four hours' sleep, but her eyes glowed and her skin tingled. She was a bad woman, she told herself. Bad wife. Bad mother. Creeping in at three and crawling into bed beside her husband, straight from another man's bed. Her gorgeous children asleep downstairs. And all she could think about was Max's hands on her breasts, her thighs, his tongue probing inside her, her straddling him and slipping on to him. She'd fallen asleep with a huge smile on her face as she replayed it all, Phil lying asleep beside her.

And then she'd woken up and showered and gone downstairs and barked out orders about homework and lost games kit and flute lessons as if none of this had ever happened.

But that was that, she told herself. She couldn't let it happen again. Once could be excused as a moment of madness, dismissed as a stupid, drunken one-night stand that no one except her and Max need ever know about. But if she saw him again . . .

Her phone rang in her bag and she felt punched in the stomach. Her hands shook as she fumbled to pull it out. Amazingly, for one of the first times ever, she managed to answer before it switched to voicemail.

'Hello, Max,' she said, marvelling at how collected she sounded.

'Hi. How are you?'

'Very well.'

'Good. Me too. I'm . . . very good. Tired. But . . . Good.'

'Glad to hear it,' she said, half terrified, half over-joyed.

'Listen, I was wondering. Can I see you again? Soon? Like tonight?'

'I . . .'

If she said no, she could be excused on grounds of a temporary lapse of sanity. It wouldn't have been an affair, just a fling. No one would ever know. She would resign from her job, move to Devon, spend the rest of her life a paragon of the PTA and baking cakes. All she had to tell him was thanks, but no thanks, it had been wonderful, but it had been a one-off thing.

'Tonight? After work?'

Was Phil doing anything tonight? Not as far as she knew.

'Tonight would be great.'

# 26

Max and Karen had seen each other three times in the past week. Well, 'seen' was a bit of an understatement, as she'd also touched him all over, tasted him, smelt him, listened to him whisper all the things he'd like to do to her. She'd managed to persuade either Ludmila or Phil to hold the fort and then she'd hurried from work to his flat, where they'd fallen upon each other like starving animals.

Whenever she looked in the mirror she wondered how something so momentous could be happening to someone who'd just filled in an online shopping list that included own-brand bleach and ant-killer. She felt like a character in a film. Who would she cast as herself, she wondered, as she sewed back a button on to her jacket that had been missing for three years. Maybe Natalie Portman? Karen laughed at her vanity. But she felt gorgeous right now: gorgeous and young and invincible.

She was in this altered state when she went to Christine and told her that – regretfully – she was resigning. She felt like a fly on the wall as Christine gave her a look so outraged it must have burned at least 2,000 calories. Karen muttered platitudes about how much she'd miss working with such an inspirational boss, how much she'd love to freelance for the supplement, how she'd do everything possible to assist in finding her replacement and how of course she understood she was tied to four months' notice.

She should have been heartbroken, but instead she just felt mildly amused. It was perverse, because of course resigning was acknowledging that soon they really would be off to Devon and that would be the end of her and Max. But she somehow couldn't acknowledge that.

On a high consisting of plenty of sex mixed up with guilt, she ploughed through her work, commissioning dozens of new ideas. If she wasn't having a stolen lunch with Max, she went for a vigorous workout in the company gym. She'd done her expenses, which dated back to 2008. At home she'd tidied the kitchen drawers and thrown out all her laddered tights and single socks.

She didn't know why. She couldn't have cared less about pleasing either Christine or Phil, but she needed to focus on those details of her life she could control when the bigger picture seemed so crazy. Dates for exchange and completion had finally been set, but when Phil talked about the move she just smiled and nodded, letting none of the normal anger and frustrations he provoked even begin to penetrate the cloud of happiness that surrounded her.

But she couldn't get away at the weekend. Max had told her not to worry, he was busy with family things. But she couldn't help it now. It was only Saturday afternoon, but she wanted to hear his voice so badly. The girls were watching lowbrow trash in the playroom; Phil was in the den watching golf, as usual. She'd picked up her phone, then put it down, about six times before she finally took the plunge and called him.

'Max, it's . . . er, me, Karen.'

'Oh. Hello.'

'Can you talk? I mean, I know it's a weekend but . . .' She felt suddenly idiotic. 'I just . . .'

'Actually, it's not a good time.'

He sounded like a robot. Karen thought she might throw up. Was this really the same man who'd been licking her nipples on Friday, stroking her hair? She shouldn't have called him.

'Sorry. I . . .'

'I'll call you later, OK? 'Bye.'

''Bye.' Karen's heart felt as if it had been gouged by an icepick. She couldn't remember ever feeling so snubbed. Or so stupid.

Eloise's voice ripped through her self-pity. 'Mum! Bea's a cow. She won't let me watch *The Secret of Moonacre*, she wants to watch *Pretty Woman*.'

'*Pretty Woman*? Starring Julia Roberts? That's not suitable for a nine-year-old.'

'That's what I told her, Mum! Tell her, tell her. She says it's about a princess but I say it's about a hooker. She's horrible, I hate her.'

Sighing, Karen stood up.

'Right. Let me sort it out.'

Dear Gwen,

How is everything? Did you get permission to have the tree cut down? All is well-ish, here – the sale of the house is pressing ahead and I can't truly say my heart leaps at the thought of moving into the house in the village, it's very damp and 'in need of complete modernization', as I believe they say. Still, it will be a challenge!

Meanwhile, I have had dinner with Richie Prescott again

and – to my surprise – he's asked me away for the weekend to Salcombe. Not far, but a place I've always loved: Sebby and I went there often as children and I have such happy memories of us playing on the beach. So off we go! I am packing my sunhat and wellies, this being the British Isles. Wish me luck. Big hugs and kisses to the girls and once the sale/move is complete I can't wait to come and visit.

All love

Grace xx

Grace sat back, a tiny smile playing on her lips, and stared out at the garden. The lime trees were in flower, and their sweet vigorous scent drifted in through the open window. She'd certainly been very surprised by Richie's invitation – first to dinner, which, if she was honest, she hadn't enjoyed terribly; Richie had drunk a lot again and then nagged her unceasingly about selling the house to Anton (who'd upped his offer first by another five thousand pounds, then another ten thousand, and then twenty), which she point blank refused to do. But then he'd invited her to go away for a weekend. That was what real, serious couples did. Couples like Sebby and Verity. It was an invitation for Grace to become one of them, to join the rest of the world. She could hardly turn it down on the basis that Richie Prescott was a bit boring. Beggars couldn't be choosers. He was her last chance for love, for a relationship, for normality and companionship – all the things that she'd willingly forfeited for Mummy but which she longed for so much now.

At night, she lay imagining finding an outlet for the passion which lay folded inside her like the petals of a bud.

She imagined her and Richie's wedding in the village church, her – having slimmed down – in Mummy's old dress, he in morning suit. Gwen's daughters as bridesmaids. Alfie and Basil as adorable pageboys. Maybe the Drakes wouldn't mind them borrowing some of Chadlicote for a small reception. And later, children. It wasn't too late. Cherie Blair had had a baby when she was three hundred and fifty-five or some such.

Since he'd asked her out again, Grace had eaten nothing but a Ryvita bar for breakfast, cottage cheese on a lettuce leaf for lunch and a small piece of grilled chicken with heaps of steamed broccoli for supper. She'd walked the dogs vigorously each day. She'd lost four pounds. She reckoned she could manage at least another four by the weekend.

She occupied herself with clearing out the house. Today she'd been piling up old clothes either to go to Oxfam or – if they were really beautiful – to keep as an incentive to continue with the weight loss. She turned back to the pile on the bed behind her. A cream silk blazer with black piping on the collar. Beautiful! She stroked it reverentially, holding it to her nose to inhale the faint fragrance of Mummy's favourite scent, Vent Vert. As always, she checked the pockets. She felt paper, its texture shiny. Pulling it out she saw a packet of seeds. The picture on the front was a vibrant splash of maroon and violet petals. 'Sweet pea "Little Sweetheart",' it said.

Without quite knowing what she was doing, Grace went downstairs to the kitchen and opened the door leading to the courtyard outside. She knelt down beside an old, chipped pot and tore open the packet. Looking around, unable to see a trowel, Grace scooped some earth from the flowerbeds with her bare hands. Then she dropped in three tiny seeds and kneaded them into the mud. She sat back on her heels, filled suddenly with new ambition, fascinated to know what would happen next.

By Saturday morning, she'd lost five more pounds and tiny shoots were beginning to germinate. Grace watered them carefully and adjusted their position as she waited for Richie to arrive. He'd said he'd pick her up about ten, though it was already quarter to eleven. She'd packed a suitcase with a fresh spongebag and new white nightie, both ordered online.

He accelerated up the drive fifteen minutes later.

'Sorry! Sorry!' he called out of the wound-down window. 'Just had a little business to attend to.' As ever there were beads of sweat on his forehead, and his complexion was more florid than even a week ago. 'Well, come on then!' he continued, patting the seat beside him. 'Let's make up for lost time!'

It was only half an hour or so's drive to Salcombe, down winding lanes edged with hedges filled with cow parsley and early forget-me-nots. The sky was a benevolent blue and the fields were full of sheep and lambs. Grace was thrilled. She loved Salcombe; she and Sebby had spent hours on its beaches making sandcastles and paddling in the freezing sea.

'It's lovely to be having a change of scene,' she burbled. 'Looking after Mummy, it was always so difficult. I've no regrets about the years I spent caring for her. What else could I have done? I mean, I wish that Sebby had helped a little more. But he and Verity were always so busy entertaining clients or doing things with the children, and they always needed plenty of notice and I never seemed to give them enough. I did go to Paris and it was rather wonderful, but when I got back Mum was in a terrible state, saying they'd tried to give her tomato soup when she only liked oxtail and the children were too noisy and Verity hadn't put her eye drops in properly.'

'I've booked a room at the Tide's Reach Hotel,' Richie said, eyes on the road. 'It's right on the beach, lovely views. I hope you like it.'

'I'm sure I will.' A room! Not two rooms. So it was going to happen tonight. Nervously, she kept gabbling. 'And then, another time, I went to my old friend Gwen's wedding in Scotland. I sort of hoped I'd meet a nice, kilted Scotsman, though I'm not sure Mummy would have been too pleased at my moving so far away, but of course I ended up seated next to a thirteen-year-old female cousin and an eighty-six-year-old deaf uncle and when I got home Lou was on the verge of resigning because Mum had screamed at her for serving dinner at five twenty-one instead of the usual five fifteen. She did offer to look after her again when she'd calmed down but it never happened. It sort of didn't seem worth it.'

'We'll be there soon,' Richie said. He paused and then added, 'So have you thought any more about Anton's offer?'

Grace glanced at him. His eyes were still fixed on the road.

'Thank you, but I've already told you no thank you.'

'And I already told you,' Richie responded lightly, 'he will do a lovely job with the house. Restore it with great care.'

'It still seems very dishonourable towards the Drakes.'

'He's prepared to offer you a hundred thousand more than them.'

'A hundred thousand?' There would be money left over that way. Perhaps Sebby would let her have some to restore the cottage. Grace wavered.

'You should tell the Drakes. They could always beat it.'

'No,' said Grace. 'No, it's not right.'

'Well, you have the weekend to think about it.' Richie's expression didn't flicker. 'And here we are now. Salcombe! "By the sea, by the sea, by the bee-yoo-ti-ful sea. You and me, you and me . . ."'

His singing was atrocious. But Grace didn't care. She was seized with childlike excitement as they drove along a narrow coastal road, busy with couples in faded T-shirts and children in matelot tops carrying buckets and spades. They parked beside the hotel, which looked over an estuary with bright blue sea and a string of sandy beaches on the other side. Grace climbed out, self-consciously inhaling the salty air. Seagulls wheeled overhead.

They checked into the cosy lobby.

'Would someone take the bags up to the room?' Richie asked. 'We need to partake of a little refreshment.'

'In the bar?' Grace asked. She was looking forward to treating herself to a sandwich with a cup of tea. No sugar. But Richie wrinkled his nose.

'Bit fusty here. I thought we'd go into town.'

Grace imagined they'd walk along the coastal road. But instead they drove, leaving the car in a municipal car park. Richie marched ahead of her, stopping at a pub. Not the bright modern gastropub with sleek blond floors and a blackboard featuring bruschetta and porcini, but a sour-smelling old-man's pub with a carpet stiff from decades of beer spills.

'I think there's a pub in the centre of town that's much nicer than this,' she tried. 'There's a back garden with sea views.'

'Overpriced nonsense,' Richie said firmly, already half-way to the bar. 'We'll just have a snifter here and then plenty of bracing sea air to blow away the cobwebs. Pint of your best bitter, squire,' he said to the barman. 'Grace?'

'I'll have a lime and soda.'

'Sure?' He pulled a face at the barman. 'Women, eh?'

'They haven't got our capacity,' the barman said, not altogether unsympathetically. Richie laughed, paid him. They sat at a table covered in damp rings from pint glasses. Grace wished there was another woman in the room.

'Well, cheers,' Richie said. 'Here's to us.'

They clinked glasses and Richie drank avidly. An old man shuffled over. He had the red nose of a habitual drinker and wore a crumpled grey jacket that had seen better days.

'Ah, well. So what are the pair of you doing in this fine establishment?'

Grace stiffened but Richie grinned. 'We're having a drink,' he cried, as if this were not the most bleeding obvious answer in the world. He patted the chair beside him. 'Come and join us.'

Soon the two men were deep in conversation about the cricket and about which was better, Tennants or Carlsberg. Grace sat feeling stiffer and stiffer. Her drink tasted like acid. A shaft of sunlight poured through the grimy windows and created a pool of light on the table. Grace wanted to be outside, enjoying it. She tried to blot out the conversation and focus on the night ahead of her. She imagined herself in the bathroom at the hotel, brushing her hair, dressed in the new nightie. She imagined opening the door and seeing Richie waiting for her on the bed. Her throat tightened with nerves.

Richie turned to her. 'Are you all right, Grace?'

'I'm fine,' she said frostily.

'My dear friend Tom here says he knows another fine watering-hole where we can quaff. Shall we?'

'I thought we were planning a walk,' Grace said, hating her querulous tone but unable to stop it.

'But this is ye finest hostelry in all olde Salcombe. Can you really resist? Come on. Don't be a spoilsport. Just the one and there'll be plenty of time to work it off before dinner.'

'Well, if the lady wants a walk,' said Tom, who even in his befuddled situation clearly retained some sensitivity.

'Ah, we'll be fine,' Richie cried. 'Come on, everybody.'

And so they ended up in another drinkers' pub. And then in another. And a third. It was past eight o'clock; all thoughts of a walk were gone. Grace thought of the menu at the Tide's Reach and her stomach growled softly like Shackleton when he was dreaming.

'It's dinner time,' she said softly to Richie when he got up to get him and Tom their fifth pint (she'd had a vodka and tonic by now to keep her spirits up).

'Ah, they won't stop serving until ten!'

Grace felt faintly tearful. She was starving, though she knew she shouldn't eat anyway. She was far from home.

Tom was getting more and more morose, ranting about how the country was going to the dogs and it was all the fault of the immigrants. 'Dogs' made her think of Shackleton and Silvester snoozing at Lou's feet, and she felt so violently homesick her head swam.

It was after half past nine when she finally persuaded Richie out of the pub, bidding fond farewells to Tom, promising to hook up with him the following day. He drove unnervingly down the narrow streets, filled with chatting holidaymakers, towards the hotel. They made the dining room at nine fifty-five.

'We are still serving but we're out of nearly everything nice,' said the teenage waitress dubiously.

'Bugger it,' Richie said loudly, making Grace cringe in embarrassment. 'Let's go to the chippie. After all, we're at the seaside. Kiss me quick and all that.' He chortled loudly and Grace cringed again.

So they ate fish and chips in silence on a bench looking over the harbour. Grace savoured the tang of vinegar on her lips, the hot lumps of cod moving down her throat. She'd been imagining this as a romantic moment but – as usual – food was the only thing she could rely on.

'A cheeky half?' asked Richie, balling up his newspaper and aiming it at the bin, which it missed by at least a foot.

'I really think we should get back now,' Grace replied.

'Eh? All right then. Lady knows best.'

The hotel was quiet as they walked across the lobby. The smiley girl on the desk waved at them.

'Beautiful night,' Richie slurred. Grace's face flamed in embarrassment.

Entering the room she saw her little suitcase on the bed and felt a pang of pathos. But Richie had other things on his mind, in the form of the mini bar.

'I know these things cost the earth,' he mumbled, surveying the contents greedily. 'But I have to toast your beauty.'

'I think you've had enough, Richie.'

'I think you've had enough, Richie,' he mimicked cruelly. 'Come on. We're on holiday. I deserve a little fun.'

'Fine,' she said. She went into the bathroom and took a long look at herself in the mirror. This might be her only chance.

She brushed her teeth, washed her face, reapplied a bit of powder and blusher to make herself look better. Then she undressed and pulled the nightie over her head. It slid down her back like icy water. Maybe she was being too hard on Richie. They *were* on holiday of sorts – his job was very stressful and he simply wanted to unwind a bit. The forecast was good for tomorrow and there'd be plenty of time then for ferry rides and walking.

She emerged shyly, almost trembling, from the bathroom.

Richie was fast asleep in the armchair by the window, snoring slightly, a little trail of dribble halfway down his chin.

Grace looked at him for a second, then turned off the main light – through the window, she gave a quick longing glance at the estuary outside, drew the thick curtains and climbed into bed. She didn't cry, she didn't allow herself to feel anything at all. In the dark, she fumbled for her bag and took out the family-sized bar of Dairy

Milk she'd hidden there for emergencies. Deftly, she peeled back the shiny silver paper and broke off a chunk of chocolate. Silently, she devoured the lot, as Richie snored in his chair.

# 27

Max was dithering. He'd wait a day before he called Karen, he decided. He'd say he was up to his eyes this week, but maybe the one after. Over the weekend he'd met up with Heather, who was tearful and bitter, accusing him of wasting her time, and who'd hit the roof when Karen had called in the middle of things, accusing him of already moving on to another woman – whose heart he was no doubt breaking too. Max had denied it, but of course she'd been spot on.

So today he was filled with recriminations. Messing with a married woman was dangerous. It could only end in pain. For both of them. The evenings they'd snatched in his flat had been like a dream, almost too blissful to be true, but he had to regard things objectively. Good sex always turned your head. And that was all it was – good sex.

He'd heard the slight shock in Karen's voice when he'd been cool to her on the phone. It had upset him at the time, and he'd wanted to call her back as soon as he'd left angry Heather in the bar. But outside in the bracing spring air he decided he'd done the right thing. Sunday too, he'd refrained from calling her, texting her, deciding it was cruel to be kind. He needed to back away. Not too quickly, because that way he might shatter what was clearly a fragile heart. But not too slowly, because then things might get even more serious. Anyway, he'd end things. And then he'd join the Foreign Legion.

Except now his mind was full of images of Karen. Her dark, slightly slanted eyes with the thick brows – Max had a thing about eyebrows. Her porcelain skin. Her dark curly hair. That tiny, slender body with the voluptuous breasts. He thought about her sly smile and the funny things she said. He felt so desperately sorry for her, being married to that arsehole. There was something about Karen, some quality Heather and the others didn't have, that made him want to look after her.

Suddenly Max didn't think he could wait to see her. After all, it wasn't as if she could be in it for anything more than a fling – she was married, had children, was about to move to the country. She didn't want anything from him, unlike Heather and the others, who'd been very clear it was a ring on the finger after six months or adios. So he'd see her again, they'd have more mind-blowing sex, he'd be very careful what he said and then he'd start slowly extracting himself.

Dear Gwen,

Thanks so much for your email and the lovely pictures of the girls. Tessa walking! How wonderful! I got back from the seaside last night. Gorgeous weather and the hotel was so smart I felt quite out of place! In the end, I came back without Richie as I was worrying about the dogs and felt on Sunday morning I should hurry home. Even though it involved catching three buses the wait between them was not long and I very much enjoyed watching the Devon scenery unroll from the windows.

Now it's Monday morning and I'm getting back to work. We have a date for exchange now, so you can imagine how

busy I am going to be. Hope you are all thriving, Can't wait to
come and see you all when things are less hectic.
G xxx

Verity was calling her from Mummy's bedroom.

'Grace! Grace! Are you there? I'm making fantastic progress with the jewellery. I've got a keep, chuck, sell and to-be-decided pile. We need to start going through it. I have to say there are some gorgeous pieces here. You and I are going to have a bit of a fight on our hands, I think.'

Grace felt numb. She didn't care any more. Let Verity take the jewellery, let the house be sold. She'd come back from Salcombe on her own after Richie had woken up on Sunday morning and announced that his head was a bit sore and how about a hair of the dog to perk himself up?

The scales had fallen from her eyes. She'd sobbed all the way home on the various buses, thanking God for her sunglasses. A taxi took her the last leg to her front door. The dogs went wild when they arrived at Lou's house to collect them.

'At least I'll always have you,' she told them on the way home.

She pushed open the bedroom door. Verity was admiring herself in the mirror, Mum's gold chain, the one that had always been Grace's particular favourite, around her neck.

'Look, say if you're mad keen on this. I'm not going to deprive you of any sentimental favourites. Of course if anything's *really* valuable we'll have to auction it.'

'Mmm,' Grace said.

'Oh, get down, Silvester. These dogs are totally out of

control. Makes me appreciate the children more. At least they can tell you they love you and they don't have little accidents on the carpet.'

'The dogs are house-trained,' Grace said indignantly.

'Well, Shackleton's not doing a very good job. He left a little puddle in the hall downstairs. And a little present on the front steps. I didn't clean it up because it was a bit bloody and I thought you should have a look at it.'

'A bit bloody?'

'Yes. Constipated I should think.'

Grace ran downstairs and outdoors to inspect. Verity was right. There was definitely blood in Shackleton's little offering. A clammy hand seized her heart. She was going to have to call the vet.

'Karen? It's Max.'

'Oh, hi.'

'I . . . Can I see you?'

She'd been sitting at her desk, practising her speech about how it had been great fun but it was just one of those things. That odd, frosty conversation they'd had on Saturday had brought her to her senses. She was crazy, she was risking her marriage, everything, for a young guy who didn't even care about her that much. She'd end it.

But then hearing him now, his voice was so sexy. *He* was so sexy. *Ignore it, Karen. Tell him.*

'Karen?'

'Not this week. I . . . Things are frantic here. But maybe next week.' Good, that gave her breathing space. After all, he'd caught her on the hop just now. She hadn't fully decided what to say.

'Next week?' He sounded hurt. She felt terrible. Karen!

'I'll text you. Got to go now, Max.'

*Damn. She doesn't want to see me now. Come on Max, it's a good thing. You'd just decided you had to end things and now you're practically begging her . . . But she sounded so cold. Has she gone off me?*

Max needed to know that that wasn't the case. He called her back.

*'This is Karen Drake. I can't answer your call right now but please leave a message . . .'*

'I . . . uh. Please let me know when you can see me. It's Max. By the way. Um. 'Bye.'

Karen had another near sleepless night. She didn't know what to do. She'd dived blissfully into this affair – kidding herself it was just a diversion, something to cheer herself up, something that no one else need ever know about. But already, she realized how naive she had been. Either way she was going to come badly out of this. Either she lost Max – and that would break her heart. Or she'd lose Phil.

But that last bit had happened anyway, she thought, rolling on her side to watch him in the moonlight that crept through the curtains. His mouth was slightly open, his eye mask was on – Phil had read that it was best to sleep with an eye mask because it increased the body's supply of melatonin, which was apparently a cancer fighter.

She'd lost him and he'd lost her. She knew that every time he looked at her he saw his disease reflected back and he couldn't stand it. She was too closely connected to his suffering for there to be any intimacy any more. The thing they both hated most in the world was the only thing they still had in common.

Apart from the girls. Whom they both adored. Worshipped.

Those girls should be more than enough to bind any two people together. But were they? Karen's dad obviously hadn't felt that way, he'd been off like a cork from a champagne bottle. Karen had never forgiven him, even though she could acknowledge that life with her manipulative, slightly deranged mother must have been hell. But now, more than half a lifetime on, she began to see where he'd been coming from. How he might not have been able to bear it any longer.

But Karen couldn't leave her girls. And with them Max wouldn't want her. She could leave Phil anyway, but could she really face life as a single parent? She could, actually, she could face the day-in, day-out slog, but what about the girls, adjusting to a dad they saw only at weekends? She couldn't do it to them.

No. This wouldn't do. She had to clear her head. Lying there as the dawn crept in and Phil muttered softly, enjoying some dream, she came to a sudden decision. She wouldn't go to work today. Karen never called in sick; Christine would automatically assume she was bunking off for sports day. But now it was time to cash in her chips, payback for all the years she'd covered for Sophie's hangovers.

She'd drive to Devon.

She arrived at Chadlicote around two. She had started the drive listening to Radio 1 but just after Swindon she switched to Radio 4. This getting with the kids stuff was ridiculous, she needed to start acting her age again. The traffic was sparse on the motorway, but when she came off at Totnes she began to feel less comfortable. The first road she took was fine, although it seemed to be jammed with over-sixty-fives doing 40 m.p.h. and braking whenever the fancy took them. But that was followed by a twisty B road with high bramble hedges that the sides of the Volvo kept scraping, and terrifying blind corners.

Karen hated driving at the best of times; she had dreadful spatial awareness and anyway – her handy excuse – it was terrible for the environment. But if she was seriously going to live here, she'd have to master this route. Gritting her teeth, she carried on down an even narrower, twistier road where you had to reverse for yards if you met a car coming the other way. She managed to spot the turning for the house, hidden between high trees. Up the long potholed drive, past the lake, round a tight bend, and Chadlicote came into view. For a tiny second, Karen was seduced by its near-perfect symmetry. How could she *not* want to live here?.

She jumped as her mobile started ringing in its cradle. She'd thought the whole of the West Country was a communications black hole. She pulled in and, seeing Max's number on the caller ID, felt her whole body tingle as if she'd been given a huge electric shock.

'Hello?'

'Karen, it's Max again. I know I'm hassling you, but . . .' The line started to crackle.

'I can't hear you.'

'It's . . .' She couldn't hear a word.

'Max,' she shouted. 'Max! I can't hear you.'

The line went dead. Sodding country where you couldn't get a signal. For some reason this was the last straw. Head reeling, suddenly knocked over with exhaustion, Karen leaned forward to rest her forehead on the steering wheel.

There was a sharp rapping on her back window. Karen screamed. She whirled round in her seat. The gentle, unassuming face of Grace Porter-Healey peered through the window.

'Hello,' she smiled.

'I'm so sorry!' Karen hastily rolled down the window. 'I . . . I was in the area looking at schools for the girls and I couldn't resist a peek.'

'You should have knocked on the door.'

'I didn't want to disturb you. And anyway, isn't it meant to be sort of unprofessional to talk to the person you're buying from? I thought we were only allowed to talk through the agents.'

'Possibly,' Grace said. The tip of her nose was bright red. She'd look so much better with just a little make-up, Karen thought. 'But I don't think we should concern ourselves too much about that. Why don't you come in? Have a cup of tea? And a biscuit.'

'Oh, no, really. I . . . I ought to be getting back to London.'

'Not without something to fuel you for the journey. Come on. I insist.'

Karen was defeated. She had no desire to sit making polite conversation with Grace Porter-Healey about how marvellous the Women's Institute was, but at the same time she was dying for the loo. And the thought of the drive back to London without a cup of tea was daunting. Of course she could try to find a service station somewhere but in this god-forsaken hole it might take hours. Plus, she told herself, why not have another look at the house? Perhaps it would be better than she remembered.

'Climb in,' she said to Grace. 'I'll drive you there.'

Twenty minutes later, Grace and Karen were sitting in the second sitting room – nursing china cups of tea. The sun had turned out to be merely passing trade: as they'd approached the house the sky had darkened and the rain began lashing down. From over the hills, towards the coast, came the sound of rumbling thunder.

'I think I'd get a bit frightened alone here when it's like this,' said Karen. 'Do you mind it?'

'Well, I haven't been alone here for *that* long. My mother only died at the end of January.'

'God, I'm sorry.' Karen ran her hand through her short hair. She looked tired, less polished than last time Grace had seen her. 'I'm so tactless. You must miss your mum a lot.'

'I do. And I don't. It was very hard towards the end, you know.'

'It must have been. She had . . .?'

'Motor neurone disease.'

'Ah. I don't know much about that. But my husband had cancer, as he told you. It's hard being a carer, isn't it? At least, it was for me. I take my hat off to the people who do it uncomplainingly. Invalids aren't always as grateful as you'd like, in my experience.'

'Mine too,' Grace said.

And they were off. Grace, apart from the odd aside to Lou, had kept buttoned up about how frustrating it had been to be at her mother's increasingly whimsical beck and call. But suddenly she couldn't stop talking.

Karen understood. 'But if you feel sorry for yourself, you feel terrible because of course you're not seriously ill, so really you have nothing to complain about.'

There was another crash of thunder. 'I did feel very isolated, very often,' Grace confessed. 'And I still do now. I didn't have time to make friends all those years I was so busy with Mummy. It will be different for you when you move here. You're a mother. You'll get to know the other mothers from the girls' school.'

'Maybe,' Karen said, sounding unconvinced. She took a sip of tea and then suddenly burst into tears. Big, sloppy glug-glug ones, like a plughole draining.

'Oh my God,' she gulped as one dripped into her tea. 'I'm so embarrassed. Sorry. Sorry.'

'Don't worry,' said Grace. She shoved a box of tissues under Karen's nose. 'Here.'

'I'm just . . . please don't take offence at this but I really don't want to move here. I mean, I know the house is beautiful and so is the countryside but . . . I've been a country mouse and I don't want to go back there.'

And now she was off, pouring her heart out about how this was all Phil's idea and she felt she couldn't let him down because he'd been so ill. Grace listened.

'I understand. It's what we were just saying. When somebody's ill you feel you can't deny them anything. Their wishes have to come first.'

Karen sniffed as she looked at her with her piercing

cobalt eyes. 'And do you ever regret the sacrifices you made?'

Grace paused. 'Yes and no. I loved my mother. I was at her side when she died. But . . . yes, now I have to build up my life from scratch and I do wonder if I should have been a little more self-centred.' She felt shocked to have expressed the thought. She continued. 'So if you really don't want to come here, you should stand your ground. Actually, there was another offer on the table.'

But Karen didn't hear her. 'It's not just that I don't want to move here. I'm . . .' She swallowed. 'I've got a friendship.'

'A friendship?' Grace looked puzzled, then the penny dropped. 'Oh my goodness. A *friendship*! You mean an affair?'

Karen shook her head.

'No, no. It's just . . . well, yes, it is. It is an affair and I'm so . . . confused.'

'Well, I've never had such an experience but I imagine so. Who is he?'

'He's the brother of an old boyfriend.' God, it sounded so tacky. 'But that's not the issue. The point is I've married the wrong man.'

'Really?' Grace didn't appear to be judging her.

'For thirteen years I've been behaving like an ostrich. Trying to convince myself that what Phil and I had wasn't crazy and passionate but that crazy and passionate was a bad idea, that what was more important was friendship, stability. And we did have that friendship. I could talk to him. He made me laugh. But I'm not sure any of that's true any more. I gave so much to Phil when he was sick, but by the time I got him through it I think my last vestiges of love for him had vanished. He survived but the love died.'

Grace said nothing. Karen carried on.

'We'd always been different and somehow we've come through something as life-changing as him almost dying even more different. He wants peace and green fields and pottering around all day talking to builders. I still want dirty streets and bright lights and noise. And we can't talk about it. He just ploughs on with his plan and I go along with it because I feel terrible not supporting him. I don't know what to do.'

'You have to talk to Phil,' Grace said. 'And you must end things with this other chap.'

'I will,' Karen said. 'I mean, I've already ended things. I'm not taking his calls even though it's killing me. And I will speak to Phil. Somewhere where there are no distractions. We'll go out for dinner. On Saturday. I'll book a table. And we won't leave the restaurant until we've thrashed this out once and for all.'

# 28

All the way home, she ran through her plan of action. She'd go to Devon. She definitely wouldn't see Max again. She would go home and *talk* to Phil. They'd go out for a romantic dinner, when they would really talk.

Who'd have thought that in the end her confidante would be Grace Porter-Healey? Grace who'd led such a sheltered life. But who had listened to her so sweetly, without interruptions or criticisms. And who was right.

Stopping at her service station, she checked her phone. A text was waiting.

Are you free this evening? M

Heart thudding, she tapped out an immediate reply.

No. Sorry. Afraid I'll be busy for the foreseeable future. Kind regards.

She pressed 'send' and leaned back in the driver's seat, dizzy with grief at what she was throwing away. But what was the alternative? Carry on a couple of months and leave anyway when she was even deeper in?

Ridiculous. She'd done the right thing. She wasn't going to think about Max any more. She was going to turn all her attention into making a new life for them all in Devon. Into what *All Woman!* would call Relationship Repair. They'd illustrate the article with a photo of couple lying on a bed divided by a zigzag line.

The thought should have made her smile, but it didn't.

Gareth stood in the middle of the so-called wobbly bridge over the Thames – the wobbles that had plagued its opening had long been sorted out but the nickname remained for perpetuity. He was killing time before a viewing on a quirky little flat in Ave Maria Lane. It should have started at three thirty, but the client had called saying he was going to be late. Gareth didn't mind. He stood admiring the view, dominated by the Gherkin: St Paul's to his left, Tate Modern to his right. Sometimes Gareth wished he was back in Dorset, but when he took in this panorama he knew he was in the greatest city in the world. He leaned against the parapet feeling master of all he surveyed.

'Hello,' said a voice beside him.

Gareth jumped. Standing beside him was Anton Beleek, gazing dolefully out at the grey river.

'Anton! Didn't see you there.'

'No? You were right beside me.' Anton snorted. 'I'm pretty missable though.' He snorted again. Gareth felt a little alarmed.

'So are you well, Anton?' he tried.

'As well as can be expected. Yourself?'

'Fine. You know, it's not been easy this past year, trying to sell houses. As you would know. But we're all surviving.' Looking at Anton's pale profile, Gareth wasn't so sure.

'Oh yes,' Anton said, and then after a second he shook his head and said, 'Sorry. What did you say?'

Gareth was uneasy now. Anton had a mind like a wheel clamp. Nothing escaped its clutches. 'I said we're all surviving.'

'Ach. Yes. I suppose so. Yes.' He paused and then said, 'It hasn't all been easy recently, Gareth. I'd begun to think about settling down. Thought I'd found the woman to do it with.'

'You and Lucinda did seem right for each other.' Gareth was uncomfortable.

'I daresay everyone's laughing at me.'

'Of course not!' Gareth lied, thinking uneasily of some of Joanne's recent remarks in the Fox & Anchor about sad old gits.

'Still, she has the right to do whatever she wants. There was never any agreement between us.' Anton turned suddenly to Gareth. His face looked like a condemned building smashed by a demolition ball. 'I thought . . . I thought I was getting on my feet again. That I could be happy with her. But fate is very cruel. Everything I love is snatched from me. I've got to accept that's just the way it goes.'

He turned and started walking back towards St Paul's. Gareth thought it best that he follow. He was scared Anton was going to throw himself in the water. But suddenly he turned back.

'It wasn't the big thing that some people made out. No woman's ever managed to nail me down, ha-ha. Nice to see you. I'm sure I can trust you not to pass on anything I've said.'

'Of course not,' Gareth said, but Anton was already

striding off into the crowd, his long raincoat flapping behind him like raven's wings.

Ludmila didn't want to babysit. 'I'm sorry but it's the annual au-pair get-together this week in Dunstable and I have been looking forward to this all year. I must attend. If I do not go I will return to Slovenia on next aeroplane.' Her bottom lip started to quiver. Karen backed off.

Fine, so no romantic dinner out. Never mind. She'd prepare a fantastic meal at home. Karen went through phases with cooking. She'd loved it before the girls were born, but years of lovingly prepared nutritious meals being thrown on the floor or rejected outright 'because the peas are touching the fish fingers' had turned it into simply another chore. Phil had made it even more onerous. Before the cancer they'd existed on pasta, alternated with fish, with a roast chicken at weekends. But since his recovery his meals had to be vegetarian, preferably vegan and all organic. If Karen ever gently pointed out how much that cost, her husband's response was the usual. 'It's only money. We can't take it with us. What price on health?'

Tonight, however, she was going to pander to Phil's every whim. As the girls sat gripped in front of *Hannah Montana* on the new HDTV screen, more spoils from Phil's post-recovery spree, she embarked on a Nigella couscous dish. Swedes, parsnips, carrots, tomatoes – you couldn't get much more bloody vegan than this. She'd make some Quorn meatballs to go with it. She'd open a bottle of organic wine. Wear a frock. Put things back on track.

Her phone beeped.

Please can we talk. At least?

'What's up?' said Phil, strolling into the room and tousling Eloise's hair, so she cried, 'Oi! Get off, Daddy!'

Guiltily, Karen shoved the phone in her pocket. She eyed her husband as if he were a stranger. Bald – well, that was hardly his fault. Deathly pale because he now never let a ray of sunshine touch his skin. Max was so much more manly, with the surprisingly dark hair on his forearms, his wide muscled back.

'What's all this cooking for?'

'I'm making us a special dinner,' she said.

'For tonight?'

'Yes.'

He looked troubled. 'But darling, didn't I tell you?'

'Tell you what?'

'I've got yoga again.'

'Phil! What is it with all this yoga? You've got all day to do it, why does it have to be in the evenings?'

'Because that is when the best classes are.'

'And you can't miss just one? I'm making us a special dinner. A treat.'

'Kaz, this is about my *health*. You can't argue about it.'

'What about us, though? Aren't we important too?'

'You're everything to me. That's why it's so important I stay healthy. Why we need to move to Devon.'

'I don't want to move to Devon,' Karen suddenly yelled. 'I love it here. I love my home, I love my friends, I love my job. I'll be miserable in the middle of the country. I can't do it.'

The impossible was achieved. The girls took their eyes off the television and stared at her.

'But Mummy, in Devon we'll have a swimming pool,' Bea said. Her eyes switched back to the screen.

A look of incredulity crossed Phil's face. A bit like the expression when the doctor had given him the diagnosis. Karen felt like the worst wife in the world. 'Kaz. What on earth are you talking about?'

'I tried to tell you. I don't want to go.'

'It's my dream, Karen. I've been focusing on this for so long. You know it's what's kept me sane, thinking of what lies in store for us.'

'For you. Not us.'

Phil inhaled deeply. 'I've given you everything. I worked for years number-crunching, commuting, wearing suits and ties just to give you the best – the best house, the best schools, to allow you to have a nanny so you could continue with your precious job. And look what it did to me. I have to think of myself for a change. I almost died, Karen.'

'But you were doing your job before you met me. And I'm not saying you should go back to it. But . . .' She lowered her voice, glancing at the girls. 'Can we really afford it? How are we going to pay for university? What about our old age?'

Phil shook his head. 'We'll be fine.' He glanced at his watch. 'Love, don't take this the wrong way but I've got to go. We'll have your delicious dinner when I get back and we'll talk about this more.'

'I may not be here when you get back,' Karen snapped, .

more loudly than she intended. Bea looked round panic-stricken.

'Mummy! You can't go out. Who will look after us?'

'She's only being silly, pumpkin,' Phil said.

Eloise stood up, her eyes full of tears. 'Why are you being so horrible to each other? What's wrong with you?'

'Sorry, darling,' Karen said. Her heart felt curled up, burnt to ash. 'We weren't really being horrible to each other, we were just . . .'

'You were being horrible. I'm not deaf, you know. Now say sorry.'

'Yeah,' Bea chimed in. 'Go on. Give Daddy a kiss. Then Daddy, you give Mummy one.'

Karen looked at Phil. She didn't love him any more. She'd married the wrong man. Married him because she was scared and insecure and thought no one else would ever love her. She'd made a terrible mistake and she'd get no second chance.

'Go on!'

Dutifully, she leaned forward and kissed Phil softly on the cheek.

'Daddy!'

He kissed her back. 'I'm sorry,' he said gruffly.

'I will be here when you get back,' Karen said, her voice level. 'But I will be in bed. Asleep. And tomorrow evening, I'm going out. So you're in charge.'

'Going where?'

'Just out. Now, off you go. You don't want to miss yoga. I'll leave some dinner out for you.'

He stared at her for a moment, then turned and left. Karen furiously started ripping off the swede's skin with a peeler. A swede made a very unsatisfactory hate object. She threw it on the floor.

'Girls,' she said. 'How about McDonald's tonight?'

They looked at her disbelievingly.

'Yay, Mum,' said Bea, as Eloise said: 'I don't know, Mummy. That food's junk.'

'Never mind that. Get your shoes on. I just need to text someone.'

She pulled out her phone and sent a message to Max.

Could I meet you tomorrow?

# 29

In the Parenthope Clinic, Bridget lay on a couch as Sian, the nurse, rubbed gel on her tummy. Sitting on a chair under the photo gallery of Parenthope babies, sent in by grateful parents, Gemma watched anxiously. Nearly a month had passed since the discovery of the ovarian cyst. Now was the moment of reckoning when they'd find out if it had gone.

'Did you watch *The Apprentice* last night?' asked Sian, who'd just scanned Gemma's womb and found it ready and willing. 'I couldn't believe it. Sacking Maggie when it was obviously all Ian's fault for ordering too many veal cutlets. Sir Alan shouldn't be allowed to get away with it. Alex not with you today?'

'No, he's waiting for the verdict on his trial. The judge summed up yesterday and the jury could return at any time. I mean, it could be a day, it could be a month.'

'Madness,' Sian said absently, peering at the screen. 'I don't know, he'll chose the wrong candidate in the end, he always does. Do you remember that year he let the dolly bird win instead of the lesbian, but then she got up the duff? Oh, sorry. I didn't mean that to sound offensive. Hmm. Good. The cyst has gone.'

'Really?' Bridget sat bolt upright. Gemma's hand flew to her mouth. How could Sian be so casual, when it was the best news in the history of the entire world?

'Really. So. Your womb is all prepped. So we're finally good to go. We can extract the eggs and take a sperm sample on . . .' She glanced at the calendar. 'Wednesday. Yes. Your husband can come in at noon to give his sample then, can't he? Not going to be too busy being Judge John Deed?'

'He'll be fine,' Gemma said. She'd insisted Alex request the judge give everyone a day off court for 'urgent medical reasons'.

'Nice one. So we'll start you on pessaries and patches to thicken your womb lining and in nine days we'll have you back here to see if it's ready to receive the embryo.'

Nick was on his way to the studio. Another couple of weeks and the album would be finished. And then they were going to be touring America. He hadn't reminded Kylie that this was imminent and she hadn't asked. Nor had he told her he was exchanging on the flat two weeks on Friday and 'completing', which meant he'd actually get his hands on the keys, a month later.

And obviously he hadn't told her that he and Lucinda had a regular thing going. They met twice a week at Flat 15 while Gemma Meehan was having reflexology, whatever that was, and they had excellent sex. After which they lay and chatted for around an hour or so – about their fathers mainly and how they wished they knew them better. Something he'd never been able to talk to Kylie about, a side of his life that he'd always kept locked in a private place, because it was too painful to take out and address. He was surprised at the connection he and Lucinda had. But a connection wasn't what Nick wanted. He wasn't looking to be close to Lucinda. He didn't love her. She was sexy. She was posh. But her prejudices drove him nuts. He hated her amazement he'd never been riding or skiing, her inability to acknowledge that you could get by perfectly well in life without a university degree. Nick had always wanted to better himself, but the more he learned about Lucinda's world, the less he was enamoured of it.

Meanwhile, Kylie continued to be her gentle, sweet self. A self who cooked him special meals and listened to each version of a new song, who ran him baths and jumped in with him. Thinking of her, Nick's heart softened like apricots soaked in milk. Why couldn't she just dress a little more subtly, have a bit more attitude?

What he really wanted, he realized, was a blend of the two women, someone with Lucinda's class but Kylie's docile nature. He was going to have to ditch both of them and keep on looking for the perfect woman. Maybe he'd find her in America.

His phone rang in his pocket. 'Hello, Charles,' said Nick, seeing the caller ID.

'Hi, mate.' As usual Charles sounded as if he'd just run up one of the Brecon Beacons. 'Just calling to see how it's all going?'

'All right. We exchange on the flat two weeks on Friday.'

'That's what I thought. I was just calling with a word of advice about that. The market's still dropping, so I think it's time you did a bit of gazundering.'

'Eh?'

'Drop your offer at the last minute. By, say, fifty grand. You'll have the sellers by the short and curlies, their sale will be about to go through and they'll have to accede.'

'Oh. Right.' Nick felt uneasy. He'd spent so much time in Flat 15 recently, he felt he'd sort of got to know the Meehans. He admired Alex M's taste in music, lots of Dylan and punk. Felt sorry for Gemma when he saw all the books on the shelves about conception and saw the dozens of nutritional supplements in the kitchen cupboards. Doing the dirty on them was . . .

'I've already dropped the offer twice.'

'So? Everyone does it. I mean, you don't *have* to but you'd be a bloody idiot, in my humble opinion.'

'Right,' said Nick. 'I'll do it.'

'You don't have to.'

'I said I'll do it,' he repeated angrily. His call waiting was bleeping. It was Lucinda. 'I've got to go,' he snapped. 'Yes?' he said to his lover.

'Oh, hello Mr Crex,' she said in her starchiest voice. She must be in the office. 'Just calling to tidy up a few details before exchange.'

'Right,' he said. 'Actually, I wanted to talk to you about that.'

'Oh, yes? Would you like to meet?'

'We could,' he said, thinking she wasn't going to like what he was going to tell her. But sod it. She was a billionaire's daughter. If she took a little cut in commission it hardly mattered, did it?

'Our usual place?' she said, but then lowered her voice and added, 'Or, for a change, I was wondering about dinner.'

'Dinner?' This was a new one. Nick really didn't want changes in the routine.

'I thought Moro. I could book it for tonight. Eight. Have you been there?'

'No I haven't,' he said.

'It's marvellous.'

Her old-fashioned turn of phrase annoyed him. 'Jolly good,' he said in just slightly sarcastic tones.

'Are you teasing me?' she asked suspiciously.

Bloody women, they were all so sensitive. 'Of course not.'

'I'll see you at eight,' she said. 'Will you be able to find it?'

'I'll find it,' he said and hung up.


As soon as Nick walked through the studio doors there were other worries to distract him. Andrew was in a state. Jack hadn't turned up.

'He's having a wobbly. The doctors say he might need a holiday.' Andrew held up a pudgy hand. 'I know, I know. I feel the same way. We've got this tour coming up, I've got to deal with all the sponsors.' A cloud of dandruff flew through the air as he scratched his head. 'I think what we all need is a week off. Why don't you take Kylie away somewhere hot? When we come back we'll all be raring to start work again.'

'Nice one!' Ian exclaimed. 'Becky's been bitching for a holiday for months. A week in Dubai, I reckon. Hey, Nick, why don't you and Kylie come with us? She's been looking so mardy recently. She needs a bit of spoiling.'

'Yeah, maybe.' Nick shrugged. 'I need to write some more songs.'

'Good man,' said Andrew, looking relieved. 'You do that.'

'You can do that in Dubai just as easily as here,' Ian said. 'Get a tan at the same time.'

Yeah, right. Dubai was Nick's idea of hell. A shopping mall on a beach. But the idea of Ian taking Becky made him feel guilty. He left the studio and took a cab home, feeling oddly uneasy. Kylie was working late tonight, so there was no reason not to go for the dinner with Lucinda. He knew the reason he was unhappy about it was because it would involve eating strange foods. Well, he'd have to tackle that fear. He was moving up in the world and part of Lucinda's job was to help with that climb.

The restaurant was crowded and buzzy. Lucinda sat at a table by the window, twisting her bracelet round her wrist. She didn't know why but she felt nervous. But then Nick always had that effect on her. They'd been seeing each other regularly for . . . what . . . just four weeks now, nothing in the scheme of things. And she knew he was still with his girlfriend. Knew what they were having was just a fling. But she couldn't help it. She was obsessed. She thought about his hard body on top of hers all the time, listened to his songs constantly. Nick had tapped a reserve of longing, of emotion, of desire that she'd never known lay inside her and she couldn't get enough of him.

Logic told her he was completely wrong for her, that there could be no future, but the bloody-minded side of her retorted, 'Why not?'

They weren't living in Saudi Arabia, she could be with whomever she chose. Why should she settle for the stuffy trust-funder her parents would earmark for her, when there was this ambitious, driven man here – just like Lucinda. All right, Nick wasn't talking marriage, but with time she could crack him.

There'd been a few weeks of non-stop sex, but now Lucinda had decided it was time to move things on to the next level. Start behaving a bit more like normal couples did. Which was why she'd booked the restaurant tonight.

He was coming towards her, looking cross, as usual. At the sight of him, her insides knotted.

'Hello,' she said, standing up. Did they kiss? Of course not. He sat down.

'So why are we here?' he asked, looking around.

'Well . . . I thought you'd enjoy it. The food's great, and . . .'

'And . . .?'

'And I thought it might make a change. You know. To have dinner. Enjoy some good food and wine. Talk. You know. The kind of things normal couples do.'

'You want us to be a normal couple?'

'Well, no. I didn't say that. But . . . you know, there's more to life than . . .'

'Than what?'

'Nothing,' she said, as a waitress appeared. 'A bottle of the Vega Sicilia,' she said firmly, determined to assert herself. 'And a bottle of . . .' She looked at him. 'Would you prefer sparkling or still?'

'Whatever the fuck you want.'

Lucinda felt as if she'd been slapped. Steeling herself not to react, she smiled graciously at the waitress.

'Still, please.'

'Do you normally swear at staff?' she asked coldly, as the waitress retreated.

'Of course not.' A pause and then, 'Sorry.'

'Something seems to have upset you. Do you not like Moroccan food?'

'That's got nothing to do with it,' he snapped. His voice softened. 'Look, I've just had a shit day. And I'm not that big on food. And I want to be close to you. Not stuck in a restaurant making small talk.'

Relief flooded over her. 'It's OK,' she said. 'We don't have to stay here. Why don't we go back to the Meehans'? They're out tonight.'

A weird look came over Nick's face. 'Look, Lucinda. The Meehans. I need to talk to you about them.'

# 30

Eight days had passed; the weather was unusually warm for early May and the streets of Clerkenwell were filled with girls in tight vests that revealed their bra straps and streaky fake-tanned legs and men in shorts smelling slightly of sweat. In the mezzanine of Flat 15 Gemma was preparing herself for summer by painting her toenails, while talking to Bridget on speakerphone.

'So how's it going with the pills?' Bridget asked.

'Well, I can't exactly say I love shoving tablets up my bottom every morning. And the hormones make me more flatulent than a cow that's just eaten a manger full of lentils. The flat stinks. Alex keeps opening all the windows.'

'Oh my God. And this is the woman who's never even peed in front of her husband!'

'That's right.' Over the years she and Bridget had had several arguments about whether bodily functions should be concealed from one's other half. 'Now I'm breaking wind all night long.'

Bridget roared.

'And ironically, the hormones have also made all my tummy muscles relax so I look three months pregnant. The other morning, a woman even offered me her seat on the tube.'

More laughter. Gemma smiled to herself. She never used to have this kind of conversation with Bridget. On so many levels, this egg donation business was bringing them closer together. Who would have guessed it?

'How about you, anyway? How are the hormone injections? And how's it going with Massimo?'

'Brilliantly. You know we've found a flat? One bedroom on Western Avenue. Bit of a tip but it's home. And he's treating me so well, Gems. Anyway, enough about me. How are you filling the weekend before egg-removal day?'

'Wedding in Sussex, tomorrow. My old friend Lalage from primary school, remember her?'

'I remember you two locking me out of your room and not letting me play with you. So she's getting married. Send her my congratulations.'

'I will. The whole thing's a pain, though, I have to say. I'd so much rather have had a quiet weekend, to give Alex's sperm maximum rest before its big day.'

'A wedding could be a good distraction.'

'Yeah.' The only thing was, Gemma loathed weddings, as she did any family gathering. They were full of mothers, wannabe mothers, children and nosy parkers who – as sure as nobody touching the Rich Tea biscuit in the variety pack – would tap her on the shoulder and ask, 'So, how long is it you've been married now? Three years! Well, can't be long before we hear the patter of tiny feet.' Although worse were the people who didn't approach her. She'd seen pregnant women dodge into doorways as if she were the bogeyman, mothers of three cross the room to avoid her. Perhaps they thought her barrenness was contagious. Or more likely, they just didn't know what to say.

'We're staying in a lovely hotel. Room service, spa. All my friends with kids talk about places like that as if they're the meaning of life, so I'm going to make the most of it. Y'know, in case we're lucky with the baby and never leave the house again.'

'You *will* be lucky. Anyway, what are you talking about? Why can't you leave the house with a baby? Kaia took hers to Glastonbury last year *and* the Big Chill.'

Gemma ignored this. She'd long decided Chudney would be a routine baby, with regular naps in a cot in a darkened room.

'And what's happening with the flat?'

'That's all good. Exchange day two weeks on Friday. Completion a month later. It means by the summer we should be in St Albans. We can have barbecues!'

'That's great,' Bridget said, as the doorbell buzzed.

'I've got to go, Bridge. Talk later.'

'Enjoy the wedding.'

Gemma waddled down the spiral staircase, determined not to smudge her coral toes. 'Who is it?' she barked into the intercom.

'Flowers.'

'Oh! Come up.' Alex had sent her flowers. How unlike him. But how lovely. She opened the front door. An enormous bunch of lilies and roses was shoved into her arms, with a barked 'Delivery for Alex Meehan.' Under its weight Gemma staggered backwards. It was one of the most lavish bouquets she'd ever seen. But who on earth would be sending Alex flowers? It must be a mistake. They must be from Alex to her. Unless he was having an affair. Panicked, she studied the card.

You saved my bacon. I'll do anything for you mate. FH

There was the sound of a key turning in the lock and the door opened again to reveal Alex, his hair standing on end and waving a bottle of champagne.

'Poochie. I won! I got Frankie Holmes off.'

'Oh my goodness!' FH. Frankie Holmes, notorious crime baron, was sending her husband lilies and violet roses.

'Unanimous verdict. He was guilty as hell, but I had the jury wrapped round my little finger. I'm king of the world, baby.'

'He just sent you these flowers.'

'Really?' Alex laughed as he regarded the bouquet in his wife's arms. 'They're not very Frankie.'

'Are you *sure* all you did was fight a court case?' Gemma wiggled her eyebrows suggestively from behind a frond, just as she emitted a small fart. The whiff of lilies blotted it out.

'Well, there were the blow jobs in the robing room. After all, he said he'd do anything for me if I got him off. I guess this is just a start. Funny, I didn't think of Frankie as being a purple flowers kind of guy. But that must have been how he thought of me.' The phone started ringing. Alex grabbed it. 'Alex Meehan,' he trumpeted, then his face changed.

'Hi, Lucinda . . . Yes . . . Yes. Well, fuck him!' There was a long pause.

'What?' Gemma mouthed. Alex held up a hand to silence her.

'How fucking dare he! No. Well, tell him the sale's off then. Goodbye.' He turned to Gemma. 'Well, that's how to ruin a good mood. Nick Crex has dropped his offer again by fifty grand. We can't accept it. We're totally screwed.'

*

327

Lucinda was sitting at her desk, twisting her bracelet round her wrist. This week was proving a disaster. Dinner at Moro had been horrible; breaking the news to the Meehans had been even worse.

In the meantime, she had to deal with Anton. Since she'd run out of Sheekey's, he'd been calling the office about six times a day and sending emails by the dozen. Marsha was getting annoyed at having to field him.

Lucinda bought her a bunch of flowers. 'I'm sorry, Marsha, but it'll only be a couple of days and then he'll get the message.'

'You could just tell him to fuck off yourself and save me the grief,' Marsha grumbled. 'I've got enough on my mind already trying to work out how to pay Duwayne's bail.' She wasn't really that cross. Lucinda could see she was enjoying a bit of intrigue.

Now she chewed her pencil, trying to see a way to make things better. She had to find the nerve and energy to call Anton and once and for all explain that it was over – except there was no 'it' to begin with. Why couldn't he just get the message? Lucinda felt exhausted. She needed a break. A holiday. She hadn't had one since she'd started at Dunraven Mackie. Perhaps Mauritius, she thought. She wondered if Nick would come with her? But she wasn't sure he'd feel comfortable at the St Géran. Moro had made him tetchy enough, how would he cope with flunkeys offering him scented hand towels on the beach and scattering rose petals on the bed? And then she had another idea.

Tobago.

Of course. Their own home. And who couldn't love it there?

Fired up again, she seized her mouse to start checking flights. They'd go first class. A bit of an indulgence – Daddy always insisted his children flew cattle, unless he was travelling too, in which case they all went in his jet. But Lucinda could afford it.

'Lucinda,' said a harsh voice behind her.

She felt as if a cold hand had grasped her innards. Slowly she turned round, a smile frozen on her face.

'Hello, Anton.'

The room was silent. Everyone was pretending not to look or listen.

'Why the hell haven't you returned my calls? My emails? Last time I saw you, you were sick. I was worried.'

'I'm sorry, Anton, I've just been so busy.'

'Don't give me busy,' he snapped. '*I'm* busy. I would never be so discourteous as not to pick up the phone and tell somebody that I was feeling better, thank you. I thought you were a well-brought-up young woman. Obviously not.'

'Shall we go outside?' she hissed. 'Discuss it there?'

She led him out of the office and round the corner.

'I just want to know what's going on,' Anton said. 'I thought we had something here, but suddenly you're ignoring my calls and my emails. I don't understand it.'

'Anton, I'm really sorry. There was nothing going on. We were just friends. And . . . I've been busy and . . . I'm sorry if you got the wrong idea.'

'I don't understand,' he said. 'I hadn't even noticed you before you sent me that Valentine. Why did you do that if you didn't want me to notice you? It said "Marry Me", for Christ's sake.'

'I was just being stupid.' Lucinda wished an alien would vaporize her. Why had she behaved so childishly? 'Messing around.'

'Messing around?' He was very pale. 'Jesus, Lucinda. I was about to ask you to marry *me*.'

Christ, the man was insane! 'Marry you? We barely know each other.'

'There's someone else, isn't there?'

'No!'

'I know there is. Well, I only hope he doesn't treat you like you treated me. You use people, Lucinda. I can see that now.'

'I was just . . .'

But he'd turned on his heel and was marching off up the road, a slim, elegant, angry figure.

Shaking, Lucinda returned to the office. As the door closed behind her, Joanne started to giggle.

Marsha shrugged. 'I told you, Luce. You should have called him.'

Niall stood up. His face was the colour of uncooked pastry; it had obviously been another bad night with the babies.

'Lucinda, could we have a word in my office?'

'Now, look,' he said as soon as the door was shut. 'You know I'm a bit of a softie, but what's up with you? What goes on with you and Anton is your own business, I understand, but if he comes into the office we all get involved. Keep it private, please. And try to pull your finger out a bit. Your targets have slumped in the past weeks. Fewer viewings. No sales. I don't know. I took you on trust and it all seemed to be working out, but . . .'

'I'm really sorry, Niall,' said Lucinda. And she was. The next bit was bullshit, though. 'I think I'm just a bit tired. I haven't had a holiday since I started and I just need to recharge.'

'You're asking for a holiday?'

Lucinda knew she was pushing it. But suddenly she needed to be in Tobago more than anywhere else in the world.

'I'm owed some leave. I'm very run down. When I get back I promise to give you my all, Niall. And I'm sorry about Anton. You know there's never been anything between us, he just . . . misunderstood.'

'Well, no more misunderstandings.' Niall was clearly hating doing this. No wonder his wife ran rings around him. 'He's a valuable agency contact. Now we'll say no more about this. Go and sell some houses.'

'I will,' she said, gratefully. And she meant it. Lucinda might be dazzled by Nick at the moment, but her career was still important. Suddenly she wanted to shine in her job more than ever, to prove to Nick she wasn't a spoilt brat, let alone a leech like Kylie. She'd call everyone on her contacts list and drum up some spectacular business. Although first she'd call Nick and suggest a meeting tonight at Flat 15. Gemma and Alex were going away to a wedding. They could even stay the night.

So much for a relaxing weekend. Gemma and Alex argued all Friday evening on the drive down to Sussex, over dinner in the Michelin-starred restaurant, over Saturday's room service breakfast, and all the way to the wedding in a hamlet six miles away.

'Alex, we have to accept the offer, otherwise we really will lose Coverley Drive,' Gemma pleaded, as they drove round and round the village, looking for a parking spot. 'We must be able to find the extra cash from somewhere.'

'We can't. We're screwed. We don't have a spare penny. Especially not with the bill from Parenthope to pay. Let's only hope . . .'

'What?'

'Let's hope that works,' he said quietly.

'What, because you'd resent having to fork out for another go! God, Alex!'

'I didn't say that,' he protested, reversing into a spot behind a people carrier. 'It's just . . . well, it is so expensive.'

'Can you put a price on a child?'

'Of course you can't. But you're not meant to buy babies anyway. Look at that for genius parking.'

Gemma didn't care that her husband had reversed into a space the size of a matchbox. 'Are you saying this is a bad idea?'

'Stop putting words in my mouth, Poochie. You're all hormonal.'

'How dare you call me that,' she snarled, stepping out of the car. A woman with what looked like a cushion up her Diane von Furstenberg dress cried, 'Hey, Gems!'

'Oh! Hey! Christina.' Gemma held out her arms to her old school friend, feeling sick as she registered that wasn't a cushion.

'How are you?' Hug. Kiss. Kiss. 'I was hoping you'd be here.' Introductions of husbands. 'You must sit with us.

Oh,' Christina added a little self-consciously, patting the bump as they hurried up the picturesque church pathway. 'Don't think I've got fat. I'm expecting. In July.'

'Oh yes!' cried Gemma, pretending to have just noticed. 'Congratulations.'

'Bit of a shock,' Christina confided under her breath. 'We'd only just started trying. I thought I'd have at least a clear year of being able to enjoy myself, but no. Wham bam, bun in the oven, mam. No more booze and ciggies for moi. I can't tell you how much I miss sushi.'

A behatted head in the pew in front turned round. 'Christina? Oh my God. I couldn't help overhearing. Look!'

There was much screaming as Christina and Nicola, another girl from their year, whom Gemma had never much liked, compared bumps. Suddenly the conversation was all due dates and forbidden foods and pregnancy yoga. Where the hell was Lalage? Alex squeezed her hand tightly.

'Sod 'em,' he whispered. 'I bet your stretchmarks will be much uglier than theirs and you won't be able even to keep toast down.'

Gemma smiled serenely. She held on to the smile all the way through the ceremony and then the reception, where their table was full of couples discussing primary school admissions, how having one child was easy and it wasn't until two that 'life really began'.

'No children yourself, I take it?' one of the mums asked, in a gap when the mum on the other side of her had gone to the loo ('Bladder not what it was! Should have done those pelvic floors'). 'God, lucky you. Christ, do you remember, Diane,' she called across the flower arrangement. 'The childless days? Being able to read a book?'

'Not having to fish poos out of the bathwater.'

They both cackled with laughter. Gemma felt Alex's foot nuzzle hers under the table.

'Where are yours this weekend?' Mum One asked Mum Two.

'Staying with Granny. I have to say, I had mixed feelings. I mean, it's lovely to get a break from the little devils but I still think it's so thoughtless. I mean, if a wedding isn't a family affair then what is? What do you do if you can't get the childcare?'

'Oh, I agree. They'll understand when they have their own.'

'Champagne?' the teenage waitress asked Gemma.

'No, thank you.' Desperate as she was, there was no way she was going to pollute her body on the eve of this momentous event.

Mum One raised an eyebrow.

'Got something to tell us? How long is it you've been married now?'

'I'm on antibiotics,' Gemma explained.

'Antibiotics, eh?' She winked. 'Congratulations,' she said under her breath. 'I won't tell anyone. I thought you had that glow about you.'

'Thank you,' Gemma said smoothly.

Despite herself, she still had some fun. Determined to get all the demons out of her system, once Dave the DJ had set up, she and Alex danced manically to the 'Vida Loca' and smooched to 'I'm Not in Love'. No further reference was made to the flat sale. They fell into bed exhausted around two and made it down to breakfast just before ten.

'Make the most of this,' Alex said, as his full English was placed in front of him. 'When Chudney comes along there'll be no more leisurely meals.'

'There'll be a screaming demon in a highchair to contend with,' Gemma agreed, popping a slice of kiwi into her mouth. 'You'll be shoving mush in its face.'

'You'll be changing its dirty nappy in the ladies.' Alex cleared his throat. 'You know, as soon as we've checked out we need to head straight back.' 'Then I can start work after lunch.'

'Not even a walk before we leave?'

'Not if you want me being a sperm donor on Wednesday morning. There's a mountain of paper to plough through.'

'God, you're a barrel of laughs,' Gemma sighed, but smiling, as her phone started ringing in her pocket.

'What's this? I suppose I'd better answer it.' She pulled it out and looked at the caller ID. An ugly foreboding dawned. 'It's Bridget. Hello?'

'Hiya!' Bridget sounded as chirpy as ever. 'How was it? Did you have fun?'

'Yes, thanks,' Gemma said. Something was up. Gemma knew it.

'Good. Listen, sorry to tell you but . . . I'm just not sure I can do Wednesday.'

She said it as if she'd realized she couldn't make the cinema because it clashed with her meditation class. Gemma felt as if something had been smashed inside her chest, that there were splinters at the base of her throat. Her ears roared.

'Why not?' she heard herself say, as evenly as she could.

'What is it?' Alex asked. She waved a hand to silence him.

'I'm sorry. I'm really sorry. Massy and I have been talking. And we think it's just a bad idea. Because you know, we want children of our own one day. Soon. And if I give you these eggs and then I find I can't have any – how am *I* going to feel? Plus, like, getting the eggs out is a really major operation. My friend Arianne who's a homoeopath was saying that having a general anaesthetic's really bad for you and I might die and Massy got really upset and said he doesn't want me to die and . . .'

Gemma stood up. She made her way to the door and out into the lobby. 'But we went through this,' she hissed through clenched teeth. 'You said you didn't mind.'

'Yes, but that was before I met Massy.'

Gemma knew it. She'd always known that was the key. Known that asking her sister how she felt about future children just days before she met the love of her life was asking for trouble. She also knew that it was completely unreasonable to try to stop her. Bridget was allowed to have doubts, permitted to back out.

'How much?' she said.

'Sorry?'

'You heard me. How much do you want to change your mind?'

There was silence down the line.

'This isn't about money.' Bridget sounded wounded. 'It's about what we discussed with the counsellor. You know. How if I gave you my egg and then I couldn't have a baby of my own I'd regret it all my life … No, Massy, let me finish … I just don't think …'

'How much?' Gemma repeated steelily.

'Massy, we'll talk in a minute, I've told you. Gemma, I'm really sorry but this is it.'

'We have to talk about this.'

'We are talking, babes. I've made up my mind.'

'Do you think you could have given me a bit more notice?'

'I told you as soon as I made a decision.'

'Text me your address. I'm coming to see you. Don't you dare go out.'

Gemma hung up. Then she sat down heavily on a chintz-upholstered armchair. She buried her face in her lap. She felt as if something inside her chest had started bleeding.

## 31

Gemma and Alex drove back to London not speaking, the car tuned to Magic FM. Alex was already immersed in his next case. Gemma was thinking about how she'd like to hang, draw and quarter her sister. The bloody flake. She'd always been about as reliable as paper shoes in the rain. Why had Gemma allowed herself to think differently?

'What was Bridget calling about?' Alex asked.

'Oh. You know. She was reading some horoscopes online and she wanted to tell me what Chudney's character might be.'

'And . . . ?'

*If it takes after its biological mother, then fucking untrustworthy. Lazy. Feckless.* 'Oh, I can't remember. All nonsense. Listen, I think I'll go shopping this afternoon. Leave you to work in peace.'

'Don't spend too much money.' Alex clearly wouldn't have registered if Gemma had said Chudney was destined to be a transexual undertaker and she was off now to buy some toy coffins for it to practise on.

'I won't. Hey, isn't this song by the Vertical Blinds?'

They listened to the jangly guitar, the snarling yet oddly heart-tugging vocals.

'Fuckers. They're on the radio all the time and then they claim poverty. I'm going to download all their music illegally and make bootleg CDs of it and sell them down the market.'

'That would do wonders for your standing as a representative of the legal profession.'

'You do it, then.'

'If you show me how.' For the first time since the call, Gemma smiled. Weakly, admittedly. But the corners of her mouth definitely turned up.

Bridget and Massy's flat was on the top floor of a shabby 1930s pebble-dashed house situated right beside a dual carriageway in west London, the kind of house – if Gemma was honest – she had driven past often on her way to minibreaks in leafy West Country villages and wondered who on earth was unfortunate enough to actually live there. She shivered as she rang the bell. It had been mild when she'd set out, a day that promised cherry blossom and tulips unfurling. But during the journey, threatening clouds had gathered. Now a low wind sent crisp packets bouncing along the ground and nipped at her legs, making her wish she'd worn tights.

She rang the bell again. Perhaps it didn't work. More likely Bridget was pinned against the wall, as if she were avoiding a sharpshooter. She was just pulling her phone out of her pocket, to start berating her, when Massy's sleepy face appeared through the glass pane.

'Bridge has gone out,' he said, as he opened the door.

'I can wait.'

'She doesn't want to see you. Says she's too embarrassed. Says you'll say you knew this would happen, that she's always been a flake.'

339

It took a violent effort of will to keep her mouth shut, but Gemma succeeded.

'She knows you're upset but really, Gemma, you are asking a lot of her. Having her body invaded like this – giving away one of her future children. I'm a Catholic, you see, so this shit is, like, major for me.'

Gemma ignored this. 'Can I just come in? Have a cup of tea. I was hoping . . . I was hoping we might be able to do some kind of deal here.'

Behind Massy's deep-set eyes, a light seemed to flicker.

'Go on, then.'

She followed him into the flat. Greying net curtains concealed the view of cars, but the traffic roar was constant. There was a shabby grey sofa bed in the living room/bedroom, a tiny bathroom with a peeling lino floor and a kitchenette, the sink overflowing with dirty dishes. The room reeked of dope and there were ashtrays everywhere, overflowing with roaches. Gemma looked around, forcing a bright smile as she wondered what marijuana might be doing to Bridget's ovaries.

'This is nice!'

Massimo laughed. 'Really?'

'All it needs is some pictures on the wall. Maybe some new curtains. It could be really cosy.'

'Yeah, right,' he snorted.

Gemma sat down.

'Like I said,' she said, glancing up at the ceiling, where a huge patch of damp spread. 'I'm quite happy to give Bridget something in return for her help . . . Have you got any central heating here?'

Massy shrugged. 'No, but it's fine. We're coming into summer.'

'Or a bath?'

'No. Just a shower.' He grimaced. 'It's a bit leaky. But that's fine. As Bridge says, in India you often go days without showering.'

Through the ceiling, a woman's voice reverberated. '*All things bright and bee-yoo-tiful.*'

'Gloria from upstairs,' Massy shrugged. 'Choir practice.'

Gemma tried to hide her discomfort. No one should live like this. How could Bridget even be thinking of bringing her own baby into such a world? Babies shouldn't grow up in holes like this. Babies would be so much better off in Coverley Drive, in the room she'd designated the nursery, overlooking the sunny garden.

'You know, I could help you get out of here,' she said.

'How much?' replied Massy, quick as a flash.

'Enough to help the pair of you put a deposit on a flat.' Gemma performed some frantic mental arithmetic. Since property had crashed, you could get an OK flat for less than two hundred grand, if her memory of programmes starring Phil and Kirstie served her well. So ten per cent would be . . .

'Forty grand.'

'Twenty,' she replied.

'Thirty-five.'

'Twenty-five.'

'Thirty.' You could see he was trying not to laugh. And there was something comical about it in a warped sort of way.

'I'll give you twenty-seven thousand five hundred pounds. And that is my final offer.' She stood up.

'Done,' Massy said. He held out a hand. They shook. His skin was much rougher than Alex's.

'Of course I'd rather have had this conversation with Bridget,' Gemma said. 'Will you get her to call me when she comes in?'

'Of course,' Massy said.

*'My song is lo-o-ove unknown.'*

Already Gemma was beginning to regret her impulsiveness. She was sure Bridget would have settled for a much lower figure. Perhaps she should have held on. But she knew what Bridget was like. She'd stay out for several days if she thought Gemma was waiting for her. When her parents had been furious because she'd stolen Mum's credit card to buy a ticket to Ibiza she'd just gone and stayed on friends' sofas until the storm subsided. It was like Alex said, she could never tough anything out, never stick at anything long enough to make a go of it, because at the first hint of trouble she went running for cover.

'I'll expect to see her on Wednesday,' Gemma said.

'Well, yeah. So long as we have the money.'

'You'll have the money. I'll get it to you tomorrow.' She opened the door. 'You think she'll be OK with this?' she added, unable to contain her anxiety.

'I'll make sure of it,' Massy said firmly.

Gloria cranked it up a notch. *'A-ha-may-zing grace, how sweet the sound.'*

''Bye, Massy.'

''Bye, Gemma.'

*

342

She got back around three. Alex jumped up from the sofa.

'Poochie. Hey! Guess what.' He gestured to a huge hamper on the breakfast bar. 'Another gift from Frankie. Totally unethical, of course. Clients aren't meant to send their counsel gifts – well, they can but they must be relatively modest, according to the Bar Council. Still, I reckon a bottle of vintage Krug counts as relatively modest. As does a whole Stilton, a ham, a load of different relishes.' He rubbed his hands together. 'I'm taking on more hardened criminals, I tell you. How are you, anyway?'

'I'm fine.' She kissed him on the forehead, then walked past him towards the kitchen and turned the kettle on.

'Where have you been?'

'Shopping, I told you.'

'Where are the bags?'

'I didn't buy anything. Tea?'

She jumped as her phone bleeped in her pocket. Rapidly, she pulled it out and scanned the message.

Have talked to Massy. Changed my mind. Sorry to mess u about. See u Weds xxxxx.

As if she was apologizing for showing up late for a gig, Gemma thought. She tried not to allow her expression to change as she pressed 'delete'.

'Who was that?' Alex asked.

'Just Lalage thanking us for coming to the wedding. Are there any fancy teas in this hamper? Or biscuits?'

'Oh, I found your bracelet,' he said.

'Bracelet?'

343

'Under the table.' He held up three rows of pearls held together by a diamond clasp.

'That's not mine. God, Alex, it's been . . . what, four years and you haven't noticed I don't own anything as bling as that.'

She held out her hand and studied the glinting diamonds, then clipped the bracelet round her wrist and tipped it this way and that, admiring the way light bounced off the huge, creamy pearls, like quail's eggs.

'That's got to be Lucinda's. She's the only person I know who wears that kind of jewellery. I'll call her in the morning and let her know she must have dropped it. As well as give her an answer on Nick Crex's new offer.'

They eyed each other warily.

'All right,' Alex said. 'I've been thinking about it. We can do it, much as it pains me, but we won't be able to make any pension contributions next year.'

'Oh, thank you!' Gemma cried, throwing her arms around him. Pensions schmensions. Who cared about their old age? Far more pressing was how to find £27,500 in twenty-four hours.

## 32

On Monday morning, Massy called Gemma.

'It took a while to talk Bridget round,' he said. 'She wasn't sure. She said you shouldn't buy a baby, that she went over all of this with the counsellor. But I said you weren't buying anything. You were just showing her appreciation for all the hard work involved.'

'Exactly,' Gemma agreed, phone tucked under her chin. She looked down at the breakfast bar. Lucinda's bracelet sat there. She needed to call her and say they were accepting Nick 'The Miser' Crex's offer. She picked the bracelet up and slipped it over her hand as she asked, 'Why can't Bridget talk to me herself?'

'You know what she's like. All sensitive.' He continued. 'And then there's this question of if we couldn't have a baby of our own. I admit, that was my fault. She mentioned to me that she'd had that discussion with the counsellor and I went sort of apeshit. I'm Italian, you see. Family means everything to me.'

'I know. You said. Catholic and all that. Every sperm is sacred.'

Massy ignored her sarcastic tone. 'You saw the shithole we're living in. I want more than that for my kids. If you could guarantee us twenty-seven and a half grand by close of play today, I'll see Bridget makes it to the clinic on Wednesday.'

Gemma's heart was racing, but she spoke very slowly. 'I'm not sure I can get you that in cash. Not by the end of the day. But I can set the wheels in motion.'

'You can do a CHAPS transfer in one day. Ask your bank how. I'll give you my account details. I want to know the money's in my account by the end of the day.'

'Shouldn't it be in Bridget's account?' Gemma was surprised at how clued up Massy was.

He sighed. 'Do you really think Bridget would have a bank account? She honestly still keeps it all under the mattress.'

'You'll get it,' she said.

She wasn't as confident as she sounded. There was three grand in the joint account and £530 in her own personal account. She started rifling through Alex's files, desperately scanning folders entitled 'Pensions', 'Investments', files which – she realized with a shock – she had never even touched before. That was men's business. What was wrong with her? How could she seriously be contemplating motherhood when she had no idea how much cash she and her husband had? Gemma felt disgust at herself, disgust for the past few years she'd spent window-shopping and lying on a bed having someone fiddle with her toes when she could have been mastering such matters.

She had no idea how to liquidate a pension. Or cash in an ISA. She was sure even trying to do so would spark a flurry of calls to Alex's chambers. She looked around the room, totting up the value of the furniture in there. The fucking zebra-skin sofa had cost three and a half grand. What on earth had they been thinking of? It wasn't even that comfortable, it was a nightmare to clean and it represented nearly a fifth of the total she had to find – the equivalent of a baby's thigh and knee.

The telly – another two grand because Alex had insisted on HDTV. The kitchen? Now that was worth twenty-five grand but she could hardly dismantle the Italian marble surfaces herself and get them on eBay by tonight.

She examined her jewellery, her clothes, her shoes. Thousands upon thousands of pounds that she'd spunked away – a bit like Alex's pointless ejaculations – on Nine West and Jigsaw, the odd thing from Nicole Farhi and a lot more from Zara. All that clobber must have been worth at least twenty-five grand, but there was no way it would fetch that much second-hand. Why hadn't she foreseen this moment and started saving years ago, putting every tenner earmarked for bubble bath into a 'bribing Bridget account'? Money had always seemed so abstract, moving frictionlessly from account to account, without you being able to touch it or see it. But its consequences were anything but abstract. They dictated the most concrete details of her life.

Gemma stared at her hands. She'd been gnawing her cuticles again. Stared at her ring finger. The band of platinum dotted with discreet diamonds, and on top of it a multi-faceted rock that Gibraltar had nothing on, surrounded by sapphires. Alex's grandmother's. The family heirloom.

Would he notice its brief absence? Unlikely. Alex was usually so absorbed in his work, he wouldn't notice if she walked around in a dirty tea towel with a pair of his boxers on her head. And if, by any fluky chance, he did, she could say she'd taken it to have it polished. He wouldn't question that.

Sitting at the computer, Gemma googled 'pawnbrokers hatton garden'.

She envisaged a dark, musty shop down an alleyway. A black cat purring on the sill of a rattly sash window. A dirty red carpet and an old man with a long white beard hobbling out of a back room crammed with dusty treasures. Instead, the pawnbrokers looked just like any other jewellers on Hatton Garden: bright, modern, with plate-glass windows displaying gold bracelets and Rolexes. Only the three discreet golden balls over the entrance hinted that you could sell as well as buy there. But still. Pawnbrokers. They were for little old ladies needing to pay the gas bill, not young women wanting to purchase the latest in fertility treatments.

Gemma pressed the bell and was buzzed in. An Asian man stepped out from behind the counter. He was in his late twenties, sharp-suited and smiling.

'Good morning, madam.'

'Good morning.' She looked around nervously. Radio 1 was playing loudly. She could see nothing suitable for extracting a pound of flesh.

'Can I help you?'

'I want to pawn something,' she said. It came out louder than she'd intended.

'Come in the back room, madam,' he said smoothly, only slightly spoiling the effect by yelling over his shoulder: 'Oi, Sharmila. Come and mind the shop, will ya?'

In the back room, she took off the ring and placed it on the table in front of him.

'You realize any loan will only be for about half the item's value,' the man – who'd introduced himself as Raf – said. 'The interest rate is four per cent a month at the moment, it's a six-month term, and if at the end you haven't paid what's owing, the item will be sold with any profits after our expenses and interest returned to you.'

'Oh!' Gemma said. This was comforting. 'So even if I can't pay you back the interest, I'll still get some money back.'

'It wouldn't be much,' Raf warned her, picking up the ring and studying it, a troubled expression on his face. 'The interest would have eaten away most of it. But better than nothing, eh?' He winked, then put a jeweller's loupe to his eye and examined the ring. There was a long pause. It was like watching the *Antiques Roadshow*, when the old woman was about to learn the ugly old teapot from her attic was worth half a million. Gemma braced herself. Probably there'd be cash left over to cover 'Stinge' Crex's shortfall.

'Um. I don't know how to tell you this.'

'Yes?' She leaned forward eagerly.

'This ring . . . did you think it was . . . ? Well, this ring's a fake. It's probably worth around thirty quid.'

'What?'

'I'm really sorry,' Raf said. 'It happens all the time. People lie about what gifts are worth.'

'My husband didn't lie! His grandmother told him. She was given it by the Rajah of somewhere-or-other Stan. When she was working in India.' Did that sound racist? Gemma blushed, but Raf just laughed.

'In the back room of the Rajah of somewhere's curry house, more like. I'm sorry, love. I can give you forty quid for it, if that helps. As a favour because you seem like a nice lady.'

Gemma felt crushed. 'Are you sure?'

'I'm sorry. I'm not trying to rip you off. We've got government regulations all over us to make sure of that.' She stood up, as Raf pointed at her right wrist. 'But that bracelet you're wearing. I could do something with that.'

Gemma looked down. Lucinda's pearls, the double row, the diamond clasp.

'That's vintage Cartier. Didn't you know?'

'No. I . . .'

Raf laughed. 'Good thing you've come to someone as honest as me. Love, that bracelet's probably worth more than these premises. I can give you thirty grand for it. Cash. The interest will be a killer, mind. So if you think you can't pay it you might want to think again. Family heirloom, is it?' He was punching numbers into a calculator. 'Here. This is what you'd have to pay per month.'

'But I could walk out of here with thirty grand?' Gemma said slowly.

'Absolutely.'

'And if I can't pay the interest, you'd sell the bracelet?'

'That's the way it works.'

Gemma began fiddling with the clasp. 'Let's go for it.'

# 33

For the next forty-eight hours Gemma barely slept. She was pretty certain everything was in place. After Raf had handed over the wodge of fifty-pound notes, she'd nervously driven across London to Massy's Costa and passed him the plastic bag of cash.

On Wednesday, Alex visited the clinic alone for the sperm donation. Gemma lied and told him she was too stressed to accompany him, reminding him that he hadn't been able to make it to any of the scans. Reluctantly, he agreed, calling three hours later from chambers to report that the selection of porn mags had been disappointing but still he'd done his duty. No, he hadn't seen Bridget but they'd told him she'd arrived at her appointed time and all had gone well.

'But you'll talk to her yourself, won't you?' he said.

'Yes, but I wanted to leave it a while,' Gemma lied. 'She's been under general anaesthetic, she needs to rest for now.'

'OK. Did you speak to Lucinda?'

Gemma cringed. She'd find a way to pay back the money, she'd return the bracelet to Lucinda one day. It would just take a couple of months.

'Yes. I said we'd accept the offer. And then I called the Drakes' lady and said we were dropping ours. Naturally she went mental.'

'Naturally,' Alex agreed. 'But chin up, Poochie. Right now my sperm's mixing with Bridget's egg.'

Phil was in the worst mood Karen had seen him in since he'd received the diagnosis. The Meehans had dropped their offer, saying they'd had no choice now their buyer had lowered his.

'I can't believe those arseholes are doing this to us,' he yelled, as he got ready for bed. 'How fucking dare they? Do they think we're still living in the Eighties or something, all backstabbing and gazundering? Next thing we'll know they'll be turning up here in stonewashed jeans and playing Kajagoogoo on top volume.'

'Darling, don't get stressed, you know it's bad for you,' Karen said. She lay in bed, watching him. His pyjama trousers were too short for his long, skinny legs. Max's legs were firm and muscular. Since Phil had chosen yoga over dinner, she'd been seeing Max as often as possible. When she was with him she was perfectly happy; the time they had seemed golden, separate, untouchable, like a butterfly suspended in amber. She still told herself firmly that it was just a fling, even though she knew it was much, much more. But why not? Why couldn't she just be happy even for a short time?

'I'll fucking get stressed if I want to. You know what Chadlicote means to me. And now our margins are getting squeezed.'

'Well,' she said. 'If it means that much to you, you'll just have to take the hit.'

'But the money's hardly there. Not when we budget what we need for renovations.'

Karen worded it carefully. 'What if I carried on working? Rented a flat. Stayed in London with the girls for a year or so. Saved every penny and then . . .'

For a moment, she thought he was going to buy it. But then he shook his head.

'No. We have to be together. Otherwise this is all pointless.' He smiled at her. 'Thanks, though, darling. I appreciate the gesture.'

'That's OK,' she said.

'I'll work something out,' Phil said. 'I am not having this taken away from me.'

Karen counted the hours until she'd see Max again.

Somehow the next two days passed. And then it was Friday morning. The day the clinic would call. Either 'Come in, the embryos are good,' or 'Sorry, don't bother, it won't be worth your while.'

The phone rang at five minutes past nine.

'Gemma, it's Donna. I'm delighted to say it's all systems go. We're eight four-celled embryos, all grade one standard. The best possible result. Could you and Alex make it here for noon? And remember, drink as much water as possible. The transfer works best on a full bladder.'

Lucinda called Nick. 'Want to meet?' she asked.

'OK,' he said flatly.

Lucinda's stomach shrivelled like a walnut. Nick had been so off with her lately. Automatically, she reached for her right wrist to twist her bracelet, then remembered she hadn't been able to find it for a few days. She had a horrible feeling she had left it at the Meehans' flat on Friday night. They'd had good sex then, but Nick had still been distant, refusing to stay the night, even though the Meehans wouldn't be back until the following afternoon. Perhaps he was going back to Kylie? Either way Lucinda needed to know where she stood. She'd booked the holiday, now she'd see how he reacted to the news.

She spoke calmly. 'Good. Gemma's got reflexology this afternoon. So I'll meet you at the flat at the usual time.'

'OK,' he said and hung up.

The room was very brightly lit. A chair with stirrups in front of it sat in the middle of the room like an instrument of torture. Monitors beeped. In a mask and gloves, Sian was almost unrecognizable.

'Can't believe this weather. You need to take your pants off, sit down, and then I'm afraid it's stirrups time again. Did you see *Relocation, Relocation* last night? It was a repeat but *such* a good one . . .'

Gemma went behind the screen provided, pulled off her knickers and skirt, after a brief second's hesitation, folded them and placed them on a hook. Her bladder was so full, she was seriously worried she'd wet herself. She climbed into the torture chair and pulled a sheet over her nether regions. Sian was talking to Alex.

'They didn't listen to a word Kirstie told them. And they were so fussy. It had to be a south-facing garden, four double bedrooms. I mean, people don't know they're born.' Alex nodded politely, as Sian pulled on a pair of white gloves. Gemma stared at the wall of babies, to distract herself from the overwhelming need to pee. She was sure there were a couple of new photos since she'd last been in.

Even now, so close, she still felt jealous of those lucky ones.

'Was that baby here before?' she asked, pointing at a chubby-faced blonde in a pink and white babygro.

Sian looked vague. 'Um, I'd have to check. Possibly. We get a lot of baby photos as you can imagine. Of course you'll be sending me yours.' A strange buzzing sound filled the air and an electronic hatch in the wall opened. On the wall-mounted TV screen, Gemma saw a swarm of cells swimming around, magnified a thousand times. They were hypnotically, compellingly beautiful. The Meehans gaped.

'Wow.' *Come on, come on, don't dilly-dally or I'll wet myself.*

'Wow, indeed,' Sian grinned. Your sister is very fertile. Of course we're only allowed to put in two embryos. Take it from me, you may want a baby but you don't want triplets. Twins'd be . . . Oh, sorry, forget I said that.'

She picked up her giant syringe and sucked up the embryo. She turned round and headed towards Gemma. *Come on, come on.* She pulled back the sheet. Gemma exhaled as Sian inserted a cold speculum inside her. *Don't pee on her hand.* She inserted the needle-like syringe.

'Stop!' yelled a voice at the door.

All heads turned. Bridget was standing there, eyes wild.

'I don't want you to do this,' she said. 'They paid for these eggs. Nobody told me. I didn't want the money. And now Massy's gone. He's gone and taken it all. I want you to stop now!'

Sian put her hand to her throat, like a Victorian seeing a table leg.

'Who let you in?'

'I tried to stop her,' said a harassed-looking Donna behind her. 'I couldn't.'

'Is it too late?' asked Bridget. Her hair was all over the place and her face was fuchsia.

'Yes, it is,' said Sian. 'And it has been since you signed the eggs away. Now out of here.' She clicked a gloved finger as if Bridget were a pesky fly.

'Gemma!'

Gemma tried to rise above the fact that her legs were in stirrups and her lady bits were on display to everyone and that any moment her bladder was going to empty itself all over the bed.

'It's too late, Bridge. You've signed the papers.'

'And anyway, the eggs have gone in now,' said Sian. 'Now out! Shoo,' she added for good measure.

'What do you mean we paid for them?' Alex said. 'We didn't pay anything.'

'Yes, you did. You paid Massy twenty-seven grand to talk me round. He told me and we had a row about it and I wanted to give the money back and now he's gone.'

'Oh, Bridge,' said Gemma.

'Did you pay Bridget?' Alex asked.

'Get her out of here,' Sian screamed. 'We are in the middle of a medical procedure.'

'Did she pay you?' Alex demanded of Bridget.

'She paid Massy. And I told you, he's taken it all.'

Gemma hauled herself on to her elbows, the pain in her stomach almost forgotten. 'Look, Bridge. I'm really sorry. Sorry I paid him. Sorry he's taken it. But this would've never happened if I'd trusted you a bit more. If I wasn't so used to you messing me around. Not playing by the rules.'

'Playing by the rules? What the fuck are you talking about? You're the one who broke the rules, paying Massy.'

'Yes,' Alex chimed in.

'I was paying *you*, not Massy. And what choice did I have? I wanted a baby so much and you were my only chance and you said yes and then you said no and . . .' Fat, hot tears streamed down her face. 'You always do this. Change your mind. Cheat.'

'Cheat? What about you? You're the one who realized you weren't going to make it as a ballerina, so you "accidentally" slipped on the steps and sprained your foot. Nicely writing a get-out clause for yourself. Not having to admit to anyone you couldn't actually hack it.'

It was like being walloped over the head. Gemma had never admitted that to anyone. She was the good, reliable sister who didn't give up when the going got tough. Spraining her foot had been the greatest excuse of all time to leave a job she hated. But how did Bridget know?

'It's true, isn't it?' Bridget challenged.

'No, it isn't!'

'Will you get out now!' Sian yelled. 'Or I will call the police, so help me God.'

'Please,' Gemma said. 'I really need the loo.'

The first thing you were supposed to do after implantation was visit the reflexologist.

'I can get a taxi,' Gemma said meekly as they walked out of the clinic.

'Don't be ridiculous. I'll drive you there.'

They sat in silence. All the beautiful thoughts Gemma had meant to be directing towards her womb were now

357

drowned out in a sea of recriminations. She'd borrowed – no, be honest, she'd stolen – Lucinda's bracelet to raise the money. And now Massy had stolen it. Bridget had been escorted out of the clinic weeping. Distraught. Saying she didn't want Gemma to bear this child.

It was a disaster. Gemma felt bad for her sister and Lucinda, and Alex and herself. But her priority was the baby. She'd lose it with all this stress. She bloody knew she would. And if that happened she would hunt Massy down and kill him very slowly, using techniques honed in Abu Ghraib.

They drove up Camden High Street towards Belsize Park, where Raquel, the reflexologist, lived. Past shops with racks of vintage dresses outside and windows full of buckled biker boots. Reggae pounded from speakers. French teenagers smoked joints. Beggars sat cross-legged next to cashpoints. In other words, life went on.

'I'm so sorry. I should have told you.'

'Where did you get the money from?' Alex said, his tone emotionless.

'I pawned . . . a piece of jewellery I had. It turned out to be more valuable than I thought.'

'Not Granny's ring!'

'No, darling,' she lied, holding out her engagement finger as proof. 'I could never ever part with that. It means so much to me. It was just an old necklace.'

'And where were you planning to find the cash to redeem this old necklace?'

She decided not to tell him her plan to flog off her entire wardrobe on eBay. 'I was stupid.'

'Right.' Alex turned to her as they stopped at a light. 'Well, if it's got us a baby it'll have been worth it.'

'Really?' Tears pricked at Gemma's eyes.

'Of course. But I do feel bad for Bridget. She went through an unpleasant medical procedure and now her boyfriend's dumped her and run off with a load of cash. We're going to have to make it up to her.'

'How?'

'I don't know. But we owe her. Owe her a lot.' Alex paused, then said, 'What she said about spraining your foot . . .'

Gemma could have confessed. But every marriage has its secrets.

'All bollocks. You know that.'

He smiled at her as he pulled up outside Raquel's. 'I'll wait here for you, Poochie. Then I'll take you home.'

'You're so lovely,' she said.

'Look, don't get all American on me. I want this baby as much as you do. Maybe more. So don't give me any of this lovely crap. I'm just being selfish, trying to perpetuate my genes.'

'You're sure?'

'Look,' he said, 'I know how much you've suffered. I know what a trouper you've been. Pretending not to be bothered every time the test was negative. All that stiff-upper-lip stuff. You've been so brave. But there's no need any more. We're in this together. If it fucks up I'll be as devastated as you. If it works . . . well, it'll be good.'

She stared at him, tears welling again.

'See you in an hour. Get the foot lady to work her magic.'

'Aye, aye, sir.'

*

359

They drove home in silence. Took the lift up to the second floor. Walked along the corridor.

'I'll run you a bath,' he said, as he put his keys into the lock, and then, stepping into the flat, 'Oh!'

'What?' But looking past him, Gemma saw. A skinny blond guy, his trousers halfway down his legs. And Lucinda, T-shirt hoiked up and fumbling with the waistband of her skirt.

'What the fuck is going on?' Alex asked.

# 34

Lucinda's face was on fire. Her hands shook uncontrollably, her legs were jelly. She thought she might be about to vomit.

She couldn't look at Nick as the lift carried them down. It had all happened in a blur. She'd mumbled something about how they'd been measuring up, and Alex Meehan had said was that what she called it and shouted at them to get out. Which they had. Pronto.

What would the agency say? What would *Daddy* say? Oh God, she'd been so unbelievably stupid. What had she been thinking of?

But she wouldn't show Nick how thrown she was. That wasn't Lucinda's style at all. If she was going down, it would be with honour: like Captain Hardy on the sinking ship. Or was it Captain Oates going out into the snow? What was going on? Lucinda was supposed to know this kind of thing.

'Sorry about that,' she said to Nick as they stepped out into Summer Street. 'We forgot to double-bolt the door. Getting careless.'

The strong sunlight had bleached out his face, so she could barely see his expression.

'Will they tell everyone about this? Will it get in the papers?'

'Of course not,' she said firmly. *Oh God, no. Not the papers.* 'I'll probably lose my job, though.'

'I'll be fucked.'

What? Lucinda stared at him. This was hardly a gallant reaction. 'Excuse me? I just said I'll probably lose my job. What will you lose?'

'My girlfriend.'

'Your girlfriend? The girlfriend you obviously care so much about, since you've been sleeping with me these past few weeks.'

'Your job, which is obviously so important because you really need the money.'

They glared at each other.

'I don't work for the money. I work because I enjoy it.'

'Yeah, right. Selling flats. How stimulating.'

'It *is* actually,' said Lucinda, shocked to feel tears stinging her eyes. Her phone started ringing in her bag. It would be the office. It would be Niall. Sacking her. She looked at the caller ID. Cass. Irritably she switched it to voicemail.

'I need to get back to work,' she said briskly. 'Receive my marching orders.'

'Right.' Nick wasn't making eye contact. Suddenly she hated him. Why wasn't he acting even the least bit concerned? She felt as if a lump of ice was wedged in her diaphragm. Had she lost her job for a man like this?

'Goodbye,' she said and, turning on her heel, marched off to meet her fate.

Gemma and Alex looked at each other and started to laugh. And laugh. And laugh.

'Unbelievable,' said Alex, when the giggles finally subsided.

'I'm calling that bunch of rip-off shysters right now and telling them what their star agent has been up to.'

'Don't do that!' Gemma yelled as he reached for his mobile.

'Why ever not? What else are we supposed to do?'

'I'd just . . .' Gemma wasn't going to tell him about the bracelet. She'd done a bad thing and now Lucinda had too. They'd cancelled each other out. 'Just I don't need the stress right now.'

'You're mad,' Alex smiled.

'Look, the sale is almost completed. They're not going to have the cheek to come back again, are they? Let's just let it ride.'

'But . . .'

'We've got enough stress with all this . . .' She laid her hand on her still-flat stomach. 'Please just leave it. Please.'

Alex stared at her, then shook his head ruefully. 'All right, Poochie. Your wish is my command.'

'I'm getting fed up with this,' Max said.

Karen swallowed hard. This was it. He was telling her it was over. He was bored. He wanted someone his own age. Who could blame him?

'OK,' she said dully.

He pulled himself up on his elbow and looked at her. His eyes were that extraordinary shade of greyish blue and his lips were so full. Karen didn't know how she'd live without kissing them again.

'Well, aren't you? All this snatched time together. Which we only spend in bed. I mean, not that being in bed with you isn't the best thing in the world. But I want more,

Karen. I want to go out with you. To eat. To the cinema. To meet my friends. I'm tired of it all being so hole-in-the-corner and rushed.'

'But what other way can it be?' she asked. 'I've got to get home to the girls. To Phil. It's hard enough to find time to see you as it is.'

'I know,' he said.

'You knew it was going to be like this. I've always told you the truth.'

'I know. But I . . . I . . .'

Karen felt giddy. She knew he was going to say something important.

'I didn't realize I was going to care so much,' he whispered.

Her heart twisted. She felt as if it might explode.

'I didn't either,' she said, leaning forward to kiss his cheek.

Max sat up. 'So what are we going to do about it? Because I'm not sure I can carry on like this. Can't you even stay the night some time?'

'You know I can't. I'd love to, but I can't.'

'Fuck.'

'Max, if only I could. If only there was some way . . .'

'Come away with me. For a weekend. Just two days and a night. It would be better than nothing.'

'I thought us girls were the ones who were meant to crave minibreaks.' She laughed at his confused expression. 'Never mind. Max, I can't. It's so hard to explain, but when you're a wife, let alone a mum, you can't just disappear for two days.'

'Other mums do it. I mean they have affairs.'

'Not many of them, that I'm aware of.' But Karen's brain was turning, like pistons on a steam train, trying to work out what she might be able to organize. A story about a hen weekend. Jamila's? Phil was so uninterested in her work friends, it was highly unlikely he'd question that. If she bought Ludmila a bottle of perfume . . .

Max saw her expression change.

'You're going to try? How about this weekend?'

'Maybe.'

'I'll book something amazing. Come on. Let's go for it.'

'I'll see what I can do.'


By the time he got home, Nick was really worried. He'd literally been caught with his trousers down. This could get all over the papers. Kylie would find out. He also had a smidgin of concern for Lucinda. She'd told him often enough that her dad was a hard, pushy bastard with a phobia about publicity. He wouldn't take this well.

He expected she'd call him, telling him she'd been sacked. But she didn't. The evening was like a timebomb. He sat with Kylie, sharing takeaway fish and chips and watching *Big Brother*. At any second the phone would ring – Andrew saying the papers had a story, Lucinda telling him she was on a plane home to Switzerland. Why? Why? It hadn't been worth it. OK, he'd shagged a beautiful posh bird but ultimately it had been a distraction, it had meant nothing to him.

Guiltily, sure it would be the last time, he made love to Kylie extra tenderly. He woke up late, after she had gone to work, on tenterhooks.

Still nothing.

In the end, he called her.

'Oh, hello, Mr Crex,' she said coolly. 'We seem to be all set for completion next week. If there are any problems in my absence you can discuss them with my colleague Gareth Mountcastle.'

'Your absence?'

'Yes. I am going on holiday tomorrow. Just a short break. Four days.'

'Right,' Nick said slowly. All his feelings about Lucinda turned on their heads. He didn't want her to go.

'Goodbye, Mr Crex.'

'Where are you going?'

'To Tobago. I have to go now.'

Tobago. She'd mentioned her family had a 'place' there. He wasn't quite sure where Tobago was. Somewhere hot.

'I . . .'

'Goodbye.'

A couple of seconds later, a text arrived.

You can come with me if you like. But need to know asap as leaving tomorrow a.m. L

Nick thought. Did he really want to go somewhere far away: somewhere sweaty, with weird food, with Lucinda? Lucinda who, he'd just decided, wasn't really worth it. But then he thought, *This is the life you want. Villas in far-off places. Smart women. Do you want to stay with a Burnley girl for the rest of your life?*

He texted back.

I'll come.

## 35

Karen was wide awake at five. Phil slept blithely beside her. She'd been awake the previous night when he came in from yoga, but she'd lain there stiffly, eyes closed, breathing loudly and regularly as he tiptoed around in the dark, getting undressed, muttering 'Shit' when he stubbed his toe in the dark. Once he'd said 'Karen? It's only ten o'clock.' She'd breathed even louder. He'd sighed and given up.

Now she sneaked downstairs into the kitchen. This was the big day. Once she'd made up her mind she'd decided to go for it sooner rather than later. She'd used the Jamila hen night story and although Phil had grumbled a bit about being in sole charge all weekend, he hadn't questioned her.

'Mummy?'

Karen jumped. Bea stood behind her in her Lola pyjamas. So tiny, frail, innocent.

'Are there any brioches?'

'No, darling. I think we've got croissants though.' Normally croissants were reserved for birthdays and Christmas, but now wasn't the moment to quibble.

'I don't like croissants. I only like brioches!'

Normally that kind of bratty remark would have acted like a touch paper, but now Karen spoke slowly. 'Well, ask Daddy to take you to the supermarket later and buy some. Because I'm away this weekend, remember?'

'Oh yeah.' Bea climbed on her knee, wrapping her skinny arms around Karen's neck. 'I'll miss you, Mum.'

'I'll miss you too,' Karen said, wondering how she could ever have thought this would work.


Nick wasn't quite sure how it had all happened. He was sitting in the first class cabin of a BA plane, halfway across the Atlantic Ocean, headphones on, watching the new Batman movie on his personal DVD player. Beside him, Lucinda was reading *The Economist*. It had all been so quick. Less than twenty-four hours after he'd said he'd come, a limo had drawn up outside the flat in Belsize Park and his phone had rung.

'I'm waiting,' said Lucinda's voice. 'I hope you have your passport.'

'Uh. Yeah.' He had a small bag as well, with a couple of T-shirts and pairs of jeans. He'd packed surreptitiously the night before when Kylie was watching *Big Brother*. 'I'll be right down.'

'Good.'

'Where are you off to?' Kylie smiled at him now from the breakfast bar, as he slung the bag over his shoulder.

He couldn't make eye contact. 'Away for a few days.'

She looked understandably aghast. 'Why didn't you tell me?'

'I thought I did.'

'Where?'

'Just away. Secret retreat. To do some songwriting. Andrew thought it would be a good idea.'

'How long will you be gone?'

'I don't know. Three or four days.' In his pocket his phone started ringing again. 'Not long.' He pecked her on the cheek. 'I'll call you.'

'But why didn't you say?' she asked, as he slammed the door on her.

Now he couldn't quite shake off the image of Kylie's woestruck face. He distracted himself, looking around. It was crazy really that an up-and-coming hot young rock star like himself had never flown first class. Or long haul come to that. The band had flown about Europe to various awards and whatever but it was usually on Easyjet or Ryanair, times being tough in the music industry.

He tried not to gawp too much at the plane's interior. Tried not to stare at Naomi Campbell and someone he was pretty sure Kylie liked from last season's *X Factor*. Tried to remember that he was one of Britain's hottest new rock stars and to conceal his panic every time the engine made a funny noise. Lucinda continued flicking the pages nonchalantly, a glass of champagne on the little table beside her. Clearly she did this kind of thing all the time.

Somehow that made it less fun. He wished he were there with Kylie, Kylie who would be nudging him, openly awestruck. He looked at the map on his TV screen. They were somewhere over the Atlantic Ocean. Another three hours to go. There was going to be a brief touchdown in Grenada, apparently, and then another hour in the air. Once again, Nick tried to dismiss his worries. It would be hot. Nick hated the heat. It made him come out in a rash. But there'd be shade, wouldn't there? It would be fine. He was living the life he'd always dreamed of.

Lucinda turned to him.

'You know we can have complete privacy in here, if we want it?'

'Oh, yeah?'

'Yeah. No one will bother us. You raise a screen by touching this button. And the chairs go back and turn into beds.'

She smiled at him. She had a slight overbite that turned him on incredibly. He felt the familiar lurch of excitement in his groin.

'What do you think?'

'Go on then,' he said. He'd made the right call. This was going to be a blast.

Max was waiting for Karen outside the Thameslink station, sitting at the wheel of his red Mini Cooper. She was used to seeing him either in one of his work suits or naked but now he was in a baggy black T-shirt and jeans. At the sight of him, Karen felt suddenly terrified. He was so young, so handsome, so carefree in comparison to her.

'So where are we going?' she asked, as they headed west along Euston Road.

'Magical mystery tour.'

'Oh, come on!' She picked the Vertical Blinds out of his pile of CDs and pushed it into the slot.

'No. You'll guess anyway when you see which way we're heading. What did you tell Phil?' he asked, eyes on the traffic.

'Hen weekend.' She felt one of her usual lurches of

remorse. 'Oh Christ, Max. I shouldn't have come. This is terrible.'

'Really? It doesn't seem terrible to me. It seems pretty . . . excellent, actually.'

Silence apart from the junkie lead singer snarling, *'We're all just cogs in a machine. Do you know what I mean?'*

'If you want us to turn round I will,' he said resignedly.

'No! Don't turn round.'

Stepping off the plane, Nick immediately felt as if he had been swaddled in wet towels. His heart fluttered like a trapped moth. How was he going to stand this? The terminal building, which he'd expected to be a gleaming air-conditioned mall, like the European airports he'd passed through with the band, was little more than a shack. A ceiling fan moved lazily overhead as they queued with their passports.

'Oh look!' said Lucinda, as they came out into a drab little hall with luggage shuffling round an ancient conveyor belt. 'There's Dolly.' She waved enthusiastically at someone in the noisy crowd on the other side of the barrier.

'Dolly?' For a second he thought she was talking about one of her childhood toys.

'Our caretaker. I've known him and his wife Mrs Marilia for ever. They're adorable. Hey, Dolly! Hey!'

A skinny, grizzled man approached them as they emerged through customs. 'Lucinda,' he replied, giving her a big hug. 'Great to see you. What a treat for us.'

'More of a treat for me! It's so lovely to smell the

Tobago air. Dolly, this is my friend Nick. Nick, Dolly.'

Nick didn't like the way Dolly scanned him. He seemed both amused and startled. But all he said was, 'Nice to meet you.'

'Likewise.'

His suitcase seemed very small, very ordinary, compared to Lucinda's Louis Vuitton one. Dolly placed them in the back of his jeep. Thankfully, it was air-conditioned inside. The car bumped along what Nick guessed passed for a motorway, although it was quarter the size of anything at home. Dusk was falling, and it was hard to see much except the odd low-roofed building and people sitting outside on deckchairs, holding beers and chatting. Reggae throbbed from a ghetto blaster.

'How's your dad, Lucinda?'

'Very well. Working too hard as ever. What about your family?'

'Got a new grandchild,' Dolly grinned. 'Her name's Jean.'

'Oh Dolly, fantastic. How old?'

'Oh, just two weeks. You'll see her. She's a noisy little creature but we love her.'

'I can't wait. You should have told me. I'd have brought her a present.'

'That's exactly why we didn't tell you.' He glanced briefly over his shoulder at Nick. 'Lucinda's a very generous girl. Too generous.'

'Oh shut up, Dolly,' Lucinda giggled. She seemed much younger here. Sweeter, in a way, but also more vulnerable. Nick wasn't sure if he liked her so much this way. The whole point about Lucinda was that she was an ice queen. A sign at a crossroads pointed incongruously to Scarborough and Plymouth. They took the Plymouth direction. The darkness was almost total, there were so few street lights. Dolly swerved to avoid a sleeping dog in the middle of the road. Nick felt nervous and bewildered. He shouldn't have come. He'd made a mistake. He wasn't going to like this at all.

# 36

'This is the M4,' Karen said. 'So we're heading west. Not to Devon, I hope.'

She was joking but Max frowned as he switched lanes.

'I thought it might be a good idea.'

'You're not serious.'

'I am.' His eyes were fixed on the road. 'Look, I know it sounds nuts but I want to look at Chadlicote with you. Help you make up your mind if you can bear it or not.'

'But I . . .'

'We're staying in a gorgeous hotel. But if you don't want to go, we won't. I'll head north on the M5 into Gloucestershire or the Cotswolds. Or straight on across the Severn Bridge into Wales. It's up to you.'

'But I hate the countryside, you know that.' She said it jokingly. 'Cows and mud.'

'And you know I hate it too. But I want to see if we both still hate it when we're together.'

It was crazy, it was totally unexpected. It meant all the things she'd wanted to forget over the weekend would now have to be faced up to. But Max was right. Things were coming to a head. She had to tackle them.

It was nearly three by the time they approached Chadlicote through the metal gates with the dilapidated lodge beside them.

'Suppose someone sees us?' Karen had told no one – not

even Max – about her visit to Chadlicote a couple of weeks ago; that was her secret.

'You're buying the place, aren't you?'

'Yes, but . . . I'm with you.'

'Say I'm your brother.'

'OK,' Karen said meekly. Grace would never believe that. They drove on. Max looked from side to side in astonishment.

'Bloody hell, Karen. This is unreal.'

'I know.'

They crossed the bridge over the stream. A deer ran across their path. The house reared up in front of them. Even more majestic than Karen remembered.

'I'm not going any closer. Pull in here.' She nodded at a clearing under a clump of elm trees.

They stared through the windscreen.

'It's amazing,' Max said. 'Phil must be absolutely loaded to afford this.'

'Not as loaded as he thinks he is.'

Max shook his head. 'Karen, you know how I'm living? In a studio flat with a kitchenette. A tiny balcony that gets no sun.'

'So?'

Max shook his head. 'I can't compete, Karen. Look at the kind of life Phil can give you.'

'Do you really think I'm that shallow?' she asked heatedly. 'Do you really think I choose people on what they can give me?'

'You said you chose Phil because he made you safe. I can't offer you anything like this. It's a bloody palace. Shit, Karen, I feel stupid now.'

'Don't feel stupid. Don't ever think this is about you offering me anything!' Karen felt desperate, as if she were arguing for her life. She felt as if all the mistakes she'd ever made were crowing in her ear, telling her it was payback time for the insecurity and greed which had – deep down she knew – been her motivation for marrying Phil. But how could Max really believe that she'd rather live in that cold, draughty house with a cold, draughty husband than be with him, in their love nest with double-decker buses rumbling past and the stuffed foxes and cats on the corner?

'I love you, Max. I never loved Phil like this. Never loved anyone. And I'll always love you, whatever . . . whatever happens.'

They looked at each other for a long moment. Then they were kissing.

'Christ,' Max said, when finally they stopped, both breathing heavily. 'I'm feeling all emotional here.' He put on a silly northern accent, trying to defuse the tension. It didn't work.

'Me too.'

They started kissing again.

'I think we urgently need to get to the hotel,' Max said hoarsely.

'I think you're right,' Karen said.

Nick woke disoriented. They were in a four-poster bed surrounded by a mosquito net, in the main bedroom of the house. House being a bit of an understatement – this was more of a mansion, up a long, dirt track that even Dolly's jeep bounced along alarmingly, and then up a steep, winding hill through high gates and on to a drive dominated by a huge white clapboard building. A veranda ran round three sides. Round the corner, in the middle of immaculate green lawns, was a floodlit swimming pool.

'The tennis courts are over there,' Lucinda had said with an airy wave. 'Maybe tomorrow we'll have a game.'

'I don't know how to play tennis.'

She'd looked a bit confused, like he'd told her he didn't speak English. 'Oh, that's right. Well, I can teach you. Might be fun.'

'Right.'

The table in the dining room was covered with dishes of what looked like some kind of stew, black peas, a sort of naan bread.

'Mrs Marilia is so sweet,' Lucinda exclaimed. 'She's made us her roti.'

'Roti?'

'It's like curry,' she said, just a trifle impatiently.

They ate some heated up in the microwave. Nick was anxious, but Lucinda was right. It *was* like curry, actually better than the takeaways Kylie ordered from the Bengal Lancer. The fridge was full of beers. Nick drank one and began to feel a bit more relaxed.

'Can you hear the sea?' Lucinda smiled. 'In the morning you'll be able to see it. We're right on top of a cliff. Got our own private beach, though it's a bit of a scrabble down the hill to get there. But worth it. I can't wait for a swim. In fact, I might have one now.'

'But it's dark.'

'So?' She started pulling off her clothes. 'Come on!'

He was ashamed to admit he couldn't really swim. So he snapped, 'I don't have to do whatever you want.'

She stared at him for a second, standing there in a mocha-coloured lacy bra and matching pants. Then slowly she said, 'No. Of course you don't. It was just a suggestion.'

She pulled off the rest of her clothes, pushed open the French doors, ran on to the lawn and dived fluidly into the pool. Nick watched as her head surfaced. She was laughing. He felt a twisting sense of inadequacy. This woman was simply outside his league. She ploughed down the pool, doing a fast, neat crawl.

'It's so warm,' she shouted, her hair slicked back from her face. 'Try it!'

'No,' he said. 'Tomorrow.' By then he'd have thought up some kind of excuse.

She swam a few more lengths and then came out, running naked and giggling to the house to find a towel. And of course she looked so gorgeous that they ended up having sex on the living room sofa. They went to sleep in the big white bed with a fan whirring gently overhead. And now dawn was creeping in through the huge shutters. Lucinda was fast asleep, looking happier than he'd ever seen her before.

Nick eased himself out of bed, padded across the wooden floor and went down the imposing main staircase to the living room. The French windows looked out over white cliffs, curving off towards the horizon. Below them, a flecked turquoise sea bubbled. There were trees everywhere – not just the palm trees he'd expected but great towering things with long, sweeping branches.

If this was Lucinda's second home, what could the first be like? Then there was the ski chalet, and somewhere by the sea in France. Nick didn't really do computers, but when he got back perhaps he should google Lucinda's dad and try to discover a bit more about him.

On the veranda rail sat an extraordinary bird with coppery feathers, a golden, tufty quiff, a long, sickle-shaped beak and sapphire round the eyes. It turned and gave Nick a cold stare. Nick stared back. The bird stared some more.

Nick blinked first.

'All right, you win,' he snapped.

The sun had just risen, but already the heat was sticky on his skin. He turned and inspected the photographs on the mantelpiece that he hadn't been able to look at the night before. This must be Lucinda's dad – a big, bluff man in chinos and a polo shirt: thick head of black hair, a little rodenty dog sitting on his lap. Behind him stood what must be her mother, a brittle-looking woman who looked as if she'd been preserved in formaldehyde, her hair styled stiffly into a blonde pony-tail, her mouth in a straight lipstick slash.

Other pictures showed presumably Lucinda's sister, a younger, slightly more relaxed version of the mother, in a stripy shirt with a turned-up collar, set off by a string of pearls. The brother wore chinos too and had an annoying smirk. A handsome, pampered bunch. Nick thought of his own family pictures – him with half his teeth missing in the scarlet school jumper, mounted on brown cardboard. A snapshot of Mum in an orange dress, laughing at Christmas dinner, her gold tooth on full display. They didn't really compare.

'You're up already,' said a voice behind him. Lucinda

stood there in tiny shorts and a black vest top. 'Isn't it glorious?'

'Beautiful,' he admitted unwillingly.

She headed to the kitchen. He followed her, slightly reluctantly. 'Mrs Marilia's left us a fruit plate,' she smiled. 'All my favourites. Yum. Star fruit. Delicious.'

'Is there any bread or anything?'

Again she shook her head with faint disapproval. 'We can buy some today. Go to the supermarket in Crown Point. But you should try the fruit. It really is amazing.'

'I'm not hungry,' he lied.

His misery was compounded when he discovered there was no tea in the house, only coffee. He drank a glass of water, while Lucinda scoffed the fruit plate and then had a large glass of freshly squeezed guava juice. Good job he'd had a big dinner on the plane.

'So today, I thought we could maybe go down to the beach,' she said. 'Do some snorkelling perhaps. Then maybe we could drive up to Englishman's Bay and have lunch at the little shack there – amazing rotis. And in the evening I've said we'll meet my friends Michelle and Angus for a drink at the Blue Haven Hotel. Gorgeous place. I mean, you can't actually get a better view than here but the cocktails are incredible. There's this rum punch . . .'

'Meeting friends?'

'Yes. Michelle and Angus. They live in a massive estate out near Argyle. Got loads of horses. We could go riding . . .'

'Why do we have to meet them?' Nick asked petulantly.

'Because they're really nice people,' Lucinda said impatiently. She smiled and kissed him on the cheek. 'Darling, I know how you'd like it just to be the two of us always. It's incredibly sweet. But life doesn't work like that, does it? You can't exist in a bubble.'

'Why not?'

She laughed. 'I love it that you're so possessive. But it'll just be one little drink. And then we'll have dinner alone. There's a great Italian restaurant in Buccoo. I could book it.'

He felt weak, like a kitten. He wished he'd never come. 'All right,' he said miserably. 'Whatever you say.'

'Nick!' Lucinda shook him. 'Nick, wake up. We've got to go.'

Nick surfaced slowly and smiled at her. He'd had a long nap, at least three hours. Lucinda thought they'd had a pretty perfect Tobago day so far. They'd clambered down a steep hillside to the private beach, where she'd swum in the crystal water while he lay on a towel. She didn't know why he wouldn't come in with her, and she wished he'd put on some sunscreen but he'd refused. Now she could see his shoulderblades and nose were deep scarlet.

She couldn't be bothered to drive to the beach hut for lunch, so instead they'd climbed back up to the house, where magical Mrs Marilia had been and cleaned up and cooked a huge lunch of more roti and delicious dumplings and callaloo, which Nick refused to taste for some reason. Then they'd had sex, which had been technically very satisfying – she'd come about three times – but, she hated to admit, lacked a certain sense of passion. Still, afterwards she'd lain with her head on his chest, which was the kind of thing lovers did, and fallen asleep to the sound of his heart pounding in his skinny ribcage.

But now they needed to get going. 'We've got to get showered and changed. We have to be at the Blue Haven for six.'

'Why?' he grumbled.

'I told you why. Because we're meeting Michelle and Angus.'

'Call them. Tell them we'll meet them tomorrow.'

'No, I shan't. That would be very bad manners. Do you want to shower first or shall I? I'd wear a smartish pair of trousers if I were you. And a long-sleeved shirt to cover the tattoo. I mean, Tobago's not a ritzy place, hardly Geneva, but when it comes to dressing up it's quite traditional.'

'But I haven't brought a smart pair of trousers. And what's wrong with the tattoo?'

Heavens, did he really have to ask? 'Well, it's just not very . . . My parents' friends might be a little shocked.'

'Tattooing isn't a chav thing, you know,' Nick responded. 'In the nineteenth century the British upper classes used to meet in drawing rooms and partially undress to show theirs off. I told you – George V had one. So did two of his sons. So did Winston Churchill. So did his mother, apparently. And a piercing.'

'Really? His *mother*? How do you know that?'

'Just . . . reading.'

'Fascinating. I'd never have known that.' But it was time to get back to the point. 'Maybe you could borrow some of Daddy's clothes. He keeps some here.'

'I'm not borrowing your father's clothes!' he exclaimed.

'They wouldn't fit you anyway. But honestly, Nick. Didn't you think?'

'No, I fucking didn't. Why should I think about packing clothes to wear to meet stupid people I couldn't give a fuck about?'

Her face froze. 'You're very rude,' she said levelly. 'I'm going to have a shower.'

Under the lukewarm water she had a rethink. Perhaps she was being a bit bossy. She'd given him very short notice of the trip. She hadn't told him what to pack. He wasn't a mindreader.

She pulled a towel round her and returned to the bedroom. He was lying on the bed, staring at the ceiling. She bent over him.

'I'm sorry. I should have warned you there'd be a little bit of socializing. I didn't mean to make all these plans, but Dolly told Michelle's maid I was coming over and she emailed me and asked if we could get together and . . . I know you're not a smart suit kind of guy. That's what I love about you.'

She wasn't sure how the 'love' had slipped out. The pause as she waited to see how he'd respond seemed to go on for ever.

'Let's go tomorrow,' he said firmly. 'I want to go back to bed now.' As he saw her hesitate, he decided to compromise a little. 'We can buy me a smart pair of trousers in the morning.'

'I . . .'

'I'm not going tonight, Lucinda. I want to be alone with you.'

'All right,' she agreed. Did she really love him? Perhaps

she did. She knew she'd been infatuated, obsessed, but the thought that this might be something even more profound made her catch her breath. It would be nice finally to be properly in love, something different, something that would give her the insight she'd always suspected she lacked into how the world really turned. But why hadn't he said, 'I love you too'?

# 37

Nick enjoyed his second day in Tobago a little bit more, although his skin had blistered and he had a permanent raging headache.

'You should wear a hat,' Lucinda said.

'I don't have one.'

'You could borrow one of Daddy's.' This time he had little choice but to agree, though when he saw the panama she produced he was appalled. But there was no one to see them on the private beach. She swam more; he sunbathed with his shirt and hat on and paddled a bit. They had another siesta. She didn't mention Michelle and Angus again (apart from to say they'd been very understanding when she'd called to cancel, saying her friend was too jet-lagged), but suggested they had dinner at the Waterwheel in Arnos Vale. He had to accept really – it was a bit weird staying at home every night. It was pitch dark by six and after that there was nothing to do, except eat Mrs Marilia's admittedly tasty food in the kitchen, watch a DVD from a dodgy collection of dusty old war movies and lame comedies starring Meg Ryan, and go to bed at around ten.

So here they were at the Waterwheel, based in an old sugar factory in the middle of the island, surrounded by middle-aged couples in pastels, talking in soft voices.

'The Caribbean food here's great,' Lucinda was saying

in her usual confident manner. 'When they try to do other cuisines is where it gets a bit ropy. I mean, caviar and crayfish salad in a raspberry vinaigrette. Please! Do what you're good at doing. Save the fancy European stuff for when you're at home.'

'Yeah, like I always do,' he said sarcastically.

'You do like to play the poor-me card, don't you?' Lucinda said. She tried to sound light-hearted. She failed. To his surprise, Nick was glad she was having a go at him. That love thing she'd said had freaked him out.

'Let's get a great bottle of wine,' he declared, as a woman cried, 'Lucinda!'

'Maureen!' Maureen was a lady of a certain age in a violently coloured kaftan accessorized with ethnic jewellery. Nick instantly loathed her. But Lucinda was standing up, kissing her, telling her her father was very well.

'Hello,' said Maureen, turning gimlet-like eyes upon him. 'My name's Maureen Berowne. And you are . . .'

'Nick,' he muttered, shaking her hand reluctantly.

'Nick Crex,' Lucinda said hastily.

'I can't believe I've bumped into you,' Maureen said, still eyeing him as if he were some weird animal in a zoo. 'You are a naughty girl coming here and not telling us. Why don't you join us?'

Nick held his breath. But Lucinda said hastily, 'Actually, if you don't mind we're a bit tired tonight . . . Maybe coffee later.'

'You want to be alone, you lovebirds. Fair enough. How about you come over to lunch tomorrow though?'

'Oh! We're leaving tomorrow. It's just a lightning visit.'

386

'But you're on the BA flight, right? That doesn't go until the evening. Come over.'

'Maureen lives in the most gorgeous house,' Lucinda said apologetically. 'You'd love it.'

Nick nodded. His headache was back and his skin was prickling more than ever. His appetite had completely disappeared.

'Karen,' Max said, eyes on the twisty road. 'I can't carry on like this any more. I know I keep saying it but I want you to make up your mind. To leave Phil. To be with me.'

It was as if all the breath had left her body. She was light-headed, she thought she might vomit. She swallowed. She tried to speak, but found she couldn't.

'I just have to have you,' he continued. 'I'll never love anyone else so much. I know it's going to be hard. I know about the girls and that divorce is hell and . . . But I'll do it. I'll fight for you. Because I can't bear the thought of life without you.'

She was still shocked. But in a happy way now. Great bubbles of joy swelled and popped in her chest. Max wanted to be with her! He could have been with any number of young, no-strings, beautiful, pneumatic-breasted girls but he wanted to be with her.

'In fact I think we should get married.'

'*What?*' For heaven's sake. A joke was a joke but this was getting silly.

'Because asking you to move in with me isn't enough. There needs to be a rock-solid commitment here. If you're going to go through with it . . . leaving Phil, I mean . . .' Seeing her incredulous face he sounded less certain now, like a little boy who'd lost sight of his mummy in the crowd. Karen said nothing, just stared at him.

'So?' he asked anxiously.

'So what?'

'So would you like to marry me?'

'Of course I would. I'd love to. I love you. But . . . oh, Max. It's only been what . . . eight – ten weeks? You don't marry anyone you've only known for eight weeks. I couldn't let you do such a ridiculous thing. Not to mention the fact I'm married already.'

'Unhappily.'

'It doesn't matter. I made . . . promises.'

'Look. I love you. You love me. Right? Or am I wrong?' Now he definitely wasn't a boy, but a grown, angry man. The contrast almost made her laugh.

'Of course you're not wrong. You know how much I love you.'

'Right. So we love each other. We have earth-moving sex. We make each other laugh. We talk. And you don't love your husband. I know you don't. He may have been ill, but he's still a manipulative bully.'

'I never said that!'

'No, you didn't. You're actually remarkably loyal about him. But he is a bully, that's obvious. You deserve better, Karen. And, look, I've always slightly pitied my friends who are married and how they never have any time to themselves and can't watch football all day, but now I want to be shackled. With another man's children. I know we won't be waltzing off into the sunset together, I know your girls will probably hate me and you will too sometimes and I'll have to learn to cook and everything and leave

388

Islington and move to the sticks but it's worth it. For you.'

'I see.'

'So?'

'Max, I'm going to have to think about this. A lot. The girls . . .'

'Lots of my friends had parents who divorced and they're fine. Much worse for parents who hated each other to have stayed together, they say.'

She shook her head, touched to her core by his love, but still not believing his argument. Couples who divorced did irreparable damage. Look at her, all messed up from Dad's betrayal all those years ago.

'So it's a no?' he said miserably, as they swept into a wide gravelled courtyard, dominated by a half-timbered building signed Faldingley House Hotel.

'Let's just check in.'

The room was cosy, chintzy, with a view over manicured gardens. The yells of children playing floated through the bay windows. Karen sat in an armchair as far away from the four-poster bed as possible. She couldn't bring sex into the equation now. She had to think. But she was so tired, more tired than she'd ever been in her life, even in the first few weeks with Eloise, even when she'd been dealing with all the fallout from the cancer. What was wrong with her? How could Max affect her more than a dying husband?

'Still a no?' Max asked gently, kneeling in front of her.

'Do you know what? I'd just really like a nap.'

'OK.' He paused and then said, 'Do you mind if I go to sleep beside you? Only I'm tired after all that driving.'

*

Lucinda glanced at Nick out of the corner of her eye. She tried hard not to laugh. His nose was red and luminous like car brake-lights, he wore an old baggy T-shirt that belonged to Benjie (his own T-shirts were too tight now he had sunburn on his shoulders) and shorts that revealed white, hairy and rather knobbly knees. He looked silly. She'd have been lying to say that this silliness didn't detract slightly from her feelings for him. Not to mention the rudeness she'd witnessed these past few days.

'There's the Dwight Yorke football stadium,' she said. 'He comes from here, you know.' She was at the wheel of the jeep; they were on their way to lunch at the dreaded Maureen's. 'It's such a sleepy place still,' she continued. 'Dogs still snoozing in the middle of the road, chickens running around. But then you hear about shootings and drug raids. It's coming from Trinidad, of course, they have a terrible drug problem there. Smugglers from Venezuela land on the beaches at night and . . . Oh, look, there's the turn-off to the Argyle waterfall. Very pretty. Maybe we should visit on the way home.'

'Lucinda, could you just quit the tour guide stuff?'

A lava of rage suddenly bubbled through her. She pulled up abruptly on the hard shoulder. '*What* is your problem?' she snapped.

'What do you mean?'

'You've been like this ever since we got here.'

'Like what?'

'So grumpy, so uninterested in everything. So hostile. I thought . . .'

'You thought what?'

'I thought you were different.'

He shrugged sullenly. 'I'm just me,' he muttered.

'So I see,' she retorted. She tried a different tack.

'Would you like to drive?'

'Nah, that's OK.'

'Sure? You might enjoy a spin at the wheel.'

'No!'

'You can't drive, can you?' she said quietly.

'Is that a crime?'

'Of course not,' she said, wondering why this revelation should make her think even less of him. Lots of adults couldn't drive, she just didn't think she'd ever met one. 'Now. Do you want to go to this lunch or not?'

A long pause followed.

'Might as well,' he said eventually.

So they drove on. Lucinda didn't speak, her mind racing. She wasn't at all sure about this. She didn't know if she wanted to introduce Nick to all Mummy and Daddy's friends. Word would get out and they would have kittens. A week ago she'd wanted them to find out like this, been looking forward to squaring up to her parents. But now she wasn't so sure. She found it difficult to admit, even to herself, but the brief fantasy that Nick was the love of her life was distinctly shaky now. She wondered if she should call Maureen, tell her the car had broken down or something.

But Lucinda was stubborn. She'd invested a lot in this relationship. She wanted to see it through. Didn't want to admit defeat. She *did* love Nick, however stupidly he might be behaving, and she was sure if they overcame this hiccup they could move on and grow stronger than before.

*

Karen thought there'd be no way that an insomniac like her could sleep in the circumstances. But her eyes closed and she fell into the heaviest sleep she'd had in months, if not years. When she woke up it was dark outside.

'Hi,' said Max on the pillow beside her.

'Hello. What time is it?'

'Around nine, I think. You were tired.'

'But I'm awake now.'

She rolled towards him. He pulled her close. They started kissing.

'We'll do it,' she whispered. 'I'll do it. I'll leave Phil. We'll be together.'

## 38

'I can't believe you did that,' Lucinda snapped.

'Did what?' They were back on the aeroplane, the same luxurious surroundings as a couple of days ago, their breakfast in front of them. But the mood couldn't have been more different. Lucinda had spent the whole flight squirming in mortification as she remembered their last afternoon in Tobago. Nick had been so rude, totally ignoring Elsa Morgan-Plaide whom he'd been seated next to, and Maureen's husband Barty, who'd done his best to welcome their taciturn guest, asking if he'd ever been on *Top of the Pops* and could you dance to his tunes. All right, they weren't exactly Jeremy Paxman level interrogations but he was only trying to be polite. And Nick had just answered with grunts and rolled eyes and sneers, like a teenager.

Now he shrugged. Something inside Lucinda snapped.

'This isn't working,' she said.

He looked at her. His nose was peeling now.

'Don't be ridiculous!'

'I'm not. I don't want to be with you any more and I don't honestly think you want to be with me. You haven't treated me very nicely at all these past few days. Most men would have loved a free holiday like this.'

'Fuck off,' he said. 'I can buy my own holiday.'

Lucinda realized how that must have sounded. 'Sorry,' she said.

There was a tiny pause and then he said, 'I'm sorry too.'

For some reason they both began to giggle.

'It's just as well,' she sighed, after a moment. 'We'd have found out sooner or later that it wasn't working, so better sooner don't you think?'

'Typical you,' he said, amused despite himself. 'Package it all up neatly. Like some kind of marketing exercise. "Oh, it didn't tick the boxes. Well, let's bin it."'

'I didn't mean it like that.' But actually, when Lucinda thought about it, she did.

'We've had some good times,' she said.

'We have,' he agreed. He kept thinking about Kylie. Thank God he hadn't told her what was going on. A week with Lucinda had made him appreciate her like never before. He'd behaved like a complete twat. He'd junk the flat – the exchange wasn't until the end of the week. He'd find a house for both of them.

But in the meantime.

'Fancy one more shag? Just for old times' sake?'

'No, thank you,' said Lucinda politely.

Nick shrugged good-naturedly. 'Fair enough,' he said. He put on his headphones and turned on the DVD of the latest James Bond. His body felt helium light with sudden relief. He couldn't believe it. It was all over. And so easily. The relationship he'd known all along hadn't been quite right had ended ideally, no tears, no recriminations, instead a kind of rueful amusement on both sides that they'd made a mistake they'd both rather forget.

'Ladies and gentlemen. We are now approaching London, Gatwick. Please fasten your seatbelts and return your tray tables to the upright position.'

Max was sleeping now. Karen looked at him, reverentially, wanting to trace his profile with her fingers, but she didn't. She didn't want him awake, she wanted to revel in this feeling of enjoying watching him breathe, of wanting to be so close to someone, wanting to run her fingers over his chest and rest her fist in his clavicle, cover his body with kisses.

They hadn't had sex. Karen couldn't. Couldn't go further than foreplay. She was too conflicted. Phil was at home. The girls were with him. How could she even be spending a night under a different roof from them? How could she be planning this – after the hell they'd already endured? Phil would give her the tiniest settlement she could imagine – she wouldn't blame him. She and Max would end up living in a poky flat, with two angry children. Two children who wouldn't have the slightest understanding or forgiveness about the fact that their parents were people too. Entitled to lives of their own. To happiness.

And they'd be right. Because no one was entitled to happiness. And no one who had a child could ever put themselves first again. It came with the territory.

Maybe they could wait until the girls had grown up? Or maybe Phil would announce he'd fallen in love with his yoga teacher and was leaving her?

Max sighed and stirred a little. Looking at him, Karen was overwhelmed with love – love she had known in relation to her daughters, but never in this adult kind of way. Not least in the past few years, when she'd trained herself not to feel too much about anything, to keep her heart in the deep freeze.

But now it was defrosting fast.

Her eyes filled, happiness and pain mingling together, and she drifted off again into another deep, dreamless, but rapturous sleep.

She woke just before dawn. Max was kissing her brown, erect nipples.

'I really mean it,' he whispered. 'I love you. I want to spend the rest of my life with you.'

'Me too.'

Afterwards they ordered breakfast in their fluffy bathrobes. Sausage, egg, bacon, black pudding, cup after cup of steaming coffee.

'How can someone as tiny as you eat so much?' Max laughed.

Guilt struck her again. It was all the forbidden foods, foods pushed off the agenda by muesli, wheatgrass, quinoa and Manuka honey. But she couldn't tell Max that – it would be as if she was laughing at Phil for wanting to stay well. What else was he supposed to do?

She glanced at her phone on the bedside table. There was no signal here. She wondered when it would come back to life again. When the outside world would start to intrude.

'It's a beautiful day,' said Max, gesturing at the window, at the view of endless, rolling green fields – a view that made the notion this was an overpopulated island on a dying planet seem as preposterous as arguing Elvis was still alive. 'Do you want to go for a walk?'

'I'd love to.' Despite his country leanings, Phil had never liked walks. Karen remembered a weekend in the Lake District shortly after they'd become an item. It was a perfect summer's evening. She wanted to walk round the lake near the hotel before dinner, but he wouldn't come with her, as the golf was on. Karen had never forgotten her fury, her exasperation, as she stormed round the lake alone, too upset to enjoy its beauty. That's when she should have walked away, when Phil refused to walk round the lake.

She swallowed and looked at Max. 'And then we'll have to get back.'

'I know. But then you'll talk to Phil.'

'Maybe not today. But I will talk to him soon.'

Max's face darkened. 'You won't back out on me, will you, Karen?'

'I won't.' She meant it. 'But just not today. I'll have to find a time when the girls are at school or something. Maybe take the day off work. I can't just drop the bombshell.'

Karen didn't want to think about it. She just wanted to enjoy the summer air on her face, watch the poppies swaying in the field, listen to the larks singing in the elm trees. Ironically, all the things she could enjoy every day if she moved here. But this wasn't about Devon versus St Albans any more. It was about Phil versus Max, a man she'd never loved wholeheartedly versus a man who consumed her.

She didn't want to think about it.

They climbed to the top of a hill, where an ancient menhir stood.

'Look at me,' said Max, pulling himself up on to it, wobbling precariously. 'I'm the King of the World. I can see for mi-i-i-les.'

She was laughing at him, arms outstretched to keep his balance, as her phone started to ring in her pocket.

'Oh my God. We have a signal.'

She pulled it out. *Phil*, said the caller ID. The ground seemed to shift beneath her as if she'd hit turbulence.

'Hello.' She braced herself for her husband's voice. But she didn't hear him. She heard Eloise.

'Mummy, it's me. Mummy, where are you?'

*Mummy?* Eloise had stopped calling her that six years ago when she'd announced out of the blue that it was 'lame' and by the way there was no such person as Santa Claus. Or the tooth fairy. Bea cried for days.

'Darling, I'm . . . away. Are you OK, sweetiepie?'

'It's not me, Mummy. It's Daddy. He's sick. Really sick. He's gone back into hospital this morning. Mummy, we need you back home. We need you now.'

'I'll give you a lift,' Lucinda told Nick, as they walked through early morning Gatwick towards passports. 'I've got a car waiting.'

It had been a snap decision to end it, but already she was mightily relieved. She knew the Tobago gossip machine would be in overdrive after the lunch, but she'd begged Dolly and Marilia to stay schtum and she was going to claim to Mummy and Daddy, or whoever, that Nick was merely an acquaintance she'd bumped into on the island, that *of course* he hadn't stayed in the villa. It felt like a narrow escape. Something she'd laugh about when she'd taken over Daddy's empire and Nick was as famous as Mick Jagger. No one would ever know, she thought smugly, as a man jumped in front of them.

'Nick! Nick!' he shouted. A flashbulb started going off.

Momentarily blinded, Nick's hand flew to his eyes.

'Lucinda!' another man shouted.

'What in heaven's name is going on?' she snapped. 'Go away.'

The man had a beer belly and a beard. He merely laughed, continuing running in front of them, his shutter snapping like the jaws of a hungry crocodile.

'I take it you haven't seen today's papers?' he asked.

'What?'

He shoved a copy of the *Sunday Post* into her hand. Lucinda stared at it aghast. '*The rock star and the heiress*', read the headline. In smaller letters underneath, she read: '*Star's girlfriend in clinic after suicide attempt*'.

The photographer continued snapping their shocked expressions.

'Welcome home,' he said.

# 39

Lucinda sat on the overstuffed sofa in the living room of her father's Claridge's suite. She kept her eyes focused on the Linley furniture. Perfectly tasteful, but *so* overpriced thanks to the fact that it was made by the Queen's nephew, cashing in on his title. She kept thinking this, hoping it would stop her crying.

'How could you have done this?' her father bellowed, standing above her. He had flown in that morning for an emergency family summit. 'You've brought shame upon the family.'

'But why not, Daddy?' she said, looking him straight in the eye and twisting her fingers together so he wouldn't see them shaking. Where was her damn bracelet? 'I'm young and single. So is he. Why shouldn't we go on holiday with whomever we like?' She was pleased with the 'whom'. Lucinda Gresham did not forget her grammar, even in moments of the gravest crisis.

Michael Gresham's face was very red. 'Because this rock star was also a client of your agency. Can't you grasp the measure of such unprofessionalism?'

'Anyway, he's not single,' Mummy said softly from her armchair in the corner where she'd been intently inspecting her manicure. 'He has a girlfriend.'

'I know,' said Lucinda, hanging her head.

'You've lost your job. You've brought terrible publicity to the family when we've always tried to be so discreet.'

'I'm really sorry, Daddy, I really am.'

'Sorry isn't good enough. You won't be coming to work for me now, you realize that?'

'Yes, Daddy.' Lucinda was devastated, but she kept her face as expressionless as possible. This wouldn't happen. Couldn't happen. She'd get another job. She'd be a brilliant success and then Daddy would beg her to join the company. She *would not* let one stupid mishap defeat her. The thought sloshed round and round her head like clothes in a washing machine.

Her father stood up.

'I'm going to stop your allowance. Evict you from the house. Someone who repays their father's generosity with this tramplike behaviour doesn't deserve any more part of it.'

'Michael!' Mummy protested. 'That's very harsh.'

'Lucinda can fend for herself. Like every other woman in the world has to. They manage fine and so will she.'

'All right, Daddy.' Lucinda kept her eyes pinned to the carpet but her mind was reeling. Where would she go? What would she do? She still had some cash from her investments but they'd taken a nasty knock recently and would only cover a month or two at best.

She had to find a job. Who could she ask?

There must be other people out there. People whom it would be less humiliating to approach. But she simply couldn't think. Cass's chinless boyfriend and his hedge fund. He'd say she could make the tea and enjoy watching her messing up the nasty strong English brews. She could go home to Switzerland, of course, but that would be even worse, living in the same town as Mummy and Daddy, doing what – working in a cuckoo-clock factory?

'Another thing you'd better know,' Daddy said. 'I've offered Benjie the job with the company that you seemed so arrogantly to think was meant for you. He's going to start after Christmas.'

All the feelings she'd been keeping a lid on burst out. 'Benjie! But he doesn't care anything about property. About what you do. All he wants to do is . . .'

'Benjie is my son. I've always felt it was right that he took over the business. Of course if he's no good at it then maybe your sister's husband would be a better candidate. Or, most probably, none of you.'

Lucinda glanced at her mother. Still gazing at her nails as if they were this week's copy of *Hello!* magazine. *Stupid cow.* But then she looked up. The concern in Gail's eyes made Lucinda's stomach turn. Made the already unbearable guilt worse than ever before. Her mother loved her and was heartbroken for her. She'd never really realized that. Until now.

'So off you go, Lucinda. I wish you luck. Hope you can get over this rocky phase. But don't expect to hear from us again.'

'But Daddy . . .'

'I spoilt you children. I see that now. But now you have to manage on your own. Benjie is returning to Geneva at the end of the week. I'll give you the same amount of time to find alternative accommodation.' He looked at his Rolex.

'Right, you'd better be off. I have a meeting in five.' He picked up his BlackBerry and began scrolling through his messages.

'Bye, Daddy.' Lucinda turned to Mummy and smiled. Chin up. Show no pain. Gail smiled back, at least as much as the services of Dr LeGrand would allow her.

''Bye, darling. I . . .'

Lucinda walked out of the room, her knees feeling as if they were on loose hinges. Down the corridor. It was as if every sound was muffled; all she could hear was the beating of her own heart. What had she been doing? She'd been so foolish. It had all been because she'd been lonely and too proud to admit it. And vain too. Nick had flattered her and she'd fallen for it unquestioningly. She was so insecure she'd risked everything for a few compliments and some good sex. How could she have done it? And she'd been so ruthless about Kylie. Poor Kylie, who had clearly known all about them and had been suffering. The papers said she was recovering, but that was scant comfort.

Lucinda realized she'd targeted Nick because that was what Daddy did. Had affairs with whomever he felt like, no regard for other people's feelings. Well, it was horrible. She'd learned her lesson. Would never do it again.

But still she'd have to take the punishment.

She pressed the button for the lift. Stepped into it, trying to think. Where would she live? Who would give her a job?

She had no friends in London to ask. She could probably find work in a café or a shop or whatever, but she didn't want that. But she didn't see how she could find a job in property without going through the proper channels, and Dunraven Mackie were hardly going to give her a reference after this fiasco. Gemma Meehan had probably grassed her up by now anyway.

It came to her as the doors pinged and she stepped out into the lobby.

Anton.

Anton owned a thriving business. He employed people with her knowldge and skills. He'd said she had some great ideas, that he wished there were more like her.

And he loved her. Well, not *love* but he certainly had strong feelings for her. Whether it was a good idea to exploit them or not was another question. Lucinda would investigate that later. Once Lucinda had an idea, she was physically incapable of stalling, she *had* to get the ball rolling.

She picked up her phone and began scrolling for his number.

Gemma was standing outside the flat on Western Avenue. She'd rung Bridget and Massy's door bell three times but clearly no one was home. She'd even braved the neighbours, but nothing.

She'd been calling Bridget every day, but every day the line went dead. Once she tried the Costa where Massy had been working. 'He's left,' said a woman. 'No, I have no idea where he go.'

Sweating slightly in the early summer heat, Gemma pulled a pen out of her bag and scribbled on a page of her notebook.

*If you do get this, I want to talk to you. I'm sorry Massy didn't tell you what was going on. I'll pay you whatever you want. G xxx*

She posted it through the door, knowing it wouldn't help but not knowing what else she could do. Then she turned back towards the Tube. For a second, her hands rested on her stomach. There were twelve more days to go before she was allowed to do a pregnancy test. She didn't know if her nerves could stand it. This was her one and only shot at motherhood. Although they'd frozen four of the remaining embryos, she didn't see how she could use them. It had been one thing to say 'too bad' to Bridget with the embryos already inside her; to remove them from the freezer and use them in cold blood, knowing her sister was against it, was quite another.

As she returned to the Tube, her eye was caught by the *Standard*'s billboard.

## THE ROCK STAR AND THE HEIRESS. BLINDS GIRLFRIEND IN COMA.

*Blinds girlfriend?* Gemma paid the vendor 50p. On the platform, waiting for a delayed train, she began to read. Six pages of coverage, including aerial shots of a mansion 'on the shores of Lake Geneva' with an indoor swimming pool, two tennis courts and its own stables. There was a brief biography of Michael Gresham, outlining how he'd capitalized on his father's fortune. A picture of a trout-mouthed mother in a pink suit with braiding around the collar and pockets, holding a pair of binoculars at some race meeting. Another of her brother and sister, and then Lucinda. 'It is believed she was working at estate agents Dunraven Mackie incognito in order to gain experience before joining her father's property empire. Colleagues told the *Daily Post* they were "gobsmacked by the news". "I always thought there was something different about her, she was very snooty and had no point of contact with planet earth whatsoever," said one, who asked not to be identified. "But Michael Gresham's daughter? We could never have guessed that.'"

Amusement at Lucinda's true identity was overlaid with horror at the thought of gentle, unassuming Kylie in a coma. Apparently she'd overdosed on discovering where her boyfriend was and been found by band member Ian's girlfriend just in time. Then Gemma was assailed by a more selfish concern. What about the flat sale? All this drama was going to hold it up again. As soon as she emerged from the Tube, she called Dunraven Mackie. The phone was answered by a man with a kind, West Country accent.

'Is Lucinda there?' she asked, although she already knew the answer.

He sounded embarrassed. 'I'm afraid Lucinda has left the company. Can I help you?'

'Yes. She was selling my flat. To the . . . er, to the man she was on holiday with.' *Whom we also found her rogering in our flat but you'll never know about that.*

She explained who she was. The man, who was called Gareth, was very sympathetic.

'Right. We are aware of the situation and we're chasing Mr Crex. He's not answering his phone at the moment, which is understandable, but I'm sure he will in the next day or so when things calm down. I'll keep you posted as soon as I hear anything, I assure you.'

'Good. Because you know we're meant to exchange soon.'

'I know. I understand. House sales are always stressful

at the best of times, without your buyer being involved in a scandal with the estate agent.'

'What I don't understand,' Gemma said, emboldened by his kindly tone, 'is why Lucinda was working as an estate agent at all?'

Gareth sighed. 'We don't understand that either. I wish she'd told me. I would have kept her secret.'

*You don't know the half of it*, Gemma thought. 'Thank you for your help. I look forward to hearing from you.'

Lucinda's phone kept ringing. Emails kept dropping into her inbox. Friends who found the scandal hilarious. Reporters wanting to talk to her. The next message cheered her up slightly.

'Wotcha. Gareth here. Hope you're OK. It's all been a bit of a drama this end, as you can imagine. Really sorry about what's happened. We're going to miss you here.' A tiny pause. 'Doubt you'll miss us, though. And – I have to say – some people were a bit pissed off with the way you and Niall kept us in the dark. Anyway, if you fancy a drink some time just give us a bell. All right. Cheers then. Er. 'Bye.'

'You are a fucking arsehole,' Martine Crex told her son.

'I know, Mum,' Nick said humbly.

'How could you do that to Kylie? After what your dad did to me? You men, you're all the arseing same.' Nick could hear her inhaling sharply on her Embassy filterless. 'Unbe-fucking-lievable.'

'Have you seen Kylie?' Nick asked. He'd returned to the flat in Belsize Park to find it stripped of her belongings.

None of her girly shit in the bathroom, the cupboards stripped bare, photos of them taken down from the shelves. The place seemed echoing, empty. He knew he was the world's biggest hypocrite to miss her, but still he did. A faint fruity smell was all that remained. The teddies littering the bed, the piles of magazines, the tampons, the handbags, the make-up. All gone. Packed up.

'What's it to you? You've got a new girlfriend now. Lucinda Gresham.' Martine cleared her nicotine-clogged throat. 'According to this, daughter of property mogul Michael Gresham, currently listed at number twenty-seven on the *Sunday Times* Rich List. Veeeery nice, Nicky. When are you going to bring her up to Burnley then, to meet your old mum?'

'It's over,' Nick said.

'Over? Fucking hell, Nicky. Then why did you do it in the first place?'

'I don't know. I didn't mean to hurt Kylie.'

'Then why didn't you work at it? Oh, don't answer! I don't want to know your pathetic excuse. You men. You're all the bloody same. So do you really want to know how Kylie is doing? I'll tell you. She's still in intensive care. They think she may be brain-damaged. Plus there was a baby and of course she's lost it.'

Nick felt dizzy.

'Are you sure?'

'Why would Sharon lie to me? My only chance of a grandchild. How could you do this to me?'

'I'm sorry, Mum, I didn't know she . . .' Nick felt flustered and hot.

'Whatever. Just fuck off. I don't know if I want to talk

408

to you any more. My own son, treating a woman like this. Didn't you learn anything from what your dad did to me?'

And she'd gone.

Nick stared at the phone. How could Kylie not have told him this? History was rapidly being rewritten in his brain. He'd never have gone to Tobago if he'd known about it. Why the hell hadn't she told him? A child. A son, obviously. Their baby. She'd killed it. How could she not even have consulted him?

Immediately, his phone rang again. Number withheld. Perhaps this was Kylie. He was surprised how visceral was his need to talk to her.

'Hello?' His voice wobbled as if he were stilt-walking.

'Hello, Nick,' said an oily voice. 'It's Charles here. I've been taking calls from your solicitors and the estate agents. They want to know what on earth has been going on with the flat while you've been off getting a tan. Forgive me, but you can't avoid the papers.'

The flat? For a second Nick genuinely didn't know what he was talking about. Then it came back to him. Flat 15. Of course. How could he have forgotten? Wasn't he meant to be paying for it next week or something? But he didn't want it now. No way. It would remind him of Lucinda and that whole sorry episode. Remind him of Kylie. Whom he'd hurt so badly. How could he have done it?

'I don't want the fucking flat,' he snarled. 'Don't bother me about it again. Just tell them to piss off. And start looking for a new one.'

# 40

Karen had hoped she'd had her lifetime's quotient of hospitals. But now here she was, back in the waiting room, feeling as if she'd entered some underwater world, where the lights were too bright and noises were muffled. Surrounded by spaced-out, hollow-eyed people. You drank vile coffee from the vending machine, you flicked through ancient copies of *Bella*, but you tasted nothing, took in nothing. Just watched the clock hands creep round.

Finally the doctor appeared.

'Mrs Drake. In here, please.'

She hadn't met this one before. He was older than Dr Munro, who had been their consultant last time, and less showy. Unlike Dr Munro, you couldn't imagine him on the golf course, boasting about the lives he'd saved today. Which surely was a good thing.

'Mrs Drake,' he said, gesturing to a green armchair. 'I'm afraid the cancer has returned. But it's moved now. To another place. On the positive side, you can be fairly confident we can treat it. Drugs in this area are very developed.'

He talked for a long time. Karen tried to concentrate but it was all a whirl. She only really cared about one thing.

'Will he . . . ? Can he?'

'He can go home with you tonight. Back in again first thing tomorrow, mind you.'

'Yes, doctor.'

\*

Gemma was online, uploading a picture of the McQueen black jacket she'd bought hoping it would make her look like a picture she'd seen of Elle Macpherson at the airport but which in fact made her resemble an extra in an am-dram production of *Oliver!* She had a plan, a plan to raise some money to give Bridget by selling off her wardrobe on eBay. She'd gone through it this morning and realized she owned twenty-seven striped T-shirts. In every shop she'd ever visited, some kind of supernatural force had drawn her to the stripy T-shirt section, and there'd always be at least one with a slightly different cut or thickness of stripes to the other two dozen stripy T-shirts she owned and she would be compelled to buy it. But now some of them had to go. The Nicole Farhis, not the Primark ones. But could she really bear to get rid of this one, which she'd bought in Bond Street to treat herself . . . ?

As she struggled to recall how she'd justified that treat, her phone rang.

'Hello?'

'It's Gareth from Dunraven Mackie, Mrs Meehan. I'm afraid I've got bad news on the flat sale.'

He spelled it out. She was amazed how calm she felt.

'It's all right,' she said. 'I expected it.'

The phone at Chadlicote rang at around five o'clock. The sun was blazing down in the summer sky and Grace was squatting over her flower pots. Watered and tended daily, the sweet peas had grown remarkably quickly. As their pink and purple flowers burst out, Grace had begun looking round the rest of the grounds, which lay under thick beds of nettles and couch grass. In the rose garden creeping convolvulus had suffocated what remained of the bushes. Grace decided she would start here. From dawn to dusk, she weeded, pruned and deadheaded, painstakingly restoring some order out of the chaos.

The evening hours she'd previously passed eating or online looking at *Doctor Who* websites were now spent browsing plant sites. After a day's raking, she sowed some salad seeds. Soon she'd be able to eat the leaves for supper. Tiny green tomatoes were already appearing. At the weekend, instead of moping, she'd visited three garden centres. Possibly she'd spent too much money, but she'd saved on biscuits and ice cream and sweets.

She began to plan. She pulled out the estate agent's map of the grounds and divided it into sections. 'Clematis' she wrote on the west wall. 'Roses' on the flower beds that would need to be dug up. Delphiniums, geraniums. The list went on and on. She'd discover something she'd set her heart on grew badly in this soil and would be temporarily dispirited. But another idea would come up.

At first she'd only been able to load the wheelbarrow with a small amount of compost. But already now she could push a whole barrow-load across the grounds to the corner she was targeting. Her muscles ached, her fingernails were gritty, her nose was full of the warm stench of turned earth, and she felt herself wonderfully at peace.

All right, so in the end it would all be in vain. The house would be sold, with acres of garden still untouched. Never mind. Grace would transform the cottage's overgrown plot. She'd put her name down for an allotment.

Phone still ringing. She'd better answer it.

'Hello?' she said, pushing a strand of hair out of her eye.

'Miss Porter-Healey. It's Nina from Bruton Bradley estate agents.'

'Yes?'

'I'm really sorry to let you know so late in the day but we've got a problem on the exchange.'

'I'm sorry?'

'We've just heard that the Drakes are having to delay the date of exchange.'

A beat. 'Sorry?'

'Philip Drake just called us. The sale of his house has fallen through so he's having to delay exchanging until he finds another buyer. I'm so sorry. I'm sure it won't be long, if it's any consolation. I gather the Drakes' house is very desirable and . . .'

'It's OK,' said Grace. 'Please don't worry.'

'I'm sorry,' Nina wailed again.

'Please don't be.' Grace smiled, noting a new blister on her hand. 'It's not your fault.'


Karen barely registered the call.

'OK,' she said distractedly. 'Just keep us posted.' She hung up. An ashen Phil was leaning back against a mountain of pillows in their bedroom. A plate of soba noodles and broccoli lay untouched on a tray in front of him.

'How are you feeling now?'

'Fine,' he said weakly. They were starting a new session of chemo in the morning. A new combination of drugs, as he'd built up resistance to the last lot. The consultant was very positive they'd work.

'Oh, Phil,' she said, her heart overflowing with pain. 'I'm so sorry. So incredibly sorry.' Sorry for him, of course. But also for what she'd done. Though he'd never find out.

'I'm sorry too,' he said, to her surprise.

'For heaven's sake. What do you have to be sorry about?' *It's me who has* . . . she thought, but she slapped the thought down like a pesky puppy. No time for self-indulgent guilt. All her energies were focused on the cancer again.

'I've let you down. I thought I was getting better. I'm sorry you married me, Karen. I'm sorry it's ruined your life.'

Tears burned in her eyes; the back of her throat was swollen and sore. 'Don't be sorry for anything, Phil. None of this is your fault. You know that.'

'I've made life so difficult for you lately. First the illness. And then organizing the move. I should have consulted you more. Not expected you to go along with me.'

'It's OK.' She'd tell him later that the move had fallen through for now. A bitter irony as, at the moment, she'd have happily decamped to the moon to have Phil well again.

'It's not OK. Devon's too far. I wasn't thinking. We'll leave this house but we don't have to go far. Just down the road will be fine with me.'

'Don't worry about it now. Please. Just get some sleep. I'll give you a pill.'

'Karen?' He looked at her beseechingly. And Karen knew. Knew that she was never going to leave Phil, no matter how ambivalent she felt about him, no matter how much she adored Max. He was her children's father. She'd seen their terrified faces, realized how much they depended on both of them as a unit. And in turn she depended on them. They were at the very centre of her being and without them she would be nothing. Whatever differences she and Phil might have, they were united in the fact that they'd created these two brilliant, precious creatures.

'Yes, darling?'

'Please don't sleep in the spare room tonight. Please stay here. With me.'

The agony at what she was going to have to give up, what she was going to suffer, tore through her. But that pain was nothing, nothing compared to what Phil and the girls were enduring.

'Of course I will, darling.'

## 41

Through the smoked-glass windows of his chauffeured limo, Nick watched the Burnley streets of his youth. The rows of dilapidated terraced houses. The teenagers in vests and cut-off jeans slumped on a doorstep drinking lager from cans, ghetto blaster booming, a Staffie at their feet. Passing a spliff from one to the other. One girl, who couldn't have been much older than fourteen, was pregnant. She'd pulled up her top, exposing her round pasty belly to the afternoon sun. Nick shuddered at the sight of her. She represented everything he'd wanted to escape. But at the same time the thought of Kylie in the same situation tore at his heart. Kylie carrying his baby. *Their* baby. Killing it by swallowing those pills because she'd found out he'd gone to Tobago with Lucinda.

He was drawing up outside her house now. Christ, the same plastic Santa Claus in the window, which stayed there all year round. The same peeling black front door with the metal gate in front to keep the bailiffs out.

'Do you want me to wait here?' asked Ken, the driver.

'Yeah,' said Nick. He got out, heart hammering. He rang the doorbell. Ding dong, it chimed. There was no reply for a while. Nick turned around, half disappointed, half relieved. But then he heard shuffling. Someone was heading towards the door. He considered dashing back to the safety of Ken's car, but it opened before he'd fully got his act together.

Michelle, Kylie's older sister, stared at him. She too was wearing a vest which did her meaty arms no favours and purple velvet tracksuit pants. She gawped at Nick as she might have done at the Queen if she'd pitched up on her doorstep on a humid summer afternoon.

'What the fuck are you doing here?'

'You know what. I've come to see Kylie. Is she in?'

Michelle stared at him for a minute with her cold, dead eyes. A Dobermann waddled up behind her and eyed Nick. Hungrily.

'She isn't.'

Nick squirmed. What was he doing here? He remembered all the things he disliked about Kylie's family. About Burnley. About his old life.

But he was here now.

'So when will she be back?'

'I wouldn't know. She's gone on holiday. To recover from what you did to her.'

'So she's OK?'

One of Michelle's many snotty children appeared at her side, dressed only in a nappy. 'Mamma, Mamma.'

'We hope so. We'll have to see. Now fuck off right now, please. Before I call the police.'

'But . . .'

'Arsehole,' she said and slammed the door in his face. A few houses along, another door opened. An old lady – what was her name? Nora Brightman – stared at him. Behind another window, a net curtain twitched. Nick headed back to the car in blind fury.

'Go home, just go home,' he snapped, climbing in.

'You mean to London?' Ken asked. He didn't sound

surprised that the visit had been so brief, because he wasn't. He'd seen it all with the idiots he had to ferry about. At least his wife loved hearing about them.

'Yeah, to London.' Was London Nick's home? It had to be. There was no place for him here any more.

Grace picked up Shackleton and placed him gently in the back of the Land Rover. Just a few months ago she'd have struggled to lift him, but now he was as light as candyfloss. After his first bloody offering, nothing had happened for a while, but then he'd started to bleed again. At the same time he'd lost weight and been so tired. So she'd called the vet.

Silvester tried to jump up beside him.

'No, darling. You can't come.' Grace tried to sound calm. Silvester, however, knew something was wrong. His doggy face was mournful and he kept whining, like one of Grace's nephews deprived of CBeebies. As soon as she put her foot on the accelerator, tears started to blind her. They were lucky to arrive at the vet's intact. Mr Jepson, the vet, looked at Shackleton carefully. Shackleton – who usually loved a bit of attention – didn't even bother to wag his tail.

'Mmm. I'm glad you brought him in,' Mr Jepson said. 'He's very close to the end now. I would recommend a shot. Put him out of his misery.'

'Shouldn't I let him go naturally?'

He shook his head. 'It's up to you, but it will only be a few more days. Maybe a week. And they will be days of suffering. I would stop it now.'

Why hadn't Grace been able to do the same thing for

her mother, she thought furiously, as she looked up at him and said, 'All right.'

'Do you want a moment with him?' Mr Jepson asked.

Grace nodded, unable to speak. She held Shackleton, crying softly into his wrinkled head. He'd been with them six years. Such a sweet little puppy, all snuffling and warm, like a hot water bottle. Silvester would be bereft when he realized his old friend had gone. Maybe she'd get another dog. But then he would die on her too. Everyone left her in the end.

'Goodbye, darling,' she said, kissing him on the head.

Mr Jepson coughed at the door. Jilly, the nurse, stood there with a huge syringe. The needle went into Shackleton's bristly coat. Grace stroked him and whispered, 'There, boy.'

He carried on wheezing for longer than she expected. Gradually, his raspy breaths grew slower. After what seemed like a very long time, they stopped.

'I think . . .' Grace said.

Mr Jepson put his stethoscope to Shackleton's wrinkled chest. 'Yes, he's gone,' he said. 'But I'm sure he had a wonderful life rambling around the grounds of Chadlicote.'

'He did,' Grace said. 'He did.'

There was a lot of paperwork to fill out before Grace returned to Chadlicote, with Shackleton's stiffening body in a box in the boot. Now she would have to think how to bury him. Was there ever going to be a day when some problem didn't present itself to her?

'Stop feeling so damn sorry for yourself,' she told herself.

She tried to focus on biscuits. After she'd cuddled Silvester she'd go and buy a huge variety tin. Grace realized with a start that she must have lost weight the past few weeks. She'd never believed women like Verity who claimed they forgot to eat but – while she had hardly skipped meals – food had no longer been at the forefront of her mind. She'd been too busy gathering up her prunings or calculating how to revive the herb garden. She'd got a tan too, and when she looked in the mirror at bedtime, she glowed from exertion. Once she'd tried to fill the gaping hole in her heart with food, but growing things was far more effective. It was almost like a love affair, but one which she was fully in control of.

Still, forget all that now. This was a biscuit night. Followed by ice cream and a family-sized bar of Dairy Milk.

Though she'd have to do the watering first.

Then she saw it. A brown Cortina, parked in the drive. Richie.

Grace fumed as she sped the last few yards along the foxglove-lined drive. What did he want? She'd come to terms with her humiliation at Richie's hands, but she certainly didn't want to undergo it again.

She got out of the car and stormed towards the front door.

'Hello, Grace,' he called from beside his bonnet.

'Hello, Richie,' she snapped over her shoulder.

'Grace! Don't be like that. Wait. Listen, I just wanted you to know I'm sorry. I messed things up with you.'

'It's OK,' she said tightly, fumbling with numb fingers for her keys.

'I . . .' He looked at his feet. 'I don't expect you to forgive

420

me. I've been having problems. That's why my wife left. Work's put me on a final warning. I've started AA.'

'Good, Richie. Goodbye, Richie.'

'I really am sorry, Grace,' he cried. 'And listen, I hear the house is back on the market. Anton . . .'

She slammed the door in his face.

Everything in Lucinda's life had changed. She'd moved out of the Kensington flat, as had Benjie, who had returned to Geneva.

'I don't want to go,' he'd moaned, chucking his back issues of *Attitude* into the recycling. 'I don't want to live at home with Mummy and Daddy. The gay scene in Geneva is rubbish.'

'Well, don't go,' Lucinda said stiffly. It was pretty hard to sympathize with him. She would have done anything to be summoned home like this and told to get to work in head office, and here was her brother moaning because there was a shortage of clubs with dungeon rooms.

'I have to. Dad says he's cutting off my allowance if I don't. Says he's fed up with having time-waster children and he wants to see me getting down to work.'

'I'll miss you.'

'I'll be back here all the time. I'll take you out to dinner on the company account.'

'Right,' Lucinda sighed.

'So where's your new place?'

'It's in Hackney. Little one-bedroom flat. Pretty central. My friend Gareth from my old job helped me find it.'

'Hackney's rough!' exclaimed her brother.

'Not really,' Lucinda lied. Actually, she'd been shaken

when she'd visited the flat for the first time. Walking out of Old Street Tube with the manic traffic, down the side streets lined by pound shops and tatty saunas, to the flat on a busy road above an off-licence. A flat which was perfectly clean, neutrally furnished, so as not to alienate anyone, with a bedroom, bathroom, sitting room and separate, albeit matchbox-sized, kitchen.

A flat she'd have sold enthusiastically to a viewer but which, for Lucinda, who had never known life without an en-suite bathroom, was a shock. Still, she was going to make it as cosy as possible, with bright posters, throws, candles, all the things she advised clients to do. And she was going to enjoy the area's bars, the cheap restaurants – lots of Vietnamese ones apparently – the avant-garde art exhibitions. Whom she would enjoy them with she had no idea. Probably nobody. Cass was up to her eyes in wedding plans and she was too proud to ask more of Gareth. But somehow she was going to retrieve something out of this experience.

'It is *so* rough round there. You lucky thing.' Benjie smiled wistfully. 'Will you enjoy it on my behalf?'

'I'll do my best.'

Karen's phone rang as she sat in the waiting room, leafing blindly through back numbers of *Grazia*, while her husband endured a chemo session. She pulled it out of her pocket and froze as she saw the number on the screen. She could hang up. But that would be too cowardly. She had to face it all head on.

'Hello?' she said cautiously.

'Karen, what's going on? I haven't heard a word from you since Sunday. Are you OK? How's Phil?'

'He's having treatment as we speak.'

'Oh.'

Karen heard the hospital clock ticking, watched an over-alled Chinese man push a trolley past bearing an old lady on an oxygen machine.

'I'm so sorry,' Max said.

'Yes.'

'Will we be able to . . .?'

'I'm sorry, Max. I have to go now.'

'But Karen . . .'

'Goodbye.' She turned the phone off.

One day at a time. That was how junkies and drunks did it. That would have to be her strategy. Focus all her energies on making Phil better. Not allow one iota of them to be wasted on what might have been.

One day at a time.


The first time Lucinda had called Anton she'd got voice-mail. So she'd hung up and then tried again. And again. On about the fifth attempt, she got through.

'Hello, Lucinda.' Not surprisingly, he sounded about as pleased to hear from her as Madonna learning the only lunch available was from Burger King.

'Anton, I'm terribly sorry to bother you. I wanted to ask your advice.'

'And why should I want to give it to you? I've been reading about your adventures.'

'You shouldn't . . . I mean, it's up to you. But I know you're a decent guy and you wouldn't like to kick anyone in the teeth.'

'Not a problem you ever seemed to have, Lucinda.'

Lucinda felt her stomach tighten. 'I know,' she acknowledged humbly. 'But I think I've learned some lessons now.'

Anton sighed. 'So what do you want?'

'I wanted to ask you for a job.'

He laughed. 'You really do have a cheek, don't you?'

'I do. But Anton, you know how passionate I am about property. You know you said I had some brilliant ideas. I could be contributing to your company. Be an asset.'

'We're doing very nicely without you, Lucinda. Even in these hard times.'

'But I could help you do better. *Please.*'

'You really do think I'm an idiot, don't you?'

'Of course I don't.' Lucinda was being sincere now, with every fibre of her being. 'If I thought that, why would I want to work for you?'

'I can't believe you didn't tell me you were Michael Gresham's daughter. Do you know how many deals I've done with him over the years?'

'Loads, I'm sure,' Lucinda said humbly.

There was a long pause.

'The pay will be bad,' Anton said.

'I can accept that.' A smile curled across Lucinda's face. 'So long as we review it after six months.'

'Bloody hell, Lucinda.' Anton exhaled. 'All right. Come in on Monday. Eight a.m. One of my contacts has tipped me off about a manor house in Devon that sounds ripe for redevelopment. I've already seen it but I'd be interested in your opinion.'

# 42

A fortnight had passed. Nick was in his room at the Comfort Inn, Cleveland, Ohio. A club sandwich sat cooling on a plate in front of him, as he flicked from television channel to television channel, all of which seemed to be showing adverts for lawyers' firms wanting to help you sue negligent sidewalk repairers.

The Vertical Blinds were halfway through their US tour. They'd already played Philadelphia, Boston, New York and Pontiac, Michigan. Parts had been really glamorous – flying across the Atlantic again (though it was only business class this time), driving across the Brooklyn Bridge in a real yellow taxi watching the Manhattan lights shimmer on the horizon.

'Wow,' yelled Ian. 'We are in Noo Yoik. We're gonna see steam coming out of the pavements. The Statue of Liberty. The Big Apple.'

'A stabbing?' Paul was ever hopeful.

'You could stay in Burnley if a stabbing's what you want. How about the Empire State Building?'

'I wanna go into a sandwich bar and order pastrami on rye. I've always wondered what that is. And a soda.'

But Nick didn't feel any desire to see New York. He just kept thinking about Kylie. Kylie in hospital, on a drip, white as a sheet. He'd done this to her by being a coward, by not having the guts to tell her it was over. By letting her find out about him and Lucinda through a call from a newspaper reporter. He'd behaved disgustingly, but he couldn't even say he'd been punished, because however much his heart ached he hadn't nearly died.

The tour had kicked off. They had a bus, like you did in the movies, which was fun initially, but the novelty of days on end trapped on a coach – even a glorified coach with giant tellies and snacks – soon wore off. The east coast of America wasn't nearly as pretty as Nick had imagined, but seemed to be endless dreary highways lined by strip malls full of beauty salons and dry cleaners and Taco Bells. The towns they visited all looked the same: Camden, New Jersey. Upper Darby, Pennsylvania. Detroit. The gigs weren't full and the reviews online were lukewarm, but nobody except Nick seemed bothered. They were too busy enjoying the groupies. Of course Nick slept with a couple – skinny blondes who screamed like police sirens as he thrust into them and scratched his back with their long nails, but half-way through he'd remember Kylie's pink face and blonde curls and his hard-on would shrivel.

Nick pushed the sandwich away, nauseated by the memory.

He kept picking up his phone, jabbing in texts. But he didn't send them. How could he? He'd ruined Kylie's life, he absolutely couldn't barge in again now. He had to respect her space, had to leave her to lead the life she'd wanted in the first place.

Gemma, also, was flicking unseeingly through the TV channels. Tomorrow, two weeks would have passed. The embryos would either have caught or not. She bought a state-of-the-art pregnancy test that also performed ballet moves, cleaned your grouting and did your tax return. But was midnight too early to do it? What about five a.m.? What about nine? Lunchtime? When was the magic hour when the embryos that had been inserted in her body suddenly, magically clamped to her womb wall?

Or – alternatively – let go in a sticky, bloody mess.

'You'll do it at seven a.m.,' Alex had decided. 'When the alarm goes off.'

'And what if it's a no?' Gemma knew without a doubt that it would be. And then her life would be over. There would be no hope.

'If it's a no, we'll get straight on the internet and start investigating adoption agencies. We will have a meeting with them sorted out by the end of the day.'

'But you said no adopting . . .'

'I changed my mind. We will get through this. Now go to sleep.'

Gemma wished they could make love, but it was out of the question. Far too risky. Though of course there were other things they could do to pass the time.

'Do you fancy a blow job?' she asked.

The gap between the digital clock clicking from 6:59 to 7 a.m. seemed to last an eternity.

'Go on, then,' said an equally sleepless Alex beside her. 'Shall I come and watch?'

'Don't be disgusting.'

Even now, they both managed a giggle.

She padded out of the bedroom into the funny bathroom that every potential buyer objected to. Unwrapped the plastic wrapper, opened the box. More foil to fumble with. In the bin. She hitched up her cotton nightie, sat on the toilet seat, stuck the stick underneath her and allowed her bladder muscles to loosen. The room filled with the warm, ammoniac smell of the first pee of the day.

She pulled out the stick. She studied the oval window. It's OK, she told herself. Because we *will* adopt. Maybe an Indian baby. Or Guatemalan. But the top space was filling up. A vertical line was developing. First faint violet, then growing darker and darker. A red line in the porthole below.

Oh, good Lord.

'Let me in,' bellowed her husband from outside the door. 'Put me out of my misery.'

'Come in.'

He pushed open the door. She stood there.

'Oh shit, I'm sorry,' he said, seeing her pale face.

Gemma looked up at him.

'No, darling. Don't be sorry. It's positive. We are going to have a baby.'


Grace was squatting in front of the courgettes. It was true what they said on the new gardening forums she'd joined, they grew like bloody billy-oh. What would she do with them all? She was eating courgette bread for lunch, pasta with garlic and courgettes for dinner, but she couldn't even begin to make a dent into this surfeit.

'Hello, Miss Porter-Healey,' a voice said behind her.

She twisted round, losing her balance and falling on to her bottom. Looking up she saw Anton Beleek.

'Oh, hello,' she said, wiping the sweat from her brow.

'Sorry! Did I take you by surprise? I rang the doorbell but nobody came and . . .'

'It's fine. I was just . . . Do you like courgettes?'

'We tend to call them zucchini where I come from. But yes, I do quite like them. They can be bland, but if you cook them in olive oil with lemon and basil, they're really very good.'

'I should try that.' She stood up, wiping her hands on her jeans. 'Now, how can I help you, Mr Beleek?'

'You know why I'm here.'

'I do. And I can't say I'm happy about it.'

'I've spoken to your brother. He's very keen for the sale to go through.'

'I'm sure he is,' she said archly.

'You have huge debts to pay, Miss Porter-Healey.'

'Please, call me Grace. Mr Beleek, I'm quite aware of the dire situation.'

'Please, call me Anton.' He was smiling.

'I'm quite aware of the dire situation and I'm quite aware we will have to sell to you in the end. If no other buyer comes forward. But that doesn't mean I can't enjoy messing you around.' *Like Richie messed me around.* She smiled at him. She was suddenly surprisingly aware of her skin glowing in the afternoon sun. She'd never had the biscuit feast after Shackleton died, instead she'd marked his burial by going online and ordering a special variety of rose to plant on his grave.

Anton Beleek looked around. 'You've been working hard at this since I last saw you. Would you like to show me what you've done? Remember, I love gardens.'

'I do remember,' said Grace with a smile. She'd been otherwise distracted that day, but he need never know that.

Karen sat in front of Christine's desk. Christine looked at her from behind the shades she was wearing to conceal yet another eye operation.

'So you're not resigning now.'

'No. The whole Devon thing is off.'

'Well, thank God for that. And how is Phil?'

'Stable. Another round of chemo in a week.'

'Christ. All that *poison* being dripped into your body. Perhaps he should try this shaman I heard about.' Christine seemed oblivious to the irony that her body was awash with Restylane and Botox. 'Shall I try to track him down for you?'

'Thanks, Christine,' Karen said, as she always did to such suggestions. People didn't *mean* to be annoying. She stood up.

'See you later.'

'Karen. There's one more thing. I'm leaving. Just handed in my notice. Jamal and I are off to India, he wants to write a novel and I . . . well, I want to put my money where my mouth's been all these years and be a good supportive wife.'

Karen gaped.

'So . . . obviously we were about to start to look for candidates. But now it seems you might be the obvious successor. Would *you* like to be editor?'

'Me?' After nine years as lady in waiting. 'I'd love to.'

'Good. Well, that was easy. I'll tell the powers that be

that you're my anointed successor. You will be able to cope with the case load, what with Phil and everything . . . ?'

'I've found the more I have to do the better I cope.'

'Good stuff.' Christine smiled. 'Congratulations, Karen, you deserve it.'

'I hope you're happy in India.'

'Me too.' Christine's phone started ringing. 'Oh, that's Jamsie now. I'd better see what he wants. Off you go. Talk later.'

Head reeling, Karen shut Christine's door. She'd never seen that coming. Christine's job. And she could take it now, now Phil had agreed they'd stay in St Albans, just in a different house.

Dazed, she walked down the corridor then turned the corner into the newsroom and slap – into Max. Her cheeks, warm from the conversation with Christine, were suddenly frozen and her hands shook.

'What are you doing here?'

'I work here.'

'But on the *Daily*. This is the *Sunday*.' What a banal thing to say to the man she loved most in the world, more than anything except her girls, whom she'd dreamed about, yearned for, cried quietly over every night. Suddenly standing two feet from her, his brown eyes locked into hers.

The temptation to shout, 'I've changed my mind, I'll be with you,' was overwhelming. But how could she with her colleagues all around her, tapping away at their keyboards? More to the point, how could she when her husband was recovering from chemo at home, her children petrified?

'I've just got to have a word with Nicky,' he said, nodding

at the news editor, sitting a few yards away. 'We need to work out which stories we're covering in the next few months. So we don't clash too much.'

'Oh. Right.' Shakily, she added, 'See you then.' She started to walk on. One leg in front of the other. Wasn't that how you did it?

'Karen!'

She turned. She must not show emotion. 'Yes?'

'I'm moving.'

'Sorry?'

'To South Africa. There's a correspondent's job up for grabs. Guns, wars, adventure. That's going to be me.' He couldn't have sounded more unhappy.

'South Africa. How wonderful!' Nor could she.

Sophie approached them, waddling slowly.

'Hey! What did Christine say? Hello, Max, how are you?'

'I'll tell you in a second,' said Karen, just as Max said, 'Hello, Sophie, I'm fine. You?'

'All right. Six weeks to go now.' Sophie's eyes grew bigger as she looked at his ashen face, then hers. She'd guessed.

'Can't wait to hear all about it,' she said to Karen, her voice laden with knowingness. She moved off, leaving them still frozen.

'How's Phil?' Max asked.

'Recovering. For now. It's going to be a long road. Though the doctors think he's got a good chance.'

'I hope so.'

'Me too.' They looked at each other. She had no idea how she could bear this. But Phil was enduring his pain, so she'd just have to put up with hers.

'Karen!' yelled a voice behind her. She wheeled round.

'Yes, Christine?'

'I need to see your cookery pages before I go for lunch. Chop, chop.'

'OK,' Karen said.

'See you,' said Max. One last look and he continued down the corridor. He didn't look back. Karen stared after him. It was as if an iceberg was in her chest.

She made it back to her desk by autopilot. Sitting down, she grabbed the mug of tea she'd made just before Christine had summoned her in. Although it was cold, its robust tannic taste seemed to thaw her icy veins somewhat, bringing her back to some kind of normality. A desperately sad normality, but still, a step further from where she'd been just a week ago. She would survive. She would get through this. She picked up the photo of Bea and Eloise, arms wrapped round each other, grinning cheesily into the camera, and – glancing around to check no one was looking – kissed both their faces. She'd slope off early tonight. Because she needed to see them both, more than she needed anything in the world.

# 43

Seven months had passed. Summer had merged into a surprisingly temperate autumn and early winter. Even now, with Christmas just weeks away and the shops full of holly and tinsel, the weather was still dry and mild.

For Gemma the time had passed agonizingly slowly. There'd been the sheer hell of the first twelve weeks, when she'd hardly dared move from the sofa, when she'd panicked because she wasn't feeling sick enough, because her breasts weren't as sore as she'd been warned. She worried because she didn't have piles or indigestion, she longed for stretchmarks that refused to arrive. There was no way this baby could stick around; miscarriages were incredibly common. She'd done a pregnancy test every day, sometimes two. Alex hadn't mocked at her, or complained. He understood.

When the day for the scan came, they were at the hospital far too early. Then the sonographer was running late. Gemma's bladder ached from the cups of water she'd consumed to make the image good. When the time came she was so desperate to pee, she'd almost forgotten what they were really there for. She lay on a couch. Cold gel was squeezed on her tummy. The sonographer, who was skinny and jolly, pressed what looked like a Hoover nozzle against it. Almost instantly two tiny semi-humans appeared on the screen. Alex and Gemma held hands and gasped. The sonographer smiled wryly.

'It's twins.'

In shock from the news, they saw a consultant. Everything seemed healthy, though of course the babies might have to come out slightly early. Gemma's tummy started growing at a rate of knots. They began breaking the news to people. A few tactful ones said, 'How lovely,' but more said, 'Double trouble' and 'Rather you than me' and 'Jesus H. Christ.'

'Why are they being like this?' Gemma asked Alex. 'Why can't they be pleased for us?'

'They're jealous because we've been twice blessed. Two babies. We'll have to come up with another name besides Chudney. What do you think of Chudwina?'

At twenty weeks they returned for the second scan.

'All's well,' said the sonographer. 'They're even both head down for now, though that will most likely change. Do you want to know the sex?'

'No!' said Alex.

'Yes!' said Gemma.

'Why?' Alex said. 'Don't you want a surprise?'

'Not really. You know I like to be in control.'

'Well, that ain't never going to happen again,' said the sonographer with a smirk. 'Not with twins. Sorry, but it's true. Get all the help you can and then some.'

'She's right,' Alex urged her. 'Come on. We've got this far. Let's just let life take us where it wants for a while.'

The sonographer printed out some muzzy grey photos. Two blobs in what seemed like a very small space. Chudney had a higher forehead than the other, Chudwina had squidgier cheeks. Gemma gazed at them for hours, like an archaeologist inspecting an ancient bit of Sumerian pottery for clues. Would one look like Alex and one like Bridget? Or perhaps there'd be some throwback and they'd end up looking like Grandpa Meehan, who had an enormous chin but a disproportionately small nose, not to mention a vile temper. It didn't matter. So long as they didn't take after her mother-in-law.

She was overcome with the need to share her news with Bridget. There was no one else in the world, she thought, who would coo over the pictures like she had, no one else who would fully share in the excitement.

But Bridget was still nowhere to be found. Texts went unanswered, and when she called her number it went straight to voicemail.

'Why don't you ask your parents?' Alex said.

Gemma was unwilling. She didn't want to alert her mother to the fact that the two daughters weren't in touch; she was stressed right now, as the neighbours had decided to build a second villa bang between her parents' lawn and their sea view. Last time she'd called Mum for an update, she'd said she was too upset to talk about it, but Gemma could get a blow-by-blow account of what was going on on her Facebook page.

Facebook.

Why on earth hadn't she thought of that before? Gemma proudly avoided Facebook, declaring it to be for sad, time-wasting losers. Meaning it was exactly the kind of place her sister would flourish. She logged in. She searched for Bridget Hobson. She found her straight away. Her sister had posted a picture of herself in a purple feather boa doing a peace sign. She had four hundred and ninety-five friends, from all over the world, collected on yoga retreats, in ashrams, on self-discovery workshops in the Brazilian rainforest, beach huts in Thailand.

She had no idea if the olive branch would be accepted. But she had to hold it out. Reluctantly, against all her principles, she made up her own Facebook page, uploaded her scan picture, and – now she was part of the system – asked Bridget to be her friend. As if they were six years old. She added a message.

> If you want to see your biological children then click on this link. I hope you're well and happy. I miss you. G xxx

The message disappeared into cyberspace. Gemma blew a kiss after it. She'd hope, but not too much.

Grace was delighted with her herb garden. The sage, thyme and lavender were already growing fast, the rosemary wasn't far behind. Even though the weather had turned and it grew dark so frustratingly early now, she was fitting in as much as possible. She'd lost two stone. Anton Beleek had been back three times to negotiate with her, once with a rather snooty young woman called Lucinda, and three times she'd shown him her progress before rejecting his offer. He'd taken it in good spirit.

Coming back into the kitchen, face scarlet, she turned her attention to the answerphone. A message. She pressed 'play'.

'Grace! It's Verity. I have just received a call from a Lucinda Gresham at Beleek Developments. Apparently, they've been trying to buy the house for months and you haven't been passing the message on to us. I can't believe it! You know how worried we are about school fees. Really,

Grace. This is awful. Call me back at once with an explanation.'

Grace smiled and pressed 'delete'. The next message rolled out.

'Grace, all right. I have a proposition for you. We buy the house. You become its gardener. We give you the gatehouse to live in for ever and you can take charge of the grounds. What do you say to that? Eh? Call me.'

Message three. 'Anton again. Why haven't you got back to me? Listen, what do you say I come down again and take you out to dinner to discuss my plan?'

Grace thought that could be an idea. She'd call him back once she'd planted the next lot of bulbs. She had to press on, the frosts would set in soon.

Alex was home early that night. He found Gemma sitting in front of the television, watching the Living Channel with its non-stop round of birth documentaries. She couldn't help it, she was addicted, crying every time the baby finally appeared. She knew she was pretty much destined for a C-section but she still wanted to discover as much as possible about every birth option and keep them all open.

'I've got news,' Alex said.

'Oh yes?' The woman who'd looked so immaculate at the start of the programme was now huffing on all fours. Gemma found it seriously alarming. Was this really what birth was like? Perhaps the C-section was the best idea after all.

'I know where Massy is.'

'What?' That had her attention.

'Frankie Holmes found him.'

'Frankie Holmes?'

'Yeah. The scumbag I got off. He owed me one. So I asked him to track Massimo Briganza down. Wasn't hard. He's living in Penge. Doing casual jobs here and there. Turns out he's a heroin addict. Got previous for robbery and fraud.'

'Oh my God. And he was Bridget's boyfriend.'

'I know. What a charmer.'

'But now we can nobble him?' Gemma imagined Massy being carried off in a Black Maria. One of the babies – Chudney, she thought – kicked to show its approval.

'No, Poochie, we can't. He didn't commit any crime. You gave him the money.'

'But it was meant for Bridget.'

'There is absolutely no proof of that. Sorry, Pooch.' Alex's eyes lit up behind his glasses. 'But it's not all bad news. Frankie's got his eye on him. He's having a word with his contacts.'

'His contacts?'

'You don't want to know. But I have a sense Massy's petty dealings will be heavily scrutinized from now on. Meaning he may end up in A & E by the end of the week. Not to mention in the Crown Court for coke dealing.'

'Frankie's done that for you?'

Alex shrugged. 'I told you. He owes me. Big time. Now will you acknowledge that my job has got some uses?'

It was Christmas Eve. At The Hawthorns, Briar Road, St Albans, Karen was squatting in front of the telly, one eye on Jonathan Ross flirting lasciviously with Girls Aloud, the other on Bea's new bicycle, which she was ambitiously trying

439

to wrap. All around her were overflowing packing cases. They'd unpacked a few cooking implements and bedding, but everything else was still buried under bubble wrap.

It had all happened so fast. A month ago, despite the distractions of Phil being in and out of hospital, she'd put the house back on the market. Property was still in the doldrums and she wasn't expecting any response, but she felt she had to do everything she could to get them out of the home where they'd suffered so much. But the very first night, the agent had called saying a couple with two small children, looking to make the move out of London, were interested. They viewed the following morning. They offered below the asking price, but they offered cash. On condition they exchanged within three weeks.

Karen heard about The Hawthorns, a rambling house on the town outskirts with a vast garden where an old lady had recently died (the girls hadn't been told that, it would freak them out). They put in an offer to the family, and they'd snapped it up, on condition of a rapid sale. They'd been out of the old house by the end of the week. Not without a certain amount of tears from Karen and the girls. But the tears had quickly dried when they'd seen the size of the garden and their new bedrooms. They'd moaned a bit when they'd had to suffer a few nights of no central heating, but Phil had quickly fixed that. Now, they were both asleep upstairs.

'Everything OK?' Phil stuck his head round the door. He'd been in the cellar, working on the finer details of Bea's new doll's house which he'd made for her all by himself. Karen would never tell him that in Bea's exacting circles doll's houses had been 'lame' for about three years. It was good for him to have a project. The chemo and radio-therapy had gone well – the next round was due in the new year, but the doctors were optimistic.

And Phil . . . Phil had been much better this time round. Still often grumpy, still snappy, but he was attempting to keep a lid on it. He appeared to be pleased about Karen's new job, and the consequent pay rise. He was distracting himself by making over The Hawthorns, and when that was done, he thought he might try to snap up another couple of properties while the market was on the skids and have them ready in time for the recovery.

So. 'Everything's fine,' Karen said, smiling. 'Do you feel better being here? Away from Coverley Drive?'

'I do. I know it's all superstitious baloney but I feel as if the demons have lifted. What I was wrong about was thinking we had to go so far. Just the other side of town is fine. And what about you? Has it broken your heart not being in Coverley Drive?'

'Nope. I've realized that much as I thought I loved Coverley Drive, you can't actually have your heart broken by a house. It's the people who are in it that count. Though it helps if the heating's working.'

'I told you I'd be able to sort it. I'm a real man now.'

Karen smiled at him. He was gaunt, still the same bleached colour as his shirt, completely bald now – almost certainly for ever. But in the twinkling lights of the tree, she could see the old Phil, the one she'd loved far more than she'd ever realized. The Phil she suddenly wanted to be curled up in bed with, celebrating the fact they'd made it through another year.

She hadn't forgotten Max. In fact, she missed him with

a fury that was physically painful. At least once a day she had to lock herself in the toilet for a secret cry. Virtually every night she dreamed about him and woke sweaty and confused. He'd been working out his notice, so occasionally she'd spotted him across the canteen, and felt as if her heart had stopped. She'd read his stories in the paper. Every now and then, a text from him had arrived. Or an email. She'd deleted them, without reading. But most days now she managed to smile at things the girls said. She'd even laughed at Sophie's reaction on realizing life with a newborn baby wasn't straight out of the Cath Kidston catalogue. Work kept her incredibly busy, making all the changes she'd itched to do years earlier, and even though circulation wasn't going up, it was staying steady, which was something in these times. Talking to doctors about Phil kept her busy. But Max was leaving for South Africa this week. By the time she returned to work in the new year he'd be gone for ever. That would make it easier. She'd get through it. In time she would be happy again.

'Can you prove it?' she asked Phil, forcing a grin. Forcing grins was the only way to get through this.

'Prove what?'

'That you're a real man.'

Phil grinned. 'Oh well,' he shrugged. 'If I must.'

He scooped her up in his arms. Karen shrieked, delighted. He couldn't be as weak as she'd feared. Either that or she'd lost weight.

'There's a lot of rooms in this house that need christening.' He smiled down at her. 'Remember when we moved into Coverley Drive? We managed the conservatory then.'

'And the shower room. And the utility room.'

'And the freezing cold attic,' he laughed.

'We'd better get a move on,' she said gamely. She wasn't in the mood, but she had to try. It wouldn't be as bad as she feared.

'Oh, I think so,' he said. 'I think the kitchen might be the place. Right over the Belfast sink.'

'Get you, Mr Drake!'

'I have got you. Luckily.'

They started to kiss. It had been a long time. Phil's hand crept up inside her shirt. Images of Max flashed through Karen's mind.

'Merry Christmas, Mrs Drake,' Phil whispered in her ear. 'You know I owe everything to you.'

'And a Merry Christmas to you too, my darling.'

Gemma was now the size of a Sumo wrestler. She sat on the sofa watching corny Christmas movies and ordering pre-wrapped presents on the internet. She had agonizing heartburn. She had piles. About nineteen hundred times a day and night she waddled to the loo. She was loving every second of it.

For the past few weeks her regular interest bills from Raf the pawnbroker had been replaced by letters warning her that if she didn't pay her debt soon, he was going to have to sell the bracelet. Just a couple of days ago one had arrived saying the bracelet was now on sale and she'd receive whatever money was left after interest and expenses were recouped. It would probably be a thousand or so quid, she calculated. When the cheque arrived she would give it to an egg donation charity.

Her parents had no desire to leave Spain and his were

visiting Alex's brother in San Francisco. So they would have a quiet Christmas at home. For Christmas dinner, he was going to prepare a duck, with red cabbage and potatoes in goose fat. No Christmas pudding, they both hated it; instead they were going to divide a chocolate log between them.

'Got to keep your strength up,' Alex grinned. He kept telling her how much he was enjoying her new, curvy body.

'If I breastfeed the twins I'll have to eat like a horse, apparently.'

'I'll order you some oats.'

She ruffled his hair contentedly.

'You know, I feel so happy here. It's funny – before I was pregnant I was fretting about how we had to be living in the perfect house, near the perfect school, that our lives just wouldn't work if everything didn't fit into the blueprint. Now I realize I'd just been watching too many property shows on telly. You don't have to live in a vast house to be happy. So long as you've got your loved ones around you and a roof over your head, that's all that matters.'

'Bloody hell,' Alex said, as she paused for breath. 'I think you missed your vocation writing Hallmark greeting cards.'

'Bugger off,' she laughed as the door buzzed.

'Can you get that? With any luck it'll be DHL delivering the baby monitor. Once they're done, I've got everyone ticked off.'

'Hello?' Alex said into the entryphone. 'Hello?' There was a tiny pause and then he said, 'Bridget. Yes. Of course you can come up.'

# 44

Lucinda and Gareth were sitting in a pub in the City, surrounded by flushed-faced workers, released for the holidays, ties removed, clinking glasses, full of Christmas goodwill to all men.

'So how's everyone at Dunraven Mackie?' she bellowed, over the jukebox. Jona Lewie was pleading to stop the cavalry. Tiddle-diddle, pum-pum. Tiddle-diddle-pum.

'The same as ever. Marsha's son's on remand for GBH now. Niall's wife's pregnant again. Joanne keeps stealing my deals. All as normal, in other words. Oh, and I had a call from a chap called Daniel Chen the other day. He wanted to let you know he's marrying the lady you found hiding in the shower. Whatever that means.'

Lucinda laughed. 'Long story.'

'Do you miss us?'

'I miss *you*. But otherwise no.'

'Well, you're doing great guns as far as I can tell. I read you acquired the site of the old hospital in Fitzroy Square. That's a fantastic location. How did you do it?'

'Aha,' Lucinda winked.

'So it's working out with Anton?' Gareth said this carefully.

'Not too badly.' Lucinda was equally cautious. 'I've slaved for him. He gave me a chance. I owe him. He's put me in charge of a huge project in Devon converting an

Elizabethan manor house into an oligarch's mansion. Everyone's bleating about how the economic climate's all wrong for it, but we're going to have the last laugh. When happy days return we'll be up and running, ready for billionaires with cash to splash on mink-lined fridges.'

'Sounds great. You know I'm from Dorset, just next door. You'll have to give me a tour some time when I'm down visiting my folks.'

'I'd love to. Come and have a tour some time. Maybe a sneaky swim in the pool. Watch a film in the cinema room.' Lucinda smiled. She'd been thinking a lot about Gareth recently. Although work was frantic and very fulfilling, she was still a bit lonely. She'd considered internet dating or speed dating, but the prospect was too depressing. After all, even in the unlikely event of meeting someone who wasn't a serial killer, she'd have to lie as usual about who she really was. No wonder she'd never got close to anyone.

Gareth had loomed in her memory. Kind, funny, reliable. Interested in property. Really very good-looking, when you thought about it. And she'd spent so much time in Devon recently she was well aware a West Country accent didn't mean you were a bit dim. Far from it, judging by the toughness with which the contractors had negotiated their deal.

'Anyway, that's me. What about you?' she continued.

'I've got a new girlfriend, actually,' Gareth said shyly.

'Oh! Right! Lovely!' Lucinda took a larger than usual sip of her gin and tonic. 'What's her name?'

'Mia.'

'How long's that been going on for?'

'Oh, just a month or so. You know. Early days. We'll see.'

Gareth shrugged, his face bright pink. 'Actually, she's going to join us in a minute. She works in a solicitor's firm near here. That's how I met her. She was doing some conveyancing.'

'Oh, that's nice,' said Lucinda, draining her glass. He wasn't actually *that* attractive. Whatever had she been thinking of? 'But, you know, I really have to get going. Got a Christmas party to attend. Sorry, I completely forgot about it when we arranged to meet.'

'That's a shame.' As ever, Gareth was giving her that look. He *knew* what had crossed her mind and he was thinking, 'Sorry, too late!' He always had had the measure of her. He shrugged. 'Some other time, maybe?'

'Absolutely,' Lucinda said over-enthusiastically. She stood up, pulling on her coat, and kissed him on both cheeks. 'Have a great Christmas.'

'You too. What are you doing? Don't tell me. Skiing at the family chalet in St Moritz. Sorry, Luce. But it was all in the papers. We wondered why you hadn't invited us. Hey, are you OK? I was just teasing.'

'I'm fine. Just feel like there's something in my eye.'

'Mia's over there.' He raised a hand. Lucinda darted into the crowd.

'Got to go,' she shouted over his head. 'I'm already late.'

She hurried out of the door. On the pavement, her breath immediately fogged up in front of her face and she felt her cheeks turn scarlet from the cold. Tears stung her eyes. The prospect of going back to her little flat was suddenly more than she could bear. How was she going to survive the next few days?

Her phone was ringing in her bag. Still snivelling, she

447

pulled it out. It would be Anton; he liked to have her on call round the clock. A relief actually. She'd have an excuse to go back to the office and work through the night, something she never minded.

But the number was a Swiss one. Probably Benjie calling, yet again, to tell her how much he hated working for Daddy.

'Hello?'

'Lucinda, darling. It's Mummy.'

'Mummy!' Lucinda literally couldn't remember the last time she'd heard her mother's voice at the end of the line. It was always Daddy, barking out orders. 'Is everything OK? Are you all right?'

'I'm fine, darling. I wanted to know how you are.'

'Really well.' But her voice was wobbling. 'Work's going fine and . . .'

'I wanted to ask you something,' Mummy said. Lucinda realized she was nervous too. 'It's about what you're doing at Christmas.'

'I'll be with friends,' Lucinda lied. 'Don't worry about me, Mummy.'

'Oh, I'm not worrying, I know you will always be OK. But I will miss you. And so will the others. So, even though Daddy won't allow you home on the actual day, I was wondering if you could join us on Boxing Day. Ginevra, Benjie and me, that is. We're going to the house in St Moritz but Daddy won't be joining us. He's off to Australia for some meetings.'

*Or more probably he'll be with one of his mistresses*, Lucinda thought. But the cynicism was overlaid by a feeling of deep, genuine gratitude. She'd see her family after all at Christmas.

Well, part of her family. The part that drove her nuts. They'd all sit around comparing their designer moon boots, and discussing whether they should give the new manicurist a go and who was doing the best après-ski cocktails. Lucinda, in her corner, with the Christmas edition of *The Economist*, would feel annoyed. A bit bored.

But – she realized now – families were meant to be annoying. Boring. It didn't matter. She still wanted to be with them.

'Mummy, of course I'll be there,' she said.

'Do you have a good ski suit? Stella McCartney is doing them, I seem to recall. Your sister has some beautiful ones. Maybe you should ask her for some tips on where to find one?'

'Mummy!' Lucinda exclaimed.

'I'm looking forward to seeing you so much.'

'Me too.' Lucinda meant it sincerely.


Grace was standing on a stepladder in the great hall, putting the finishing touches to decorating the Christmas tree that Lou's son had delivered. The wooden angel with red wings that Mum had brought back from a parents-only holiday in Austria. A faded gold bauble that had belonged to her grandmother. A pink plastic clown that had come out of a cracker a few years ago.

The temperature had dropped dramatically. Grace was wearing thermal tights, two vests, two T-shirts, two jumpers and a fleece over it all and she was *still* frozen solid. At night, she slept with her coat on, snuggled up to a hot water bottle. But she'd never have to endure this cold again. This time next year she'd be in the lodge. The lodge which

Beleek Developments was fully modernizing for her. This time next year she'd decorate the tree wearing a skimpy silk dress to celebrate the double glazing and under-floor heating. This time next year her plans for the garden would be fully under way.

No time for thinking about it now. Grace had to get changed. Into the size fourteen dress she'd bought from a little boutique in Totnes. Because Anton Beleek was taking her out to dinner tonight at the hotel he was staying in, in Dartmouth. Grace didn't know for sure but she had a feeling this time she might be staying the night.

Gemma's heart was in her mouth as Bridget made her way up in the lift. What would she want? Would she be angry with her? Would she announce she'd launched a custody case? Slowly, she manoeuvred herself off the sofa and waddled towards the mezzanine rail.

There was a banging on the door to the flat.

'Go on,' she said to Alex, who was looking uncharacteristically nervous. He went to open up. Trying to bend over the rail, Gemma couldn't see anything, just hear voices at the threshold.

'Hey! How are you?' Alex sounded about as genuine as a bottle of perfume on an East End market stall.

'Sooo good. Great to see you. I'm taking it Gems is here?'

'Of course, come in, come in.'

And there was her sister, standing in the living area below. Hair its usual bird's nest. Face pink from the cold. Wrapped in a cardigan that, even by Bridget standards, was horrid, with a design of what looked like a polar bear's droppings. And she'd put on weight again. Gemma couldn't believe how delighted she was to see her.

'Gems!'

'Bridge! Where the hell have you been?'

'Oh, you know me. All over the shop. But now it's time to come home to roost. God, it's hot in here.' She started pulling at her cardigan ties. 'Or is it just me?'

As the cardigan fell to the floor, Gemma saw a bump under her sister's top. This wasn't a bump from too many mango lassis.

'You're . . . Oh my God, Bridget!'

Bridget grinned, that old, familiar irrepressible grin that Gemma had missed so much.

'I am. But only one foetus, I'm happy to say. Not like you, you greedy cow.'

'When's it due?'

'February the second.'

'No, but I'm . . .'

'February the fourth. I did look at your link. But if you're having twins they'll almost certainly come out earlier.'

'Oh my God.' Gemma tried to compute what was actually blindingly obvious. 'So they must have been conceived . . .'

'More or less on the same day, yeah. The last time I shagged that twazzock.'

'So three babies are going to be born.'

'All with the same mother,' Bridget said – then, seeing Gemma's face, added, 'I mean, I know you'll be the twins' birth mother but I'll be their biological mum. We talked to the counsellor about all this. I'll be a mum of three.'

'Fascinating social experiment,' said Alex. 'How our two turn out, compared to yours.'

'But where are you going to live?' Gemma interrupted. 'What are you going to do?'

'I'm on the council house list. Going to jump straight to the top now I'm a single mum.' She held up a hand. 'I know, Alex. I'm sorry. But the system's there, so why not abuse it? Or I might go to Spain. Stay with Mum and Dad for a bit. The Spanish love children, don't they? *Bambinos.*'

'*Niños.*' Alex couldn't help himself.

'And will Massy play any part in this?'

'Who?' Bridget hooted. 'I shouldn't think so for one tiny second. I mean, he doesn't even know I'm pregnant for a start. And I've no plans to tell him.' Laboriously she began climbing the spiral stairs to her sister. 'Come on, give me a hug. Oh, bloody hell. For the first and last time, you're fatter than me. Alex, get the camera out to record this historical moment.'

They hugged. Bellies bumped.

'So what are you doing this Christmas?' Gemma said into her sister's hair. The familiar smell of patchouli made her want to gag and cry with delight at the same time. Over her shoulder she saw Alex roll his eyes and make a wild gesture towards the living area below.

'Didn't you see my suitcase? I mean, you can tell me to piss off if you want to, even though you are my sister. But given you owe me one, I thought I might stay until the baby's born. Sort of keep you company. But then me and the baba will find somewhere. What kind of birth are you planning, anyway? I'm so into self-hypnosis.'

*

Nick and Martine Crex were sitting in front of his enormous plasma screen. They'd just watched a DVD of the latest James Bond and in a moment they'd order a takeaway. Chinese or Indian. That was the question.

'That Daniel Craig is well fit,' said Martine, approvingly. 'I'd give him one.'

'Right.'

'Get me another can of Special Brew from the fridge, love? Shit, my fags are running low. Will that newsagent's on the corner be open now?'

'Probably. Do you want me to go out for you?'

It was freezing outside. But Nick wasn't sure he could stand another second in this fetid, smoky room.

'Would ya?' She made an unconvincing gesture towards her purse.

'Mum, don't worry. It's on me.'

'Ta, love,' she said, picking up the remote and flicking to QVC.

Outside, Nick took a deep breath of frosty air. He prayed no one would ever find out about this Christmas. Having Mum to stay with him in London seemed utterly shameful. The other two boys from the band were in Barbados. Jack, of course, was back in the Priory. He should have gone away too, but he hadn't organized himself in time. He wondered where Lucinda was. Probably back in Tobago. Or skiing. Yes. She'd be skiing.

And what about Kylie? He'd written to her several times. Nothing. Contacted her via Bebo. Sent her flowers. Texts.

She didn't want to know.

Mum had said she was with Robbie Gwyther now. She'd

found a job back at the old salon. She was doing fine. Nick wondered what she'd be doing right at this minute. She'd driven him nuts last Christmas, putting fairy lights up all round the flat and playing her naff compilation CD with Slade and Wham! on it. Insisting on a plastic tree with a fairy on top.

He wished she was there irritating him now.

The US tour had been a failure. The critics dismissed them as over-praised and over-hyped British imports. The venues had been only half full, and the fans that had come had been scathing in their web reviews. The new album was due out in the spring and the label were still claiming to be very excited, but Nick wasn't sure. Maybe he should have stayed in Burnley. Never got involved in any of this.

He couldn't resist any longer. He pulled his phone out of his pocket and dialled. Miles north, it rang. He waited for it to go to the O2 voicemail service, like it always did.

'Nicky?' That soft voice. It was like an arrow through his heart.

'How are you?' he asked gruffly.

A tiny pause and then she said, 'I'm fine. And you?'

'Did you get my letters?'

'Yes.'

'Kylie, I'm sorry, I really am.' He paused. 'I miss you. I was an idiot. I'd do anything to make it up to you.'

A group of drunk office workers wearing Santa hats and tinsel staggered past him, arms around each other's necks. *'God rest you merry gentlemen.'*

'Can I come and visit?' he asked.

A long pause.

*'Good tidings of comfort and joy,'* the workers sang.

'I'd like it if you did,' she said.
*'Comfort and joy.'*
Fireworks exploded in Nick's chest.
'I'll see you on Christmas morning,' he said eagerly.
*'Good tidings of comfort and joy.'*

# Win a sofa

# from sofa:com

**Sofa.com** offer comfy sofas and beds covered in beautiful natural fabrics. They're just the sort of thing you'd love to curl up on to enjoy a Julia Llewellyn novel!

And we've teamed up with them to bring you this fabulous competition prize.

**Simply visit www.sofa.com/lovenest to enter and win a sofa worth up to £1,500!**

**Closing date April 30th 2010**

For full terms and conditions and details of how to enter visit www.sofa.com/lovenest